the CONDEMNED and CROWNED

BOOK TWO *of* REVIVAL OF THE FALL

STELLA HOPE

Print ISBN: 979-8-9918400-2-6

Ebook ISBN: 979-8-9918400-3-3

This novel is entirely a work of fiction. The names, characters, places, and incidents portrayed in it are the work of the author's imagination. Any resemblance to actual persons, living or dead, events or localities is entirely coincidental.

Stella Hope asserts the moral right to be identified as the author of this work.

Book Cover by MiblArt

Copy editing by Nicola Hodgson

First edition.

DEDICATION

For my husband,
thank you for supporting my writing.
Looking back, I realize how lucky I was to be the object of your high
school infatuation. Now I'm reminded of it daily. I'm lucky to be
able to love you.

For my son,
I'm glad you enjoyed listening to the fight scene in the Assembly
headquarters.
My sneaky little one, you're still too young for my books. Thank
you for being patient with your mama while she worked on this
book
Love you, kiddo.

Pronunciation Guide

Characters

Cerys: "Kehr-ihz"
Creiddylad: "Cree-thil-ahd"
Glais: "Glice"; rhymes with "slice"
Guillermo: "Gee-yair-moh"; Will's full given name
Gwyn: "Gwen"
Gwythyr: "Gwenth-yere"
Nudd Llaw Eraint: "Nee-th"; the "th" sound is soft in "Thau-Errent"

Creatures

Afanc: "Avank"
Dullahan: "Dule-a-han"
Gwyllgi: "Gwith-gi"
Jorōgumo: "Jor-oh-gum-oh"
Leshy: "Lesh-ee"; rhymes with "slushy"
Nguruvilu: "Nnn-gooroo-veeloo"
Púca: "Poo-ka"
Skogsrå: "Skogs-row"

Yōkai: "Yow-kai," collective word for supernatural beings, spirits, or monsters in Japanese folklore.

Other

Annwn: "An-noon," the Otherworld in Celtic Welsh mythology

Sláinte: "Slawn-che," Irish way of saying "Cheers!"

CONTENTS

Chapter One

It Does the Body Good

Esme

"Hey, Jacob, so do you remember when you asked if you needed to grab your tarp, shovel, and rope to help me hide a body?"

Jacob, Esme's long suffering mentor, local Archmage in all but name, and grandfather in all but blood, let out a deep, exasperated sigh through her car's speakers. He replied, "Well, good evening to you too, Esmeralda. Please try to remember your manners, darling."

Unphased by his reprimand, Esme soldiered on. "We have twelve."

From the passenger seat, Abby added, "Six are horses, though."

A small sputtering sound reached their ears. "Is that Christi's daughter?"

Esme rolled her eyes and tightened her grip on the steering wheel. She was trying very hard to stay right at the speed limit.

Getting pulled over covered in blood would cause more problems than she wanted to deal with.

"Yes, Jacob. Abby is with me. Long story short, I know she's a Corded Brother. But the thing is, there really are a dozen dead bodies in Christi's backyard right now. We need a clean-up crew or something. I don't know... Whatever you all do when more than one malevolent gets killed at once."

Abby tapped Esme's arm lightly, a silent rebuke for her impatience, and said, "Bastion, we arranged a parley with the man Esme, Miles, and Finn ran into while hunting the gwyllgi a few weeks back. The purpose was to learn more about his motives for seeking out Miles. We got the information we needed and even established a potential alliance with Gwyn. But our meeting was disrupted by an attack from six Dullahan."

The other end of the line went so quiet, Esme thought Jacob had accidentally hung up. By this point, she was so tired and sore from getting knocked on her ass by a charging horse and tackled by its 300-pound, fully armored undead rider that she just wanted the conversation over with.

She said, "They attacked Gwyn. So, I did what I always do and ran in without thinking. I wasn't about to let Abby's boyfriend die in front of us. Oh, yeah, she didn't know Gwyn was our guy until last night, so that's a whole other thing..."

Esme chewed her lip, realizing she was completely botching this report. "Anyway... Abby helped too. You should have seen the metal behemoth she used to T-bone one horse."

Despite Abby's groan, Esme continued. "Miles had been following Gwyn after a lead he got about a new mage matching the description you'd been circulating. He showed up and joined the fight, which was lucky because Gwyn almost died. Gwyn is in Miles' car right now, headed back to Seattle. Miles healed him as much as he could, and Abby stitched him up."

Esme hastily added, "We really need that clean-up crew. Pretty please with a cherry on top?"

Jacob's slightly intimidating, official Assembly voice came through the speakers. "Abigail O'Malley, upon your honor as a Corded Brother, I require an honest answer."

In her peripheral vision, Esme saw Abby sit up straighter in her seat.

He asked, "Are you working with that leprechaun to play a trick on me, or is this a genuine issue?"

Esme wanted to laugh but bit her lip to stop what would probably come out as a mad giggle. Jacob thought Finn, Esme's magic mentor and infamous thorn in his side, was behind it all. To be fair, she wouldn't put it past Finn to do something like that.

Abby slapped both hands over her face and muttered, "Jacob, this isn't a joke. At all."

In his upper-crust British accent, Jacob replied, "Well, bloody hell," and the giggle Esme had been holding back finally escaped.

Abby had kindly offered to let Gwyn recover at her apartment, but both Esme and Miles vehemently objected. Although Esme now had a great deal of respect for Gwyn, they just didn't know enough about him to trust him. Esme argued that the man who healed him would be the better caregiver during his recovery, while Miles maintained that Abby's safety was their primary concern. Abby fell silent at that—she'd been just as dumbstruck to see Miles' healing powers at work, knitting Gwyn's lung and bones back together, as Esme had been the first time she'd seen his magic.

Miles lived in one of Seattle's famous floating houses. It was small, but the view from the dock was unparalleled. When they reached the parking lot, they realized they had a blood-covered, Gwyn-sized problem. He was still unconscious, and they needed to get him down the dock without anyone calling the cops. Luckily, it was dark, so the simplest non-magical solution was to carry him like he was blackout drunk. The Dullahan's whip had sliced through his muscles, ribs, and into his lung, so carrying him like that, even after the healing, would have been excruciating if he were awake.

With Lily and Cerys trailing behind, Abby rushed ahead to open the door and prepare the guest bed. Carrying Gwyn was easy enough, but when they tried to lay him down, Esme fumbled, and he flopped onto the bed like a sack of bloody potatoes. She wasn't surprised she managed to mess up something so simple with how drained she was feeling.

"Oops," she muttered into the silence.

Miles said, "Eh, he'll be alright," in a chilly tone she hadn't heard from him in many months. Cerys' lambent eyes studied them for a moment, hopped onto the bed and curled protectively around her master.

They all stood there for a pensive moment, looking at Gwyn and Cerys. The past twenty-four hours had been a living nightmare, and they were all completely spent.

Finally allowing her shoulders to sag, Esme suggested, "Can we all just go to bed now?"

Face determined, Abby insisted, "I'm not leaving Gwyn."

Miles shrugged weakly. A bruise was forming under his left eye. "I've got a sleeping bag."

She surprised him with a hug. "Great. I can sleep anywhere. My bag's in Esme's car, and I can just... jump in the lake to clean off."

Miles gave her a quizzical look. "It's eight degrees centigrade outside. And I have a shower, Abby."

A bit sadly, Esme commented, "So we're having a bestie sleepover at Miles' and all we're going to do is sleep. No movies. No special snacks. Nothing. *Lame.*"

Abby and Miles both looked at her wearily.

She sighed. "Yeah, you're right. Honestly, a full night of sleep sounds like heaven right now. Being over thirty has definite drawbacks."

Even though she was exhausted, Esme's mind refused to rest as she lay next to Miles. The only sound in the room was the little puffing sounds Lily occasionally made while dreaming at the foot of the bed. She shifted her position to face him and watched the gentle rise and fall of his chest. If things were different, she would have reached out for his warmth, but her hand hesitated in the space between them.

Gwyn had claimed Miles was his father, the legendary Welsh king Nudd Llaw Eraint. It was impossible to dismiss the idea completely—everything they'd learned about Miles lined up with what was known about Nudd. She had seen Gwyn fight with a sword against the Dullahan like he was born to it, and then Miles had done the impossible, re-knitting his organs, bones, and muscles with magic. As far as she knew, magic wasn't supposed to work that way.

She pulled the blanket tighter around herself, trying to ward off the doubts creeping into her mind. Even if he was Nudd, it wasn't like he'd lied to her. He just hadn't told her everything. She rolled onto her back, staring up at the ceiling. The minutes dragged into hours, and the cold expanse of mattress between them became a chasm she couldn't cross.

The night felt endless as her silent battle between weariness and doubt raged on.

The next morning

"How much longer can you hold out?" Esme muttered, feeling more than a little annoyed as she was already half-covered in dust from the early morning battle. Her grip tightened on her opponent and her weapon.

She'd be the first to admit she was taking her frustration out on something that didn't deserve it, but it felt damn good. The lack of sleep and the bruises covering her from head to toe after the previous day only made her grumpier.

Something had to give. They had to talk about this. It was eating her up inside. The next twelve hours offered no hope for improvement, either. Miles and Abby had to work. Since Esme was the only one with a job she could skip, she would act as Gwyn's nurse for the day.

Only Lily rose to say goodbye as she slipped out of his house a little before five in the morning to return home. When she woke up, Miles was still fast asleep next to her, his body looking as battered as she felt. Peeking through the cracked door, she saw Abby asleep on the floor next to Gwyn's bed.

Now, back at home, Esme was taking out some of her frustration while planning on indulging in copious amounts of sugar. She tossed the stump of the carrot she'd been grating into the batter and grabbed the muffin pan.

Carrot and walnut muffins for the health nuts and double chocolate for her. She had just enough time to get both batches baked before she needed to head back over to Miles' house to take over nursing duty.

Carrying twenty-two muffins, she tiptoed through his front door, having already eaten two of the chocolate ones. She found Miles awake, dressed for work, and standing by the coffeemaker. His face transformed upon seeing her and her baked burden.

"Hey there." He greeted her quietly.

She cracked a smile at the relieved expression he wore. "You thought I left again, didn't you?" she teased.

"Technically, you did." He pointed at what she was carrying. "I'm just glad you're back."

"Is Abby awake yet?"

"You just missed her. She's off already."

"Ugh, now I have all these muffins and too few stomachs to fill."

He walked toward her and exaggerated his Welsh accent as he asked, "Hang on now, what kind of muffins?"

By the time he reached her, she could feel herself being pulled into his gravitational field. She set the muffins down and pulled him close, holding him tightly. For a long moment, they simply stood there, breathing and existing together in the little time their responsibilities allowed. Whenever he held her close, she felt as though the rest of the world could fade away, and she wouldn't care.

She'd known him for less than a year, but somehow, he already felt like home—warm, safe, and comforting. Yet her mind whispered with every heartbeat that he might not be the man she wanted, or needed, him to be. He could be the jailer of the injured man in the guestroom, his father, a man older than gunpowder or paper money. A legend who had become part of mythology itself.

Shattering the tranquility of the moment, she said, "When you get home, we have to talk."

"Should I be scared?" he asked, jangling his house keys in one hand and sending her a crooked smile. "Those are terrifying words for any male."

Unable to find the right words, she kissed him instead, filling the space where her answer should have been. She feared the right response to his question was, "I'm probably the one who should be."

To keep herself entertained while taking care of Gwyn, Esme brought a book. She'd waited for months to get it from the library, but she wouldn't mind if she accidentally drifted off to sleep after the abysmal night she'd had.

Right as she was about to get to the best part of her book, Gwyn groaned in pain. Trying not to overreact to his discomfort, she walked to the spare bedroom that doubled as Miles' office and knocked. "Hey sleepyhead, how are you doing?"

"Esmeralda!" His voice was strained, but underneath it, she heard a hint of relief at seeing a familiar face. "It is nice to hear your voice this morning."

She cracked the door open wider. Cerys glanced at her with mild interest before settling back down to rest.

"May I come in? I'm your nurse today." She allowed a bit of a laugh to color her last statement because, of everyone who'd been there when he was injured, she was the only one vastly underqualified for the job.

"Yes, of course. But I should warn you, I seem to be somewhat underdressed." He looked around himself. "Do you know where my shirt went? And, uh... where exactly am I?"

She opened the door fully to see him lying in bed, bandages covering half his chest. He looked exhausted. Trying to lighten the mood, she said, "I'm surprised Miles didn't heal you completely this morning. You're in his guest room."

Gwyn clearly didn't consider her statement to be a joke. He responded ruefully, "Your man is a psychopath. I hope you understand that."

She didn't know the limitations of Miles' healing and she refused to make assumptions about the whys of this whole situation. She was trying to be congenial with him. But damnit, he hit a nerve first thing. She snapped back, "I'm part demon. Is there even a difference? And whether or not he's 'my man' is still up in the air."

Offhandedly, Gwyn replied, "Of course, there is a difference. He is enjoying my suffering."

Her sarcasm came out in full force. "Wow, I did not take you for the 'woe is me' type. But here we are."

That seemed to have struck a nerve with him as well, because his face fell. He said, "Apologies, Esmeralda. You're so much like her. I..."

He let out a long breath. The movement tugged at his bandages, causing fresh blood to stain them.

As if summoned by this, Lily pattered into the room and sat by Gwyn's bed. Apparently, the gwyllgi and the wolfhound had become fast friends because Cerys looked at her like a puppy looks at its newest playmate, with unmitigated adoration. Esme rummaged in the medical kit for fresh bandages and sat on the edge of the bed without asking for permission.

"Let's change this out, shall we?"

Unconcerned, she proceeded with the familiar action without a second thought. Even though he was injured, she'd witnessed him fight with magic and a sword. The man laying next to her was still a lion, even if he acted like a lamb.

With one hand removing the tape and the other holding his bandage in place, she couldn't help but notice the artificial smile he displayed for her.

With manufactured levity, he said, "I believe you are in a dangerous area. I'm quite certain that I smell horribly. I commend you for your bravery and for your aid."

She scrunched her nose in mock-horror. "Only a little smelly."

She'd learned during her work with the Assembly that switching topics without warning often caught people off guard, making them answer more truthfully. "Real talk time, bud. It's hard to believe the things you said about who you are when this injury suggests otherwise."

"Yes. After I broke free from my confinement, I was surprised by my newfound ability to bleed." He started chuckling but quickly restrained his movement, trying to cover his wince of pain. "What I said when we talked near the beach with your leprechaun friend wasn't me playing the dramatic bard. I am not the Gwyn ap Nudd I once was."

He paused for a long moment, wincing again as she pulled away the most sodden part of the bandage. Finally, he added, "I have lost my ascension. I am less. Now, I am nothing but a man."

It made her wonder if something similar had stripped Nudd of his power, turning him into the man she knew as Miles. She tried to reject the thought, but the uncertainty lingered. She rolled her eyes at her own thoughts. They seemed too far-fetched to even consider.

"N—," he started, then corrected himself, "Miles told me you requested my healing. Sincerely, thank you, Esmeralda."

His tone made it sound like she'd threatened to fall on her own infernal sword if Miles didn't heal him. She muttered, "Uh, yeah. We couldn't exactly let you die."

Out of nowhere, he said, "Your eyes are just like hers. The blue so dark that it's nearly purple."

"Are we talking about Elena again?" Esme asked, her tone edging into frustration.

According to Gwyn, Elena was the woman Nudd had loved but couldn't be with due to societal pressures. Esme felt the "please stop talking about my ex" glare she was giving him, but she couldn't help herself.

"Gwyn, Gwyn, Gwyn, I feel like we keep stepping off the path I want to travel down right now."

There was a hint of sadness in his response, but he made it clear that he understood her intentions. "Honestly, Esmeralda, I don't know how to prove it. Maybe you should ask your Miles these questions instead of me."

Lily moved closer to Gwyn's injury, her snout twitching as she sniffed. Esme shifted, positioning herself between Lily and his wound. She couldn't blame Lily for following her instincts. Petting the wolfhound to redirect her attention, Esme said, "No, silly girl. I'll get you a treat in a minute."

Of course, what she needed from the medical kit next was the farthest away from her. She had to lean off the bed to reach it. In the split second between leaning over and reseating herself, Lily had wedged her body between them, an easy feat for a massive dog, and was already licking at Gwyn's stitches. Cerys, watching from Gywn's other side, seemed to approve.

When Esme reached to redirect Lily, her hands stopped mid-movement. Then her heart skipped two full beats as she saw the faintest candlelight glow emit from Lily's tongue as she licked at the blood on Gwyn's torso.

Neither of them moved, as if afraid they'd break whatever spell was happening. They gawked as the skin under the stitches slowly knit itself together beneath Lily's ministrations.

Esme remembered what Finn had said the night she learned about her demon heritage and Miles' god-touched status: "I suppose I can be fair and mention that his hound is too."

She must have been staring blankly, because Gwyn's quiet murmur of "Diolch" startled her. It seemed like he was thanking the dog.

Gwyn's face darkened as he addressed her. "If I needed more proof that Miles is Nudd, Lily's healing power would be more than enough."

Gods and goddesses, was it true?

Her mouth shot off, defending Miles again, even after what she'd just witnessed. "Whoa now, Finn said that Lily was also god-touched, with a weak halo, just like Miles. Which, remember, Nudd did not have. In case you haven't noticed, I trust Finn."

She ended this tirade by standing up from the bed and growling like a rabid bear, her frustration outweighing any potential embarrassment.

She didn't need to finish bandaging him now, because Gwyn sat up smoothly, already apologizing. "Esmeralda, I'm so—"

She cut him off. "But, hey Gwyn, you had six freaking Dullahan come after you and you have a pet gwyllgi. Plus, you can fight with a sword—people can't do that anymore! So maybe you're not a complete lunatic. I'm somewhere halfway between believing you and thinking that you're a basket-case."

She walked out of the room and quickly grabbed a random t-shirt of Miles'. Returning, she tossed the replacement shirt at the no-longer-invalid. She knew she wasn't being fair to him, but she was too exhausted in mind and body to hold it back.

"Your shirt and jacket are in pieces. While you hop in the shower, I'll warm up a couple of muffins and make some more coffee. The four of us are talking about this tonight, calmly, like friggin' adults! Do you understand?"

When she looked at him for a response to her scolding, she saw he was holding back a laugh that bordered on tears.

"I'll look for some scissors and tweezers so you can pull the stitches out. I'll find your shoes too, because I'm pretty sure poor Cerys is long overdue for a potty break. I was too afraid to take her out."

She hastily shut the door and walked back into the kitchen, still flustered. She needed that chocolate muffin.

For the rest of the afternoon they mostly ignored each other, her by reading, him by brooding in his bed. The peace only lasted until Miles got home.

CHAPTER TWO

A DIVINE INTERVENTION

Miles

It pained him to leave Esme alone with Gwyn, but she'd insisted it would be fine. To her face he agreed, but he still placed a binding ward on Gwyn's magic before they went to sleep that night. The clever Fae trick he'd learned rendered his would-be assassin magically impotent as long as he remained within Miles' home. Just in case, Miles had kept Gwyn's injuries only partially healed, ensuring he couldn't pose an overwhelming physical threat to Esme either.

The previous night had been a blur; everyone too exhausted to talk much. But from what he gathered, it seemed like Abby was getting too close to the bastard for comfort. Still, there had to be more to why they were all at Christi's house when the Dullahan attacked. Miles hoped he'd come home to a peaceful evening and finally get some answers.

When he opened his front door, instead of being greeted by the amethyst eyes and golden-brown hair that he'd expected, he saw the scowling face of the last person he wanted to see moving around.

The bastard had used magic to open the door, because Gwyn was still sitting at his kitchen table eating one of his muffins, acting like this was a normal thing that he had any right to be doing. He was even wearing one of his Oxford shirts. The gwyllgi sat next to him, staring intently at Miles.

But where was Esme? His hand reached for the weapon that wasn't at his side. The only thing that stopped him from second-degree murder was the sight of Lily jumping off the couch, tail wagging in his peripheral vision. Her movement uncovered a waking Esme.

"Sorry, I fell asleep," she said groggily.

His spiking heart rate eased. She'd been napping on the couch with his dog.

Footsteps echoed on the dock behind him. Abby ducked under his outstretched arm, which was still holding the door open, and peeked inside.

Abby said, "Well, this is not what I expected when Esme texted me to come over."

Gwyn, glancing first at Abby and then at Miles, gave a smug nod and lifted the side of his—Miles'—shirt to reveal a healed torso.

Esme started speaking quickly. "Oh, right, you're probably wondering about the stitches. I didn't see any medical scissors, so we kinda... sorta... used your kitchen shears to cut them out. I cleaned them with rubbing alcohol, though!"

What the actual fuck had happened? Miles replied mechanically, "Okay."

Esme added, "And I ordered teriyaki for everyone. It should be here soon."

Bloody hell. Abby was right. This wasn't what he'd expected, either.

Esme

Esme had never seen Miles look as confused as he did at that moment. He squinted at her, his head tilted slightly, a million questions written on his face. "Is anyone going to tell me what happened while I was gone?"

She could tell that he wasn't angry, exactly. It seemed like the response of a man accustomed to handling any situation with ease, walking into a fubar not of his own making.

She could feel Gwyn's eyes practically burning a hole into her back. She nodded toward Gwyn. "Pretty sure he's afraid I'm going to scream at him like a crazed banshee again, so he's keeping quiet."

For the third time in as many minutes, Miles' face darkened with murderous intent. In hindsight, it probably wasn't the best moment to crack a joke—especially not that one.

Clearing her throat to regain his attention, Esme began backtracking. "What I mean is, we're all here to talk about yesterday. Not just the Dullahan attack, but about everything."

Miles stepped aside to allow Abby to enter. She was still in her scrubs, carrying the same backpack she'd brought from Christi's house.

After he closed the door, Miles' expression was unreadable, but his stance suggested he was resigned to the upcoming conversation—and the presence of a gwyllgi in his living room. It was a miserable thought for Esme to have, but she saw his defeated expression as a favorable sign.

A knock came at the door. Miles checked the peephole and, seeing nothing, said, "Must be the food delivery."

He opened the door to reveal Finn standing next to a bag of food, holding a six-pack of beer. The leprechaun wore a glamored shirt that read, "I love Nudd!" with a heart shape in place of the word "love."

Esme instantly wanted to throttle the mischievous Fae. Hopefully, it wouldn't set Miles on edge before they had a chance to talk about Gwyn's assertions. The atmosphere was already tense, and she didn't need a silly shirt making it worse.

His shirt reverted back to its original form in an instant.

Finn's height was the result of magic. Esme had yet to hear the full story, but the short version was that an ifrit had broken her magically binding promise to him. Consequently, Finn was granted her magic in recompense. Now, he stood at least two feet taller than any other leprechaun, with a magical arsenal that included the firepower of desert demons. For beings partially made of magic like ifrit, breaking such a promise was a death sentence. For humans, losing one's magic would merely feel like one.

Esme had met Finn during an interrogation over his threats toward a dryad who had been dating a seated Assembly member. The incident of his misconduct coincided with the mysterious death of a child near both Finn and the dryad's home. Despite their initial tense introduction, all of which was Esme's fault, she and Finn became fast friends. Later, she interrupted Miles, who was taking his turn at interrogating a drugged Finn. But Miles was more concerned about the leprechaun's prior encounter with a banshee. He also wanted to recruit Finn to join the Corded Brotherhood. Her threat toward Miles during the encounter prompted him to disclose the increasing danger posed by the returning malevolents. From that point on, the trajectory of Esme's life had changed forever.

Finn greeted them cheerfully. "Heyo! I'm here for the party! I see we've invited the spooky one." He was referring to Gwyn.

Esme instinctively covered her mouth with consternation. "Amazing timing, Finn, as always."

Miles was deadly still for an instant. Collecting himself before taking a long breath, he asked, "Should I expect Jacob to show up next?" He pointed one accusing bionic finger at Gwyn. "And how is he healed?"

Before answering, Esme ordered, "Finn, shut the door."

Finn never took his eyes off the gwyllgi and Gwyn as he shut the world out of their conversation. Then, with seemingly no effort at all, he shook off his nerves. Acting nonchalantly, as if there were nothing strange about a villain and a malevolent sitting in the dining room, Finn returned to his relaxed demeanor.

Finally, Esme answered Miles. "He's healed because Lily healed him."

Miles paused halfway through removing his coat, one arm hanging free while the other remained in the sleeve.

She explained. "While I was helping change Gwyn's bandage, Lily snuck in. She licked his wound, and her tongue glowed just like your hands do when you heal."

Miles' disbelieving eyes tracked from Esme, to Lily, and back to Esme again. Noticing his attention, Lily wagged her tail expectantly. Miles finished hanging up his coat and called Lily over, gently smoothing the fur around her eyes, searching for something in her canine gaze.

Finn shattered this moment of deep contemplation. "Wound? What did I miss?"

Esme couldn't resist provoking him, so she replied with playful nonchalance, "Dullahan."

The leprechaun had already opened a beer. He spluttered, nearly spitting out his last mouthful. Miles shot him a reproving look.

Finn said, "Aye, sorry, boss. I won't make a mess. Want one?"

After Miles' denial, he added, "Just feckin' what now? Dullahan, plural?" In slow motion, he placed his beer back on the kitchen counter.

Since Miles was busy looking at Lily as if she were an alien and Abby was ogling Gwyn's abs in the guise of examining his now-healed injury, Esme stepped up to explain. "Six of them attacked Gwyn at Abby's parents' house. We joined the fight. One of their whips struck Gwyn and messed him up pretty badly."

She made a gesture encompassing everyone now gathered in the room. "In short, we won."

Abby ceased her ogling and perked up. "Oh, speaking of whips!" She grabbed the backpack she'd arrived with. "I drove back to my parents' house on my lunch break to check if the cleanup crew was done since Mom is out of town. I took this as a little trophy for Gwyn."

What she pulled out was not what Esme would call a "little trophy." A human tibia wrapped in leather made up the pommel, grip, and guard of the whip's handle. The length was several feet of human vertebrae, linked together in a grisly chain. Abby had driven through most of her lunch break to do some good old-fashioned corpse robbing. Abby was a harpy without wings when she was angry, but this was a whole new side to

Esme's best friend. The unexpected gesture made Esme think that maybe Abby and Gwyn were a brilliant match after all.

Finn gasped, whispering, "It's a soddin'—"

Gwyn's eyes sparkled like a kid who was getting exactly what he wanted for Christmas. Abby then pulled the short sword Gwyn had used the day before from her backpack.

"We forgot to grab your sword in the chaos. Sorry! I figured you'd appreciate a little war prize and your sword back during your recovery."

With a face like a child who received only coal for Christmas, Finn commented, "I wish I'd been there. How could ya leave me out of the fun?"

At first, Gwyn cradled the whip as if it were a newborn babe. After running his fingers over the chain, he held it up, allowing its full length to cascade downward.

He said, "Thank you, Abigail. This is... incredible."

He gazed adoringly at it a little longer before rewrapping it and placing it on the nearby table alongside his sword.

Miles' eyes tracked each millimeter of movement that Gwyn made with both weapons. While Esme understood his attitude, it was time that Miles knew the whole of what was going on. It was time to turn on her 'Assembly Enforcer' mode.

She announced, "Gwyn, we fought for you. Miles healed you. You owe us answers." She emphasized the *owe*. "What did the Dullahan want?"

Abby had joined Gwyn at the small dining table and was looking at Esme as if she'd morphed into a completely different person. Esme regarded this as simply another part of her confession to Abby about her covert operations for the Assembly for the past ten years.

Gwyn shifted in his seat to better address each of the people surrounding him. The sparkle in his eyes from Abby's gift faded back to the exhaustion Esme had noticed earlier. "You are quite correct, Esmeralda. Please accept my gratitude for everything done in my name."

Miles stood from his inspection of Lily and crossed his arms over his chest, facing Gwyn squarely. Gwyn's eyes tracked the posturing movement. An acknowledging, tight-lipped smile grew on Gwyn's face.

Esme could already see she was in for a tiresome time with the two of them.

Gwyn continued. "To ease the hostility in the room, allow me to make a promise to you all." He scooted the bone whip and short sword aside and turned his palms upward in his lap. "Upon my magic, I pledge I shall not act in any way that would purposely harm anyone in this room, unless I am attacked first, while I am a guest in this house."

Finn slapped the table, startling Esme. His palm emitted a flash of light as he said, "It is marked."

Gwyn nodded at him.

It wasn't the first time Finn had made that move when a promise was made or kept, but Esme still didn't know what the slapping and puff of magic meant. She'd ask him eventually.

While everyone's attention was focused on Gwyn, Finn cut in with wide eyes and a hopeful grin. "Can I inspect the whip for a minute?"

Gwyn lifted the whip up in one hand and Finn walked over, almost reverentially, to take it.

"I'll be…"

Esme rudely snapped her fingers at Gwyn, back in the guise of an Enforcer. "Well, out with it, Gwyn."

Finn handed the whip back and whisper-yelled conspiratorially to Abby, "She's done this bit on every male in the room! Fun to watch; not so fun to be on the receivin' end."

Miles hid a grin by rubbing his beard.

Gwyn began his story. "The Dullahan were there for me. Because of who I am... who I was. They sought leadership for their group. When I denied them, they protested."

Miles interrupted, "Who are you?"

Gods below, so much had happened in the past few days that Esme had never talked to Miles about who the stranger he'd killed for, then healed and cared for, then allowed to stay in his house overnight, was. He'd done all of that on her word alone—for her. But the idea that Miles might already know Gwyn's true identity quickly overrode her regret for not telling him sooner.

Gwyn stood and raised his arms dramatically in the air. He was playing the storyteller again. "I am Gwyn ap Nudd, son of Nudd Llaw Eraint and recently released convict. I regret we could not exchange words when we ran into each other in the forest while I was collecting my gwyllgi. Miles, she is well behaved; may she remain in the house for now?"

Miles smiled, a full grin spreading across his face, hinting at an imminent burst of laughter. "Gwyn ap Nudd," he chuckled, "Mate, that sounds like a load of bollocks."

But then he looked around and saw that no one else thought that it was a joke.

Gwyn replied with a strained smile. "I'm glad a countryman has heard of me. Cerys sits before you. You saw the Dullahan. What further proof do you need?"

Esme knew snapping her fingers for a second time wouldn't work amid the tension, so she clapped like an exasperated summer camp counselor. "Back to the original question, gentle-men."

Gwyn nodded slightly, and Miles took half a step back, crossing his arms again. Good; they were willing to play nice-ly.

Gwyn continued. "The Dullahan desired my leadership. When I told them I no longer wore the Wild Hunt's mantle, they were not pleased—as you witnessed firsthand. Next, they sensed the two of you." He pointed at Esme and Miles. "My refusal to serve them was made worse by your presence. They believed I was withholding... pets to bolster my own power."

"Pets!" Esme blurted out. "What does that mean?"

"Esmeralda, your kind has always been valued as warriors."

"Okay—" that was easy for her to accept, "but what about Miles?"

Gwyn waved his hand smoothly in the air. "Perhaps they sensed his special abilities or his true identity. I truly do not know what they thought they could gain from either of you. I give you my word on that, though I have suspicions."

Esme's response was clipped. "Air them."

She thought better of her demand for a moment, then added, "But spare us the daddy issues for now, please. This is about why six Dullahan came for you."

Gwyn inclined his head regally. "I will respect your wishes, for now. I owe you that much at least."

He sighed. "My time in the magical prison changed me in abilities, body, and mind. Since you all have seen me bleed, you know this to be true. I am human again. I have told you this, Esmeralda, but I will clarify for all present in good faith because some of you may have answers I need."

Miles cut in, "Prison?"

"We believe I was imprisoned during the magical event you call the Extinction. Yes, I left the world along with the malevolents. I believe that I was imprisoned unfairly, but I will temporarily refrain from voicing my concerns out of respect for Ms. Turner's wishes."

Esme was getting to know Miles' little tells. The puzzle pieces of her request to heal Gwyn were coming together in his mind. She'd begged, "Please, Miles, he might be the only person who can help us stop the malevolents from returning." If Gwyn was telling the truth, he was the only link to the past, to the failing magic that bound the malevolents, that any of them had. Who knew what solutions to the malevolent problem they'd find if they got him talking openly?

Gwyn explained. "Upon release, every being that emerges from one of those magical prisons is severely weakened. I have lost my immortality. So too did the Dullahan. We have proof of that. My magic is still strong but also diminished—like theirs. Perhaps they think they can use the power of someone with unique," he looked at Miles, "powerful," Gwyn pointed at himself, "or magic similar to theirs," he finally pointed at Esme.

Esme hummed thoughtfully. "Your theory makes sense, especially since we attract the malevolents we're hunting by putting on a display of magic."

Even Miles seemed to consider the possibility.

Gwyn seized the lull in conversation to say, "Abigail, I also owe you a debt of gratitude for coming to my aid without obligation. I know how much courage it took to run through that battlefield without a weapon. I am proud to name you as a friend."

Esme saw that Abby's pale cheeks were turning pink. Before her friend could start diminishing her own efforts, Esme hastily spoke up, "You should have seen the enchanted behemoth she summoned in under five seconds. It flattened one of the horses."

Gwyn beamed at Abby as if she'd hung the moon. "I'm eager to hear that story."

Then he cleared his throat. "I owe Mr. Goodwin a debt as well. First, for defending myself and you two as well. Second, for saving my life, even if it was... under some duress. And third, for offering me hospitality. Speaking of which, I will have to find new lodgings immediately."

Abby glanced at Esme, silently asking if she should offer Gwyn her apartment. Esme shook her head.

"I can call Jacob," Esme offered. "He has plenty of space."

"No," Miles said. "He should stay here."

This began another round of "I know exactly what you're doing" glares between Gwyn and Miles.

Finn interrupted, changing the topic. "I don't care where he stays. Are we ever gonna eat this delicious-smellin' food?"

Was the apocalypse coming? Because, for once, *Finn* was the voice of reason.

CHAPTER THREE

ARE YOU HE?

Esme

The sky was a thick cover of gray clouds. Once again, Esme and Miles found themselves on his porch, sitting under the same blanket they'd shared on a similar night before. Beneath them, Lily rested her head on her paws, her body acting as their feet warmer. The same city lights reflected on the lake's small waves. Back then, they'd talked about Esme's guilt. Tonight, she hoped the conversation would be about clearing Miles of his.

Esme tried to bridge the space between them that wasn't of their own making. She sat close to him, resting her head on his shoulder, their hands intertwined on their touching thighs. There was something almost magical about how their hands fit together, like puzzle pieces that had always been meant to meet.

The present moment felt so far removed from the past that it seemed like an eternity had passed. Abby and Finn had returned home, and Gwyn and Cerys were back in his makeshift room, probably brooding.

The outdoors became their private space as it grew late and colder. It was a time just for them—to speak and to listen.

Miles said, "Undoubtedly, Finn is at Jacob's now, filling him in on everything we talked about tonight. Jacob called me earlier and mentioned that the containment unit had completed their work, so Abby's parents' backyard should be back to rights."

Esme shook her head at the phrasing. "Jacob called it a containment unit? The old man's been watching too many cop procedurals."

Miles' only response was a restrained huff of laughter. He was always quiet, but that night he was even quieter than usual.

Esme asked, "So, what do you think about Lily's magical showcase today?"

Miles blew out a stressed breath and scratched at his beard, a gesture that she'd learned signaled his anxiety. "Honestly, it's hard to believe. Bloody hell, Esme, all of this is."

"Yeah... I know."

She didn't want to break the peaceful moment, but it wasn't fair to either of them to leave Gwyn's questions hanging between them. She finally mustered the courage to speak again.

"Are you in a good place, emotionally, to handle a real discussion right now?"

He gave her the most aggrieved expression she'd ever seen. "For you? Always, lovely. Especially if it'll get you to open up about what's been bothering you the past few days."

Esme tried to fight a grimace from appearing on her face. "Yeah, if you can't tell, I need time alone to deal with my emotional baggage. It's not my best quality; sorry."

"Let's not start apologizing for who we are again, yeah?" he reminded her.

The last time they'd sat like this, comforting each other, she'd confessed her fears about losing control again. She'd unleashed the brutally violent power of her demon side without her mental checks in place when Juniper, a tree spirit possessed by a pishacha, had taken Will and Maureen as its food stores. During the confrontation, Juniper had knocked out Miles and beaten Finn to a pulp, leaving Esme to defend herself and all of her friends on her own. Back then, Miles had been less than pleased when Esme used the word 'tainted' to describe herself—a term often used as a slur against her and other cambion.

Not moving her head from its resting place, she asked, "Speaking of who we are, how old are you?"

"Uhh... thirty-six." She felt the rumble of a chuckle deep in his chest. "Sorry, I had to think about it. I don't get asked that question often."

Just come out and say it. "Gwyn says you're more like fifteen hundred years old."

"Huh?"

She sat up to face him, as if having a face-to-face conversation might make what she was about to say seem less ridiculous. "Gwyn thinks you're his father."

Miles squinted, his expression turning into an almost comical portrayal of incredulity. "Did Finn put you up to a prank?"

"No." She gripped his hands, making it clear that she was being sincere. "If you dig into his father's background, you'll find a ton of similarities between you and him. That, plus the whole god-touched thing..."

He responded after a second's pause. "So you all are actually buying into his claims? You're seriously talking about Nudd Llaw Eraint?"

The grimace returned to her face. "Right. I figured you would have learned about him in school, growing up there."

He was still looking at her as if she'd lost her mind. She changed tack. "Okay, let's treat this like it's an academic argument because I did research. I used my brain; *amazing*, right?"

He showed no sign of going along with her self-deprecating comment. Well, she wasn't magically going to become less melodramatic overnight.

"Let's go back one step farther than Nudd Llaw Eraint. From what I've read, the Celtic god Nodens is associated with healing," she pointed at him, "Water," she gestured at their surroundings, "Hunting," she made a gun with her fingers, "And dogs. He had a wolfhound who could heal people by licking them."

She balled her hands into fists to keep from gesturing wildly at Lily.

"Later, sometime around the Roman occupation of Britain, everything that people believed about Nodens, they believed about Nudd. Nudd was supposed to have been a true king of the people. The epithet 'Silver Hand' was given to him because he lost his hand in battle and had it replaced with a magical silver one." She lightly squeezed his prosthetic hand. "Oh, and obviously, Nudd was Welsh. All of that, plus your 'god-blessed' status and your unique power to heal..."

Esme shrugged. While it felt good to have it all out in the open, she also felt foolish for confessing her partial belief in it.

Miles leaned in, placing his elbows on his knees and resting his head on his clasped hands. His voice was flat when he said, "Okay."

His tightly controlled disposition made him difficult to read, which made her anxious. When he raised his face to meet hers, she expected a mocking grin or laughter wrinkling the edges of his eyes. What she saw instead was something close to sadness.

"I can say with certainty that I am not Nudd. And I'm definitely not fifteen hundred years old. I can't believe I actually had to say that. Hang on." He leaned slightly to pull his phone out of his back pocket. "My mum sent me a few pics of me growing up last week." He unlocked it and navigated to find the photos.

He showed Esme a slightly grainy picture of a little boy with chestnut brown hair, smiling widely. He was wearing a sweater over a button-up shirt with a striped tie. It must have been his school uniform. Next he swiped to a picture of the same boy as a teenager, complete with acne spots, mid-kick on a soccer field. Finally, he opened up his own photos and showed her a picture of him in his graduation regalia. He looked to be in his early twenties. He had two complete hands in every photo.

Almost as an afterthought, he added, "I'll show Gwyn these. With any luck, they'll cause a break in his psychiatric condition."

Esme cast a wary, suspicious glance in his direction. "Yeah, if you two don't kill each other first. Speaking of Gwyn, what are you planning for him? Why did you say that he should stay *here*?"

Miles, back in the roguish guise he seemed to show no one else, grinned like he'd just won a high-stakes bet. "I picked up a little Fae trick a few years back. While Gwyn was unconscious, I placed a ward on him that constrains his magic within my house. He's magically impotent."

Eyes still narrow, she asked, "You purposefully left him half-healed too, didn't you?"

"Initially, I did it to ensure an easier interrogation when he regained consciousness. But then you insisted on staying to take care of him while Abby and I went to work." He shrugged. "Why take a chance when I don't have to?"

Esme's lips tightened as she shook her head, wondering at the landscape of his mind. How could someone so protective and gentle also harbor such a calculating and ruthless side?

It didn't take long for her to figure out that the answer lay in the reflection of any mirror.

"Fine." She rolled her eyes. "You know you're going to have to teach me the magic."

A knowing smirk was her answer.

"What are we going to do with Gwyn? I mean, besides you watching him like he's a bug that you'll squash the second he makes the wrong move," Esme asked.

"Maybe we should leave that up to Jacob. Who knows; maybe the Bastion can think of a way to make his presence... beneficial. Plus, he must have a purpose for sticking around other than assuming I'm someone else."

She had a hunch that the reason had curly blonde hair, but didn't see the need to bring that up yet. Maybe when Miles saw Gwyn as something other than an overt threat, it would be worth mentioning.

She snuggled back up against him, resting her head back on his shoulder. He was her shield against the creeping cold of the night.

That reminded her. "Oh, hey, would you like to be my date to the Solstice Gala? It's the biggest event of the year for mages in Seattle."

He asked, "A gala? Like, with fancy clothing and hors d'oeuvres?"

She smiled at the thought of him in another suit. "The Assembly is technically a nonprofit in the United States. So, our branch at least puts on a gala every year downtown as a fake fundraiser so we can cross t's and dot i's on tax forms. Everyone gets dressed to the nines and has a good time."

He pulled her closer, tightening the embrace. "Just tell me what color you'll be wearing."

She let out a soft snort. "As long as you don't match Finn again, I think we'll be okay. He was distraught when you both showed up at the last Assembly meeting wearing navy blue."

Their conversation had helped to shrink the distance between them back down to nearly nothing. No one knew how magic worked. That's what made it magic. She had no real reason to distrust what Miles said and only a few reasons to *begin* to trust Gwyn. As she waited for his response, she enjoyed the comforting warmth his closeness provided.

He squeezed her shoulder once, then moved to kneel before her. His eyes held the soft, gentle green of new spring leaves. "Anyway, lovely, about what Gwyn said. Maybe I'm just an accident of magic. Or maybe I'm a genetic freak. Maybe his confusion is because I'm god-touched or whatever Finn says. I don't know. But I know that I'm not Nudd. Coincidences happen."

He placed both hands high on her thighs. She hoped that reignited intimacy might make any lingering distance between them disappear completely.

What he said next only increased her anticipation. "And you, Esme, you've been the happiest surprise of my move to Seattle. For months, I tried to deny what I felt about you. The only thing on my mind today was the anticipation of returning home and being back here with you. All I want is for you to feel the same way."

The fairy-tale king that he occasionally turned into when it was just the two of them was back. She reveled in it.

But his next words were like a firehose, dousing the delicious heat building within her from the closeness of his hands.

"That's also why I think you should go home tonight. I can't risk you being taken by surprise while sleeping. Especially with him fully healed in the next room. I *won't*." His words were a final decree.

Damn his overprotectiveness. She wanted to tell him that he was being ridiculous, but the worry she saw etched in the subtle lines of his face stopped her. Even if he made a valid argument, she didn't have to like it.

As Esme drove back to her empty house that night, she couldn't shake the feeling that there was still something lingering between them—something he wasn't telling her. Looking back, she wondered if his last words about Nudd were mainly said to convince himself.

CHAPTER FOUR

THE ATTACK

Miles

The King turned away from his shieldmaiden's crestfallen expression. As the unwilling guest in his memory, Miles felt how heavily the crown rested upon his head. This was not the first time Miles had witnessed the King doing what he thought was right, but ultimately was also something he knew would hurt her.

If the constraints of propriety didn't exist, the King would eagerly make her his wife until his dying breath. Despite being a widower for many years, accepting her into his service had eliminated that possibility for them. He could not change the past. His discipline and duty to his people meant the enchantment she held over him would remain buried, given life only within his mind and now Miles'.

Miles felt his own attention wander to study the room as the King became lost in thought. The royal bedroom was austere, its cold stone walls adorned with a tapestry of a boar hunt, and the faint gleam of a polished bronze mirror reflected the fire burning in a nearby brazier. A bed, with a canopy and draped in undyed wool and woad-dyed blue linens, was the only luxury in the room, placed on a rough stone floor with a fur rug at its edges. The emphasis was on surviving rather than luxury, and any hints of power were balanced by practicality. The room reminded Miles of the man.

The King, and Miles within, were abruptly jolted back to reality as his loyal dog, a massive wolfhound with a shaggy gray coat, stirred from her spot on the rug to wary attention. His shield-maiden also straightened to readiness, her frown replaced with a flat expression. The melancholy building inside him vanished as the sound of running armored feet filled the air.

Moving swiftly, the King reached his window, dodging the shieldmaiden's attempt to stop him from venturing too close to a position susceptible to an archer's assault. He looked down and saw Glais rapidly approaching the door below his private meeting rooms.

The wolfhound joined the sudden cacophony by letting out a series of frantic barks that echoed through the keep. The keep was stirring; preparing for another attack. But from whom?

Miles jolted awake to the sound of Lily's frantic barking. He'd been having another new dream. He recognized the man, Glais, and the warrior woman from prior dreams. Eventually, there would be a right time and place to tell Esme about his dreams. But not with Gwyn's mad ravings still fresh in everyone's minds. That would only lead to further confusion.

He heard scratching. It sounded like it was coming from outside. Suspicion crept in. Could it be his houseguest, former patient, and his potential killer, all wrapped up in one, plotting at four in the morning? But as Lily's barks turned to deep growls, he pushed his suspicions aside. Much to Miles' dismay, his gentle-hearted hound was infatuated with the aggravating man.

His insistence that Esme stay home that night now seemed doubly wise—though she wasn't pleased about it at the time. He hurriedly unplugged his prosthetic hand from the charger and clipped it on. Then he grabbed the daggers from beneath what he now thought of as Esme's pillow and headed to investigate.

Opening his bedroom door, he saw Gwyn and Cerys already awake, standing in the hallway. They'd left the guestroom to see what the noise was about. In front of them, the front door rattled on its hinges. Lily's growls grew louder as she crouched, ready to spring. Cerys' glowing eyes sharpened as she did the same.

"Lily, quiet! Back," Miles ordered.

"Are burglaries common here?" Gwyn asked.

"Not at all," Miles replied.

Just as he considered it might be a drunkard staggering around and trying to open the wrong door, the overwhelming feeling of malevolent magic hit them. Instantly, Miles erected a magical shield while Gwyn dove for his short sword, hidden in plain sight near the coat rack. He reached his feet gracefully, ready, as the door shook again.

Miles noticed Gwyn's posture was tense, but not directed at him, meaning he'd have an ally in this. His fight against malevolent creatures had been a solitary one, with Lily as his only backup, until Esme and Finn came into his life. Knowing that his would-be killer was entering the battle on his side eased the hostility he felt toward the other man, if only slightly.

It had only been two days since Miles had patched Gwyn's ribcage back together—an injury that had left bone and muscle looking more like ground meat than anything recognizable as anatomy. It should have been fatal. Lily's touch had completed the healing just the day before, but now, with an unknown foe at the door, Miles could only hope that their work would hold together when it mattered most.

Miles couldn't risk using his gun. It would wake neighbors where the barking of dogs or the pounding of doors would not. "On three," he whispered, "I'm going to open the door. We need to bring whatever it is inside and finish it *quietly*."

The door had stopped rattling, replaced by scratching sounds from the porch.

Gwyn tilted his head, evaluating the situation, and responded calmly, "No fire. On your count."

Miles shuffled over to the door on silent feet. As it shook once more, he counted down, grabbing the doorknob. "... Two." He felt a trickle of anticipatory sweat creep down his elbow. "...Three." He unlocked the deadbolt and swung the door open.

Icy wind gusted through the open door and a creature that looked something like a red fox with a body stretched out like a snake's scrambled in. The bulk of its elongated body crashed through the door, writhing on short legs that sported claws, dripping water everywhere. Incongruous to the rest of its form, the claws looked like those of a great bird of prey. Miles didn't recognize the monster, but the magic it was emitting was all he needed to decide what to do next.

The vulpine serpent headed straight for the dogs on four scurrying legs that were balanced out by its belly, which it used like a massive fifth leg. Lily and Cerys were quick to react, splitting off in different directions. The creature snapped its foxlike head full of sharp fangs at Lily as she rushed out of the way—just in time.

Out of its throat came a hacking bark like a seal's, albeit an angry one. This was followed by a deep, painful-sounding bellow. Miles wrenched his attention away from Lily to see that Gwyn had plunged his short sword into the side of its writhing tail.

Well done.

The cut hadn't driven home into the creature's spine because it still thrashed to nearly knock Gwyn off his feet, away from his sword that was still stuck in its rear. Miles dropped his personal shield and used magic to close the front door, hoping to muffle the sounds of their struggle from his neighbors. Hopefully, the gesture wasn't too late. The last thing they needed right then was mundane attention.

Driven by a vengeful rage, the creature fixated on Gwyn. Miles took this opening to sneak behind it into the kitchen to gather more weapons. When he looked up from his spot by the knife block, he saw that Gwyn had erected his own working shield. The dogs were harrying the creature from two sides, nipping at its legs in turns, so that each could disengage as needed. Setting aside his personal squabbles, Miles focused on working with Gwyn as efficiently as the dogs were during the fight.

Miles kept his voice as quiet as possible, while hoping that he could be understood. "Keep it entertained."

Miles' coffee table was now in pieces and Gwyn was standing on his couch. The creature wriggled its heavy body across the wooden wreckage of Miles' furniture. It lashed out, tearing and ripping at Gwyn's perch in a frenzy.

Miles crouched on the kitchen counter with the knives he'd grabbed from his room clutched in both hands. Then he set about performing the telekinetic magic necessary to launch a few additional smaller steak knives from the nearby knife block at the creature. These would be backup for the two in his hands. In the time that this took, Gwyn had somehow grabbed his sword from the tail of the creature and was using it to slash at its biting maw. Reluctantly, Miles found himself impressed, yet again, by what he saw.

Getting too much resistance from Gwyn, the creature's body coiled tightly, ready to strike at Cerys with its threatening jaws. Suddenly, it turned without warning toward Miles. His use of magic must have attracted the creature's attention. The fox's snakelike tail whipped upward, slicing the ceiling, to balance the long distribution of its body's weight. On the way down, the tail's tip nearly rocked Miles' television off the wall.

The magic he'd worked on the knives hummed with power as the beast completed its turn in his direction. Once it was all the way around, Miles loosed a flurry of flying blades. They rocketed across the kitchen and into the living room. One knife hit home on the monster's furry shoulder. One bounced off the thick ruff of fur along its back. The third and fourth barely sliced glancing blows along its flank.

Normally, Miles would see this as a terrible waste of magic. But this time the action had distracted the creature for just long enough that Gwyn was able to thrust his sword squarely into the place where the spine met the monster's hips. Its back legs went dead immediately, but its front claws and horrific teeth still thrashed in Miles' direction. Only a few inches separated him from being sliced to ribbons.

Miles sprang off the counter and landed, thrusting his daggers downward on top of the thing's back. He rolled off and jumped up into a ready crouch, leaving the daggers behind. It was the same trick he'd used on the afanc the first time Esme had gone monster hunting with him. The twin handles heaved upward a few times as the creature made its last struggles to fight before death overcame it.

A tense few minutes later, Lily and Cerys sniffed the corpse in turn. Miles could tell from their careful but unguarded stances that the creature was indeed deceased. He watched as Gwyn fell backward onto the nearly destroyed couch, breathing heavily. From his spot nearby, Miles could tell that one leg of his borrowed sweatpants had torn, revealing a glimpse of blood beneath. The creature must have raked Gwyn with a claw before he'd generated his own shield.

Eventually, Lily broke off from her inspection of the corpse to examine Gwyn. He wasn't moaning in pain, so Miles figured that he'd just received a glancing blow. But, perhaps that was an impression born from too many years dealing with dramatic civilian patients hoping to receive the maximum number of painkillers.

Gwyn petted both dogs as they crowded him. As Miles approached, he noticed Lily sniff his leg with interest. He heard him speak quietly to her in horribly garbled Welsh. All he could pick out from the phrase was, "No, girl."

Once close enough to see what was happening, Miles noticed that the skin on the front of Gwyn's calf was sliced cleanly. He could see a tiny sliver of white through the red of his flesh; a bit of his tibia was peeking through. That gash was nasty. Based on his experience, he could tell that the bone's top layer had also been impacted. That had to be agonizing.

When Lily licked Gwyn's injury, Miles finally understood how others felt when they saw him heal for the first time. He thought he probably looked like a goggling baboon as he watched the faintest glow emit from her tongue. Trusting Esme and seeing it for himself were two very different things.

He stared in amazement as Gwyn's flesh knit back together under Lily's ministrations. His dog was quietly performing the same healing magic that he had kept hidden for all these years. How? Had his power transferred to her somehow, or...

Gwyn scoffed as Miles looked at him a little dumbly; not a familiar feeling for Miles. "So you see the truth of it now? Let us remove the body before sunrise, yes?"

Mentioning the corpse of the creature at his feet snapped Miles back into action. He grunted his agreement and bent down to grab the top half of the body. But he stopped mid-movement as a thought struck him.

"We'll need a visual and auditory illusion to get this body out of the house without being noticed. I'm physically stronger than you are—" Gwyn's face soured at this comment, "But I'm shite at illusions. Can you manage the magic while I drag this to the water's edge? It should sink."

Gwyn stood there, just stood there, doing nothing for one minute too long for Miles' patience to endure it. For all Miles knew, the lunatic was gearing up for another speech about their true identity.

Miles had just worked a full day at the hospital while the man who wanted to kill him stayed at his house alone with his girlfriend after he'd battled Dullahan the day before. Then he'd been startled awake during the middle of what should have been a night only interrupted by his dreams, since Esme was gone. He refused to entertain the insane man's repeated claims that he was his father while they stood in front of a bleeding malevolent corpse in the middle of his shattered living room.

Miles barked in his military voice, "Oi! Can we just get this bloody carcass out the door, mate? We can deal with your psychological damage later. *Move!*"

CHAPTER FIVE

MEETING WITH THE BOSS

Gwyn

After the prison that had kept him sealed away from the real world collapsed, Gwyn awoke, newly human, on the peak of Dinas Emrys. In the year since, he'd devoted himself to two pursuits: learning how to communicate while adjusting to living in the modern world, and plotting.

Gwyn had come to Seattle in search of the man who bore his father's magic and appearance, convinced he was the key to uncovering the truth. Months after his awakening, the void in Gwyn's memory haunted him. He remembered his past—Gwyn ap Nudd, prince and leader of the Wild Hunt—but the circumstances of his fall remained a mystery. Stripped of his demigod status, he was now a mere mage consumed by one desperate question for Nudd: "Why?"

It was his second night in Miles' home. The tension between them was unbearable, taut as a bowstring about to snap. Gwyn's instinct screamed to flee, but his mission demanded patience. Observing Miles up close offered the best chance to uncover the truth—whether Nudd truly inhabited this man or was merely playing an elaborate charade.

Gwyn hadn't heard Miles leave that morning, but when he entered the kitchen, a note waited for him on the counter. It read:

> *The Leader of the Assembly of Mages has summoned you.*
> *A hired car (mundane) will pick you up by 13:15.*
> *Lily's walker will come by later. Take Cerys with you.*
> *Don't make the <u>mistake</u> of lying to him.*

Perhaps Gwyn had been in this powerful mage's territory all along without realizing it. Maybe the man even expected a formal greeting from him.

Attending this meeting would provide a respite from the dream that felt like a memory that was currently haunting him. Gwyn still felt weak from blood loss, so it was possible that it was just a fever dream. Plus, it was simply beyond the realm of possibility that he could have stolen two souls from Annwn. Wasn't it?

Yet, he couldn't shake the feeling that he'd done something cosmically unforgivable. If it was true, he'd done it for love. It felt like a worthy excuse, but perhaps that was his human mind shading the morality of what he'd done gray.

No stories he knew of spoke of such a crime among his people, for Annwn was a realm of serenity. To steal a soul from its rightful rest was not only cruel, it was unthinkable. And yet, love had driven men to commit unforgivable sins before.

Even if he had once dared to commit such a sin, what had he truly saved? A stolen soul could never return unchanged. It would be someone, but not the one he had lost. Creiddylad, if he had taken her, would have been altered in ways beyond reckoning. Death was immutable, and even he was not above its truth.

He wanted to believe that his past self had known better. But what if he hadn't? What if love had made him reckless?

If he had stolen from the depths of Annwn itself? Then Arawn, lord of Annwn, would not allow such a sin to stand. He was no cruel god, no petty king. He was not the type to rage, nor did he forgive. His justice was quiet, inevitable, and absolute.

A flicker of memory, half-formed and fragile, stirred at the edges of Gwyn's mind. A cold shudder passed through him—something deeper than fear.

The thought of Abigail as his Creiddylad and Esmeralda as their Elena brought him to the brink of overwhelming emotions—sheer joy and profound dread. How could he tell them? Should he even tell them?

Not until he knew more.

Resigned, Gwyn pulled on Miles' borrowed sweater, his own clothes still abandoned at the hotel. A stolen muffin provided a small act of defiance before he leashed Lily and glamored Cerys to look like a Rottweiler. They enjoyed a quick walk along the shoreline until his ride arrived.

The car dropped Gwyn and Cerys off in front of a gated home. While searching for a way in through the gate, he heard the popping sound of mist walking. The patter of hurried steps soon followed. Without turning around, Gwyn said, "You are much alike to your kin, leprechaun, appearing when mischief is afoot, especially in matters best kept *private*."

Finn's voice came from behind him. "Uff, beggin' yer pardon, but the geezer wanted me here."

Finn punched a code on the security post at the front gate and led them inside. Just as the gate clanged shut behind Gwyn, he dropped the gwyllgi's glamor. Maintaining the illusion too long was exhausting—glamors never held well on hellhounds.

With his longer strides, Gwyn reached the front door before Finn and lifted the knocker. The leprechaun caught up and pointed at the button on the side of the door.

Finn said, "Ya know, there is a doorbell just there. Would probably work better since his hearin' isn't the best."

"I do doubt that our coming is unknown to the Lord," Gwyn declared, but his finger still gravitated toward the button, eager to experience pressing one for the first time. In this modern life, Gwyn hadn't yet had many chances to ring doorbells. Since his return, his life had been one of loneliness and bleakness—until, by some chance, one night, he had encountered Abby.

A servant ushered all of them, including Cerys, into the house. The congenial middle-aged woman guided them to what appeared to be an office. Mahogany paneling and tasteful sconces framed a heavy wooden desk at the room's center.

Their host sat in the central chair, awaiting his guests. Despite his slightly stooped form, Gwyn could tell that his presence still commanded respect. His pressed robes were as neatly coiffed as his white hair. Gwyn read weary attentiveness in the deep lines of his host's face.

Still, Gwyn's years of dealing with men like him had taught him never to overlook even the slightest indication of ruthlessness in their gaze. The eyes allowed mortal men to peer into another's soul, into their true self. What he found there revealed that this man certainly hadn't softened with age.

Gwyn relaxed a bit. He hadn't completely lost his fear of the situation; the opposite, actually. But now he understood the ground he stood upon. Men like this one were common in his time, and were not to be underestimated in wit or in their willingness to do anything. Underestimating such a man could be a fatal mistake.

Just as Gwyn bowed, the wicked leprechaun declared, "Heyo. We're here, yer benevolence."

With a subtle look of disdain, the Archmage's eyes scanned Finn's, but he held back the biting comment that was surely on the tip of his tongue. Instead, he waved his hand toward the empty seats in front of him, inviting them to sit down.

Gwyn took a seat and made a deliberate show of relaxing. Posturing had its time and place, but so too did feigned indifference. Cerys perched on her hind legs, her posture alert, sensing her master's tension but thankfully not giving the game away with her hackles raised. Finn, meanwhile, flopped unceremoniously into the oversized chair next to Gwyn and crossed his legs.

His host introduced himself. "I am Jacob, the leader of the Northwest Assembly of Mages. And, because you are well apprised of the malevolent situation, I am also the Bastion of the Corded Brotherhood in the United States."

Gwyn's understanding of the meaning behind those titles was weak at best, but it was his turn to introduce himself.

"Lord Jacob, since you summoned me, I assume you already know who I am. I trust you're aware of everything else I've said to your vassals. I would add that I prefer that you call me simply 'Gwyn'."

"Vassals." Jacob snorted at the term, then inclined his head in assent. "I am no lord. Dispose of the title. Very well; we shall dispense with the 'about me' section of this interview."

One gnarled finger pointed at the leprechaun sitting primly next to him. "Finnegan, you will be quiet while I ask him some questions."

Finn rubbed his hands together fiendishly. "Aye, ya both know me, so I'll skip my introduction. I'll zip my gabber for now. In the meantime, I'll be hangin' on every word."

Jacob made a derisive sound but instantly recovered and turned to Gwyn, his face the picture of seriousness. The Bastion swirled his teaspoon in his teacup and took a deliberately slow sip. Then he tapped the spoon, producing a sound much quieter than expected with the movement.

He said, "Now, let's clear a few things. Miles doesn't buy your story. You must admit, it sounds outlandish. I have far too many reasons to trust him and only a single, flimsy reason to trust you. Up until now, you have endangered none of my people. Apart from that minor incident in the forest, during which your intentions still remain unverifiable... Certain members of our community have spoken in your favor. That helps your case."

Was he referring to Abigail and Esmeralda?

Jacob sighed. "Still, no one in Europe knows anything about you other than what they've observed since spring. Yes, they've been watching you since the first time you stepped foot in that run-down inn in the middle of nowhere Caernarfonshire wearing illusory clothing and speaking passable Latin."

Gwyn shifted in his seat. Jacob had just confirmed his unspoken question of whether he was being tracked. It also reminded him of his debt to Edgar, the man who'd taken him in when he was at his lowest for nothing in return.

Jacob continued. "I'm sure you'll be happy to know that the magic you used to manipulate the plant growth near the inn is still in effect. The botanical garden you've encouraged to grow there has made his inn a popular spot for visitors to snap photos and enjoy refreshments at. I know several curious individuals who would love to discover how you've preserved the enchantment, independent of your active presence there."

So, the little trick Gwyn tried on the way out of the inn had paid off. Good. At the time, magic was the only method he could use to convey his appreciation beyond words, as he was utterly penniless. He told Jacob, "My mother's side was gifted in druidry."

The small smile the older man had been wearing dropped into a scowl. "Good for you. Never do it again! It is against international mage law. The reasons we keep our existence secret are innumerable."

Then Jacob's face contorted with anger, hinting at bloody retribution. The man's words were sharp, like a butcher's knife carving away the unnecessary. His voice sharpened as he cut. "I know who you claim to be, but we know what your insides look like and they appear to be fully human. You bleed just as easily as the rest of us. So, Gwyn, let's deal."

Gwyn watched Finn's sudden change in expression out of the corner of his eye. The leprechaun's head jerked back in sheltered surprise, and a grimace formed on his face. This re-action confirmed that such behavior was out of character for Jacob, at least as far as the leprechaun knew. Gwyn suspected this side of him was reserved for special situations.

Jacob said, "I am not a betting man, Gwyn. You are an unknown quantity who could pose a serious threat to my people."

This, Gwyn understood well. This was an aspect of leadership that weak men never came to recognize—your people were the foundation of your strength. If they could not recognize a threat in their midst, it was the leader's duty to remove it.

Gwyn said simply, "I understand."

Unexpectedly, the elderly mage shifted tactics. "So, how does it feel to be sitting in front of a wizened old man who holds a small amount of power over your future?"

Out of all the scenarios he had envisioned for this conversation, Jacob aiming directly for his private fears was the least expected. Nudd always said that his hubris would be his undoing one day. Was Jacob testing him?

Gwyn remained silent.

"Well, that's what you have given me in coming here, no? Power. You don't even have an identity. You've been relying on reloadable debit cards and illusory identification to get you through the last few months. And we've checked: your funds are running dangerously low unless you pack up and venture outside the county to try your luck at gambling again. But good luck with that. Most casinos in the state have ties to our perceptive First Nations allies."

Where a lesser man would wear triumph on his face for landing such a blow against him, Jacob's facial expression didn't change from calm anger—the most dangerous type.

Gwyn considered his current situation. He could simply leave, but that would only lead him farther away from getting information out of Nudd and farther away from discovering if he'd truly committed the sin his recent dream had hinted at. He patted Cerys sitting on the floor to appear more casual than he felt.

His injury and its aftermath placed him into a situation in which force was no longer a viable option for achieving his desires. One hard-earned lesson stood out in his mind: if a man draws his weapon and you have no intention of fighting him, dissuade and disarm.

"You are not wanting for wealth or power. Men such as you seek but one thing," Gwyn said at last.

Jacob raised an eyebrow. "Speak it then."

"The security of your people. I *am* a betting man, and I'm willing to wager that we are moving toward my muzzling."

Jacob let out a single, barking laugh. "You would be correct."

Gwyn was growing tired of this song and dance, but what else could he expect as an outsider? He held both hands palm up in the air on the table before them and said, "Upon my magic, I do swear that from this hour until the moon's waning after the winter solstice, I shall bring no deliberate harm to any person unless myself, or your allies, are attacked first."

Gwyn knew he had once existed in a dimension so incomprehensible that no ordinary human could grasp it. Occasionally, he could almost remember what it felt like to stand before the gate between the worlds of the living and the dead. Sometimes he could dredge up an image that hinted at unlocking his past power, but it would slip away as surely as the tides.

Yet all those vague memories meant less than nothing when faced with the need to survive—to stay alive. The taste of death was still fresh on his tongue. He was alive, even if he had fallen so far that he couldn't truly comprehend the distance.

On the more tactical side of things, his promise might grant him the time he needed to uncover what Nudd was up to.

The leprechaun marked the binding moment with magic, storing the memory of it within Fae magic itself.

A cunning smile grew on Jacob's face.

"We do not know you well enough to trust you, Gwyn. But I will allow you to stay if you can answer one question to my satisfaction. You have no connection to this place other than your ludicrous belief that Miles is your father, *who wronged you so.*"

Jacob continued. "You left Wales. You left England easily. You could go anywhere, escape the mage eyes watching you here, and do whatever you wish. You could make better preparations for revenge if that's what you are bent on. So, my question is: what other reason do you have for wanting to stay here?"

Because he had nothing. Because he had no one anywhere else.

Gwyn swallowed the lump forming in his throat. He admitted, "Because what you say about Mr. Goodwin may hold some merit."

Years at court had taught him to meet Jacob's intelligent, challenging gaze unflinchingly. "I've based my actions on fragments of a past that is clouded even to myself. I no longer deny the possibility that I could be wrong about his identity. Recently, I've noticed two sides of the man—one very similar to Nudd and the other completely different. My uncertainty is part of the reason I stay. To leave might grant me freedom, yet it would not allow me to act with a clear conscience. I am no villain."

Allowing some of his imperturbable facade to slip, he spoke candidly. "As you've so eloquently stated, I am human. I have begun to care about things—about people—here."

Finn abruptly piped in, "It's so touchin' I might cry."

Leprechauns.

Jacob took another long sip of his tea, keeping his eyes locked on Gwyn. "Very well," he said, placing the cup back in its saucer. "I am satisfied. But, before we turn to what you can do for me, please report on this attack that Miles alluded to briefly."

Was Gwyn now a foot soldier reporting to his commander? So be it. It was a small price to pay. Reporting on battles to his father's bannermen in his youth made this a familiar task.

Gwyn recounted the creature scratching at the dock and rattling the door in the middle of the night. He emphasized their caution in avoiding mundane attention and summarized Miles' planning and every step of combat. He described how his paralyzing blow to its rear allowed Miles to slay the beast with a pair of daggers. He admitted using illusory magic to conceal the disposal of the corpse.

Jacob said, "I fear that this may have been a nguruvilu. You said it looked like an elongated fox and was dripping with water? They originate in the rivers of Chile. The Assembly thanks you for your service. Your use of magic out of doors is excused in this case."

Miles had instructed him to share all the details with Jacob, so Gwyn said, "I must also report that I sustained an injury in the fight. Magic healed my injury. As I'm certain you know, Miles has that ability."

Gwyn allowed a wicked I-told-you-so smile to dance over his lips. "But it wasn't Miles' magic who healed me. It was Lily's, twice over. She manifested the power to heal with a lick in exactly the same way as Nudd's loyal hound. Your written accounts confirm that detail."

Gwyn observed that Jacob could also wear a mask of imperturbability. He harrumphed. "Yes, I think that what Esmeralda said is correct. You need to get out of Dr. Goodwin's house."

Finn agreed with a wisecrack. "Two squabblin' cats they are."

"Yes, but there is also the matter of two powerful magic users, one with unique talents and the other yet undecided," he glanced at Gwyn sidelong, "and two magical dogs, one of which has the whiff of malevolent magic, living under one tiny roof that is easily accessible from the water. The concentration of power will attract malevolents. We must split you up."

Gwyn sat up straighter and leaned forward slightly in his seat. He was both thrilled and troubled by the idea. While the constant quarreling with his host was exhausting, it did allow him to keep an eye on Nudd. Still, he recognized that the situation was slipping away from his control.

So, he used one of his favorite modern words. One that encompassed agreement, satisfaction, obeisance, and an indication of suitability all in one simple word.

"Okay," Gwyn said.

"Now we are getting to the part where we discuss what you can do for me." Jacob practically smiled. "Some suggest that you may have knowledge that can help us in our fight against the malevolents. First, you will spend a great deal of your time recalling events and various other magical pursuits from your past with a scribe or on recordings she sets up. That way, your ramblings will only waste the time of two people."

Gwyn suspected Jacob actually sought magical knowledge to strengthen his position; an understandable goal.

"Second," Jacob's gaze encompassed both Gwyn and Finn, "you'll teach Esmeralda how to wield her new talent for conjuring infernal weapons. What she did fighting the Dullahan was extremely dangerous, and I'd prefer to minimize her risk."

Gwyn hadn't seen her mount a conjured pike just in time to slay the Dullahan's charging steed. Neither had he seen when she'd summoned an infernal sword to cut down another Dullahan that she'd thought incapable of threat. By that point, Gwyn had been lying in a pool of his own blood, near to death.

Finn was swinging his dangling legs in the air and grinning wickedly, as if he knew something that Gwyn didn't. Jacob noticed his display and ordered, "Stop that childish movement!"

Jacob went on, "Fionn will observe all of your training with Esmeralda. She, incidentally, also assured me that your scribe would be safe in your presence. Do not make her into a liar, boy."

Gwyn's heart skipped a beat. That could only mean that Abigail would be his scribe. Neither of these duties would be a hardship to Gwyn.

Jacob grabbed the walking stick that had been leaning on his desk within reach. He stood, rather quickly for his advanced age, and pointed the end of the stick menacingly at Gwyn.

"One more thing. I reckon you will be far less pleased with this stipulation, but it is one that I cannot leave unattended. You will join Miles in ridding the area of the malevolent beings that are returning. For all intents and purposes, you are a Corded Brother visiting from Wales now. Stick to the lie and we shouldn't have too many problems. Am I understood?"

Gwyn felt his face break into an unkind smile that he quickly smoothed out to appear as a sign of blithe acceptance. After all, it was an opportunity to continue watching Nudd and rejoining a hunt for the wicked had its appeal.

Jacob added, "Esmeralda will be returning to her work in the bar. You will take her place in the field. I will work on obtaining a false identity for you in the meantime. That will be your ticket to freedom once you've proven yourself."

So be it. This did not differ from what Gwyn expected of any lord in the past. If you wanted something, you had to provide something of value in return. Why would a modern lord be any different?

CHAPTER SIX

MENAGERIE OF NIGHTMARES

Him

"Easy, now," he muttered softly, his voice kept low to calm and coax. "Dinner."

The forest was quiet, save for the occasional rustle of evergreen needles in the frosty wind. The moon hung low in the sky, beams barely reaching past the clouds. Just enough light cast a pale glow over the clearing he'd created for his charges.

It was a perfect night for monsters.

The air thickened with the rancid stench of old potatoes and the pungent musk of freshly killed deer as he tossed the gruesome mix toward the beast. The magical cage he'd constructed was the only thing standing between him and the elephant-sized malevolent—a massive dire boar with three sets of jagged tusks ready and eager to tear him apart.

The creature paid no attention to the food. It charged, slamming its thick skull into the side of the cage. The structure groaned, but held. The boar, frustrated at its inability to reach him, paced within its enclosure, circling, eyes blazing with raw fury.

He hated to see it in such a state; hated what he had to do to it. But it had to learn, for the sake of everyone depending on him. The fire that arced from his hand was measured, controlled.

Scorched patches on its thick hide and fur released the acrid smell of burned hair and the beginnings of sizzling meat that clawed at his throat. The unbearable, piercing sound that assaulted his ears forced him to cover them—desperate to silence the squeal.

The cage rattled again as the boar smashed against it, the violent impact reverberating through the stillness. Its teeth were bared in silent outrage. It wasn't just a matter of breaking its will. It was about control—keeping it focused, functional.

He flicked more tendrils of flame toward the beast until it slumped in submission, sedated by pain, and the smell of something like bacon wafted to fill the forest clearing.

Each time the magic landed, it felt like a piece of his soul was burning away with its flesh. But what choice did he have? He whispered a quiet apology; not that it would understand.

It wasn't ideal. None of this was. But the stakes were too high to falter now.

He left the boar. Gripping the leg of the deer he'd butchered, he moved to the pit he'd dug nearby, clearing away the branches he'd used to conceal it. With a toss, he threw the severed leg into the gap between the remaining branches. In an instant, the dirt walls came alive with frantic scratching.

Peering down, he saw his other mindless tool inside. The ghoul's eyes were glowing like hot coals in its sunken, rotting skull. Its decayed flesh clung to its bones, twisted and grotesque, with fang-like teeth and claws that scraped the fresh earth around it. He dropped a second leg into the pit and replaced the branches. The sounds that followed, horrible, wet slurping and popping, were sickening, but expected.

He loathed these creatures for their mindlessness, but in them, he saw a reflection of the world—chaotic, ugly, and violent. And that made them easy to control. He didn't control them out of cruelty; he did it because there was no other way.

If only he could control them like...

No, returning to those tainted memories only exacerbated his misery. With each remembrance, pieces of his identity drifted away like a leaf on the wind. He needed to retain his mental clarity, even if only for a few more weeks.

The skogsrå in the city and the nøkk in the alpine lake were better tools: more intelligent, and easier to manipulate. At least they could be reasoned with, to some extent. He'd forced their agreement to feed only upon the wicked—a perfect alignment with his own moral compass.

The necessity placed upon his shoulders compelled him to make these difficult choices, to make sacrifices, and to prepare accordingly.

The Alp scuttled near his feet before climbing up his back, sinking its claws into his flesh as it settled on his shoulders. As a malevolent animal that subsisted entirely on the life force it drained from its victims during nightmares, it posed no threat to him during the day. It remained by his side instead of looking for prey because he had ensorcelled it to believe that only he could satiate its hunger.

Its coal-black eyes gleamed through its thick, matted black fur, and it bared its wicked fangs in silent frustration. It was hungry.

But so was he—for justice, for balance. He just needed to be patient. A bit of suffering now was worth saving what needed to be saved.

At least, that's what he told himself.

There was one more task left. The enormous white sac appeared to be exactly as he'd left it a few days before. It still emitted no scent; nothing vibrated or squirmed within. With the Alp still on his shoulders, he reached out and touched its surface. It was cool—far too cool for the creatures to hatch, but not frozen. Perfect.

Because their mother was difficult to control, he'd used magic to sedate her, then kept her body temperature low to leave her lethargic and sluggish until he was ready for her services. She slept in a sheltered crack in the mountainside. There was no need to bother with her that day. He'd ensured she would wake only when needed, hungry and enraged. Everything had to be precise.

He was just like these monsters, now more than ever before. They were expendable parts of a greater plan—a plan that could save everything.

CHAPTER SEVEN

THE DEMON'S IN THE DETAILS

Esme

"Y'all kinda suck at this," Will said, crossing his arms and scowling theatrically.

"He says, being a crappy teacher!" Esme shot back. They'd been at it for three hours already.

Abby shrugged in a "she's not wrong" kind of way toward Will. Esme appreciated the backup, however slight.

Abby had shown them into the Assembly's secret library for the magic practice session. They sat at a table that looked like it belonged in a high school chemistry lab, rather than in a library surrounded by thousands of ancient books.

"Well, excuse me," Will said with a pout. "I didn't exactly sign up for this."

He was right. Will had been voluntold by Jacob to start teaching his secret method of seeing magic to anyone who might interact with a returned malevolent being. The idea was, if they could see malevolent magic, they could track the beings without having to spend hours or even days setting up traps. Jacob believed that teaching his friends first would make things easier for Will.

"Easy" was not a word that Esme would use to describe the learning experience so far. Still, Will didn't deserve her grumpiness. He'd been through enough over the past few months. Esme quickly apologized. "You're right. I'm sorry."

Will sighed. "No, I'm sorry. I came up with this by accident when I was a teenager. I've been doing it unconsciously for such a long time that I can't explain it."

Esme became aware that Abby was no longer paying attention, her eyes unfocused. Usually, this meant Abby was close to solving a problem or coming up with a great idea. Esme was desperate for anything, any spark of genius that might come out of that beautiful brain, to end the excruciating torture they called "practicing."

Abby asked, "What's the first thing most of us learn after minor telekinesis?"

Will looked at Esme, expecting her to supply the answer. Seeing his look, she threw up her hands in denial.

"I didn't even know magic existed until I was seventeen! I don't know because I learned everything out of order—and all at once."

Esme's parents had hidden her magical lineage. Only this past spring had she discovered the true reason behind their secrecy: demon blood ran through her veins, just as it had through theirs.

"Yeah, I forgot you were a late bloomer," Will smirked. "I'm gonna guess illusions, Abby."

Abby pointed at him, her excitement growing. "Right! You said you were really young when you performed the magic for the first time. Compared to now, your magical toolbox was much smaller back then."

"I mean, was my toolbox really that much smaller back then?" Will said, trying to make a joke about his relatively weak magic compared to either Esme or Abby's.

Esme intentionally took what he said in the wrong way. "No one wants to know about your toolbox, Cruz."

"Children! Both of you," Abby grumbled. "What if, every time you do the magic, you're unconsciously creating an illusion that only you can see? Like a personal illusion that floats on top of the magic your other senses perceive."

Will scratched thoughtfully at the scruff growing on his neck. "Short stuff, you might be onto something. It's worth experimenting with, at least."

The click of the door latch reverberated through the supposedly secure chamber, jolting them from their relaxed conversation. In walked a stunning woman. Esme felt an unconscious tug that captured her entire focus. The woman was probably Esme's height but slimmer, with dark brown hair and very fair skin.

Abby seemed surprised to see her there. "Katia?"

"Esmeralda and Guillermo," Katia said. "You two took down that pishacha. Very nice."

The pain of remembering Juniper's death seemed to fade when this woman looked at her with pride in her eyes—when Esme should feel the exact opposite. What was going on? Gods above, was even Will blushing? So she wasn't the only one affected by this woman's presence.

Abby introduced her. "Katia is the lead researcher of all things malevolent for the Assembly. She's taught me everything I know."

"That's an exaggeration," Katia said with a smile. "But I'm happy to finally meet you both."

She placed her oversized tote bag on the table beside them. "Today I'm acting as a messenger. The 'top dog' wanted a message delivered to you by word of mouth alone."

Esme was captivated by the way Katia's accent added charm to her words, though she couldn't pinpoint where it was from. Somewhere between eastern Asia and eastern Europe, or maybe both.

"The boss man wants the two of you," her eyes took in Will and Esme, "to keep your ears open tonight at the bar. Apparently, tongues have been wagging about either demons or Dullahan, or both. I don't know. He wants to know the extent and type of rumors so we can plan accordingly."

Esme had worked at The Sanctuary of Spirits, a bar catering to the magical community of Seattle, for over a decade. That night, she was prepared for her first shift in quite a long time, but she hadn't expected to dive back into her covert work for the Assembly as well.

Esme glanced at Will. The barback often worked the same shifts as her, but she knew this was outside his usual role. As far as she knew, all Will had agreed to do was teach magic sight, not spy for the Assembly. But she also knew this was how the taskmasters ensnared you—starting with the easy ask.

Smirking, Katia added, "I think your leprechaun friend will be there doing the same. More boots on the ground and all that..."

"Okay with me. Will might be a different story, though... Katia, I've never seen you around at the bar before," Esme said, hinting at the ask.

Katia's perfect smirk morphed into a perfect smile. "I don't drink and I certainly don't go to bars. Because when I've tried, I end up doing many things that I should not." Then she winked. Like wink winked at Esme. What the hell was that supposed to mean?

Esme looked the other woman over. She felt a strange prickle of unease, a sneaking suspicion that Katia's charm was more than just natural; that she was using some form of magic on them.

Grabbing her bag from the table, Katia said, "Alright, that covers everything for me. If I don't return home soon with a block of Parmigiano Reggiano, my partner will refuse to make the pasta I've been craving. I hope to see you all again soon."

Before Katia turned to walk away, Esme caught a glimpse of something familiar: a subtle recognition registered in Katia's violet eyes as she glanced back. A shared understanding silently connected them for a single instant. Then, as if nothing had happened between them, Katia waved farewell and left the room.

Esme wasn't certain if she wanted to breathe out a sigh of relief or distress as the door clicked closed again. She couldn't keep her thoughts bottled up, or they'd become yet another heavy weight she'd be carrying alone.

"Hey, Abby. We know there are different types of demons, right?"

Abby, puzzled by the off-topic question, still answered, "Yeah... lots."

Esme leaned back in her chair, putting on a show of casualness. "I'm no expert, but I think we just met a watered-down succubus. Kinda makes me wonder which flavor of demon I am."

Will let out a gusty breath, his speaking volume raised beyond his normal range. "Phew. Oh, dear gods and goddesses, I was afraid that I was starting to bat for both teams for a moment there."

Abby's eyes widened, and she made a strangled sound of comprehension. Her cheeks flushed, but she conceded, "I... think you might be right."

***

That evening, The Sanctuary of Spirits was alive with chatter and a bit of magic. While Jacob may have set out to decorate the bar as if it were a posh club catering to the upper echelons of society, its patrons treated it more like a dive bar. Arguments were as common as intimate conversations, and loud complaints about bad luck in games of chance filled the air along with laughter and jibes.

Esme wasn't exactly sweating, but mentally, she was tiring. Over her shoulder she confided in Will, "I forgot how frantic this could be."

He retorted sharply, "Yeah, it probably wouldn't feel so bad if you could find your way to work every once in a while, slacker."

Esme stuck out her tongue in his direction while absentmindedly starting the underbar glass washer. She had used her additional bar shifts as leverage to persuade Jacob to buy the machine for them. The ugly, silver monstrosity of technology had already captured her heart because of all the time it was saving them in washing glasses.

As she looked out over the room filled with mages and non-humans, co-existing in harmony, she realized there was something about the bar that made her feel a sense of anticipation every time she walked through the door. Maybe it was because she didn't grow up knowing about magic, or maybe it was because she'd made the bar her home away from home. Either way, the atmosphere there seemed to hum with possibility. Maybe a little hope, too.

Esme loved that she never knew what the night would bring. Mages and magical beings from across the world regularly popped in for a pint. If a stranger seemed friendly or lonely, she'd ask them to tell her a story or to show off a fun bit of magic. Most nights were filled with light-hearted banter, but every so often, she could release some pent-up frustration by breaking up a bar fight.

For all these reasons, she was still happy to be back, even if it was because Jacob was trying to shelter her like a child. She gently scooted a pint of stout across the table, ensuring the perfect foam head she'd achieved remained intact. The leprechaun's eyes practically sparkled with wonder as he received it.

Finn asked, "So, ya excited to start yer special trainin' with the mad dog?"

It was obvious to Finn how much she wanted to start training with Gwyn. Esme's enthusiasm was practically overflowing her body. Her excitement was too much to hide, and she clapped with childlike joy at his question. Though she'd come close to death more times than she cared to remember fighting malevolents recently, the change gave her life a sense of purpose and direction.

Miles was unhappy that she'd be spending so much time with Gwyn, but he was satisfied that Finn would be there for her as backup. Even he couldn't deny the logic behind her seeking training. She adored Miles, but his protective streak was sometimes frustrating. She'd dodged injury twice while summoning weapons to fight the Dullahan. Would she get lucky a third time? To justify trying this new magic again, she had to minimize the risk involved.

She answered Finn cheerily, "Of course. It'll feel like going to the Ren Faire without having to wait in a ton of lines."

Finn snorted. "I hope it'll be less smelly than it was in times before modern plumbing."

Esme could feel her face betray her shock. It had taken months, but this was her first clue as to Finn's true age.

In a lame effort to mask her astonishment, she remarked, "I bet you miss the fashion from yesteryear, though."

In a departure from the leprechaun stereotype, Finn's obsession with fashion focused more on clothing than footwear. If he wasn't overdressed, he acted as though he were a slovenly pig wearing rags.

He said, "'Twas far more elegant. But spandex has its merits. I'm off to work. See ya later, lassie."

"Have a good night, Finn."

She had her own listening to do. As the bar got busier, she had a sense that the atmosphere of the bar was growing off. Attributing that impression to her extended absence, she tuned her ears to the murmur of the surrounding conversations, keen to pick up anything about demons or Dullahan.

At a four-top, two middle-aged couples cast occasional furtive glances her way. Their faces were familiar, but their names escaped her memory. They weren't frequent visitors to the bar or mage social events.

When her instincts told her not to overlook their surreptitious glances, she listened. She edged closer to the group, pretending to wipe down a nearby table. She'd always known her hearing was exceptional, but after discovering it stemmed from her demon heritage, she'd started to fully leverage it.

"...can't be a coincidence. Twice in one month?" A female voice.

"You think she had something to do with it?" A second male voice, she couldn't tell whose, responded in a hushed tone.

The other male said, "Think about it. She's a conjuration mage. Who knows what kind of creatures she can summon?"

Holy smokes, were they talking about her? Esme's heart skipped a beat, but she kept her face neutral, focusing on rearranging the menus on the nearby tables. She wasn't the only conjuration mage in town. There were plenty about, so there was no reason for her to assume that they were referring to her.

More concerning was their implication of a recurring problem. "Twice in one month" might reference the death of one Assembly member and the mysterious injury of another. The first was Philip Luis, who had disappeared mysteriously one night. In reality, Philip had been murdered long before he "vanished." A doppelgänger took his place until Miles killed it when it attacked Esme near the bar. They had the body incinerated by a greedy mortician. The second incident could be when Maureen showed up to Assembly functions with broken bones and bruises after being imprisoned by the pishacha.

While Esme's hands were in motion, every bit of her sensory attention zeroed in on that table. It was an effort not to inch closer to them. Their failure to create a ward of silence around their table while gossiping about someone in the same freaking room as them suggested either rudeness or a lack of magical ability. She was betting on them being affected by both conditions.

A third voice, one of the women, joined in, speaking hesitantly, "But she's been around for years, and everything has been great."

Only silence followed. But as Esme moved on to clean a different table, the second voice piped up: "Don't forget about her parents. You know what the rumors were, both before and after they died. They were asking for trouble with what they were up to."

That was beyond a doubt confirmation. They were definitely talking about her.

Esme placed the menus back on the table. Each step back to the bar shook her emotions together—confusion, fear, and an undercurrent of fury, combining them into something potent and dangerous. It was supposed to have been an easy night of slinging drinks and listening. But given the last eight months of lies unraveling at every turn, that was probably a naïve expectation. She should expect to encounter more challenging truths. After learning about malevolents and her cambion heritage, she thought she was done with lies. Now this—what did her parents have to do with anything? She was one wrong comment away from losing her fucking mind.

According to Jacob, only a handful of people knew about her heritage. If rumors like this spread, everyone with magic in Seattle would know within weeks. It was disheartening that the community could turn on her so easily, especially if accusations like the one that man made gained traction.

Esme had a tendency to skip right past sadness and instead channel her emotions into anger. Whether it was directed at herself, her circumstances, or someone else, the result was always the same. After killing Juniper to save her friends, and herself, she'd learned that her anger had real consequences if allowed to run unchecked. So, she took a deep breath, feeling the tension ease from her shoulders, and allowed herself a single, bitchy look in the direction of the group. Anything more would risk her needing to control her demonic emotions in a way she didn't feel capable of doing well just then.

She didn't want to believe that there could be something more that her parents had hidden, but it wouldn't be surprising. What made it worse was that they'd been loving and supportive. She never felt unsafe or neglected. They were always there for her—until the day they died.

Her parents' deceptions were resurfacing, and strangers knowing more about them than she did was eating her alive. Hearing that their deaths had magical significance threatened the stability she'd fought to rebuild. She'd picked up exercise and self-defense classes. Her magic had grown thanks to training with Finn. Tomorrow, she'd learn how to wield conjured infernal weapons properly. And dammit, she finally had a man who made her feel both strong—she could be herself around him.

She'd spent years working as the Assembly's errand girl, feeling little pieces of her soul being eaten away each time they asked her to "apply pressure" when they deemed it required. Her job at the bar was fulfilling in some ways, but even that was half at the Assembly's behest—they needed a spy there, and she filled the role.

This information dragged her back toward a past she'd worked to escape. Tonight, she'd listen, gather information, and feign stability.

The stakes had risen, and this was just the beginning—she could feel it. More bloodthirsty malevolents were returning to the world daily. So much so that Jacob had pressed Gwyn into service. And now, in addition to fighting monsters, Esme might have to face her own peers over rumors.

Sword training with Gwyn tomorrow might clear her head enough to calmly ask the right questions to the right people. Given who the "right people" were, her being close to calm was probably all she could hope for.

CHAPTER EIGHT

PLAYING WITH CUTTING THINGS

Esme

The drizzling rain barely reached them under the towering western hemlock canopy. Esme wiggled her toes in her hiking boots, the chill creeping in as her wool socks gradually lost their battle against the cold. At least the short sword she gripped, forged from brimstone and a shadowy, indescribable substance, radiated comforting warmth in her hands. She had fashioned her summoned sword to resemble the one Gwyn had taunted her with all morning.

A few of his instructions had already taken root in her brain, twining around her gray matter like invasive vines. In her dreams tonight, she was certain a terrifying creature with cold blue eyes would visit her—not to devour her, but to critique her foot placement. The black-haired monster would shout, "Feet shoulder-width apart! Turn your rear foot to a forty-five-degree angle, and sink into your legs!" Inevitably, this would be followed by, "Esmeralda, did you fail basic maths? Forty-five, not thirty!"

Oh, wait, that was her real life, not a dream.

She had tried arguing that she didn't need to hold her sword "like a tiny bird" because it was conjured, not real. But Gwyn's victory came when he pointed out that if a malevolent Fae had a child's throat in its grasp, she would need real cold iron to solve the problem.

The only positive outcome of the argument was that it gave her a chance to convince Jacob (and Miles) that she needed a real weapon. It wasn't that she needed their permission to buy one; she just didn't want to endure the inevitable lectures that would follow; treating her like a fragile object and suffocating her with their concerns. Ever since the Dullahan fight, their shared trait had become tiresome. She was nearly thirty-two. If she wanted to play with sharp objects, they should watch her do it without comment, dammit.

Finn's intermittent tinkling laughter, provoked by Esme's tumbles on damp leaves and failed parries against Gwyn, only fueled her mounting frustration. Finn was the worst kind of spectator. Their other spectator, Cerys, was blameless. She contentedly watched the debacle they called "training" playing out with her spooky gwyllgi eyes. At least the hound seemed entertained. Esme made a mental note to bring a couple of dog toys and treats the next time they trained together.

The monster from her daydreams turned flesh barked orders at her like a drill sergeant who could only accept perfection. "Keep one foot planted while you move at all times and power your movements from your hips. Never twist your knee inward! React after the cue, then act!"

Esme performed the actions over and over, without rest.

"We have to make up for years of lost training time. Esmeralda, your demon blood will help you catch up, but you'll need to work hard for it—it won't do all the work for you!"

During one bout, she advanced and slashed at his side. Gwyn easily parried her slow movement, deflecting the momentum sideways. Trying to catch him off guard, she turned his deflection into a riposte, chopping downward in a bid to score a shoulder tap of victory.

But once again, he blocked her attack with frustrating ease. She accepted that he was bigger and stronger, but at this stage, she expected to see some progress. Failure after failure was increasingly pissing her off.

Esme's eyes flickered to black for just a moment, but it was long enough for her to make him strain. Pushing forward, she relished the small triumph as the infernal power she accidentally, and unknowingly, pulled from that realm during her heightened emotion surged through her muscles. She forced him to lose ground, centimeter by centimeter, as he struggled to keep her conjured sword away from his head and neck.

That was all she wanted. Just a small degree of satisfaction for her effort; no injuries. Later, she'd regret being a jerk, but in that moment, the twisted joy was too sweet.

Gwyn backed away and resumed his at-ease stance, allowing his sword to rest near his thigh.

He said, "Your safety is more important than damaging your opponent. Esmeralda, you don't need to imbue your movements with anger in the same way that you do your infernal magic. Or... have I offended you?"

She snapped back, the truth of her feelings boiling over. "Oh, I don't know, Gwyn. Maybe I have all this pent-up energy right now because I haven't been laid since you moved in!"

Finn started laughing so hard that he fell over sideways, collapsing onto the damp hemlock-needle-covered ground.

Gwyn's pedantic expression turned to dejection. "Esmeralda, I... I had no idea that I was occupying your room at Miles' home. Without proper identification, I cannot rent an apartment easily. Though, I have not heard of any progress in obtaining it."

Gwyn's misunderstanding of the word "laid" sent Finn into hysterics. The leprechaun looked like he was having a seizure.

Esme smirked and answered quickly, hoping to cover up for the misunderstanding. "I'm not upset that you're still living with Miles. I'm just messing with you because I'm frustrated with my skills."

Esme dismissed her conjured sword, adding in an exasperated tone, "And the leprechaun won't shut his mouth!"

Gwyn frowned, perplexed. "Yes, he seems to be in some sort of prolonged fit. Have I missed something?"

Finn managed to choke out between gasps of laughter, "La d... she wants to practice... sword fightin'," he emphasized the innuendo, "with her preferred partner, if ya get my meaning."

Horrified, Gwyn blushed, causing Esme's cheeks to burn in sympathy. All her other friends had modern views on sexuality and senses of humor, but she feared she had gone too far for his sensibilities.

Gwyn shuddered with disgust, probably because he was still convinced that Miles was his father in disguise. Regaining composure, he forced a quick smile. "I have some good news to lift your spirits, then. I'll be spending several hours at Abigail's soon to fulfill some scribing duties."

Esme pretended great emotion, clutching her heart tightly with her hands. She said, "You're wingmanning me right now? We've reached a new level of friendship. I'm touched."

Finn, still giggling, was cut off by her next threat.

She snarled, "Finn, if you don't stop it, when I get home, I will throw the cookie batter I have in the fridge straight into the trashcan."

That caught his attention. Treats and booze always did. He sat up straight from his position on the ground, wet, dirty, and covered in leaves, and said, "Right. Well, I suppose I can do some of my teacherly duties while we're at it."

Esme rolled her eyes. But her mentor didn't notice the gesture because he was too busy mist walking. In an instant, Finn vanished and then materialized right behind her. She squawked like a dying bird and jumped a few feet forward in surprise. The rascal had gotten exactly the response he was aiming for out of her.

"That's it!" she shouted. "Your Christmas present will be something with bells on it. That way, I'll always know where you are, you mischievous brat!"

Through a triumphant smile, Finn asked, "What did the scorpion say to the fox, lassie?"

He waited but got no response from a stone-faced Esme. Gwyn's expression of impassivity was as stony as her own. Finn giggled as he eventually answered the question for everyone, "'Tis my nature.' It's been so long since I've had such a reaction outta ya. Can't blame me for tryin'."

Gwyn watched this exchange with his arms crossed until his patience reached a breaking point. "Leprechaun," he said in an authoritative tone, "You mentioned training her. May we proceed?"

Finn turned his head to face Gwyn and blew a raspberry. Utterly confused by this, Gwyn squinted and moved his head back slightly, as if trying to create more space between them.

Regaining his composure, Finn said, "Esme, I think ya transferred infernal power to yer muscles back there. Ya almost had him break! And yer eyes eclipsed."

She had felt the flicker but brushed it off as a side effect of her heightened emotion. His comment about using magic to strengthen her muscles intrigued her, though. She hadn't known it was possible.

Gwyn chimed in, "Esmeralda, have you never transferred general magic to strengthen yourself? To fight a Dullahan in hand-to-hand combat like Miles did, he must have used that magic."

"What..." It wasn't eloquent, but that was all she could come up with to answer both of his thoughts.

Finn answered for her. "Aye, this must be another one of those things she never learned. Probably on purpose, because the old codger didn't want her usin' infernal magic accidentally."

She asked, "So you're saying I can use two different types of magic to make me a better ass kicker?"

A wicked smile spread across her face; the idea filled her with a fresh burst of energy. Eagerly she delved back into the darkness to summon a fresh sword and suggested, "Let's keep drilling then, Gwynnyboy."

The sputtering he made in response to his new nickname was music to her ears.

During their snack break a little while later, Gwyn's demeanor shifted from pedantic to contemplative. Shaking the jerky he'd been sharing with Cerys, he said, "Esmeralda, I have come to realize that my world was quite small compared to this one. I didn't even know that there were lands so far to the east. Now you say there are malevolent creatures returning to here from these far-away lands. I think I should gain a small understanding of these histories. I may visit the library in Seattle this afternoon."

Esme said, "Oh! I love libraries. Can I join? I have something slightly esoteric I'd like to keep out of my browser history."

Secretly, she was curious about the schemes attributed to cambions in legend and folklore. If she could understand the range of things her parents might have been involved in before their deaths, it might soften the blow when the full truth came out.

Gwyn hesitated briefly, then said, "Of course, you may join. But what is a browser history?"

Esme waved the question away. "Doesn't matter unless you're looking for sexy eighteen-year-olds like this pervert," she said, pointing at Finn.

Gwyn didn't know that Finn had glamored himself to act as nubile bait for an afanc months before, so he took her comment seriously. Attempting humor for the first time in Esme's presence, Gwyn quipped, "Isn't that a bit young for you, leprechaun?"

Finn didn't deny it. He just giggled and laid back on the log he was sitting on.

Esme asked, "Finn, wanna join our library party after we all get cleaned up?"

"Nah, too quiet for my liking," Finn groaned. "Besides, I've got plans this afternoon."

"Hot date?" Esme teased.

"I wish," Finn replied. "Do you see the pitiful condition I've been reduced to? I'm a friggin' leprechaun, makin' wishes, while surrounded by humans. It should be the other way 'round."

Miles

Will stopped suddenly when he saw Miles getting out of his car.

Will said, "If you're here for a walk on the wild side, I can't help you. I would never play my girl. Even if you look like that." He made a small washing motion toward him with his hand raised in the air.

Miles remained frozen in shock for a moment before realizing that he had acted like a bloody fool. The timing of his arrival at Will's apartment, just as he was arriving home, would appear either highly suspicious or desperate.

In truth, he was desperate. Since Esme had mentioned Nudd Llaw Eraint, he'd been driven to a maddening distraction. He had already frantically searched through every scrap of information he could find about Nudd. It pained him to admit it, but Gwyn was right about the great number of similarities between himself and the legendary king. One story about the three plagues that ravaged Nudd's kingdom featured him prominently. Yet, in most accounts, he was barely a side character, hardly significant. This story held the one crucial difference between him and Nudd, the one thing he clung to as proof against Gwyn's claims that he was just like his supposed father. Nudd had a brother; Miles was an only child.

Desperate for answers, Miles wanted to determine whether his healing magic was fundamentally different from general magic. He'd already concluded that if they looked the same, Gwyn's assertion that he was somehow connected to Nudd had to be false. It would prove that Gwyn's misjudgment of his identity was due only to a similarity between his "god-touched" gift and his father's. It wasn't unheard of for people to look alike without being related. The gene pool that coded for facial features was only so big. There were lists of famous actors who looked exactly like historical figures from paintings.

Perhaps his dreams were a side effect of the gift as well.

Regardless, Miles needed to know before he went completely mad. Miles rubbed at his beard, even knowing that it was a nervous gesture recently pointed out to him by Esme.

"I'm actually here to talk about something that's a different type of magical," he said.

Will's face scrunched up in surprise before his expression was replaced by a smile. Miles, not naturally inclined toward humor, had observed Will's interactions with Esme enough to know that a well-timed joke could help him open up.

Will said, "Okay... but I'm not standing out in this rain. Come in. Len's not home, so it's no big deal."

Miles had met Will's roommate a month ago while searching for Will after his kidnapping by the pishacha.

"Grand, thank you," Miles said sincerely.

He followed Will up the steps to his apartment. The living room was still an art gallery and studio in all but name. Len used their alteration powers to sculpt clay and glass into works of art. Because Len wasn't home working, the protective plastic sheet that had lain in the center of the room the last time Miles had been there was now gone.

Will suggested Miles take a seat on the uncovered couch and went to the kitchen to grab water. Miles was usually a planner, but what he was doing was impulsive, so he spent the quiet minute alone, alternately rubbing at his beard and nervously bouncing his legs. He trusted Will because Esme did, but revealing his secret about healing magic would open a door that couldn't be closed.

Will returned with two glasses of water and sat on the adjacent loveseat.

"So, what's up, Romeo? Is this about the non-progress we've made in training them on my magic sight?" Will asked.

Will had hit on half the reason Miles was about to bring him in on his most dangerous secret. All mages could feel magic. They could feel it on their skin as it was being cast and the traces that it left behind. But Will had figured out a way to see magic.

Miles considered. "Yes, and no. I want to borrow your ability to see magic for a test."

Will groaned, burying his face in his hands. "I knew once this got out, it would follow me around."

"I understand the sentiment far better than you know," Miles said, unable to conceal his grimace of shared pain. "That's actually why I'm here."

"Okay, golden boy." Will's face was the picture of skepticism.

Miles asked, "Can you see if the magic I cast is different when I try two things?"

Will was surprised by the simplicity of the question. "That's it?"

"That's it."

Will looked relieved. "Phew, you showing up here like that had me worried. I thought you were going to suggest something crazy. Give me a second..."

He shook his head like a dog for a moment, then said, "Go for it."

But when he glanced up at Miles, he flopped back in the chair with a disturbed expression on his face. And they hadn't even started the test yet.

Oh hell, Will must be seeing this halo others had mentioned.

"Let me guess," Miles sighed. "My head is glowing?"

Will's reply was deadpan. "Uh, yeah, it fucking is."

"Mate, that's part of the reason for this test. I'll explain after, yeah?"

"Uh, sure. Do your thing, actually-fuckin'-golden boy."

Given that fragile art pieces surrounded him, Miles thought it would be best to do something non-destructive as a show of his general magic. So, he levitated the pillow on the couch next to him.

Checking in, he asked, "General magic, got it?"

"Yeah, boss. It looked like telekinesis always looks. Your head still doesn't look right, though."

Ignoring the comment about his head, Miles prompted, "Great. Noted about the head. Now pay attention and see if the magic I'm about to do looks different. You'll see a visible glow, but please ignore that and only look at the magic itself. I cannot stress that enough."

He flipped the push dagger out of the holster that was strapped to his arm. In his back pocket, he had a package of gauze that was individually wrapped, and he proceeded to take it out and open it. Will's eyes grew wide at the sight of this, but he took it in stride.

But his calm acceptance crumpled when Miles lifted his sleeve and made a neat slice on the muscular part of his forearm, just above his prosthesis, carefully avoiding the veins so as not to make too much mess.

"Gods a-fucking-bove!" Will gasped in horror.

Miles urged, "Just watch, mate! I'm sorry I didn't warn you. I see that I should have now."

He wiped at the blood dripping from the cut with the clean pad of gauze, then caught Will's eye. "Ready? Ignore the mundanely visible light and focus on the magic."

Will, one hand still over his mouth, pale and wide-eyed, mutely nodded.

For some unknown reason, Miles had always found healing himself less effective than healing others. The energy it pulled from him felt like he was doing much more than healing this minor cut, but he pressed on.

Bright candlelight glow emitted from his hand where he placed it over his arm. The warm tingling it left on his skin was a pleasant balm to the lingering pain he felt from the damage he'd inflicted upon himself. He checked again to see that Will was watching, and completed the healing.

He wiped off the rest of the blood and asked, "So?"

Will's voice was half an octave higher when he asked, "Did you just stab yourself on my couch like it was no big deal, then fucking heal it?"

Impatient, Miles pushed, "Yes, I can heal using magic. But did the magic *look* any different?"

Will stood up from his seat on the couch and said, "Bro, it was the same color as your head. What the *actual* fuck?"

Hell. There went his hopes of finding an easy answer. He was back to square one in furthering his self-imposed denial.

Holding up the bloody gauze, Miles asked, "Where's the rubbish bin so I can discard this? Then, let's talk."

CHAPTER NINE

DOWNTOWN CONVERGENCES

Gwyn

While on his way to the library, a garish advertisement on the side of a bus answered a question that had tormented Gwyn for years. There was a name for the creeping melancholy that invaded his nights and days, for the illness of his mind that caused him to lash out at friends when it was at its worst, for the darkness that smothered his soul until he thought the sun would never shine again. Its name seemed so simple, so elementary. Its name almost felt too small for the thing that had ruled so much of his life—depression.

But depression wasn't the topic Gwyn was trying to hide his keen interest in. In fact, he hoped that his research that day might help lessen at least some of the melancholy he felt. He needed answers. The possibility that he had been the architect of his own imprisonment gnawed at him every time he looked at either Abigail or Esmeralda's faces.

The books he wanted were spread across three of the four floors of the non-fiction section. Some were found under 200. Many were listed under 398, which felt farcical to him once he learned they were popularly dubbed "fairy tales." The rest were filed in 891 for tales from his home and neighbors. Esme hadn't agreed to meet him for a while yet, but he still wanted to get a head start on gathering the materials he needed.

He searched for the most incriminating titles first. Anything with "afterlife" or "underworld" on the spine, he considered the most damning. The library was quite busy that afternoon, so he kept an eye out for an empty table while he browsed the shelves. His secrecy on the subject was likely absurd, but hiding his vulnerability had always been second nature to him. Plus, he'd rather Nudd not be informed about this one recalled memory, assuming that's what the dream was.

Gwyn loved libraries. During the months following his release from the magical prison, libraries became his sanctuary, where he learned English and discovered fragments of his history. Even though the sunlight was just as weak in Seattle as it was in Wales, this library's vast walls, made entirely of glass, allowed enough light to see by without electricity. It was a marvel that the structure, stories high, could even stand with walls so fragile.

After completing his first round of the non-fiction section—another farcical term in his opinion—he did a second lap of the seating areas and found a single open table nearby. The moment he placed his items down, another east Asian man carrying a similarly sized pile of books did likewise at the other end of the table.

"Oh, sorry," the stranger said with a friendly smile.

Gwyn hesitated, then decided to stay, remembering Abigail's initial invitation.

"I gladly share," Gwyn said to the other man, "but I warn you, my talkative companion is joining me shortly."

Gwyn noted that most modern men lacked physical fitness, but this man was an exception. His physique suggested a rigorous training regimen. The stranger appeared to be in his thirties. He had black hair and high cheekbones that supported thick-rimmed glasses, which slightly obscured his almond-shaped eyes.

"That's no problem. I'm also a bit of a chatterbox," the stranger replied brightly.

The man unburdened himself of his stack of books and pulled out the chair diagonally across from Gwyn. At a cursory glance, there was nothing noteworthy about the man's appearance. Yet as he sat down, Gwyn felt a slight pause—an intuition, a gut feeling rather than from any noticeable change in the man's behavior. Given how much strangeness his new life brought daily, Gwyn's instincts were no longer reliable, so he ignored the feeling. After all, modern men didn't walk around bearing weapons, and there was no sense of magic about him. The chances of him being a threat beyond his physicality seemed very low, so he didn't mind sharing the table.

Gwyn barely had time to read a single page on Egyptian concepts of life after death before the man began talking, confirming his earlier claim. Showing Gwyn the title of his first book, *The Aeneid*, he remarked, "Seems like our interests align."

"Oh?" Gwyn asked, attempting to balance politeness with avoiding further conversation.

In truth, he'd had countless nightmares about translating that epic poem as a boy. His tutor considered it an adventurous tale, perfect for teaching a young boy Latin, which was true. However, Gwyn had been forced to translate the tale, bent over a table with weak candlelight, for up to twelve hours a day as an eleven-year-old. At that age, all he'd wanted to do was practice swordcraft, not sit in one place. Even the memory of his hand cramping up felt like torture.

Unfortunately, the stranger took his simple response as encouragement. "You could say I've taken a professional interest in stories about the underworld recently."

Gwyn's interest piqued. If this man was a professional in magic histories, talking with him could be an invaluable shortcut to finding the information Gwyn sought.

"My interest is more... curiosity at the moment. What drew your attention to that text?" Gwyn inquired. He still occasionally struggled to find the right word.

A young woman at a nearby table shushed them.

Undeterred, the stranger lowered his voice. "I can't remember if Aeneas actually retrieved a soul from the underworld or if he just visited."

"Aeneas merely visited," Gwyn replied with forced casualness. The question skirted far too close to his own secret interests for comfort, but he still asked, "Are there other tales of souls brought forth from the afterlife you might share?"

"I know of a few..." The man's voice trailed off as a strange smile spread across his face. There it was again—that nagging unease.

But as he felt Esmeralda draw closer, her magic preceding her, Gwyn realized her presence might explain the man's misplaced smile. Nothing more sinister. She was attractive, and he understood the sentiment.

She whispered, "Oh, hey Gwynnyboy! You've made a new mage friend! How sweet!" Since she wasn't carrying a stack of books half as big as herself like he had, she must have headed straight for his table.

Mage friend? The stranger had no whiff of magic about him. But at the same time, Esmeralda was not an incautious person. She wouldn't call someone a mage without reason.

Gwyn narrowed his eyes, suspicious and concerned by his inability to sense the man's magic. "It appears so. And one with similar interests."

The man's smile faltered slightly as Gwyn's tone shifted.

Esme's movements became slightly tense as she reached to pull out the chair next to Gwyn's. She paused halfway through taking her seat, then gave the man a once-over before hastily returning her attention to Gwyn. He had to give her credit. She had an uncanny ability to read unspoken cues. Just like Elena.

The stranger remarked, his grin regaining its full strength, "I see that I should read about demons in addition to the afterlife if I want to stay apprised of the goings-on in Seattle."

Esme stood abruptly, startling Gwyn with the speed of her movement, and forcefully slammed the stranger's book closed, surprising everyone.

The man's smile vanished as quickly as it had reappeared.

A few tables looked over in surprise but quickly returned to minding their own business. The same young woman who had shushed them earlier tried again with Esme, but received a rude gesture in response. Huffing with indignation, the woman gathered her materials and fled.

Barely above a whisper, Esme snarled, "This isn't a chance meeting, is it?"

"In some ways, yes. In others, no," the man answered.

Esme's eye twitched. "I really like straight answers, friend."

"I'm not the best at them, I'm afraid." A sly smile returned to the stranger's face. "But for you, I might just try."

Gwyn's hackles rose as the stranger looked at her with an unsettling, almost clumsy lecherousness. Gwyn suspected that this was an attempt to disarm her, rather than flirting.

She, however, seemed unfazed by his attention, not wavering when she asked, "What do you want?"

The stranger held up both hands in a gesture of surrender. "I apologize for my... forwardness."

He snapped his fingers, the whites of his eyes eclipsing to absolute black. In an instant, a ward of silence manifested around their table. Esme retook her seat, settling back into the chair with a resigned sigh.

With the outside world now shut out of their conversation, the stranger said, "When something extraordinary comes my way, I give it my full enthusiasm. I didn't mean to cause any... discomfort. I'm just someone who likes to go all in when I see potential."

Gwyn noted, "I've recently learned that what you just did is...what's the word?"

"Illegal," Esme supplied. "His use of a ward in public is illegal. Also, the last time I wore a glamor as thick as this guy's, I was bent over in a piss-filled alley struggling not to vomit from the concoction I had to drink to get it that way. If he's not stupid, he'll keep it on long enough for justice to lose his trail."

Gwyn found it deeply concerning that he couldn't detect the man's glamor either. It was almost as if the stranger was deliberately blocking only his magical abilities.

"My thanks," Gwyn said, deliberately excluding her name. "His words must be extremely important if they can justify breaking the law."

The stranger smiled like a salesman trying to charm his customers during a pitch. "This may surprise you, but I'm not here to cause problems." He shrugged, hands rising again. "In fact, I'm here to help solve one or two if I can."

"Tempt us with details then," Gwyn urged him. What had started out as a research session was feeling more like a game of high-stakes poker, which coincidentally, had paid for Gwyn's trip to America. He had to assume that the stranger had deliberately used the words "demon" and "afterlife" in his inflammatory statement.

The stranger's focus shifted back to Gwyn's face, scrutinizing every detail as if he couldn't believe they were actually speaking face to face.

Frustrated with the lack of answers, Gwyn snapped, "You've already admired my appearance. Will you flirt with me as well, or will you finally speak plainly?"

The stranger flashed another brilliant yet insincere smile, his eyes crinkling at the edges.

"I heard a rumor I couldn't ignore and came to the area to check it out. I never imagined that what I would uncover would surpass what I set out to find."

Beside him, Esme's eyes narrowed. "Straight answers, friend," she reminded him.

"I mentioned that I wasn't very good at them. Look, I don't want to agitate either of you. So, let's meet here again in, say, one week at the same time? Let me dangle some bait, though..."

He pointed at Esme and said, "It's rumored that there is a bevy of demonic problems in the area, including a few wagging tongues. I am uniquely suited to help you in that arena. To balance things out, I've already started a few counter-rumors. I just wish I'd known it was you and I'd have done a better job.

You probably have questions about a few demonic things, and I have answers."

He behaved in a way that suggested he had some connection to Esmeralda, but her behavior showed no recognition of him.

Turning to Gwyn, the stranger spoke in a language Gwyn hadn't heard aloud in a millennium. He said, "To you, Bull of Battle, I could be an invaluable ally... if you accept my partnership."

With his last word, he broke the ward of silence.

He stood, gathered his books, and said, "Well, thanks for sharing the table. See you both next week."

Once his head disappeared down the stairs, Esme nudged Gwyn's arm, asking, "What did he say to you at the end?"

Gwyn drummed his fingers on the top of his stack of books. "He... called me by my old title."

"And?" she urged.

"Was it not enough that he spoke a tongue long dead, Esmeralda?"

The flat look she gave him was just shy of calling his bluff. "Just saying that was a lot of words for a title."

"A long title for a very important man," he returned, attempting to downplay it.

Despite his growing trust in Esme, he had to keep a few cards close to his chest.

She rolled her eyes. "There's no way he's going to attack us in the middle of the public library. So, we're definitely showing up at that meeting."

If anything, Gwyn needed Esme there because he felt blind and deaf to the stranger's magic.

Curious if she would convince Miles to go, he asked, "Will you be inviting Miles, then?"

Given the stranger's flawless Brythonic and his mention of being an ally, it was highly probable that he had knowledge of Nudd—or something from Gwyn's past. Gwyn couldn't pass up that opportunity.

Esme grimaced. "He said 'you two,' not 'you three.' What does my boyfriend have to do with finding out about my heritage? Will you invite Abby?"

Gwyn sighed. "Fair point. Let's see what this glamored man has to say."

Esme

"Have you met Beatrice at all?" Esme asked, taking a sip of her decaf. As soon as she'd left the library, she headed straight to the coffee shop for another meeting. At least this one had been planned.

Katia had agreed to meet her at the same place Esme had taken Finn to before his obligatory public introduction to the Seattle Assembly. As Jacob's messenger, Esme figured Katia might provide answers he was hesitant to give. Despite her succubus allure, Katia seemed like a cool person. Even if Esme didn't get any new information from this meeting, the possibility of making a new friend made it worthwhile.

The dark-haired woman across from her smiled knowingly, her eyes shining with a hint of mischief. "You mean the water nymph? Yes. The answer to your second, unasked but burning in your eyes all the same, question is yes, Esme," she chuckled quietly. "And the answer to your third unasked question is also yes."

Esme squinted. "So, are we confirming both what you are and who and what you've done?"

"The nymphs can be very accommodating, as you've already guessed. And it's only fair that I share because I've known some of your secrets longer than you have."

"About what I am?" Esme asked.

"Indeed. But I couldn't bring it up, not even with my 'sister,' because Jacob made me promise not to."

Damn Jacob for withholding a valuable resource like Katia from her all these years. The thought didn't make her plan to approach him about her parents the next day any easier.

Esme said, "Again, thanks for coming. I overheard a few things at the bar last night, but I wanted to talk with you about it before reporting to Jacob."

Esme had been certain that training with Gwyn and Finn in the morning would help ease her dread about what she had overheard. And it had helped. Until the unknown cambion man had shown up at the library and brought everything back by reminding her about her own involvement in the swirling rumors.

Katia raised an eyebrow at Esme's last comment. "If I can answer, sure."

"Do you know what tipped Jacob off about the rumors?"

Katia's response was both honest and casual. "His position being threatened, of course."

Had Esme become a liability to Jacob? Lugging around the weight of her past mistakes wasn't exactly enjoyable. Being an asset to the Assembly had unknowingly given her a sense of security for so many years. The idea that she might now be a hindrance—to them, to him—was hard to swallow.

Katia filled the silence. "Those who know about us and who've noticed the recent fluctuation of the seated membership board have started blaming his support of our kind, calling it a symptom of his problematic leadership."

"Are they trying to remove Jacob from power?"

"Not yet. Whether they try depends on how well he handles his public image during this period of acute attention."

That made sense. If Jacob were to stay in power, things needed to go smoothly for a while. But Esme still couldn't make sense of how Jacob's support of cambions connected to whatever her parents had been doing before they died. Katia seemed too young to know much about her parents, but it was still worth asking.

"Do you know anything about my parents?"

"Almost nothing. I was living in Russia when they died."

Well, that confirmed the sort of Russian accent.

"Oh, okay..." Esme shook off her disappointment and moved on to the next question.

"But those people can't know about Philip Luis and why Sylas has gone into hiding, right? Jacob said that information wasn't leaving the ears of the Brotherhood. Well, and me, of course."

Katia shrugged delicately. "We have a leak somewhere. A number of people in your parents' generation were knowledgeable about their ancestry."

"Fuck..."

Katia's smirk was infectious, and Esme found herself grinning despite everything.

"Hey! Don't blaspheme what keeps me alive." Quite the joke for a succubus to make.

Esme, inspired by Katia's joke, couldn't resist asking about the mystery that had been weighing on her mind ever since their initial meeting. "Yeah, so how does that work exactly? I can reach into the infernal to increase my strength and magic. What can you do?"

The nearly empty coffee shop made Esme hope no one was eavesdropping. To mundane ears, and even some mage ones, she'd sound completely insane.

Katia answered, "I could probably strengthen my body too, but not as well as you. My... genetics have a few upsides and many downsides. Since my connection to the infernal never fully closes, I have to sustain myself with sips of vitality. If I don't feed it, my hunger and my allure become... unsustainable. I have to be careful not to take too much. The upside is I'm a spoiled brat because I get whatever I want. I heal more quickly than I have any right to and I should have a very long life."

"Healing and a long life sound great. So... how old are you?"

"Eighty-eight."

Esme nearly spat out her coffee. Katia looked—at most—thirty-eight. The succubus grinned like a Cheshire cat, clearly enjoying her reaction.

When Esme's shock subsided, she finally asked, "So, what are we going to do about it?"

"About the rumors? I've already started whispering doubts about the persistence of demon blood to a few select people. Like I said, I usually get my way." A smug smile played on her lips. "Jacob's craftiness makes it impossible to know what he's planning behind the scenes."

"I just feel guilty for bringing trouble down on Jacob's head, ya know?"

Katia's laugh wasn't the delicate sound one might expect from a woman who looked like her. It was full-bodied, leaving her clutching her middle from the strain of it.

When she finally recovered, she said, "Ah, Esme. He brings enough trouble onto his own head without your help. To my knowledge—and I know a lot—you've been nothing but a boon to him. You asked about your parents earlier. Go ask him and don't be too nice about it."

Oh, Esme planned on it. Right after visiting the biggest pain in her side first.

Chapter Ten

An Urban Hunting Party

Gwyn

Miles fumed. "How many times do I have to tell you that I'm not your bloody father?" His dark hair was even more unruly than normal as he tugged his jacket over his prosthesis. Gwyn remembered his father's hand. *That* was a thing of magic. This one was almost entirely driven by technology, except when Miles occasionally used magic to enhance its capabilities.

Gwyn looked at Miles with undisguised disgust. He sneered, contorting his expression into one of contempt. "And yet you truly excel at demonstrating his worst qualities."

As the tension in the room escalated, Lily and Cerys wisely moved to safer spots, out of the line of verbal fire. Miles' fists clenched at his sides, and his seething anger propelled him to take a single, threatening step closer to Gwyn. "You think I enjoy having you around? At best, you're a liability; at worst, a threat. The only reason you're still here is the convenience of keeping you leashed."

Gwyn smirked, knowing but not caring that he was pushing the situation dangerously close to blows. "The feeling is mutual. I would not pretend civility if revenge was more important to me than the truth."

"Oh, you're *so* noble. There is no truth to find, you paranoid idiot! You're obsessed with a fantasy, and it's driving both of us insane."

Gwyn's temper flared. "Deny it as you will. I know what manner of man you are—even if magic has brought this upon you. And I will prove it."

"Bollocks," Miles spat, teetering on the edge of violence.

Gwyn could see the effort it took for Miles to force his tone to be more conciliatory. His jaw was so tight the muscles were straining beneath his scruff. Miles suggested, his voice tight, as if trying to put the situation to bed, "Let's just go. We have bigger problems than your insanity to deal with."

The argument was going nowhere, a rehashed, tired debate. Gwyn saw two sides to the man called Miles Goodwin. To the world, he was Dr. Goodwin, stalwart and fastidious, a shining example of success. But to Gwyn, he was something else entirely—arrogant, superior, and hostile to his every action.

As Miles opened the front door, the bite of the autumn air sliced through Gwyn's open coat, chilling his skin. Miles had mentioned something about a windstorm, but Gwyn had mostly ignored the weather. During his time, bodily comforts didn't matter during the hunt. Focus, the thrill of the chase—that's what was important. Gwyn was determined not to let modern luxuries weaken his former resilience.

His host muttered from his place in the doorway with a reminder, "Not talking is always preferable."

As Miles released the door, it swung back forcefully, nearly colliding with Gwyn's face. Rather than succumbing to another outburst of rage, Gwyn made the most of the moment, exchanging final goodbyes with a sleepy Cerys and Lily before venturing out into the city for their hunt.

The sky outside was as dim as his mood. Thick gray clouds hung low in the night sky, allowing only a fraction of the moon's light through. Only artificial lighting illuminated the ground enough for them to navigate by. Both men allowed the wind to carry away their bitter exchange, leaving room for silence between them once more.

As they walked to Miles' car, Gwyn realized that he'd just thought of the other man as Miles and not Nudd. When Miles allowed the door to slam in his face, it was the act of the modern mage—not the relic of Gwyn's past. That was something Nudd would never have done. His father, always proper and composed, would never have engaged in such childish behavior.

Regardless, there were simply too many similarities between the man he'd once known and this version for comfort. The shifting nature of Miles' personality, combined with all the other similarities between the two men, made Gwyn wonder if he was actually dealing with two men in one body. Nudd Llaw Eraint, the man he knew, wouldn't hesitate to take over an innocent man's life if he believed the sacrifice of one had a greater purpose for the many.

Nevertheless, Gwyn adamantly rejected the idea of embracing villainy. He'd be certain before enacting any form of violent interrogation or retribution—even if it was tempting at the moment.

This line of thinking inevitably brought Gwyn back to the dream he'd had during his recuperation. His "depression," as he now called his pervasive melancholy, had a way of pulling his thoughts into a dark abyss, leaving him lost in gloomy reflections. If that dream turned out to be real, was he truly any better than what he accused his father of doing to him?

He tried to ignore its absurd suggestion, dismissing it as a feverish hallucination. No one, not even an ascended, could cross the door to the afterlife and return, much less bring two souls back with them. Still, Gwyn couldn't stop his heart from fooling his soul into believing in the possibility of the impossible. Maybe he was the romantic his father accused him of being.

Life was full of coincidences, and magic only amplified their probability. He had to accept that and move on.

There was another, harder-to-accept possibility: that Gwyn was seeing purpose in Miles' actions where there was none. He knew his excessive pride and depression had fueled these arguments more often than necessary. He remembered the dark periods when it felt like the sun would never shine upon him again. When the melancholy settled in, shadows haunted his mind, making him imagine enemies where there were none. He lashed out at those around him, often unjustly.

His pride still mourned the loss of his power, leaving a bitter taste in his mouth. So, was his soul slipping back into that dark space?

Perhaps. Yet there was no denying that mysterious circumstances had thrown him more than a thousand years into the future. And the one person who could help him understand it remained a frustrating mystery to him.

Regardless, they all shared a common, more pressing concern that Gwyn had deliberately committed himself to resolving. All over the world, the failure of the magic that contained malevolent creatures was degrading, seemingly more rapidly than ever before. He'd seen what it was like in his time when families were ripped apart by malevolent savagery. If Gwyn had any power to stop it, while serving his other purposes, he wouldn't just stand by and watch.

It had been a week, but he hadn't heard anything about moving houses from the Archmage Jacob. Perhaps the man needed to see a return before investing any further in Gwyn. *That* he could understand. He would prove himself tonight. In the meantime, he would bide his time, watching, waiting.

The city sped by in a blur, the silence heavy with unspoken tension. The thought of Abigail joining them on the hunt left Gwyn with mixed emotions. He admired her courage and willingness to fight the Dullahan, but it was obvious she was more of a scholar than a warrior. Her safety would be his priority.

Yet, he'd be a marked liar if he claimed he wasn't excited for a hunt regardless. Hunting was what Gwyn ap Nudd was known for, after all.

Abby

Everything was set. Abby, used to night shifts in the ER, had managed to fall asleep by 8:30 pm and was anxiously awaiting her ride by 2:00 am. Her apartment, perched at the corner of the building, was high enough that she could peek through the two living room windows to see if Miles' car was approaching.

She nibbled on an energy bar while double-checking the supplies in her small backpack. Lip balm, more snacks, bear spray—because human mace wouldn't cut it if a monster was in your face. Check, check, check.

Tonight would be her first outing as a Corded Brother field agent. While she had a hunch that Jacob wanted her there to keep Gwyn in line, she didn't mind. This case was special to Abby because she'd been the one to bring it to the Corded Brotherhood's attention. It would be the first chance she'd ever had at seeing a malevolent case all the way through to the end.

She'd spotted the problem while working as the nurse for a patient suffering from a suspected overdose. The EMTs had administered medication, but the man wasn't improving. As Abby ran through her usual intake routine, she froze at the foot of his bed. The man was practically covered in magic, and her Brotherhood training told her it was malevolent.

Despite their efforts to save him, his heart gave out, as sometimes happened with the elderly. Except this man wasn't elderly. He was no older than thirty, looked fit, and had no signs of being a drug user.

She had called Jacob on her break that night, and he started digging into it immediately. Three other men had died in similar circumstances downtown over the past year. Jacob pulled some strings and had the bodies exhumed, where possible, to check for lingering magic. Only two other corpses had been available—they both confirmed their suspicions. A malevolent was feeding on men downtown. Each death had occurred at regular intervals, about every three months.

They suspected some kind of life-stealing human imitator was at fault, but there were so many types, they couldn't make a guess without more evidence.

When her phone rang, she was midway through running back and forth to her bedroom, double checking that she had all the supplies she needed. Seeing Gwyn's name on the screen, she didn't wait for his greeting before saying, "Be right down!" and accidentally hung up on him in her eagerness. Whoops.

Apologizing to Gwyn for the mishap, she climbed into the back seat of Miles' car. The atmosphere in the car was decidedly frosty when she first entered. She didn't think this was because of her hanging up on him. No, they were probably arguing again.

Trying to break the tension, she asked, "So, where are we headed?"

Miles replied, "King Street Station area. Your guy and the other two we confirmed with magic on their bodies lived in the area. So that's where we're starting."

Abby couldn't hold back a slight flinch. Gwyn noticed.

"Abigail seems concerned. Is this area particularly dangerous?" he asked.

Miles scoffed. "Dangerous? No. But it is sketchy after dark."

"Sketchy? Does this word mean that we place Abigail at risk?"

"No, Gwyn." She paused, trying to understand his unique perspective before clarifying, "'Sketchy' means questionable." After a brief pause, she added, "The world has changed a lot recently. Women have way more freedom and rights than they used to, but it's still tough to feel safe out there sometimes. You know?"

Seeing his concerned expression, she reassured him. "Luckily, I have magic. I can defend myself easily if I need to."

To drive the point home, she performed a small spell, heating the air around her finger. Extending her hand between the front seats, she said with a teasing smile, "Go ahead, touch my hand."

Gwyn turned in his seat as he appraised her with a raised eyebrow, coincidentally catching her in the act of winking at Miles' silent laughter reflected in the rearview mirror.

"Well, go on," she urged him.

Gwyn reached forward but quickly yanked his hand back, wincing from the intense heat.

He conceded, "Impressive, Abigail."

"That's only half of the heat that I can generate on a single finger. I can't blast fire like you can, but I've got hot hands. Also, I can generate a passable aegis."

Like most mages, she could manage a little of every kind of magic, but her strengths lay in enchanting objects, with telekinesis as a close second. She suspected that telekinesis developed out of necessity, helping her move enchanted objects into place. Compared to what Miles could do, her shield wasn't great, but it would block most attacks for a while, short of a bullet.

After a short drive through the sleepy downtown, Miles found a place to parallel park a few blocks away from the station.

As they took off their seatbelts, she asked, "So, what's the plan, boss?"

Miles replied, "Here's what I'm thinking. Gwyn and I will sweep the pedestrian-only areas separately."

Abby nodded. "Makes sense. A woman wouldn't be wandering alone in one of those places at this time of night."

Gwyn interjected, "Abigail and I could travel there together."

Abby shook her head. "That's fine for a bit, but most of the creatures we're after wouldn't reveal themselves to a group, let alone attack one. We need them to leave their hiding spots."

Miles agreed. "Right. My thought is, Abby stays street-side. Some of the pedestrian areas are lower, with roads above. The streets below are far more isolated and dangerous than the bustling streets above. If she's up there, we'll have a pair of eyes overhead to see what we can't from below and she'll be safer."

She reminded them both, "I have my phone. Keep your ringers on."

Miles nodded. "So, is it a plan? And remember, Gwyn, no visible magic."

Gwyn glanced back at Abby in the rear seat and nodded. "Let's hunt."

They filed out of the car and walked in silence along the quiet streets. Downtown blocked most of the wind, but Abby's hair still whipped across her face, prompting her to pull up her hood. Only the occasional seagull call and the hum of a car engine interrupted the sound of their footsteps. Miles broke off first, giving a low wave as he descended the steps toward the football stadium. Abby continued walking with Gwyn for another block.

"You realize that's the only way down, right?" she pointed out.

"I understand that now," Gwyn admitted with a small smile. "I'll be honest—I didn't want to leave you."

"I'll be fine. You're at a much higher risk down there than I am. Up here there are cars passing by and plenty of witnesses that should keep most danger away."

Despite her confidence, anxiety fluttered in her chest, and she instinctively leaned toward him for comfort. She hugged him impulsively. After a brief hesitation, he hugged her back. It dawned on her that this was the first meaningful touch they'd shared, rather than a fleeting brush of hands.

The embrace lingered, with neither of them in a rush to leave the warmth of their bodies pressed together. She hoped that this hinted that there could still be a deeper connection between them; something beyond just friendship after the truth of who he was came out. She was the first to retreat, though his absence left her with an ache of longing. He turned on his heel and followed Miles down the steps.

Abby walked north along the main street for a few more blocks before exploring the side streets. She tried to use a modified version of Will's method to detect magic, but it was hard to tell if it worked. Even her instincts told her nothing was happening around her. Neither had she received any texts or calls, which meant the guys weren't having much luck either. Bored with failure, she circled back to check the underpasses where Gwyn and Miles were hunting.

When she reached the old tunnel that connected to the nearby Sounder light rail station, she spotted a familiar dark shape. The angle made it hard to tell whether it was Miles or Gwyn, but she guessed it was Gwyn because of the leaner build. Except he wasn't alone. A smaller figure stood a few feet in front of him.

Were they... talking? Abby quickened her pace but then stopped suddenly. When the figure stepped out of the shadows, Abby could see through the glamor the creature was projecting that the back half of her body wasn't human at all. The woman's hairless, skinless lower half resembled a decaying tree stump, hidden only by her clothing. Malevolent magic radiated from her.

Abby grabbed her phone and called Miles.

When he answered, she whispered urgently, "The old train underpass. Now!" She hung up, her attention snapping back to Gwyn as he stepped toward the woman, who was reaching out to him.

No.

Gwyn

"A mage!" The woman's voice was bright, almost cheerful. The way she'd moved under the dark city streets didn't fit the expected behavior of a young woman out alone. Gwyn was immediately suspicious.

Until he forgot to be...

Another language of his childhood, a language of nostalgia. Her voice reminded him of home. It reminded him of traveling traders and fishermen with their ruddy faces, and ever-present battle ax at their sides. They would hawk their foreign wares to the nobility at outrageous rates, claiming their prices were fair due to the epic journey they'd undertaken to reach farthest Wales.

The memories left him feeling unsteady. They made him forget what he was there for. He shifting his feet to balance on the railroad ties instead of the rough-and-tumble ballast rocks that supported them. Even footing would serve him well, whatever situation he found himself in—that lesson too far ingrained in his psyche to ever forget.

"It must nearly be time for the gathering. He must have sent you to deliver my promised attire!"

The voice stepped into the light cast from a streetlamp above, revealing a petite woman with waist-length blonde hair so fair it was nearly white. Her clothes were disheveled, as if she'd scavenged them from the streets. But her eyes—glimmering, translucent blue—held him captive. Her skin glowed with an otherworldly radiance that made it impossible to look away.

"No. I'm…" But his denial caught in his throat as her smile vanished. With no discernible reason for the change, everything suddenly shifted.

The warm tingling spreading through his body quieted the voice in his mind, urging caution. His posture relaxed, and his worries melted away. He suddenly knew, without a doubt, that this woman needed his help—his protection. The weight of her frown felt like a punishment, and the very thought of displeasing her filled him with dread.

His foot slipped off the railroad tie, and his balance faltered on the rocky ballast. Yet, as he stepped forward, he craved nothing more than to bask in her radiance. As the woman reached her hand out to him, Gwyn wanted to allow her anything she desired, without limits. He couldn't fail her again. The idea of disappointing her felt like a fate worse than death.

Despite the sound of rocks quietly scraping and shifting nearby, the enchanting woman held his gaze steadily. She had his undivided attention. Nothing could break it.

Nothing except the sudden fury that ripped through him when a ballast rock fell from above, crashing onto her outstretched arm. The glow of her skin flared to a blazing brightness, nearly blinding him, as a scream tore from her throat—a hollow sound, like a child blowing with all their might into a broken horn.

Gwyn's memories of battles from his former life were vivid. His spiraling worries and unanswered questions about his previous lives, both human and ascended, often kept him awake late into the night. Even in sleep, battle memories would jolt him awake, his heart racing, his body drenched in cold sweat. So he recognized the sickening squishing, crunching sound he associated with the blade of an ax or a sword meeting an unhelmeted head as the rocks slammed into her, sizzling from magical heat. Three more, even larger, burning hot rocks, fell from above, crushing the woman's unprotected head and shoulders.

He stumbled backward, feeling as though he had taken a blow to the midsection from one of the falling rocks, though there had been no physical impact. The sound—or perhaps the creature's death—had viciously broken the enchantment she had held over him. Losing his footing, Gwyn fell hard onto his backside.

Footsteps rapidly approached from behind. Miles stopped just short of him and offered a hand.

Abby's worried voice carried down to them. "Is he okay?"

Gwyn accepted Miles' hand with a moment's hesitation and dusted off his trousers.

"He's fine," Miles answered for him. Then he turned to Gwyn. "What happened?"

Gwyn glanced up, seeing a crown of blonde curls about twenty feet away on the street above. Looking up at her, he managed a feeble smile. "Our quarry is dead, thanks to Abigail. I think it was a skogsrå. They drain the life energy from their male victims."

Miles frowned, confused. "So where's the body, then?"

Gwyn looked around and spotted a pile of rotten wood a few feet away. He pointed at it.

"Convenient," Miles muttered, pleased they wouldn't have to clean up.

Still agitated and murmuring angrily to herself, Abby shouted down at them, "To hell with the edict!" She stomped furiously toward the stairs leading down to them.

The harpy she had transformed into was everything Gwyn remembered about his past love—and more. Memories, long buried, resurfaced at the sight of her fierce beauty and power, leaving him breathless. The secret he had been toying with now seemed even more possible, frightening him more than the skogsrå ever had.

But he... he was still less of a man than he hoped to be. His ego had taken a hit. His confidence in the hunt had been naïve and foolish. He'd underestimated the dangers they would face and overestimated his own readiness, leaving him vulnerable and indecisive at a crucial moment.

Now, he had to decipher the skogsrå's words. "Gathering?" "Attire?" And who was the 'he' she spoke of?

The easiest person to imagine as the skogsrå's conspirator was the man from the library only the day before. But he'd called himself an ally. Gwyn needed to consider her words before he made himself look like a fool in front of Abigail once again.

Amid the hubbub following the successful hunt, no one noticed the pair of stylish shoes attached to two short legs scurrying away at a suspiciously brisk pace.

Chapter Eleven

The Underdog Loses

Esme

Three people for sure knew something about the controversy surrounding Esme's parents' deaths. One of them was probably still raging in the forest because Esme had killed his girlfriend in self-defense. An angry leshy, especially one powerful enough to sit on the Assembly, was not someone to trifle with. To avoid upsetting Sylas, Esme decided to wait patiently for him to come to her when he was ready, no matter how much it hurt.

The next person who came to mind was Jacob, but he'd been tight-lipped about her parents on more than one occasion. It didn't seem worth pushing for answers from him just yet. No, the key was the third person: Maureen Mitchell—Esme's former bully, a seated member of the Assembly of Mages, and a powerful evocation mage.

After Esme first learned of her demonic heritage, Jacob explained that there was a faction that regarded those with demon blood as inherently untrustworthy, corrupted humans. Maureen was one of those people. But she had been silent about Esme's "tainted" status ever since Esme had saved her from the pishacha—twice. Friendship seemed unlikely, but if Maureen would stop bullying her, at least their interactions would be tolerable. Given their past, it seemed entirely possible that someone like Maureen would jump at the chance to gossip about Esme's parents.

That thought process brought Esme to Maureen's doorstep, dressed in demure clothing and slightly perspiring, despite the cold, humid air, and holding a basket of baked goods. This wasn't her first visit to Maureen's home, but it was her first time coming voluntarily. Months ago, Esme had been called in to clean up enchanted rats at Maureen's house—pest control wasn't exactly an option when magic was involved. Being on the Assembly's payroll, Esme had used her conjured minions to remove the rats one by one.

In her red raincoat, she felt like Little Red Riding Hood about to greet the Big Bad Wolf disguised as Grandma. If Maureen refused to see her, the only things Esme would lose were the driving time and a bit of her dignity, but she was well-practiced at the latter.

She rang the doorbell and watched as the light showing she was being recorded by the attached camera flashed on. Esme plastered a cheery smile on her face and waved for the camera, lifting the basket to show she was also bearing gifts.

A moment later, she heard the sliding click of a deadbolt being thrown open. Maureen's day job was in finance—probably something fiscally vampiric in nature—so Esme was used to seeing her in stuffy business attire. But when the woman, in her late forties, opened the door, she was dressed far more casually than Esme had ever seen her, in a loose University of Washington sweatsuit.

After she recovered from her shock, Esme spoke hastily, partially because she'd practiced her initial speech on the drive over and partially because she wanted to get the rejection over with if it was coming. "Good morning! I know I didn't call first, but I wanted to talk to you about something personal—if you have a few minutes. And I brought muffins and scones!" She held up the basket as if it contained gold instead of glutinous delights.

In lieu of a greeting, Maureen asked, "Aren't muffins and scones basically the same thing?"

No. Not at all. Muffins were more cake-like, while scones were more bread-like, but this wasn't the time for arguing over food. So, Esme laughed and said, "Haha, yeah. The muffins are blueberry since I know your husband likes blueberry drinks, and the scones are vanilla bean—they'll go well with coffee or tea."

Maureen gave Esme an up-and-down look, clearly assessing her motives. Given their history, Esme couldn't blame the woman for questioning her motivations to show up at her house unexpectedly. So, Esme offered a bit of truth.

"It's about my parents. I don't trust other people to be honest with me about some of the bad things they might have done."

Still standing in the doorway, Maureen visibly struggled to mask her reaction. Esme had dangled a juicy piece of gossip, and Maureen had taken the bait. She opened the door wider. "Well, come in then."

Victory.

Maureen's home in the Leschi neighborhood was as old as Esme's bungalow, but much larger and nicer. Hers was the sort of home that should have lively parties in the backyard on a sunny day. Instead, the beautiful home hosted an adult bully and her overly timid husband.

Maureen led her to the front sitting room, a rarely used relic in houses of this era. She took the basket and left Esme sitting alone for a few minutes while she fetched coffee.

Esme's focus shifted to her breathing, a conscious effort to manage her anxiety and hostility for a more fruitful conversation. By the time Maureen returned, Esme already felt much better than she had when she first walked through the door.

Placing the cups on fancy coasters, Maureen prompted, "So, what's this all about, Esme?"

Esme took a sip of her coffee, hoping it wasn't poisoned, to give her mouth a moment to catch up with her racing thoughts. *Just spit it out.*

"I recently found out that my parents might have been up to some morally questionable things around the time they died." She exhaled slowly and placed her mug back on the coaster. That was too much, too fast. She needed to start again.

"Look, Maureen, I don't know what you know about my past, but my parents worked hard to keep me away from the community, from magic, from everything. I didn't even know magic was real until I was seventeen because they hid it all from me. I didn't even know I was a cambion until like, six months ago."

Maureen's body relaxed in her chair, as if taken aback.

Esme scoffed. "Bet ya didn't know I was ignorant on top of all the other things you've called me." Gods above, she hadn't planned on such hastily spoken vitriol. But this woman always got under her skin.

She added, trying to smooth things over, "I'm not here to fight. Like I said, I don't trust other people to be honest with me about my parents. They hid so much from me."

Maureen cleared her throat and asked, "You truly didn't know about your demonic roots?"

Esme sent her a flat look. "No." *Thanks for treating me like shit over it for years.*

"Jacob never said a word about it to you?"

Esme barely maintained her composure. "No."

"Well... That is news to me. Fine," Maureen huffed, "What do you want to know?"

"Someone mentioned my parents were up to something shady before they died. I'm trying to figure out what."

"Ah," she mumbled. Then Maureen sat silent for a long minute, thinking carefully about her answer.

Eventually she said, "Your parents were messing with powers they never should've touched."

"Like what?"

Maureen studied her for a moment and, as if coming to a decision, said, "I saw what you did in the forest when you saved us, Esme. I know you've touched infernal power at least once."

"Yes," Esme admitted, hoping some honesty might earn her the same in return.

"Who taught you to do that?"

"I did it accidentally." This was a half-truth. In reality, Finn had encouraged her to imbue her conjurations with "angry magic" after teaching her the differences between malevolent, Fae, and general magic.

Maureen barked, "Don't do it again! That's a door best kept closed." Now this was the Maureen Esme was more familiar with—unreasonable and hostile.

"But why?" Esme asked.

"You really are ignorant, aren't you?"

Yes. She was tired of feeling that way, too.

"I saw the aftermath of what you did in the forest. Can you honestly tell me that any sane person would do that?"

That hit Esme right in the solar plexus. With so much happening in her life, she managed to suppress the nagging guilt she felt over killing Juniper on most days. But Maureen's words brought the scene back, clear as a horror film. Maureen couldn't have known that Esme was mentally riding with the eldritch beast while she used it to tear into the dryad's flesh, sap draining out of her like blood. She couldn't know the depths of darkness Esme had sunk into. But Esme said none of this. Because if someone like Maureen knew, Esme would be the first mage to be burned at the stake in a couple hundred years.

Maureen filled the quiet. "Infernal power is a drug, Esme. It will control and consume you."

There was some truth to that, but not the way Maureen meant. When the lives of her friend and herself were at stake, Esme had no choice but to visit the dark place that infernal magic required. Her desperation had driven her deeper into its pull than ever before. She'd lost track of herself in the process, but since that incident, she had deliberately come into contact with the infernal again, without further issues.

To Esme, the dark place didn't feel like a drug like Maureen described it; it felt more like a place to hide.

Sounding almost surprised, Maureen said, "I can't believe I'm about to say this, but I believe you, Esme. I believe your ignorance was real, and you used the power accidentally. You saved us from that demon. I guess it takes one to kill one, right?"

She had the audacity to snort in Esme's face after that back-handed compliment.

Maureen added, "You've done good work for the Assembly for years."

Was that a straightforward compliment coming immediately after the backhanded one? Esme might have a heart attack from the shock.

"So here's the truth, "Maureen explained. "Your parents were trying to harness infernal power to control malevolents. The idea was that, since malevolent magic is an offshoot of infernal magic, the older form might hold sway over the newer type. Kind of like how the rules of general magic override what the Fae try to do with their brand of devilry."

So her parents also knew about the malevolent problem and never said a word to her. *Typical.*

"What?" Esme asked, not really knowing what she even meant by the question.

Maureen sounded like she was teaching a lesson, not dropping a bombshell. "It got them killed, Esme. They didn't die in a car accident."

Something as big as the International Space Station must have fallen out of the sky and hit her because Esme felt flattened. She closed her eyes, shutting out the world. The warm image of her parents' beaming faces greeted her there.

But her next thought, knowing exactly what the malevolents were capable of, made her open her eyes wide. She wouldn't hide. She refused to let her thoughts go in that direction. It had been over ten years since their deaths, and she had finally found some true happiness in her life. This news would not—could not—destroy her.

Esme had to keep going.

She told Maureen, sincerely for once, "Thank you for telling me. And for the coffee." She stood and walked straight to the front door in a daze without saying another word.

Maureen stopped her as soon as her fingers were grasping the handle. "Jacob will confirm it."

That was exactly what Esme planned on finding out... immediately.

As Esme walked to her car, she realized there had been far too many hushed conversations between her parents when she was a teen. Were they talking about normal "can't let the kid hear this" stuff, or was it something more? Gods, she'd been a naïve child to miss so much.

She still had the option to turn back, even now. She could walk away and never think about it again. Her life was just starting to be lived, to be enjoyed. She didn't have to stir up trouble. The problem was, Esmeralda Morgana Turner did not like loose ends.

She drove straight to Jacob's house. He was home more often than not these days, so it was a safe bet she could simply drop in on him. She keyed in the gate code and parked close to the front door. Now, she felt like Little Red Riding Hood in her raincoat, heading to the woodcutter's house.

She let herself in using the keys he'd given her years ago. The multitude of magical alarms in his house recognized her, so they didn't activate. It was nearly lunchtime, so Jacob should be awake. She called for him, more out of habit than expectation. Despite being hard of hearing, Jacob refused to wear his hearing aids at home, so this tactic rarely worked.

She made a beeline for the library, where she often found him either napping or flipping through old books. Even though he could afford a huge house with a garden in one of the city's nicer areas, he often fell asleep in the same ratty old recliner he refused to replace. He was one hundred and six years old, so she supposed she couldn't blame him for his eccentricities.

His library was a gorgeous example of the classic style done right, with floor-to-ceiling bookshelves filled with tomes of magic, classical literature, and modern works. To her surprise, Jacob was wide awake.

He looked up from the desk where he was working and said, "I know that look, darling. What did I do this time?" His Received Pronunciation was in full force. It appeared he was taking notes on a relatively modern book about wards. Interesting.

The fact that he'd said "this time" was telling. But if she jumped straight into questions about her parents, she'd screw it all up. Plus, she was an adult, and being a total jerk wouldn't help her get the answers she was after.

With forced cordiality, she said, "Hi Jacob, how are you?"

His lips formed a flat smile. He saw right through her bluff. "I am doing relatively well, Esmeralda. How are you? Is this visit a follow-up on the listening you did at the bar?"

It wasn't the first or the twentieth time she'd shown up at his house unannounced. She'd worked with—and for—Jacob for more than a decade. He was practically her adopted grandfather, having supported her through the grieving process and handling the overwhelming paperwork that came with death. He had also been her mentor, though recently she'd begun training with Finn instead.

She started the conversation by addressing the smaller of the two issues that were currently bothering her.

"I'm... surviving. Anyway," she shook her head vigorously, as if trying to dislodge a bothersome thought. "What's the holdup with finding a place for Gwyn? Are you stalling? He and Miles are not getting along."

Tension at Miles' house was palpable, the kind of energy where murderous thoughts seemed to pulse from both men. It was exhausting just being there when they were both present.

Jacob huffed out a small laugh. "Esmeralda, you could ask your beau that question."

Labels again. She really needed to talk to Miles about that, about their exclusivity and titles, but she currently didn't have the energy to argue with Jacob.

"Yes, I know Miles is in his overprotective mode, wanting to monitor Gwyn, but it's making him miserable!"

Jacob closed the book he'd been working on and pushed it aside. "Yes, well, he's a grown man, and I'm here to help, not hinder."

Help, not hinder? Really? Any moment steam would rise from the stifled anger burning within her.

Jacob added, "I know this may sound harsh to you, but we have to make sound business decisions. We're still waiting for Gwyn to prove himself worthy of investment."

"Killing two Dullahan and nearly dying in the process wasn't enough? And training me, hunting malevolents with Miles, plus telling his entire life story while Abby records it, which you hope to get some new magic out of, isn't enough?"

Jacob shrugged. "Gwyn came here with questionable intent. He has a tall mountain to climb to win my trust."

She had paced so much in that exact spot she was standing on that she expected there to be scuff marks on the floor by now. But, no, Jacob's house was as immaculate as ever.

"Trust," she said, continuing to pace—some things never change. "I need to be able to trust you, Jacob."

She blew out a huge breath. "I'm trying to stay calm and collected, but I'm really upset right now. Yes, this is about the listening I did at the bar."

He turned in his seat to face her squarely. Despite his fragile appearance, he possessed immense inner strength.

"I overheard people debating whether I had something to do with"—she made air quotes with her fingers, mimicking the voice of the man who had said it—"'twice in one month... who knows what kind of creatures she can summon.'"

He brushed off her worries with a dismissive tone. "I have no doubt that this will blow over, darling. They'll find something else to occupy their minds and tongues with soon enough."

"But I know that some of this has blown back on you!"

"These things happen, Esmeralda. Don't worry about me."

It seemed he thought that was the end of the conversation. Unfortunately, she had to disabuse him of that notion.

"Wait, there's more. The same group of older couples followed up with something like, 'Don't forget about her parents. You know what the rumors were. They were just asking for problems with what they were up to.'"

She stopped pacing and faced him directly. "I talked to Maureen about an hour ago. She told me my parents were trying to use infernal magic to control malevolents. Why didn't you ever tell me?"

Jacob's expression morphed, growing somber as he replied, "For starters, we have not talked about their deaths in quite some time."

Her mouth tasted sour from the bitterness of deceit. "That doesn't excuse the omission, Jacob. Is it true?"

Jacob's lips flattened into a tight line, and with a nod, he said, "Yes."

She had to hold back tears. "Why didn't you tell me in the months since I've learned about malevolents?"

He averted his gaze, scanning the room as if desperately seeking an answer that might placate her.

But then his face turned stony.

For the first time in her life, his voice carried a sharp undertone of anger, directed at her. "You want the truth, Esmeralda. Fine. Here's the truth. You've messed around with harnessing infernal power in new ways twice without proper supervision. I wasn't about to allow you to make it a third, *possibly fatal*, time."

Her voice was very small when she asked, "What do you think I was going to do with this information, Jacob?"

"Exactly what they did. Run headfirst into 'solving the problem' with zero plan other than intuition. You can't tell me your personality wouldn't lend itself to such rash actions."

The painful truth cut deep, but the underlying reason behind it was even more agonizing.

"You're right, Jacob. Now that I think about it, that's probably exactly why you wanted me working for the Assembly. My hotheadedness adds that extra special something; that intensity you need in a minion you used to apply pressure on bad eggs."

The worst part was that he was right. But that still didn't excuse him from keeping the truth from her for so long.

But she wasn't finished yet. "Jacob, I'm thirty-one years old. I have no children, no husband, and no living relatives. I have a bachelor's degree, yet I work in a bar you own, occasionally doing things you order me to do 'in the name of all magekind.' All because I feel indebted to the Assembly for helping me after my parents died. If I'm rash, it's because I don't have much to lose, thanks to your influence over the choices I've made. And sure, my own incompetence played a part in blindly following you—up until now."

"Esmeralda..." he started, but she cut him off.

"No." She waved a hand, forestalling him. "I'm leaving. I need to contemplate the course my life is taking if I want to become someone who can be trusted with the truth."

She grabbed her purse and coat from the chair nearby where she left them and held back her tears until she was out of the house.

If only she'd glanced back, she would have seen the sorrow, regret, and love in Jacob's eyes as a single tear slid down his cheek.

CHAPTER TWELVE

DINNER DATE

Esme

Esme changed their plan for a cozy dinner at Miles' house to celebrate their brief freedom. The constant arguments with Gwyn had ruined the welcoming atmosphere there. It had been a month since their encounter with the ensorcelled Sylas, and she still felt the need to repay Miles for the surprise soup and hot chocolate he'd brought on their hike. So, instead, she'd made a homemade dinner for them to share at her house. She had even doubled the recipe to ensure they both would have enough leftovers for lunch the next day—anything to reduce their current stress levels.

As she applied a bit of makeup, she tried to bury the weight of the day—an impossible task, but one that was worth attempting, anyway. For their first sort-of date, she ditched sweatpants for her favorite jeans and a fitted top. For all they'd been through, they hadn't even had a real dinner out or even at home together yet. She hoped the night ahead would make up for that.

After her emotionally draining encounters that morning, she longed to replace the day's negativity with something positive. So, naturally, she almost pounced on Miles as soon as she opened the front door to greet him. He was still in work clothes—tailored trousers, leather shoes, and a button-up shirt. Even his hair looked unusually neat.

Once he stepped over the threshold, she closed the door behind him with a telekinetic flick and looped her arms over his shoulders, pulling him closer. With her face pressed against his chest, she murmured, "Hey."

He stroked her back as she lingered, unwilling to leave the comfort of his arms.

"Bad day?" he asked.

Still pressed against him, she replied, "Yep. Wanna make it better?"

He gently squeezed her. "Of course," he said, then kissed the top of her head.

She lingered a moment longer against his chest, the steady rise and fall of his breath calming her. Then, almost reluctantly, she tipped her head back, seeking his lips like they were a lifeline back to him. Her kiss wasn't just longing—it was the kiss of a woman thirsty for affection in a sea of negativity.

He returned her ardor with equal passion. His beard, grown longer than usual over the chaotic past few weeks, was pleasantly soft against her skin. As she released his upper lip, he whispered, "I've missed you."

That was all it took for her to lead him to the bedroom. She had deliberately prepared food that could be reheated later because this long-overdue reunion couldn't wait. How could she have gone more than a year without being with anyone and now feel like a starving woman when it hadn't been that long since they'd been together?

There was an undeniable intensity to their connection. Maybe it was the nature of their work together. Maybe it was the constant danger. Or maybe it was simply because everything felt right with him. Whatever the reason, it was indisputable.

While preparing their dinner earlier, Finn dropped by to grab the cookies she'd promised during sword training. The problem was that while she was too busy working in the kitchen to think about it, their never-ending game of tricks and mischief had continued.

So, as soon as Esme shifted her weight onto the bed, hoping to get into a more horizontal position with Miles, a whoopee cushion exploded with a crude sound. Esme curled onto her side, laughing uncontrollably, which revealed several more of the offensive toys hidden in her sheets. She looked up to find Miles grinning, leaning against the wall. Her affections had already mussed his typically unruly chestnut-brown hair into a wild, disheveled state that suited him perfectly.

Miles knew how mischievous she and Finn could be when they teamed up. The fact that he was still standing there, looking at her with affection shining in his green eyes after all that, suited her perfectly, too.

She asked him, "The night is still salvageable, right? Otherwise, I'll have to get that leprechaun back ten—no, one hundred—times over."

He answered her question with another kiss.

Later, as she lay sprawled out on the bed, feeling completely at ease for the first time that day, her stomach growled loudly, demanding food. Moments later, Miles' stomach growled in agreement. It took some effort, but they eventually made their way to the kitchen.

As they talked over dinner, she eagerly peppered him with questions about the hunt that Gwyn and Abby accompanied him on. Using a tried-and-true delaying tactic was the best way to avoid discussing her rough day for as long as possible.

"So, Abby pelted the skogsrå with rocks from the train tracks and then yelled, 'To hell with the edict?' Priceless! This story is absolutely going into my pick-on-Abby repertoire."

Miles chuckled. "It's worth thinking about, though. The number of malevolents that specifically feed on one gender isn't small. It might be wise to implement a rule that if the target is unknown, a varied team goes out."

"I like this idea," she said. "It might convince Jacob to send me back out instead of saying I 'need more training first.'" She impersonated his accent to mask the deep wound his words had left. "I'd love to get back out there with you again."

As usual, Miles was too observant. His face showed concern as he looked at her from across the table. By this point, he'd polished off his meal, leaving only an empty plate. He started, "Okay, so we're avoiding talking about something..."

He was a much faster eater than she was, so he pushed his plate away and folded his arms on the table thoughtfully.

In a playful gesture, she threw her arms in the air, pretending to surrender. "Fine. You got me. Yes, I'm not ready to talk about something just yet, but I'll get around to it, I promise."

She wanted to share her discoveries but didn't want to offload a ton of negative emotions during their first sorta-date.

"Alright, lovely, what do you want to talk about then?"

"You."

With a wary look, he uttered, "Alright."

Miles was probably the most accomplished person she'd ever met. But how did he get there? How did he become the person who Jacob trusted implicitly? Even though she felt more connected to him than she'd ever felt with someone else in the past, she really didn't know a lot about his background.

"What is the story behind your joining the Corded Brotherhood? I can't believe I've never asked you that question before."

"It makes more sense if I start the story earlier than my vows, yeah?"

She could hardly contain her excitement, her hands itching to clap. "Yes, *please*, I want to know everything."

"I think I had the opposite experience with magic as a teen to yours. When I was eleven, my mum got a nasty cut from a broken glass. I healed it without knowing what I was doing. She looked at me like I'd sprouted a second head."

His small laugh was genuine, like most of the hurt of the moment was gone. "My parents are both fairly weak mages. So, they really didn't know what to do with me after that. They basically shipped me off to a boarding school that was in the control of the London Assembly."

"Boarding school, really? How very British of you," she joked.

"It wasn't half bad. Having a good school on my resume helped me get into the medical program at university. I did well there and made a few friends. Anyhow, when I was around fifteen, a bogle managed to sneak into the boys' dormitory. I don't know if you're familiar with them, but they're bald Fae with large pointed ears, dark blue skin, and wicked fangs. This one was maybe half a meter tall, so it must have been an adolescent. When I caught it going through things in my room, it attacked me."

He pointed at the scar on his cheek. "That's where this is from. The bugger tried to eat my face off! I won't go into the details of how over dinner, but I won the fight. I guess knowing I could fight and heal made me interesting to the leader of the London Assembly."

Miles grimaced, tugging at the scar on his cheek. "By the time I was starting my A levels, I was training daily. They wanted me to heal. They wanted me to kill. I became a tool to them."

Even if his expression hadn't changed, Esme was still starting to regret asking the question. These sounded like painful memories.

"That's why I joined the military, to escape the pressure they were putting on me. Obviously, my plan failed because I walked right back into the fold after my hand was blown off. But, by that point, I'd seen enough to know what I could do with my skills. I'd seen enough suffering and violence to know what I thought was *right*, if that makes any sense. At least the Corded Brotherhood's fight is clear-cut. Sure, sometimes the way we handle the problem is... debatable. But I think I needed to do something I thought was unquestionably right after everything I saw while fighting against humans."

From everything he said, it was like the Assembly leadership in London had meticulously shaped him to serve their own interests, disregarding his own, molding him into the man he'd become. It made her wonder if her situation with Jacob was like what happened between Miles and the leader of the Assembly there. Many of her life decisions after her parents' deaths had been driven by a desire to make Jacob happy and proud. Could he have felt the same way about this other Assembly leader?

"Are you still in contact with the leader of the London Assembly?"

He responded with an uncharacteristically curt "No."

She had a feeling that whatever was behind that must be part of the reason he moved clear across the world to Seattle.

Now that she'd temporarily parted ways with Jacob, now that she'd attempted to escape from her own metaphorical cage... What would she do next?

Miles reached across the table and grabbed her hand with his prosthetic one. "Alright, lovely, I answered your question. Now it's my turn. Please tell me what's going on. You know I'm with you, especially when things get difficult."

Of course, he just had to go with that last sugary line that never failed to pull on her heartstrings. It was the same thing he had said after she'd admitted her fears that she wasn't good enough for him after their first night together. Some mornings she still woke up wondering why he was with her, when he could easily have someone more like him, an expert in some field with their life perfectly mapped out. But then every once in a while he pulled out that line again, and she turned into a puddle of adoring goo.

Still, Esme stalled in answering by clearing the table and loading the dishes into the dishwasher. They were having such a great night so far and she knew what she wanted to talk about would ruin the mood. To delay further, she grabbed two over-sized cookies that she'd spared from Finn's clutches and brought them into the dining room with two glasses of milk.

Miles took one look at the treats and huffed out a laugh. "You're going to give me, and yourself, diabetes with all the baking you've been doing lately."

"What? It's therapeutic. Can you blame me, with everything that's been going on?"

He answered with a roguish grin. "I suppose not."

"Plus, I'm really banking on the small part of me that isn't human to neutralize that whole metabolic threat. It occurred to me that my parents never mentioned any relatives with cancer, diabetes, heart attacks, or any diet-related health issues. Heck, I might be wrong, though, because I still gain weight."

"Huh, that would be nice, considering how much of it we see in medicine nowadays. Anyway, Esme... if you feel you can talk about it, please let me know what's going on so I can help."

Miles was a natural fixer. If there was a problem, he had to resolve it immediately. It was probably torment for him to sit there while she delayed again and again.

His eyebrows shot up in surprise as she recounted what she'd overheard at the bar. When she explained how she went to Maureen's house seeking the truth and got much more of that particular commodity than she originally bargained for, he was far more subdued.

"I'm not surprised she opened the door," he said. "You saved her. So, do you believe her about your parents?"

"Well... That was only my first stop this morning." She grimaced. "I went to Jacob's house to confirm it. I'm fed up with people I should be able to trust constantly lying to me."

"But you can trust Jacob," he said, gripping her hand tighter. "He wants nothing more than to keep you safe."

Her anger flared, immediately erecting a shield of hostility to protect herself. She yanked her hand away from his. Was it too much for her to ask for her boyfriend, if that is what he was, to be on her side? Her heart ached, the wound was still fresh, and his cold logic felt like a blow in her already wounded state. She felt alone and misunderstood.

"Can I?" She hated that her voice wavered. "He's hidden the truth for years. About them. About me. Those aren't little white lies, Miles. And, sure, you can justify it by noting the secrecy around the malevolents, but he still didn't tell me after I knew about them!"

She added glumly, "On top of that, he practically admitted he doesn't trust me to handle my infernal powers responsibly."

She caught Miles' expression before he could mask it—surprise, maybe guilt?

Completely raw from the day's pain, she blurted out foolishly, "And you..." she swallowed hard. "You're hiding something, too. But I've let it slide, figuring you'd tell me when you were ready. What are we even, Miles? I have a key to your house, but I don't even know if we're exclusive."

He started to say something, but she cut him off, not wanting to see the still-guarded look on his face. She couldn't handle being brushed off again today. "You know what? I need to get a good night's sleep. Given everything that happened today, now's not the time for a deep conversation."

Just as she thought he would, Miles respected her boundaries and left. Because he was a good guy like that—too good. The only words he mustered were a sincere, "I'm sorry, lovely."

She'd whispered, "Me too" as he walked out her front door.

The realization that she'd anticipated that too-perfect response from him came to her quickly. Esme had been relying on him to continue his perfectly consistent behavior of respect. She was trying to push him away, to run and hide like she always did when the world became too much, after she'd already fought. A part of her was disappointed because she wanted him to stay and fight, but the larger part of her was overwhelmed and needed to be shut off for a while.

In the end, all she ever did was tear things apart—her metaphorical cage, her trust, her relationships. And tonight, like always, she had no idea how to fix what she'd destroyed.

The room felt too quiet after Miles left. The half-eaten cookies taunted her with reminders of the tranquil, domestic scene that could have been. She stared at the door for a long moment, waiting for something—anything—until she heard a faint scratching of claws, begging to be let in.

CHAPTER THIRTEEN

SHE WRITES

Abby

Abby chewed on the cap of her pen, a habit she couldn't quite break, even though she was planning to type everything Gwyn said. This was their second scribing session, but his first time at her house, making her anxious. Having met only days earlier at Jacob's, their initial meeting felt more businesslike and less intimate than this one.

She'd cleaned her entire apartment from top to bottom that morning, yet somehow, after Gwyn arrived, she still managed to find two small piles of dirty laundry. Her forearms were tired from the monumental effort it took to make her apartment presentable. She could use enchanted cleaning, but it wasn't as effective as elbow grease. Truth be told, Abby was a bit of a slob. Cleaning didn't register high on her list of priorities when there were so many more interesting and important things to do.

With her laptop on the table in front of her, Abby sat at her rarely used dining table, facing Gwyn. After welcoming him and offering refreshments, she insisted he get comfortable.

Yet he still sat stiffly. Should she offer him a blanket or something? She knew she was overthinking things, wanting everything to be perfect. Weeks after their first "date," everything about their dynamic had changed.

When they'd toured Pike Place Market together, she'd thought of him as just a normal guy who was new to Seattle, new to the US. But now, she knew he was probably the Gwyn ap Nudd of legend. His vivid description of the past and the average mages' immense power during their first scribing session further convinced her he might be telling the truth.

She'd seen him take down one Dullahan with the strength of his sword arm and another with pyromantic magic. Who was she to him now? The woman who'd caved in the side of a rampaging stallion using enchanted patio furniture? Or was she still the woman he'd met in The Sanctuary of Spirits, who'd shared a table and a drink with him? Did it matter?

She knew she was putting too much pressure on herself and on the situation. The only solution was to get to work. That's why he was there, after all—this was decidedly not a second date, even if she still wanted it to be.

Abby cleared her throat and said, "Last time, we talked a lot about the past in general. For a change, let's explore our sparse historical records. Historians say Nudd's reign suffered three plagues. Weird word to apply to an invading army, a giant thief, and dragons, but okay."

Gwyn responded matter-of-factly to her joke, "Yes, my memory is quite clear on the first one. I had not yet ascended."

It felt ridiculous having him seated in her dining room, in a chair that looked too small for him, while he casually talked about transforming into a demigod.

"Okay... well, if you were there, let's talk about the feast with the Coranians," she suggested. It seemed like a good place to start, and there might be some interesting magic in the methods they used to rid Wales of the dwarven invaders.

He leaned forward with interest, seeming genuinely pleased to revisit and share the memory. "In those days, even in the grandest keeps, everything was built from wood and stone. We couldn't conceive of the construction methods the Romans used. Do you have some paper I could draw on?"

She hopped up to grab the required materials from a kitchen drawer. Taking the pencil, he drew a large rectangle representing the great hall of Nudd's keep. Inside, he sketched a thin capital "I" in the center, which he explained was the great fire pit that warmed and lit the room. At the top of the "I," he drew a smaller rectangle perpendicular to the great hall's shape, showing where the throne and raised dais were situated.

"For good reason, my father was distracted that evening, so Creiddylad was able to sit by me at the high table for part of the meal."

Why did they have to immediately wander into the most awkward topic concerning Gwyn's history? The legends said Gwyn tried to steal Creiddylad, his sister, from her husband on their wedding day. She didn't want to hear the answer, but damn it, Abby had to ask. "She was your sister... right?"

"By all the magic... No!" he nearly shouted his refusal.

She'd clearly hit a sore spot; Gwyn was flustered and probably offended. "Creiddylad was Nudd's ward, fostered by her family with us to prevent disputes between our kingdoms. Your historians have written perversities upon my life."

He deflated at her expression. "I apologize, Abigail. The rewriting of her parentage has been the most disgusting revelation I've had about my reputation since my reemergence. This angers me more than even those who say I ride with demon dogs and consort with the devil. It besmirches her name, not just mine… I'll continue.

"Your legend is wrong about who gave Nudd the idea for the potion that killed the Coranians. Llefelys had nothing to do with it. Nudd had no love for his brother. He never would have contacted him for help, for anything. My grandfather had a good reason to give Llefelys the place you now call France. If their homes had been any closer, their constant fighting would have escalated into war."

Gwyn finally relaxed his posture enough to rest his arms on the table. "But I suppose it's not unusual for men to erase the victories of women, especially when the victory was as great as this one."

Abby asked, "Are you hinting that Creiddylad created the solution?"

"Yes. She was quite clever. Her intelligence and scholarship made men uncomfortable. That's probably why that ulcer of a human being, Gwythyr, was the only one who would marry her. She rightfully made men feel small in comparison."

Abby found it refreshing that Gwyn appreciated Creiddylad's less traditionally feminine role in their society. She'd expected a man from his time to be more aggressively misogynistic.

His words showed his deep regard for Creiddylad. Listening to him talk about her, Abby felt a twinge of envy for a woman who had died a millennium ago. She realized, despite the absurdity, that Creiddylad possessed things Abby wanted but could probably never have.

Curious, she asked, "If she wasn't your sister, what stopped you from marrying her?"

Gwyn smiled ruefully as he scrawled a word above the drawing of Nudd's hall. She couldn't read it. It looked like a large pi symbol with a "v" and a lowercase "d" that might also be an "a."

Seeing her confusion, he explained, "Nudd."

"Oh."

"I was held in reserve for when my political usefulness was highest. Before that happened, I ascended and lost my value as a pawn in the game of marriage." Now he looked triumphant.

"Oh," she repeated, feeling a bit stupid.

"Back to the story," he continued. "As these things go, Creiddylad's task that evening was mainly to be pretty and engage in pleasant dinner conversation for our most prestigious guests. But, of course, she was the mastermind behind their demise. I remember her smiling as she watched them die. She was a force of wrath when threatened. It was beautiful."

Abby cleared her throat, trying to dislodge her ridiculous growing feeling of inadequacy. "So, how did she figure out that boiling some kind of insect in water and throwing them at the Coranians would kill them?"

Gwyn's laugh was genuine and joyful, not at all like a man mourning a lost love. Maybe he'd come to terms with it since his reemergence.

"We didn't boil the poor creatures to death," he said. "She found that immersing the beetles in water boiled with fragrant beans from a wandering merchant stirred them to such... energy that their flapping wings deafened the Coranians, whose hearing was their greatest power."

Was the solution they'd used to defeat a magical army truly that simple? She asked, "Like coffee beans?" A small chuckle escaped her lips. "Was she getting them amped up on caffeine?"

Gwyn's eyes widened in understanding. "Yes, that might be it. We traded far and wide back then. Perhaps it was coffee. Brilliant, Abigail."

She allowed herself a small smile at his praise. Sometimes, a girl had to take compliments where she could get them.

"So, if the insects didn't kill them, what did?"

"Well-honed blades."

A little disappointed, she said, "Well, that's not incredibly magical or exciting."

He spread his hands in the air, a resigned agreement.

Abby asked, "What happened to her?"

When her typing caught up to his words, she looked up and noticed him watching her intently, now with a sad expression.

"This is one of the gaps in my memory from those days. All I remember is that she died sometime later of a plague that killed indiscriminately."

His words said one thing, but they felt loaded with something more, like an apology for telling her the truth rather than mourning his lover's passing.

He changed the subject abruptly. "Speaking of significant events, Abigail, I wanted to talk about what happened with the skogsrå."

She buried her face in her hands. This was the conversation she'd been dreading. The brief car ride back to her apartment filled with Miles' incessant questions on the way had kept them from really talking after the hunt. She'd killed a creature by dropping super-heated jagged rocks on her head, less than six feet from him. If the skogsrå had been human, Gwyn would have been drenched in her blood from Abby's action.

Her words tumbled out in a rush as she apologized, face still hiding behind her hands. "I'm sorry. I just saw that she wasn't human and freaked out when she reached for you."

His concerned voice broke through her feeble attempts to shield herself from the world.

"You did the proper thing. I acted too carelessly that night. Abigail, you spared me from terrible harm. Thank you for your swift action. I... will do better in the future."

He drummed a frantic pattern on the tabletop with his left hand. "My concern isn't about the creature's death. I'm more curious if there's a special event coming up for mages. The skogsrå said something that's been stuck in my mind. She thought I was a messenger for someone. She mentioned a 'gathering' and said 'he' must have sent me to bring her some promised attire. What stands out is that she used a very specific word for clothing—with a formal meaning."

Abby's eyebrows nearly climbed off her forehead. "Formal meaning? She wasn't speaking English?"

"No. The language of northern peoples across the ocean from Wales. I do not know their modern name."

Maybe he meant old Norse. But then his words finally struck her, a cold dread seeped in and her heart stuttered in her chest. There was only one event that came to mind.

She finally answered, "The Solstice Gala."

He started to ask, "Do you think that..."

She cut him off, finishing his thought. "...someone invited malevolents to an event full of mages? Yes. Cover up her back half with a fancy dress and formal cape and that skogsrå could pass for Fae. Why not when six Dullahan just showed up at my parents' house? With that and the rumors flying around about movement at the top of the Assembly, something is going on in Seattle. We have to tell the Corded Brotherhood about this. ASAP."

She thought for a moment, then said, "But that can wait until tomorrow. No good will come of sending out the alert at this hour, when we still have a few weeks to prepare. Do you have any plans for tonight? I think we should write out your encounter with the skogsrå in detail for the report."

Gwyn shifted uncomfortably in the too-small chair. "I had thought to take a long walk after our meeting, perhaps to partake of a drink at The Sanctuary. I would welcome your company for either."

She could tell he wasn't trying very hard to disguise a lie. "Let me guess: you and Miles are back to squabbling like children, and you need to get out of the house?"

"In my mind, I refer to it as my floating prison," he half-joked. Picking at imaginary lint on his clothes, he casually added, "Esmeralda called it 'wingmanning.'"

Abby was not the least bit surprised. A knowing smile spread across her face. "Wow, she pulled an Esme on you."

"A what?"

She smiled ruefully. "You'll figure it out, eventually."

She waved his concern away. "Want to finish this, then watch a movie after instead?"

"A movie?"

"Yeah, we can download action, comedy, whatever."

"You'll have to show me what to do."

The realization struck her. He didn't know what a movie was. She could have the great honor of introducing him to a fictional world with elves, orcs, wizards, and magical jewelry.

"Wait, have you ever had popcorn before?"

"No."

"Gods and goddesses," she gasped, "go sit on the couch and get comfortable. We have to see to your modern education. I'm texting Esme to say you'll be home late because we're watching the director's cut."

If she couldn't have it all, she'd at least share a new experience with him for a few more hours.

Gwyn

Gwyn had spent the past months moving from camping outdoors to shelters and between hotels, so he was used to waking up in unfamiliar surroundings. But this was the first time he'd awakened in the early hours of the morning, cradling something warm. It was also the first time in what felt like weeks he'd slept without keeping one eye open, waiting for Nudd to strike first.

Abby had fallen asleep on the couch next to him while they watched the movie. He'd stayed awake, letting her rest while he marveled at the story playing out on the screen. At first, she slept sitting up, head thrown back, but as the movie went on, she gradually leaned sideways until her head rested on his shoulder.

When the screen went black, he found the device Abby had used to turn the television on and powered it off, but he still couldn't bring himself to wake her. He'd hesitated long enough that his head dropped back, and his eyes closed involuntarily.

Somehow, in their sleep, they'd shifted until his body was supporting hers in the narrow space of the couch.

Eyes cracked open to the darkness surrounding them, he still didn't want to move. So he closed his eyes and breathed in the scent of happier days, wishing he could reach out and touch her with meaning.

CHAPTER FOURTEEN

EVERYTHING SUCKS

Miles

Sleep had once again become a rare and broken thing for Miles. He felt sluggish, his muscles sore due to the lack of proper rest. His nights were punctuated by brief, restless spells of fitful dreams, each one haunted by the king.

With Gwyn now living with him and Esme gone, the visions had taken on a more vivid quality. Every creak of the house made him flinch, expecting betrayal in the dark. The constant stress of always watching his back, fearing that the man sharing his home would finally complete the job he'd started months ago in the forest, was most likely triggering the resurgence.

His restlessness made him painfully aware of Gwyn's absence as he lay awake the night after his first fight with Esme, counting how many times he woke up. When he woke the final time at five o'clock and still hadn't heard from her and Gwyn still hadn't come home, panic set in.

His phone screen blinked on again. Still no response from Abby after all the messages he'd sent her. His fingers hovered over the call button, twitching with uncertainty before he finally dropped it, decision made. He'd gladly seek forgiveness for waking Abby if it meant knowing she was safe. The fact that he hadn't spoken to Esme since leaving her the night before only compounded his stress.

Her flaws, the ones that still sometimes frustrated him, felt like pieces of her he wouldn't change for the world. Esme had a way of making him feel seen, in a way no one else ever had—as if she truly understood the parts of him he tried to keep hidden. She could make him laugh in ways no one else could. It was like she knew every secret key to unlocking the joy he'd buried six feet underground years ago. Even in the middle of their first argument, there was never a moment where he didn't want to reach out and touch her, just to feel connected. He'd probably screwed up royally by not staying to talk, but he thought it might be best to give her the space she requested.

Now he just needed to do something, anything to fix... something.

He grabbed his jacket and decided to stop by Abby's apartment on his way to work. He didn't hesitate to use magic to bypass the building's security. Morality wasn't at the top of his mind just then. He climbed the stairs and, pausing briefly, knocked loudly three times on her door.

A thump was followed by a muffled, feminine "Ouch" from the other side. Relief washed over him, quickly replaced by regret. He mentally berated himself for his anxiety, planning to make it up to her with a few lunches in the hospital cafeteria.

Abby opened the door, squinting against the bright hallway light. Her rumpled clothes and the sleep lines creasing her cheeks told him everything. She leaned against the doorframe, arms crossed, and mumbled in a groggy voice, "Hey. Uh, why are you here?" Her tone made it clear: he'd screwed up, and there'd be a price to pay.

His reply was accompanied by a phony smile. "Good morning. Sorry to wake you, but I was worried since you didn't respond to my texts and calls. I'm looking for Gwyn."

If Gwyn had skipped town, Miles would throw a party at The Sanctuary of Spirits. But if he was causing trouble in the city, Miles needed to know.

Abby opened the door wider, revealing a sleep-rumpled Gwyn, barely awake, pulling himself up from the couch in the same clothes as yesterday. Miles shot him a deadly glare, wordlessly conveying his opinion on Gwyn's continued presence in Abby's apartment. Gwyn's casual yawn before walking over only stoked Miles' irritation further.

Abby must not have appreciated his lapse in composure because she added snarkily, "I told Esme he was staying to watch a movie. It's not his fault she was too distracted to mention it."

So, Abby did not know they'd had a row the night before, either. For the second time in minutes, Miles must have given himself away because Abby's attention turned decidedly predatory. The intensity of her scrutinizing gaze only served to magnify the guilt he felt for not staying to talk, for not staying to fight with Esme the night before.

He needed to pull himself together. He forced his face to composure, refusing to let any further hint of emotion show.

Abby added, "Although, I guess Esme didn't know we fell asleep on the couch. Sorry. My bad for picking a long movie."

Gwyn came up behind her, and she glanced at him before shaking her head slightly—the kind of silent communication couples use. Nope, Miles didn't like that either.

She turned back to Miles and, raising an eyebrow, asked, "Anyway, why are you here so early?"

"I'm on my way to the gym before work."

"Okay... I think I know what's going on here." Now fully awake and clearly irritated, Abby re-crossed her arms. "Frankly, I shouldn't even have to explain this to you. I might be a tiny person with unimpressive... skills," she glanced around, probably ensuring the hallway was empty, "But I'm an adult who can make her own freaking choices, Miles. If I wanted to have Gwyn over for a massive fuck fest, I can. We fell asleep on the couch watching the movie. Get over it."

He'd definitely messed up.

"And while we're at it," she continued, her agitation rising, "you've been generous letting Gwyn stay with you, but let's not pretend it was a completely altruistic choice. He's not a prisoner. He's capable of making his own choices, too."

She ended with a sharp, "You're being a dick, Miles."

Gwyn's grin stretched wider, feeding off Abby's words like a satisfied malevolent. Abby began to close the door but paused. "Oh, and one more thing—don't forget it's Esme's birthday. But something tells me you already have."

The word 'birthday' hit him like a cold slap to the face. He groaned, a very American 'fuck' slipping out, as the realization settled in that he hadn't known that it was her birthday at all.

With a flick of her fingers, not even a full wave, Abby bid him farewell and telekinetically shut the door in his face.

Well, that had gone splendidly. He had some serious groveling to do after work and a long overdue conversation with Esme about something he'd never told another living soul.

Esme

Esme stood in the clearing where she often met Finn for magical training. The moon was full, shining through the tree branches above, but she wasn't cold—yet. Where was that leprechaun? He was probably hiding, planning to jump out and scare her as part of one of his ridiculous training methods. It was already odd enough they were training at night.

She sensed movement in the undergrowth nearby. A shadow flickered at the edge of her vision. One minute, everything was fine. She was prepared to be surprised. The next, a suffocating sense of dread settled over her. A primal instinct, a deep-seated feeling, told her that the rustling in the bushes wasn't Finn.

It was hunting her.

But what could she do? She felt paralyzed with indecision. Summoning a blade came easily this time, but it materialized, twisted and warped. The smooth edge she'd planned for it was instead serrated like the teeth of a monster. But there was no time to worry about her faulty casting.

A beast from her worst nightmares, eyes glowing red with malevolent magic, burst from the undergrowth, charging her.

The creature was a twisted amalgamation—tentacles flailing from its nightmarish form. Its muscular lower body resembled her shadowcat's in build. But the thick, mane-like scruff that covered the creature's neck led to a face bearing the jaws and fangs of a hellhound.

The eldritch horror she'd lost herself in when she'd lost control of her demonic side was back to complete the job it had started. It craved her full surrender to the magic, to the fury.

Desperation and fear fueled her magic, lending it speed. She sent infernal power to increase the strength and haste of the muscles in her shoulders and back. She struck. Her warped blade bit into the creature's wooden flesh. Shadows and brimstone rose in a fog of destruction from where the eldritch beast had fallen, obscuring her vision of what lay beyond.

Esme panicked, struggling to hold her ground, as she waited for the creature to leap back out of the smoke to finish what it started with her. Out of nowhere, a powerful gust of wind swept through, rustling the leaves and causing the tree branches to rock. She barely kept her footing. It blew the shadows and brimstone away, revealing the broken and bloodied body of Juniper.

Esme dropped to her knees on the forest floor beside her fallen friend. Liquid streamed down her face; not tears, but the thick sap that had leaked from Juniper's body as she tore it apart. A mournful scream, devoid of words but full of anguish, tore from her throat.

But no one was there to hear it. Her voice dissipated into the stillness, unheard and uncared for by anyone.

Beside Juniper's mutilated head, where her wild green hair didn't obscure the ground, an invisible hand inscribed a single word that sent a shudder through Esme: *Murderer.*

Then the forest shifted, and Esme realized she was at Finn's house, slumped in one of his too-small chairs. It was the same chair she'd sat in the first time they'd met, back when she had him tied to his bed, interrogating him. She pushed the thought aside. It was more disturbing that she had fallen asleep so easily. Knowing Finn, the teasing about it would be relentless.

Esme shook off the nightmare and looked around. She finally spotted him, cowering in a corner with his hands raised protectively over his head. Was he continuing some prank that she'd forgotten about when she dozed off? Then she heard the first crash in a long line of destructive noises.

Finn peeked through his arms at her as she stood to investigate. "Esmeralda, dove, yer awake. Please! I won't... I'll disappear, I promise. Please."

He looked as bloody and bruised as he'd been when the pishacha had imprisoned him with Will and Maureen. All three of her conjured trolls filed out of Finn's conservatory. She knew, even without seeing, that they'd destroyed the lush, meticulously planted, and lovingly cared-for garden it held.

But they weren't done yet. Somehow, she just knew. They picked up any piece of heavy, hand-hewn furniture they could find and smashed them into the whitewashed cob walls. The golden decorations and tableware that once adorned every available surface flew wildly across the room as the trolls found new furniture to destroy.

All three of her minions were warped by infernal power. They'd always been hideous creatures, but now they appeared as wicked, twisted versions of themselves. Their yellowish-gray skin sprouted spikes, and all of their teeth had elongated to form fangs. Their eyes blazed with malevolent magic, and their fingers had sharpened into claws.

Then Tom spotted Finn, and Esme knew, just as in her dream, that they were hunting him. She looked down to see that her hands were bloody and bruised, like a boxer's after a no-gloves match.

Had she...?

She yanked on her connection to her conjurations, but the link was sluggish. All three turned to face the cowering leprechaun and advanced. Why wasn't he standing and fighting them? Then she realized that his main offensive weapon, his ifrit fire, would also burn down everything around them, killing them both. She was powerless.

"No, no, no, no, no!" she screamed.

That scream seemed to unlock something because the world slowed down around her. Something clicked—this wasn't real. This had to be yet another dream. As this thought occurred to her, the same invisible hand materialized a neon sign in the air: *Ruinous*.

"This isn't real," she whispered, the truth dawning on her. "I'm dreaming."

But the nightmares had just begun.

The creature latched onto Esme's chest, fangs piercing the skin near her collarbone, was feeding off her torment and fear. With every passing moment, her body withered a little more as the creature grew fatter from its feast.

CHAPTER FIFTEEN

UNHAPPY BIRTHDAY TO YOU

Abby

The sun was setting by the time Abby and Gwyn showed up at Esme's front porch, hours after their tense encounter with Miles that morning. Abby banged on the door and rang the doorbell simultaneously. Pressing her face against the door, she shouted, "Woman, I know you're here! Your car is in the driveway. Open the door, or I'm coming in with my key and your birthday present!"

Gwyn fidgeted, clearly uneasy about the legality of their actions, yet he remained where he was. Abby had spent most of the morning thrift shopping for new clothes with him. It didn't seem right for him to keep borrowing Miles' clothes, especially since they weren't even the same size. Now he wore a vintage leather motorcycle jacket they'd found for a steal, along with black jeans and his old, worn hiking boots.

Lowering her voice, Abby hissed through the door, "You cannot ghost me like this on your birthday without it being a cry for help, Esme. We're coming in!"

She pulled out her keys and flipped to the one with an orange tabby cat painted on it, a nod to Mr. Snuffles, the beloved cat who was supposed to belong to Esme's next-door neighbor, although Esme liked to pretend he was hers. Abby opened the door, peeking inside to find nothing out of place in the living room. They walked into the kitchen—everything looked fine there, too.

Then she heard white noise coming from Esme's bedroom. Esme was a light sleeper—something they now knew was due to her enhanced hearing—so she always slept with a machine blaring to muffle street sounds. Still, it was hard to believe that Esme could sleep through the banging, doorbell, and multiple phone calls, even with the machine on. Maybe she was simply too sick to get up and grab her phone in between bouts of paying homage to the porcelain gods. Regardless, Abby needed to know and help.

"Stay here," she told Gwyn. "I'm going into her bedroom to check on her. That sound is a machine she uses to help her sleep."

He nodded, his worried expression stark. That same worry crept into her thoughts—an unwelcome intruder.

Abby cracked the door open. "Esme, I'm coming in. If you're sick, you know I've seen worse."

She opened the door and immediately knew she'd been dead wrong. She hadn't seen worse. Her stomach dropped all the way to her feet while her heart and mind raced together, throbbing with adrenaline.

"Gwyn!" she shouted, her voice full of fear and panic.

Her hands heated up as Gwyn's boots pounded down the hallway. With his height advantage, he easily peered over her shoulder to take in the scene before them.

Esme was sprawled out on her bed, still covered with her blankets, but a furry black creature the size of a small dog was lying on her chest.

Abby's shock grew as she realized that the creature didn't budge or make a sound in response to her entry or her shout. Stunned, she asked, "Why isn't it doing anything?"

"By all the magic..." Gwyn whispered.

Then Abby pushed him aside and ran to the kitchen, allowing her hot hands to cool down as she grabbed two of the largest knives she could find. When she returned, Gwyn was still standing there, not acting. What was his problem? Why wasn't he attacking it?

Angered, she shoved him aside again, knives ready in her hands, intent on stabbing the malevolent. Because that's what it was. She felt the magic plain as day once she entered the room.

"Stop!" Gwyn's command was so forceful it caught her off guard. Fumbling, the knives fell from her grasp, clattering as they hit the floor on either side of her.

He joined her midway to the bed. "It is an Alp. I have never seen one myself, but I have heard countless stories of them. They are usually invisible. That we can see it is probably a part of its diminishment post-emergence."

He lightly touched her shoulder. "Let us approach calmly. I do not think it will react."

"Why did you stop me?" Abby asked with more than a touch of hostility.

"Harming it will only hurt Esmeralda worse than it already has. It can heal itself by draining her of vitality."

Abby growled, "But can it heal a chopped-off head?"

He smiled wickedly, giving her what she hoped was an approving glance. "I do not know. I doubt you would be willing to risk Esmeralda's life to find out, however."

Together, they moved closer to the bed. Abby sighed in relief; Esme was still breathing. Purple bruises darkened her eyes, her cheeks were hollow, and streaks of dried blood marked where the beast's fangs had pierced her skin.

Abby's distress was tangible as she asked, "Then what do we do?" Her voice trembled. "I've heard of Alp. Let me think…"

She snapped her fingers as an idea hit her. She grabbed the knives off the floor and handed them to Gwyn. "A lemon!"

Abby raced back into the kitchen and flung open Esme's refrigerator. She let out a cathartic sound of delight when she found what she needed. She sliced the lemon into wedges and sprinted back to the bedroom, dripping pieces in hand.

Gwyn stared at her, baffled. "Abigail, what are you planning to do with that fruit?"

"Legend has it that if you want an Alp to detach from its victim, you need to place a lemon in its mouth." She rushed on, explaining, "I can't heat my hands or do any effective enchanting while I hold the lemons, so the first strike is all on you. Get ready to slice and dice or kill it with magic if this works. Got it?"

The look of approval was back on his face, lifting her spirits somewhat. "Clever. Let's try it. I am ready."

He looked ready, gripping the knives like he wasn't just a swordsman but a knife fighter. For all she knew, maybe he was.

As Abby leaned over to place the lemon slices in the Alp's mouth, a worrying thought hit her. Hating that she was allowing her fears to delay her, she asked, "It's not going to bite me, is it?"

Gwyn's face betrayed uncertainty. "Let us hope not. It cannot feed on you if you are awake, so you are safe."

"Alright," she muttered, rolling her shoulders, preparing herself for battle. Her heart raced and her trembling hands betrayed the rush of adrenaline surging through her veins. It felt ridiculous to have such a strong physical reaction to this relatively insignificant threat—she'd fought six Dullahan recently. She could dismiss this as a newbie's nerves. Even so, it felt like another mark of cowardice. Just get it done.

First, she touched the creature's back to test its reaction. Its fur felt rough and wiry, like some breeds of dogs have on their hackles. The malevolent didn't flinch. Gaining confidence, she trailed her hands up its body to its ears, then its eyes. Ready now, she gripped the lemon wedges tightly and shoved them between the creature's lips and teeth.

Nothing happened. It remained unresponsive.

When she turned around to see what Gwyn thought about this development, she saw he was still standing ready, knees bent, knives poised.

"Wait," he cautioned.

Backing away from Esme, Abby prepared her hot-hands spell. Steam rose from her hands as she poured more magic into the effort, hoping it would be enough to burn through the creature's thick fur quickly enough to make a difference.

After several minutes of no change, Abby declared, "It's time to summon the cavalry. How long until there's irreparable damage?"

Gwyn shrugged, uncomfortable. He was usually more outspoken, which made Abby even more anxious.

She forced her jaw to unclench and her shoulders to relax. "I'll call Miles, then Finn. They'll get Jacob involved for us."

Miles arrived in under thirty minutes, likely skipping patients and breaking speed records on the way. Abby sat on the bed with Esme, holding her hand, hoping Esme knew her friends were there for her.

When Miles stormed through the front door and rushed into the bedroom, he immediately grabbed Esme's other hand, clasping it in both of his and kissing the back of it. He whispered, his voice nearly breaking, "I should have stayed and fought with you. It would have been worth it to never see you like this. I'm so sorry, lovely."

His head snapped up to Abby's, and he barked, "You've tried lemons. Anything else?"

She shook her head. "No. Gwyn says that if we attack it, it'll just heal itself using Esme's energy."

Miles looked away from Abby and growled like a feral animal.

Abby flinched and saw Gwyn do the same in her peripheral vision. Miles had always been composed, even when fighting against malevolents. This was... different.

"I'm going to try healing her wound where the fangs are puncturing her skin. Be ready."

There was no mistaking the last sentence was a direct order.

Within moments, the golden candlelight glow of his power emanated from his hands as he placed them on Esme's collarbone. The Alp writhed, seemingly torn between staying latched on and fleeing from Miles' magic. With every movement, fresh blood spilled from the puncture wounds near Esme's throat.

Miles cut off his magic and glanced up at Abby once more. His voice was hollow. "I don't think healing her is enough."

Abby replied, "But it clearly didn't like your magic. Have you called Jacob?"

He shook his head, his face now a shade paler than when he'd entered the room. Abby had been sure he would have called Jacob straight away.

She steadied herself. "I'll call Jacob and update him." She gestured for Gwyn to follow, giving Miles a moment alone with Esme.

Jacob answered on the first ring. She put him on speaker so Gwyn could hear.

When she finished updating him on the situation, Jacob was silent for so long that Abby wondered if the call had dropped. Meanwhile, Gwyn paced tiny circles in the kitchen, moving his hands as if silently arguing with himself. Eventually, he devolved into muttering angrily in another language. Like Abby, he was restless and agitated.

When Jacob finally spoke, Gwyn stopped pacing to listen. "I'm going to send Guillermo your way. When he arrives, call me back. He'll get there faster than I can at any rate."

The Bastion of the Corded Brotherhood, known for his strict adherence to manners, hung up the phone on her without saying goodbye.

Gwyn looked at her quizzically and asked, "Who is Guillermo?"

Will pulled off his jacket as he walked through the house to join everyone else in the bedroom. "Jacob said that if I didn't show up ASAP, he was going to fry my ass, so here I am."

Abby snapped, "Stop pretending you're not as worried as we are. I'm calling Jacob back, so zip it. Capiche?"

The man who usually acted more like a nymph than the human he was, rolled his eyes and walked to Esme's side. From the moment he sat down next to her, Miles hadn't moved an inch from her side. Honestly, Abby was surprised he hadn't curled up next to her by now. It was obvious to everyone that he was head over heels for her, even if Esme didn't know it yet.

Esme's condition hadn't worsened since Miles used his magic on the Alp. Her cheeks were still slightly sunken and her eyes were ringed with purple, but she didn't look any worse. Maybe Miles' magic had slowed the creature's feeding.

When the call reconnected, Abby turned on the speaker, skipping the pleasantries just as Jacob had skipped saying good-bye. "Jacob? Will's here and, thank the gods, Esme hasn't gotten visibly worse. Tell us what to do."

The tone that Jacob usually reserved for Assembly meetings came through the connection. "Miles, I trust you can figure this out once I explain the procedure to your assistants. I'll focus on their tasks. Understood?"

Hearing his name seemed to jolt Miles awake, and he answered affirmatively.

"Good," Jacob continued. "Given that the creature seems to be reactive to Miles' healing magic, we are going to attempt to override its malevolent magic with his. Our biggest problem is that we cannot identify where precisely the malevolent magic is operating. That is where Mr. Cruz comes in."

"Uh oh," Will muttered under his breath. Jacob only used last names when things got serious.

"For Dr. Goodwin to know where to focus, Guillermo must observe the magic and create an illusion to highlight it. I trust you can manage simple illusions, Mr. Cruz?"

"Yeah, yep," Will replied, sweating like a student being grilled by their least favorite teacher.

"Now, unfortunately, Guillermo does not have the strength required to do this alone. In order for him to succeed, Gwyn, you must transfer power to him. If you are who you claim to be, this should be simple. Gwyn, I'm relying on your cooperation. Can you manage it?"

Jacob's tone carried an uncharacteristic challenge, but Gwyn only smiled in a devil-may-care way. "Anything for my sister... in magic." He added the last part belatedly.

"Good. If you can't pull this off, our efforts will fail. Abigail, darling, you'll be backup, providing extra power as needed—and, if necessary, kill the blasted thing if the others are overtaxed afterward."

Desperately, Abby argued, "But I don't know how to channel my magic into someone else!"

"You are more capable than you give yourself credit for. Now, here's how it will work. Mr. Cruz, will you please cast the simplest, least draining, sustained magic you can think of? Gwyn and Ms. O'Malley will feel your magic."

Will appeared more confident than he had been a few minutes ago, knowing that he'd have a backup power source. He said, "Got it. I'll cast a simple light spell."

Abby reached out and touched the glowing orb. It felt slightly warmer than the surrounding air. It tingled in a pattern as unique to Will as his fingerprints. One of the odd quirks of magic was how, with the passage of time, the unique signature attached to it faded. While traces lingered to let you know that magic had been used, within a very short time, it became impossible to discern exactly who had been the caster.

Gwyn followed Abby in studying Will's signature. It took Abby a long minute to be certain she knew the feeling of Will's magic well enough to answer Jacob in the affirmative.

"We've got it, Jacob. Can we move on now?" Her worry for Esme outweighed any care for being terse with the boss.

Jacob grumbled, "We're only halfway there, Ms. O'Malley. Now imagine pouring your magic into Mr. Cruz. The act is less like two instruments playing a duet and more like mixing a cocktail. Your magics should become intertwined. Do you understand?"

"Yes, I guess. Let's just get on with it!" Trusting in Gwyn's strength, Abby grabbed her knives again and braced for a fight.

Miles sat through the instructions with an expression of detachment. He was still pale, but he only had eyes for the woman lying comatose in the bed.

Jacob said, "If you're ready, there's no point in delaying. I'll stay on the line for questions. Begin."

CHAPTER SIXTEEN

SLEEPING BEAUTY

Esme

This time, Esme sat on Miles' front porch, watching the waves dance on Lake Washington. She knew her nightmares would soon darken, but for now, she savored this brief respite.

It didn't take long for a nightmare version of Miles to appear, walking toward her down the pier. He never wore his doctor's coat outside work, but in this nightmare, he made an exception. A look of disgust contorted his features at the sight of her. That single expression told her this nightmare would be full of a different kind of suffering.

He stopped in front of her, his expression hostile, and asked, "Why are you here?"

Against her will, she replied snottily, "We aren't done yet."

This time, the nightmare had stripped away her ability to control her own body.

He opened the door telekinetically and marched inside without looking back. She felt her legs carry her into his living room, her magic closing the door behind them. He slammed his brief-case onto the counter, his eyes a tempest of rage.

"Esmeralda," he said, "you've shown your true self to every-one. I don't even know why I'm indulging you right now."

He laughed with sarcastic derision.

With no control over her mouth, she asked in a haughty voice, "And just who am I, Miles?"

"Abusive trash who can't leave well enough alone. Get out of my house." His magic flung the door open again, pointing to the world beyond—a world that didn't include them.

She felt herself sink into the infernal—into the place of seclusion and gloom where she'd hidden during the darkest night of her life. Just as she knew in the first nightmare that something was hunting her, just as she knew her trolls were hunting Finn, she knew she was going to attack Miles. And she had no choice but to be a participant. She couldn't close her eyes either.

In her mind, Esme screamed expletives. She screamed and begged for forgiveness from everyone she'd wronged. If only she could find a way to fix it.

She cried out to her friends, begging them to intervene, to end the nightmares, to take any action, even if it meant hurting her, just to spare her from witnessing what was sure to come next.

But no one came.

Esme felt the nightmare version of herself conjure its own twin—but as a gorgon. Her golden-brown hair became writhing snakes, her body long and serpentine, both a sickly green color that her mind associated with infection and death. She kicked and thrashed, trying to stop the force compelling her consciousness to merge with the gorgon's, just as she had joined with the eldritch abomination when she killed Juniper.

The nightmare's author forced Esme to join in the agony of tearing Miles apart. She tore off his prosthetic limb, then she kept ripping. The violence only grew more grim from there. She fought against the force controlling her, but it didn't listen to her pleas.

After enduring the agonizing torment of experiencing every action in excruciating detail, the invisible hand wrote a single word on the wall in Miles' blood: *Belligerent.*

Gwyn

The malevolent magic that blanketed Esme never ceased its constant movement. It swirled like red smoke, writhing and clinging to her skin, invading her mouth and nose.

But all Gwyn could do was channel a steady stream of power to Will. Abigail stood off to the side, a shieldmaiden ready for battle, while Miles studied the blood-red magic with a clinical detachment.

Gwyn understood his hesitation. Starting something, knowing it might not succeed, was as terrifying as the failure you were trying to prevent. But Gwyn's concern for Esme's well-being outweighed his conflict with the other man. The problem was that his human body didn't have unlimited power reserves, and they were steadily burning through them while maintaining the illusion.

"Miles," Gwyn snapped, "your Bastion ordered you to begin."

Gwyn's sharp command had the desired effect. Miles immediately came back to his senses and grasped the Alp's face, ready to begin.

Golden light flared from his hands, swirling over Esme's skin. Everywhere it touched, it pushed against the oppressive red smoke. Where it met the malevolent magic, the blight recoiled, retreating like a snake driven back into its hole. The golden glow entered Esme's mouth and nose, chasing the malady away. Inch by inch, the red shrank, its furious twisting weakening under the relentless push of Miles' magic.

A small cry escaped Abby's throat. He couldn't agree with the sentiment more. The sight before them was marvelous to behold. And to him, it was a reminder of his father—another unshakable similarity.

The golden light flowing with precision and control triggered a memory of the meticulous grace his father had wielded in one of his darkest moments, when Nudd didn't think he was being watched. The moment was a mirror to his past, to Nudd's, to Elena's.

The memory nearly made Gwyn falter. But for Esme, he would keep going. He still had energy left.

Esme

The world around Esme shook violently, and she felt like she might fall apart. Was this next nightmare going to be watching all her friends die during the cataclysmic earthquake supposedly overdue for the Cascades? She was standing on the sidewalk in front of her house, but everything was warped from the tremors.

When she looked at the sky, it wasn't its usual blue or black, but a familiar shade of gold.

She *knew* that color.

In control of her body once more, she shouted, unable to contain her joy.

Gwyn

A sudden movement nearly distracted Gwyn from feeding Will's magic as he watched the swirling illusion. With a hiss, the Alp withdrew its fangs from Esmeralda, spraying Miles with bloody spittle. Its elongated mouth was grotesque next to its tiny, beady, black eyes. Despite the creature's threat, Miles remained focused, his attention solely on repelling the malevolent magic, which was quickly losing ground.

Gwyn heard a knife clatter to the ground and watched as Abby lunged forward, grabbing the beast by its scruff, the other kitchen knife still in her hand. With a sudden burst of strength, she slammed it to the floor, momentarily stunning it. Seizing the opportunity, she drove the knife in her hand through the back of its ribs with unexpected precision and force.

On the heels of her savagery, the golden light pouring from Miles' hands ceased abruptly. He tipped backward. Will lunged forward, ending his illusion spell, and caught Miles before he fell off the bed. Miles had overexerted himself, pouring too much magic into Esmeralda and paying the price.

Abigail continued her relentless assault on the malevolent creature, plunging the second fallen knife into its flesh. Gwyn grabbed Miles' legs as Will held up his upper half. Together, they repositioned him onto the bed so he could recover by her side.

It was remarkable that Abby wasn't covered in blood after the brutal attack. Leaving the Alp's corpse where it lay, she moved to the other side of the bed, opposite Miles. Kneeling down, she gently brushed a stray hair out of Esmeralda's face.

"Esme?" Abby coaxed, shaking her gently. The puncture wounds where the Alp had latched on were now sealed, but Esme's skin was still streaked with both fresh and dried blood. Abby checked her pulse, placing two fingers on Esmeralda's neck. "Her pulse is good."

Slowly, Esmeralda's eyelids fluttered open. Without lifting her head, she looked around at the faces surrounding her. The intense gratitude and awe in her expression nearly brought Gwyn to his knees. It felt like he was reliving the resolution of two tragedies from different eras simultaneously.

As Gwyn watched Esme's eyes fill with life once more, a profound realization struck him. Despite his suspicions and animosity, he couldn't deny the truth: Miles, whether he was Nudd or not, had discovered and safeguarded them. He had protected the two women whose very existence and current struggles might be the fault of Gwyn's own past actions.

Esme's gaze pierced through Gwyn's hardened exterior, melting away a layer of bitterness. For all his flaws and secrets, Gwyn could not deny that Miles was capable of unwavering dedication.

A booming voice resounded from the forgotten phone sitting on the bedside table, demanding, "Did it work?"

Weakly, Esmeralda croaked, "Yeah."

Abby added, "Jacob, stay on the line. We need to talk once I've got Esme settled." Then she turned to the others. "Will, get Esme water—plastic or paper cup, no glass. Gwyn, take off Miles' shoes."

Will grinned. "Hah! I get the good job."

Once those tasks were completed, Abby shifted into her nurse mode. "Since you got the 'good job' last time, Will, now you can throw the corpse in the trash and take it outside to the bin. No need to keep it in Esme's fridge until trash day with how cold it is. Shoo."

She handed Gwyn the phone with Jacob still on the line. "Here, take over while I ask her personal questions. Also, shoo!" Then she ushered both men out of the bedroom, saying she'd tend to Esme's private medical needs.

Back in the living room, Gwyn collapsed onto the couch. Will followed, washing his hands with a spring in his step.

"That felt amazing," Will declared, far too cheerful for the current climate. "Is that what you feel like all the time?"

Gwyn shrugged lazily. He felt drained.

"Well, if you ever stop being obsessed with the blonde beast in there, you know where to find me."

Jacob's voice crackled over the speaker. "Mr. Cruz, do you think this is an appropriate time for flirting?"

Will replied, "Sorry, bossman, I kind of forgot that you were on the line. Plus, I can't help it—the man is beautiful."

Jacob snorted.

Will said, "Anyway, y'all, I gotta go. I'm late already. Gwyn, tell Abby she'd better update me on Esme or else. You, tall, dark, and handsome... if you ever wanna try magic channeling again, call me. That was as good as..."

Jacob interrupted, ordering, "Do not finish that sentence, Mr. Cruz."

Gwyn didn't dare ask, "As good as what?" He kept his mouth tightly shut.

Will pulled a sour face at the phone and left. After the door clicked shut behind him, Jacob asked, "Blonde beast?"

The memory brought a wide grin to Gwyn's face.

Abby

When Abby returned from the bedroom, she plopped down heavily on the couch next to Gwyn.

"Jacob, I'm back. Esme's going to be alright physically, but she's lost a few pounds. I've never seen anything like it. Honestly, given what she's been through this year, I think therapy would benefit her. We must have someone on staff who can work with her, right?"

Jacob sighed heavily. "Yes, I agree. Is that all? I have concerns you need to check on."

"No, there's more, but let's address your concerns first," she answered.

"Very well. Investigate how it got in. I know Esmeralda's house is warded against most forms of entry. I personally placed multiple wards that don't require daily renewal. And it's too cold to think she went to bed with a window open. I'm not asking; I'm ordering you to check immediately."

Abby sighed. "Jacob, we know you're worried about her. You don't need to give us orders. We want to help."

"I sincerely apologize for my tone. I am... quite agitated."

"I remember her window was closed, and so was the one in the ensuite bathroom."

Gwyn joined her as they walked through the house, checking the windows and doors to confirm they were all shut and locked. "You're right—everything is locked up tight."

Abby bent to scratch her leg, and her keys clinked to the floor. Seeing the key that was painted to look like an orange tabby cat sparked an idea. "Mr. Snuffles! Alp can shapeshift. What if it disguised itself as her neighbor's cat? Esme would definitely have let it in."

As they made their way back to the couch, Gwyn added, "But she'd have to fall asleep with the Alp still in the house, correct?"

Abby nodded. "Yeah, but if that flea-ridden mongrel showed interest in cuddling, I think Esme would allow it."

Jacob said, "That's plausible, but it doesn't explain why the Alp targeted a demon-blooded mage in a warded house instead of one of the million defenseless humans in the city."

"I agree. Alp have a reputation for being intelligent. In folklore, they wear clothing, play tricks, and, of course, kill."

Gwyn speculated, "Her demonic blood might have attracted it."

Jacob agreed. "Unfortunately, that is a possibility. I'll make a trip out to her house to fortify her wards tomorrow, since I'm assuming that Miles will stay there tonight. Now, let's discuss your concerns."

Abby said, "First, have you heard from Finn? I called him for information on the Alp, but he hasn't responded. That's unusual for him."

Jacob grunted in displeasure. She noted he didn't actually answer the question. Instead, he asked, "Anything else?"

She touched Gwyn's leg, saying, "Tell him about the skogsrå."

Gwyn said, "When I approached the creature, she knew I had magic, which wasn't surprising. But instead of aggression or fear, she acted as if she expected to meet a mage. She mentioned that the time for the 'gathering' must be approaching if I was there with her 'promised attire.' As I told Abigail, the word she used to describe the clothing is very specific to formal clothing."

When he was done, Abby asked, "Jacob, I know this sounds crazy, but do you think that someone could be using malevolents? The first thing I thought of when Gwyn mentioned formal clothing was the Solstice Gala. If someone is using them to attack mages…"

Jacob said, "Given your discovery, it would be reckless to assume there isn't someone behind this attack. I'm starting to think that what Gwyn mentioned is connected to what happened with Esmeralda. If she said formal wear, she might have meant business attire. Which means we also need to consider the fourth-quarter meeting as a second possible target."

He added, "Or perhaps we are thinking in the wrong direction. Perhaps whoever sent the Alp simply knows that Esmeralda works for the Assembly. If that's the case, any of you could be targeted next. Let me make this clear: if she or anyone else in the community is being targeted, we are dealing with a highly critical situation."

Everything was going to shit, but Esme was going to be okay. Plus, when Jacob said any of them could be targeted, Gwyn had grabbed Abby's hand and squeezed meaningfully. Maybe, even amid the chaos, she still had something to hold on to.

CHAPTER SEVENTEEN

AN EYE OPENER

Miles

Flickering torchlight cast jagged shadows over bodies strewn across the floors and tables of the great hall. Miles, an unwilling guest in the king's body, surveyed the carnage and felt the twisted satisfaction curling the monarch's lips. His host wasn't a vicious man by nature, so there had to be some justification for the slaughter.

A sudden shout jolted him from his thoughts, leaving him puzzled by the king's uncharacteristic cruelty.

"Sire!" A guardsman ran his way, stopping just short of the dais. Bowing, he said, "There has been a fight with casualties. The guards of some of your nobles have been slain. But your son is worried that your shieldmaiden may pass from this world soon if you cannot make it in time to heal her."

There was only one person the guardsman could mean. "Lead on," the king ordered, his voice laced with worry—an indication that his host's thoughts mirrored his own.

The king's body was just starting to show signs of aging, but Miles felt none of it as they rushed through the halls toward the chambers he had assigned her—the only female in his household guard. When they rounded the corner, Miles found himself staring at a face he knew all too well. Gwyn, slightly younger, stood there, dressed in a princely robe, blocking the king's view of the bed's occupant.

Gwyn's temper exploded. He yelled, "Father, your nobles conspired to murder her. They orchestrated an ambush with their guards. I warned you this would happen!"

The king's usually calm voice turned into a fierce growl. "Move aside!"

Gwyn stepped aside, revealing the broken figure of the guardswoman. She lay still, drenched with so much blood that it couldn't all have been her own. She appeared much paler than he had ever seen her, a result of the blood loss she was grappling with as she struggled to breathe. Her violet eyes remained closed, moving only sluggishly in response to the torchlight.

The room grew silent, tension lingering heavily like a suffocating fog. The king extended his hands—one flawless, the other silver, glowing softly like candlelight. Miles' trained eye watched as he first stopped her internal bleeding. Next, he closed the wounds on her torso and arm, stopping the immediate threat of further blood loss.

The king sensed the fractures in her right arm and at her wrist. A shield, or many shields, if what Gwyn said was accurate, must have hammered her sword arm with substantial force for it to be so destroyed. The king gripped it tightly, eliciting a weak moan of pain from her, and commanded his magic to heal the bones. Miles knew their proper healing depended entirely on the king's firm grip.

Miles was not yet capable of the precision he felt the king use. He sent precisely measured tendrils of his healing magic aimed at exactly the correct angle for maximum success. Miles paid close attention, hoping that someday he would reach the level of expertise he was studying.

Panting slightly from the exertion, but still trying to hide his weakness, the king ordered, "Everyone, out!" The remaining guards filed out. Through the king's eyes, Miles experienced the unwavering glare he aimed at Gwyn, whose only crime was standing stubbornly by his friend's side.

"Out!" the king shouted again.

Dream-Gwyn looked back at him with a wounded expression before leaving the room. Miles felt a rare flicker of sympathy for him.

The reason behind the king's heartlessness became clear to Miles when he felt tears rolling down his host's face. The king braced himself on one arm to brush the hair away from her face, pausing briefly to linger on the feeling of her skin. A small motion made the king glance at where he braced himself on the bed. With the fragile strength of a newborn, she sought his hand and held onto it. It was hers to keep.

The king resumed healing her, but now using only one hand.

The dream dissolved like mist, leaving the warmth of a thumb gently stroking his arm. Miles blinked, the memory of the king's tears clinging to him as a curtain of golden-brown hair greeted his vision, leaving no doubt that she was lying beside him. He was here, not in the past. Yet, the significance of his dream remained.

With her keen senses, Esme probably knew he was awake, but he needed a moment to absorb the dream he had while unconscious. Logic suggested that his brain was processing recent events through these dreams. The similarity between what had happened to the guardswoman and Esme supported that. But each time he saw Gwyn's younger face in his dreams—because this hadn't been the first time—it seemed less like coincidence and more like a warning or a premonition.

Could it be that Gwyn wasn't entirely insane? If he truly was the Gwyn ap Nudd of legend, and if Miles had somehow inherited his father's magic—and his face—then where did that leave them? Maybe it was time for a frank conversation instead of constant bickering. The woman lying next to him deserved more than that. She needed stability, not their endless childish games, given everything she'd endured this past year.

He had to choose his first words carefully. They had to be the right words. "Happy birthday, Esme."

Her voice trembled, barely audible. "I...forgot it was today."

He gently moved her hair aside, lifting himself onto one elbow so he could see her face. Keeping his voice low to match hers, he replied, "Abby didn't."

"Yeah, well, Abby also just helped me pee and wash up, so she's kind of amazing. I think I heard them leave."

"They're probably going to take care of the dogs..."

Time seemed to stand still as their eyes met, a silent understanding that almost too much had passed between them to put it all into words at once. But he'd try.

He started to speak. "Esme, I..."

He had a growing list of failures and needed to apologize for all of them. He'd allowed himself to be knocked out by the pishacha, forcing her to make her first kill to save him. Juniper's blood was on his hands. He hadn't stayed last night to talk it out because of a secret he was keeping from her, and that nearly cost her life. She deserved more than a weak man. She deserved the truth.

She squeezed his arm gently, silencing him. "Please, I have to say something first... Thank you for getting me out of there."

"I had a lot of help."

"I know, I know. While I was in there, it got to a point where the only positive thing I could imagine was the short intermission between scenes. I couldn't stop what the nightmares made me do—what they made me watch. Then I saw your magic in one, and it felt like... like I could hope again."

She squeezed his arm again, and a sly smile crossed her face. He braced for the joke she was about to make, her usual defense mechanism.

"But, hey, I guess the upside of all this is that I don't have to worry about gaining any weight from baking for a while."

And there it was.

"Esme, lovely, I don't care if your muffin tops give you a muffin top. All I care about is having you around for a long, long time."

Even from this angle, Miles could tell that Esme's body had suffered from the Alp's feeding. She'd lost some of the muscle she'd worked so hard to build.

Tears welled in her eyes, and his heart broke. In some ways, he could imagine what she'd been through because of the dreams and nightmares of another man's life thrust upon him. But on a personal level, he had never experienced his worst fears becoming real in his own mind while he watched, powerless.

He lay back down and kissed the spot where her neck met her collarbone, wishing away her dark thoughts. "I'm staying with you tonight if you'll allow it."

She nodded, though she was still trembling, fighting back more tears. He draped his arm across her chest and returned the gentle caresses she'd given him. "Just let it out, lovely. I'm here."

She curled into a ball, turning away from him but letting his arm stay over her. He held her close as the torment she'd been holding in finally caught up with her. When her sobs subsided, she whispered, "I'm such a terrible person. I don't deserve anything from you, and yet you're still here."

"I can't imagine wanting to be anywhere else."

Sensing the importance of getting his message across clearly, he sat up straight next to her on the bed so that he could look directly into her eyes as he confessed. "Esme, I care about a lot—my patients, protecting people from the malevolents, my Brothers and friends. I do everything in my power to keep everyone safe. But you... you're the one thing I want for myself. You're the one thing I want to be selfish with, to be mine."

Now came the hard part. "And that means that I owe you an explanation about last night, and everything else that has been going on with me lately."

Was it selfish to reveal his truths now? Maybe. But it was the only way he knew to keep her from running or pushing him away again. Frustrated by memories of his repeated failures, he paused to release a deep breath—a technique he'd picked up from her.

Rubbing his temples, he admitted, "There are things I haven't told you. Honestly, I've kept them hidden for so long that it's half out of habit and half because I was trying to figure it out myself. In retrospect, I see that I've isolated myself from you and everyone else as I've navigated through my confusion. I still haven't figured it all out yet. But I'm just going to say it as simply as I can, because it sounds bloody insane."

She gently grasped his hand, and he gave it a small squeeze.

"The dreams started when my healing magic manifested—around eleven or twelve. At first, I thought they were just nightmares, but they felt... too real. Like memories. It's like I'm a guest in someone else's body, reliving the same man's life night after night."

She tried to sit up, but her movement was still unsteady.

"Relax, lovely. I'll explain. Unless you need something?"

Esme shook her head and laid back down.

"Most of the dreams cycle, playing out exactly the same way each time. But in the last few months, I've had a break from those to experience a whole host of new ones. And it seems you've been the catalyst for that."

"Me?" she asked hesitantly.

Miles barely held back a laugh at the absurdity of it all. "Yes, you. The first night we spent together was the first night in memory I didn't have those dreams. Esme, it was the first night I slept soundly in what feels like forever. That's probably why I didn't wake when you snuck out."

Even in her weakened state, the minx defiantly grinned up at him, a mischievous glint in her eyes. "I mean, I know I'm good, but not that good."

He never wanted to leave this room; never wanted to leave her side.

He confided, "I've never discussed this with anyone before, except for you now. Honestly, I didn't want anyone to think I was crazy. I had enough to handle with trying to hide my magic and dealing with the Assembly trying to use me."

Another heavy sigh escaped him as he grappled with the undeniable reality of what he was about to disclose.

"But that's only half of it. The truly unsettling part is that my life has always mirrored my dream host's. I feel like my identity was shaped by a stranger who wore my face sometime in the past. It's like all the big events in my life—losing my hand, my time in the military, my magic, even having the same type of dog—had already happened to him. Turn after turn, year after year, everything about me has mirrored his life. It's as though my entire existence is a reflection of his."

Esme asked earnestly, "Isn't that how dreams work, though? Your brain processes your waking issues at night using dreams and nightmares?"

Her voice wavered slightly on the last word. He squeezed her hand again, hoping she'd understand he recognized what she was dealing with beneath their conversation. As much as this was about him, it was about her, too.

"That's what I tried to believe for years. But when you said that Gwyn thought I was his father, I realized the dreams might not just be a product of my mind."

Her face went slack as she grasped the significance of what he meant.

He confirmed her suspicions. "The man my dreams follow must be Nudd Llaw Eraint. I just woke up from a dream about him healing his guardswoman."

Esme whispered, her voice barely audible, "Her name was Elena."

She spoke so softly that he wasn't certain that he heard her right. "What was that, lovely?"

She repeated, louder this time, "His guardswoman's name was Elena. That's what Gwyn told me. Have... have you seen Gwyn in your dreams?"

Miles couldn't bear to let her see the fury that was certain to be written across his face, so he stood up and turned away from her. "Yes."

Behind him, he heard the soft rustle of sheets as she sat up in bed. "You said you've felt like someone else already made all your choices, like they've happened before. Miles... I'm a cambion, just like Elena was. Did he love her like Gwyn says?"

Her voice broke. "Am I even *your* choice?"

All the pent-up frustration at his lack of agency, at his lack of control over his own life, that had been simmering for over two decades, finally erupted from within him, compelling him to speak the unfiltered truth.

"Yes!" he nearly shouted. "He never chose love. But I am."

The rustling of sheets stilled.

When he turned to look at her, tears were streaming down her face again. Consumed by the fear that this was evidence of her slipping away, he sank to his knees beside the bed and bared his soul to her.

"I think love is something that grows when a person finds the thing they never knew they needed until they saw it in someone else. You're the person I didn't know I needed my entire life."

He looked down at the sheets just long enough to gather his thoughts and then met her gaze.

"When my parents started pushing me away because they didn't understand me, I honestly stopped feeling loved. Over the course of time, I started to view care and concern as a substitute for it. I thought that love was a rare commodity—not meant for me or my lifestyle. But you give love so freely... Your ability to make everyone feel cherished and loved leaves me in awe of you. You're funny, and a hell of a lot smarter than you think. Being around you is like walking into the sunlight on a freezing day. You're full of life. I love that you're sweet just as much as I love how aggressive you can be. The things I lack, you have in abundance. Esme, you're everything I need. I've felt stifled, controlled my entire life. But with you, I can just *be*. I'm not an officer or a doctor. I'm not a Corded Brother or an agent. With you, I'm just Miles. So, to answer your question from earlier, you're not a terrible person, Esme. I love you."

Finally, he implored, with the solemnity of the penitent at prayer. "Please, please, let me have you."

She laughed through her tears and said, "Gods above, golden boy, that was *so good*."

CHAPTER EIGHTEEN

GHOULS JUST WANT TO HAVE FUN

Jacob

As soon as Jacob hung up with Abigail, another call came through on his home line.

Katia's voice blasted over the speaker the moment he answered. "Jacob? Yes, hello. Sorry for calling so late, but I wanted to let you know I'm locked in an office supply closet at HQ because someone let a ghoul into the restricted access area. You know: a typical weekday for me."

The weariness that had settled in once he knew Esmeralda was safe faded instantly. "What do you mean by 'let in'?"

"Well, for starters, it didn't set off any wards. That was clue number one."

Her tone shifted to exasperation. "The other clue nearly hit me in the face when it surprised me while I was working. Jacob, it had a building access card jammed into the rotting flesh between the bones just above its wrist."

"Blast it all," he whispered. Two attacks in one night, both targeting demon-blooded mages. This couldn't be a coincidence. Katia had made the smart move to barricade herself. Her particular skills weren't useful against the undead, nor was she a trained fighter physically or magically.

"You're safe for now, yes? Do we need the quicker option of Maureen? Or do you think you're safe enough to wait for me? You know I'm slow."

Katia made an unladylike noise, a habit likely picked up from her father, Jacob's old friend Konstantin. "Eh, I'll be fine until you get here. Maureen is... not pleasant."

He'd expected that. Maureen had been hard on Katia for years; no matter what he did, he couldn't convince her that their demon-blooded kin weren't a threat. Though the experience of being saved from the pishacha by Esme was starting to make her reconsider.

Jacob pressed his fingers to his temples. Katia was sharp, but she always danced too close to the edge, just like her father. "I must ask, since you say we have time... It's not just work, is it? You've been slipping on feeding again?"

She made an unhappy sound that wasn't strictly an answer, so he continued. "Heather is on board. She understands your needs, darling. Look, I don't want to walk in there, only to restrain you the moment you remove the barricade."

"Trust me, Jacob, it's not that. I just... overindulged at my last event and got 'tipsy.' Heather had to pick me up afterward. I'm burying myself in work to forget. No harm done, but I still hate myself a little. It's embarrassing."

The safest way to control her hunger was with multiple partners, taking small amounts each time. Katia's "tipsy" meant she'd taken too much vitality in one feeding. When that happened, she would appear intoxicated—hardly a safe state for a succubus at an orgy. In those situations, she became the threat, not the vulnerable. He knew she hated the necessity her heritage forced upon her, but she'd been lucky enough to find a supportive partner in Heather.

"I think I understand... Apologies, Katia. I'll be there soon."

He was going to have to take a bevy of anti-inflammatories in the morning to deal with the repercussions of this late night foray.

Katia's tone changed abruptly, going from despondent to amused. "Thanks, Jacob! Esme showed me a new mobile game I can play while I wait. Ta-ta for now!"

Of course, Esmeralda had shown her a new game. It was a relief to hear Katia sounding secure about her situation rather than terrified. He hung up the phone, relieved that he hadn't already prepared for bed. Of all the indignities, slaying a ghoul in pajamas would top the list for him.

They obviously had a problem on their hands. The pattern was undeniable. Cambions first. The rest of the Assembly would soon be in the crosshairs. Before killing this malevolent once and for all, he'd grab the building access card the ghoul was carrying and find out exactly who had placed it there.

Him

"Do I look like I have enough gray hairs to take the reins yet?" Maureen snorted. "No, I'm just saying that when one apple spoils, you don't toss the whole bunch. You get rid of the rotten one and keep the rest."

He'd carefully planned her visit to The Sanctuary of Spirits at a time when the three people he needed to avoid would not be there. No one had the courage to question Maureen's choice of wearing a glamor inside the bar. She was the perfect disguise. On top of that, she'd earned a reputation as an outspoken critic of the cambion presence.

He spoke with her voice through her lips. "That's what's going on in Seattle right now. Something is rotten at the center, and it reeks of an old man who doesn't even notice the smell of sulfur, if you catch my drift."

Maureen's tablemates nodded in agreement. They needed to see the truth, to understand that their community's survival depended on removing at least one member of it. He had to make them see.

"I've had to clean up too many of his messes. I'm tired of the fumbling. He's too old. It's time for a change. Mark my words, soon enough, he's going to crack, and the aftermath is going to be messy."

As he stood, he tossed two hundred-dollar bills on the table. "Drinks on me, everyone. I'm heading out. I've got some after-hours trades to look over before the markets open up tomorrow. Cheers!"

The smiles that followed him out of the bar were unsettling in their simplicity. It had been a productive night's work with minimal effort. They trusted him; believed him. For their sake, he couldn't let them down.

He'd already burned the dress he'd gotten for the skogsrå to wear to infiltrate the gala. That day he'd originally come into the city to see if he could find another intelligent malevolent to recruit since he'd recently lost her. Instead, he'd found failure after failure. The work he'd just done was his only recent success. But he couldn't stop now. He wouldn't stop.

With his own eyes, he had seen Jacob entering the Assembly headquarters to save the succubus. Sadly, he was painfully aware of his own limits. Realizing he couldn't confront Jacob head-on and survive without trickery, he was forced to accept that this attempt to remove the life-stealer had failed.

But with Esmeralda... he'd been so sure the Alp would succeed. There was no known method to stop one mid-feed without inflicting serious, irreversible damage on the host.

He suppressed the memories of happier days that tried to flood back into his mind. The memories were bright, shining things and, like the full force of the sun, neither would be shining upon his face ever again.

The only explanation for her survival was the Brother. His unique magic...

Her death still wasn't something he wanted to witness himself—he wasn't that far gone yet. But it was something that needed to be done.

Leaving the city behind, he felt an overwhelming sense of relief as he shed his glamor. He could feel his magic changing, twisting, and he hated every second of it. The short days and long nights of this season worked to his advantage, allowing him to continue his work even during the daylight. He was thankful for the heavy clouds covering the sky, as the full light of day had begun to drain him lately.

He knew what he was becoming. His kind's heightened sensitivity to the pull of darkness had made him naturally vigilant throughout his life. It was the nature of creatures whose very existence was tied to magic.

Unlike humans, whose souls alone suffered from wicked actions, creatures of magic underwent a transformative change if they succumbed to malevolent intentions for too long. It was an inevitability he had accepted. Joyfully, he offered himself as a sacrifice for them all.

The crunch of his footsteps merged with the discordant sounds of his single remaining pet. Looking down, he saw that his toenails were starting to gnarl. Soon his gait would change to force him into heavy, plodding steps. While he suffered through the transformation of his legs, his budding claws made every step a misery.

Purity was never an option; perfection was never possible. But order? Order was within his grasp, and he would restore it—no matter the cost to himself. Mistakes weren't just setbacks, they were also lessons. Every failure had sharpened his focus.

The cost didn't matter anymore. Sacrifices had to be made—for their sake, not his. For the community. For the future. He only hoped it would be worth it in the end.

CHAPTER NINETEEN

TINGLY IN ALL THE WRONG PLACES

Esme

Esme narrowed her eyes at Gwyn sitting across the table. She'd thrown one of Miles' hoodies (that she'd shamelessly pilfered) over her pajamas and called it good enough for the day at home. He, on the other hand, proudly sported a new ensemble, courtesy of his thrifting adventure with Abby the day before. Abby had done a great job. He looked much more put together than he had when borrowing Miles' clothes.

"Alright, Gwynnyboy, let's deal. I'll teach you to cook something if you teach me about demons."

It was the perfect topic to get some information out of him while avoiding any mention of Nudd. After Miles' revelations, that subject felt too weighty to bring up without him present. If she wasn't so exhausted, she'd be walking on cloud nine after his speech last night.

Gwyn's devilish grin mirrored hers. "Deal."

With Abby and Miles at work, Gwyn was assigned as Esme's babysitter for the day. To her, helping Gwyn after his injury was different. He could hardly sit up without assistance, while she was just worn out. Being supervised not only made her feel infantilized by others but also left her feeling like a child stuck at home while the adults were out working—again. The societal devaluation of her work as a bartender sometimes made it hard to remember that its merit was equal to theirs. People needed a place to relax and unwind and sometimes a willing ear to listen, and she provided that.

Still, Esme allowed their overprotection for three reasons: she wanted to learn about demons, dreaded being alone after her nightmares, and suspected Miles wanted her to keep an eye on Gwyn, not the other way around.

It was strange to feel so optimistic and yet equally vulnerable after nearly dying. Something had shifted between Miles and Gwyn—the tension had eased, and Miles hadn't demanded another binding promise from Gwyn. It was progress, however fragile. She just hoped it lasted.

Thinking back on cooking, Esme suggested, "I'm not going to insult you with some recipe you can find on the back of a box, so how about omelets? Abby loves them, but her mornings are always too hectic to make them."

As she'd hoped, that last part caught his attention, though he tried to hide it. She added, "While we cook, you can teach me about what variety of demon I'm supposed to be."

She could use a hearty meal herself. She'd lost nearly ten pounds from the Alp's feeding. While the number itself wasn't catastrophic, losing that much weight in a day wasn't healthy. The aftermath left her feeling drained and sluggish.

Esme grabbed the ingredients and placed them on the counter. Both dogs, who'd been napping on the floor nearby, perked up at the smell of bacon. She made sure to save an extra cooked piece for them to share.

While she showed Gwyn how to use the stove, something nagged at the back of her mind, a strange sensation. It almost felt like magic, but she swore she could hear someone walking around outside. Given that it was daytime, there was probably no need for alarm. The dogs didn't seem bothered by it either, so she set the thought aside and focused on their preparations.

"We're keeping it simple today. Just bacon and cheese as the filler." She showed him how to prepare bacon in a pan, the easiest method for a total newbie.

"So," she asked, "what kind of demon do you think I am?"

He responded while skillfully chopping the bacon into tiny pieces. At least she didn't have to teach him knife skills.

"Don't forget to save some bacon for the dogs."

Gwyn sliced a piece in half and flipped both pieces, using the flat of the blade, one by one, into the waiting hounds' mouths. "Nergalian. I'd bet what little money I have on it."

"Ner-freaking-what?"

He smirked. "You have a habit of making up nonsense words."

She shot him a playful look. "Uh, it's called expletive infixation, gosh."

A flicker of confusion crossed his face before he replied seriously, "I have no idea what that means, so I will answer your first question instead."

As she showed him the right amount of oil—in this case, more bacon grease—to prevent sticking, he explained, "Nergal is the primary demon associated with war, death, and less so with disease."

Without missing a beat, she quipped, "I'll take the first two and pass on the third."

"How often have you been very sick in your life, Esmeralda?"

She thought about it while helping him sprinkle the cheese and chopped bacon onto the waiting eggs. "I mean, I've had colds like anyone else but, damn, you're right. I almost never get more than a few sniffles. Does that mean both of my parents were Nergalian? Was Elena also Nergalian?"

He raised a brow and stole a bite of the completed omelet.

She scolded him. "Hey! This one's mine. You get to eat whatever you screw up making yourself!"

With a weighing motion of his head, Gwyn replied, "You may have the good omelet... Yes, Elena was Nergalian. Concerning your parents... I have no idea. One had to have been, at least."

"Bets on my mother for that role. She was a force. Have you ever heard of a begotten being able to control malevolents?"

His forehead wrinkled, and he blinked slowly, absorbing the idea. "I... no. I don't think so. Maybe. It is an interesting idea."

The idea left him as perplexed as it had left her. At least she tried. His last comment made it sound like she might have a willing practice partner if she ever decided to test the idea. Given Jacob's warnings during their last meeting, she had to remind herself it was "if," not "when."

Just as she sat down to eat her second breakfast for the day, while coaching Gwyn from the sidelines, the doorbell rang. Instead of getting up, she rudely yelled at the door from her seat, making Gwyn jump, "Who is it?"

A familiar voice called back, "It's yer best-dressed bestie, lassie!"

She shouted back, "Abby is way better looking than you!"

Finn argued, "I didn't say attractive. I've seen meself in the mirror. I said best-dressed."

"I don't know. Gwyn is giving you a run for your money today!" As she stuffed another bite of her omelet into her mouth, she asked Gwyn, "Can you open that? I'm not getting up." She'd exploit this brief break for all it was worth.

"I have zero interest in burning my breakfast for the leprechaun." His brow quirked again as he gestured at the door, unlocking both locks at once telekinetically and sliding the door open.

Finn sauntered in, sniffing the air all the way to the kitchen. Esme warned him, "We don't have extra, but you can raid the fridge for leftovers."

"I'm not here for the food this time." He winked, sitting down. "I'm here to see you! What the hell happened to ya?"

She wiped her mouth with a napkin and leaned back in her chair, allowing her food baby room to breathe. With a somber expression, undoubtedly aided by her newly pale complexion, she said, "Gwyn, don't you think Finn would be a good training stand-in for all those child-sized malevolents I might need to slice up with my conjured sword? Maybe we should arrange for Miles to be around next time we train, just in case we accidentally find out how easy it is to make leprechauns bleed."

While Finn mimed shock, Gwyn looked baffled at the abrupt topic shift.

Esme affected fury. "Two words: Whoopie cushion."

For once, Finn didn't fall out of his chair in a fit of laughter. Instead, he looked smug. "I can't wait ta hear the story."

"Yeah, that's never happening. Where were you yesterday?"

He waggled his eyebrows knowingly before answering. "Honestly, I was kind of avoidin' you due to the whole whoopie cushion trick. I was gardenin' and watching a new show." His joviality turned serious. "Lassie, what happened?"

Gwyn answered for her, taking a third chair. Hunched over but stiff, he had a somewhat predatory look. "An Alp broke into the house and fed on her for over twelve hours. Your presence, or simply your communication, could have been beneficial, *bestie*. Abigail is quite cross with you."

Finn scoffed. "By all the magic... I stick to my own company for one day, and suddenly I'm persona non grata. Esme, I'm really sorry, dove."

Esme reassured him, "For what it's worth, Finn. I'm not 'cross' with you. I'm sure you'd have been here if you'd known."

Gwyn added, chastising, "You also missed Esmeralda's birthday because of it."

Finn snorted. "Ya must be jokin'."

Gwyn's demeanor turned dangerously serious. "It will be quite clear when I choose to be humorous with you, leprechaun."

"Uff, yer right about your lack of humor." He snorted derisively. "Esme, sorry for missing your birthday. When you're feelin' better, let's celebrate, yeah?"

That strange sensation came back again. Finn's question barely registered as the overwhelming distraction consumed all of her attention. She asked, "Do you guys hear... or feel that?"

Finn asked, "Kinda tingly in all the wrong places?"

"Exactly that," she answered.

"Ah, that's just your ole fella settin' up new wards outside. He's looking mighty serious about the business, too."

"Jacob is here?" Esme asked.

Gwyn didn't seem surprised at all. She must've missed something.

"Aye. I got the impression that he aims to speak with ya, too."

Two days ago, she couldn't imagine letting Jacob back in so soon, desperate to carve out her own path without him. Now, standing on the other side of death, it felt like those old grudges were insignificant. She was ready to cast aside their grievances and start fresh. Facing death had changed how she saw herself—and with that, she realized how some of her personality traits might have been hard for Jacob to accept.

The invisible author behind her nightmares had called her many things, but three stood out: murderer, ruinous, and belligerent. Seeing those sides of herself play out in vivid, terrifying detail had left her feeling both empowered and shaken. Empowered because she'd faced her darkest moments repeatedly and emerged almost numb to the shock of her own violence. Shaken because these were not the qualities she wanted tied to her identity. But the shame gnawed at her—those words were chains, binding her to a version of herself she didn't want to be.

It felt like forever ago, but it hadn't been that long since Jacob had revealed that she was a cambion. On that same night, she had realized he treated her like a father would a grown child: giving her space, respecting her independence, but still seeing her as his responsibility, his granddaughter in all the ways that counted. She now understood why he had kept the truth about her parents' deaths from her. His attempt to protect her had been misguided, but still came from a place of best intentions and love. Sure, she could still be a bit sullen, but banishing him from her life had been too extreme.

Her fingers scrubbed at her makeup-free skin, trying to wipe away the grime of the past days, her breath shaky as she struggled to find the peace she needed. "Finn, will you please ask him to come inside when he's done? I'm going to freshen up and put on some real clothes."

When she finally dragged herself back into the living room, she found Jacob lounging comfortably in her recliner, feet up. He looked tired. Whatever he'd been doing outside must have drained him. "I see that you're already in your happy place, Jacob."

Gwyn and Finn sat together on Esme's couch, looking like a very odd couple—Gwyn, long and lean with angular features and raven-black hair, and Finn, squat but sturdily built with blond hair and stubble. While Gwyn sat upright, almost at attention, Finn was cross-legged, his bare feet on her couch.

Jacob shifted in the recliner, straightening it with a creak, and let out an aggrieved sigh. "Oh, Esmeralda, first, let me wish you a belated happy birthday! Unfortunately, your gift is still being crafted. The specifications I requested were more intricate than expected."

Finn grimaced as Gwyn shot him another withering look.

Unaware of the earlier tension, Jacob continued. "My dear, we have a problem on our hands. I would wait for Miles and Abigail, but this affects you most directly, and it can't wait."

She asked, "Is this about the Alp?"

"Yes, and more. There was another attack last night—the only other cambion in Seattle proper was targeted."

Esme's eyes widened. "Is Katia alright?"

"She's fine. Apparently, she played that ridiculous phone game you introduced her to while locked in a closet at Assembly HQ. I dispatched the ghoul sent to kill her."

The ghoul sent to kill her? What the... But of course, Finn's mind latched onto something else entirely.

The leprechaun's eyebrows shot up. "There's another cambion in Seattle?"

Esme stifled a laugh at the thought of love-struck Finn meeting a succubus for the first time. "Yeah, let's hope you never meet her. After how you reacted to meeting Abby, you might actually die... perish... kick the eternal bucket if you meet Katia."

She would be lying if she said she didn't luxuriate in the stink-eyed glare Gwyn shot Finn. Gwyn hadn't been there the night Esme introduced Finn to Abby and Miles. At the time, it seemed like the poor leprechaun was instantly smitten with Abby. Now, looking back, she wondered at that. Even before Gwyn was in the picture, Finn had never so much as flirted with Abby. Perhaps Esme had misinterpreted the situation. She was still going to tease him about it, regardless.

After a moment of enjoying Finn's confused stare, Esme clarified. "She's a succubus."

Naturally, Finn didn't seem the least bit put off by the idea of a person who leached a bit of vitality from their sexual partners. The way his hands fidgeted and the huge grin on his face made Esme instantly regret telling him about Katia.

Jacob cleared his throat, steering the conversation back on track. "We have evidence that someone with access to the building, and enough magical expertise to bypass the wards, targeted her. I don't think it's a coincidence that both cambions were attacked the same night. And after talking with Gwyn about what he discovered on their last malevolent hunt, we believe someone is planning to target the winter Assembly meeting or the Solstice Gala."

Jacob's bushy eyebrows lifted, his expression turning serious. "My dear, this can only mean that we have someone inside the

Assembly creating a serious problem. I fear attacking you was just the first step. You are not safe as things stand currently. I need you to have a companion at all times."

Great; more babysitters.

"So, what are we going to do about it?" Though she suspected Jacob already had a plan.

"I have a few ideas... And I have made a few calls."

Bingo. Esme just hoped she'd like whatever changes he was cooking up.

CHAPTER TWENTY

BUFF DUDES REBUFFED

Esme

The spectacle playing out before her eyes made it a great day to be Esmeralda Morgana Turner. She couldn't quite decide if she wanted to see the brilliant finish it seemed to be headed toward or if she wanted it to keep going. Will would die of jealousy when she told him about this.

The newcomer, with his dark blond hair, intense brown eyes, and a face that defied traditional masculinity, squaring off against Miles, exuded an aura of danger. His swagger, radiating self-assurance, only amplified the palpable threat he exuded. Though shorter than Miles and Gwyn, his bravado filled the room. His demeanor expressed that he was not to be trifled with.

With steady breaths, the smaller man shot under Miles' leading leg. Wrapping both arms around Miles' thigh, he held on, pushing violently upward with his legs and core. Miles reeled on one foot, but only for a split second.

Wham! If the gym had been an American football field, the smaller man would have just completed a successful tackle—dumping Miles onto the floor like a sack of potatoes.

But the fight wasn't over. Miles used the muscles of his trapped thigh, combined with the momentum from being taken down, to twist his torso behind the smaller man, swirling like a corkscrew. The thigh, once trapped, became an advantage as Miles used his free leg to wrap around both of his opponent's legs, throwing him off balance and taking him down to the mat.

It had been two years since Esme had seen Colin, and his late twenties suited him. She couldn't help but admit that he had become quite good-looking. She thought he'd been busy building his Public Relations career in Los Angeles, but she soon learned that was only half the story.

Esme nudged Gwyn. "So, Gwynnyboy, you up next?"

In his characteristically arrogant manner, he replied, "I have considered it."

She quickly backtracked. "Maybe not with Miles, though. Let that feud rest for a bit, please."

He smirked, amused. True to his character, he gracefully obliged her request.

"Abigail's brother?" he suggested.

Abby wasn't even around to see this little sparring session, so the only point of a fight between them could be to address the friction she'd sensed rolling off Colin toward Gwyn. It was classic "stay away from my sister until I approve of you" crap that brothers sometimes try to pull. Esme suspected only Abby and Gwyn had failed to notice their growing connection—Colin had in just six hours.

Gwyn leaned over and whispered, "Also, I just remembered we failed to meet at the library as planned."

Oh no.

Seeing her expression, he added, "Perhaps we will see our fount of knowledge again. He seemed... eager."

With a nod, she felt a twinge of regret for the potential knowledge she could have gained. How had she forgotten? Oh, right—she'd been comatose.

The sparring match was at its finale. On the mat, Miles had Colin's outstretched leg painfully immobilized between his own, leaving Colin no room to escape. Esme winced in empathy, knowing all too well the pain of having your knee twisted the wrong way, teetering on the edge of a break. As predicted, Colin tapped out, and the two men got up, exchanging friendly pats on the back.

When the pair walked over, Esme confided, "I always thought you gave off assassin vibes. Turns out I was right!"

Sweat dripped from Miles' brow as he shook his head in amusement. Colin, still catching his breath, grinned shyly. He seemed as unaccustomed to Esme's presence in their world of Corded Brothers as she had once been to learning the truth about malevolents.

Colin suggested, "Miles says you've been training. How about a round?"

"I'm still weak from the Alp, but I think this guy," she pointed at Gwyn, "could use a good workout."

As far as she knew, Colin didn't know how they'd defeated the Alp, just that it had been done. Miles' magic was still a secret, even from his Brothers, as was Gwyn's (maybe) true identity. Talking about it now would only complicate things, especially with a potential saboteur lurking in the Assembly.

On that front, Jacob had called in "people" to comb through databases and scrutinize security camera footage, but no solid leads had emerged on who authorized the access card. The ghoul seemed to suddenly materialize, its rotten fingers scraping against the doors of Assembly headquarters. Eventually, its arm brushed against the card scanner, granting it entry. It repeated this process on each door and scanner until it reached the only food available in the building—Katia.

It was obvious that a powerful magic user had assisted its transference through mist walking, a skill for which Finn was famous, to the door. Yet how the ghoul got past the wards was still a mystery. Jacob claimed to have a few ideas about that, but he was keeping tight-lipped "for now." Though Esme found it frustrating, she had to trust that he had good reasons for his secrecy.

Because they didn't know who had set up the ghoul or who targeted Esme, they kept the malevolent attacks a secret from all levels of the Seattle Assembly. Only the Corded Brotherhood was alerted. Within twenty-four hours, they had mobilized agents from outside the region.

Unfortunately, since the Brotherhood's numbers were already spread thin across the country, most field agents were unable to leave their assigned region. Still, Jacob kept them on the search, questioning locals in hopes of uncovering any nearby leads. Even so, they found the perfect field agent to join them undercover in Seattle—Abby's brother, Colin. After all, the Corded Brotherhood was a family business for the O'Malleys. His presence was easily explained as a family visit for the holidays, making him the discreet backup they needed. Esme just hoped their numbers were enough.

Now, because it was a Saturday and Colin had just landed a few hours before, they were enjoying a bit of downtime at the gym. Esme and Miles had been training together at this particular gym for months after their normal operating hours. She'd always wondered how Miles had managed to secure such special treatment. Now, she knew. The mundane gym owners knew about magic because their daughter had been attacked by a malevolent. She survived only because a Corded Brother was tracking the winged cat creature when it attacked. The girl had been just four years old, so her memory of the event was easily chalked up to imagination. Her parents, however, had fought the monster until the Corded Brother arrived, leaving them with memories too sticky to be rewritten so easily. Granted the unique privilege of retaining their knowledge of the mages, they became enthusiastic advocates. The little girl came through the ordeal with nothing more than a few stitches and a fantastical story about a monster.

Esme would be the only one not joining Jacob and the others that evening. Though Jacob wanted her to join the meeting to plan how they would find the attacker instead of going to the bar, Esme refused to go into hiding. She reasoned that by continuing to act oblivious, they could deceive their enemy into believing the planned attack was still a secret. So, tonight, she would be back at work, with eyes and ears open for any scrap of information that might lead them to the person orchestrating everything.

Gwyn didn't have hand wraps, so Miles let him borrow an extra pair from his bag for the sparring match against Colin. Was this a small gesture of goodwill from Miles after opening up to her about Nudd, or was it just him hoping to see Gwyn get his ass kicked? Time would tell. A million unresolved issues still lingered between them, yet Esme would refrain from trying to force either of them to discuss it unless their feud escalated again.

A sweaty Miles joined her, leaning against the wall as they watched the match begin. Every time he smiled at her, that slow, lazy smile of his, it felt like the ground shifted beneath her feet.

Gwyn stood in a combat-ready stance, while Colin stood stick-straight in place.

"Gwyn! You have to bow to start the fight," Esme reminded him.

Instead of a typical martial arts-style bow, Gwyn performed a courtly one, confusing Colin. But they proceeded anyway. The beginning of the match was uneventful, with both men measuring and prodding each other.

Miles' phone rang. "It's the on-call doctor, probably wanting a quick consult. I'll be right back." He kissed Esme on the cheek and stepped outside to take the call.

Colin attempted a few exploratory kicks. Being so much shorter than Gwyn, his options for effective punches were limited. After a few of these, Gwyn threw a punch, missing as Colin ducked beneath his right hook. While still ducked down, Colin easily slipped under Gwyn's reach to land a left hook into Gwyn's liver. The resounding thud told Esme the hit was a bit too hard for a sparring match. *Ouch.*

Not to be outdone, Gwyn grabbed Colin as he rose, locking both arms around the back of his neck. As Colin tried to stand to full height, Gwyn wrenched him downward, and Colin's sternum met Gwyn's knee. Unlike the shot Colin had just landed, Gwyn showed more appropriate restraint in the force he used on the smaller man.

Just when things were getting interesting, Esme's phone also rang. She glanced at the screen—it was Maureen.

Her disbelief was obvious in her voice. "Uh, hello?"

"Hey, Esme," came the voice of her long-time nemesis turned... what was she now? Esme felt uneasy in this unfamiliar territory.

Esme asked, "Do you need something, or are you calling to unveil a few more scathing truths?"

The older woman snorted, a sound too rough for someone who presented as prim and proper to the world. "Neither, actually. This is a courtesy call. We've got a problem."

Esme's interest piqued. Jacob had said none of the Assembly members knew about the attacks on her and Katia—not even Abby's mother, Christi. Maureen couldn't possibly know about the suspected attack.

"Another one? Okay, you have my attention." She only whined a little.

"Look, Esme, I know I've been hard on you. I won't say everything I've said was wrong, but I owe you for what happened in the forest. You're in danger."

Esme struggled to keep her snarky remarks to herself. "Considering all we've witnessed, that's hardly surprising news to me."

Given their history, Esme couldn't help but suspect Maureen might be the one partnering with or even manipulating the malevolents. It was within the realm of possibility that she had the magical chops required to be the person in question. Plus, she'd been possessed by a pishacha only a few weeks before. Could they be entirely certain that they'd actually killed the demon?

Just as Esme glanced back at the fight, Colin's head smashed into Gwyn's chin in a vicious headbutt. It wasn't sparring anymore. This was something else entirely—at least for Colin. Miles was still outside on his consultation call. It was up to her to stop the fight from escalating any further.

Maureen's voice snapped her attention back to the call. "Someone's been using a glamor to impersonate me. I found out when a friend mentioned a conversation we never had. Esme, they're dragging you through the mud, and they're trying to get Jacob—wait, what's that sound?"

Esme rushed through her words, already starting her sprint toward Colin and Gwyn. "Two idiots fighting! I have to go, like, right now. Can we meet at the bar tonight to finish this? Free drinks for the trouble."

"Fine! See you at seven then."

What should have been a fun break had devolved into conflict they didn't need, fueling her annoyance. The fight had deteriorated into both men aiming for headshots in close quarters. Esme tossed her phone aside where it bounced off the padded mats a few times before coming to a stop.

Three strides later, she reached them, and, without slowing down, she slammed straight into Colin's side, knocking him off Gwyn. She quickly stood back, giving them both a moment to catch their breath and regain their feet.

But Colin had other ideas. The moment he stood back up, he launched himself fist-first toward Gwyn. Esme's annoyance turned into cold anger, giving her clarity. To drive home the point that the fight was over, she had only one option that would not look like magic if caught by the gym's cameras. Even if the gym owners knew about magic, she still had to be careful.

She allowed her frustration to fuel her reach into the infernal. A touch of her blood's magic surged into her muscles. As her eyes eclipsed, she ripped Colin off Gwyn, throwing him so hard that he rolled twice after hitting the mats. As Colin rose, she was already crouched and ready for round two if he forced it.

Esme growled, "The match is over, Colin."

The moment she said his name, clarity returned to his eyes, as if he'd been completely lost to the fight. Gwyn stood a few feet away, seemingly untroubled by the events of the last minute, but Esme knew better.

Breathing heavily, Colin slowly got to his feet. He walked a step closer to her and said, incredulously, "You're tainted?"

Esme relied solely on the unenhanced power of her own muscles to sucker-punch him directly in the face.

"I'm what, exactly?" she screeched. The talk with Maureen just a scant few minutes before hadn't done wonders for her temper. But, damn it, he was being a speciesist.

Colin didn't retaliate. Instead, he responded by raising his hands in a defensive, open-palmed gesture—his expression showing surprise rather than anger. He didn't step back or accuse her of going too far, though the pain was clear in the wince he tried to hide. His reaction wasn't one of aggression. It was one of understanding. He nodded slightly, as if to acknowledge he probably deserved it.

It was at this moment that Miles returned inside to find Esme standing, fist still raised, Colin sporting a now-bloody nose, and a fight-rumpled Gwyn making a placating gesture at Colin with both hands.

History repeated itself as Miles looked around and asked, "Is anyone gonna tell me what happened while I was gone?" For added emphasis, he threw his hands in the air this time around.

Beneath the prickly aggression Colin was showing, Esme knew he was fundamentally a good person. Still, she criticized him, "I've known you since you were a kid in high school, Colin Henry O'Malley, and yet you still say that crap? I thought you were a Corded Brother!"

With a sad, defeated expression, Colin looked Esme straight in the eyes and said, "I deserved that. I'm sorry... I didn't mean it like that." His voice was thick with regret. "I was just so surprised when I saw your eyes, and that term gets tossed around, it just slipped out." His voice was soft, not defensive, his posture open—almost vulnerable.

Using the back of his hand wrap, he wiped at the blood dribbling from his nose. Straightening up, Colin said, "Esme, that was really shitty of me. Even if I didn't mean it that way, I deserved what I got. I'm sorry."

Gwyn snidely remarked, "Even I know better than to insult a Nergalian demoness to her face."

Miles' expression remained flat. Esme realized that the outcome of this encounter for him depended entirely on her response. Knowing Colin's good nature, she wasted no time in forgiving him.

Colin returned her hug halfway, using one arm to stem the flow of blood down his face. Meanwhile, Miles walked to the bathroom and grabbed a wad of hand towels for him, already mollified by Esme's decision.

Stepping away, she added, "Maybe you and Gwyn should talk about whatever the hell was going on between you two during that match like big boys."

"That's easy," Colin replied. "This unemployed loser can stop sniffing around my sister."

Gwyn's eyes narrowed, a flicker of offense flashing across his features. "What is it with you people and applying canine metaphors to me? I cannot oblige you, Colin. Your Bastion has ordered it."

Colin's face scrunched in disbelief. "Sounds like a load of shit to me."

With arrogance in full force, Gwyn replied, "I assure you, it is not."

Esme felt compelled to back Gwyn up. She said, "Eh, he's a special case. Also, Abby is a grown woman. Let it go."

"See," Gwyn gestured widely with one hand. "I'm special."

Miles buried his face in both hands and groaned, while Esme rubbed his back, cooing softly, "I know, babe, I know. We're stuck with him... You know what, we can go home and cuddle with Lily for a bit before I have to go to work."

The aftermath of the Alp and ghoul attacks had already begun to reshape the landscape of their lives. Jacob's adamance that Esme had someone with her at all times seemed to be the excuse Miles needed for him and Lily to all but move in with her.

Gwyn was already relishing the newfound space in Miles' empty house, allowing him and Cerys to breathe more freely. It was heartening to see that Miles was willing to put aside his constant surveillance of Gwyn for once. It made Esme hopeful about a future where they could set aside their grievances and work together—they'd be unstoppable.

Expecting Maureen's usual mix of unpleasantness and insults, Esme wasn't eager to hear what the other woman had to say later that night. She already knew that someone was targeting her, yet, given their history, she still remained skeptical of Maureen's intentions. Before getting distracted by the noises of the fight coming through her speaker, Maureen had briefly mentioned something about Jacob. That, at least, deserved further investigation.

Esme would ready herself for yet another verbal battle in The Sanctuary of Spirits.

CHAPTER TWENTY-ONE

CH-CH-CH-CHANGES

Esme

"Sitkum, my man! I haven't seen you since this summer!"

Esme offered her raised fist for a friendly bump to the Sasquatch sauntering up to the bar. He obliged, making the obligatory exploding sound as their fists ricocheted off each other. Sitkum was still considered a young adult by Sasquatch standards, despite being nearly Jacob's age. Chatting with him gave her the odd experience of talking to someone who occasionally used old-fashioned speech but loved the newest trends in music and media. By Sasquatch standards, he was small, at just under seven feet tall, which is how he earned the nickname "half."

"Esmeralda, how's it going? You know I try to stay in the mountains during the winter—fewer hikers and hunters to become a pain in my ass when it's cold."

"Right?" she joked. "Sorry about my kind. We're like locusts."

"Not you, though; you're welcome up anytime." He winked his heavy brow at her.

"Hey, no more flirting. I have a boyfriend now." He wasn't truly flirting with her. She wasn't hairy enough for his tastes, but they liked to play up the joke because it always gave them a good laugh.

Sitkum was a man who loved love. From their prior conversations, she knew he couldn't wait to find a mate. She had the impression that, in Sasquatch culture, his family would likely be heavily involved in this process, but she avoided bringing it up after the one time she did—it made him terribly sad. And a sad Sasquatch was a sight too miserable to behold.

"Do I know your boyfriend?" he asked. Talking to Sitkum felt like cracking open a six-pack while sitting on your front porch with your bestie on a summer's afternoon—laid-back and easygoing. She loved him for it.

If she were speaking to a human, she'd describe Miles' age, hair color, job, etc., but since she was talking to a person who claimed telling the difference between humans was like differentiating between two bald, wrinkly Sphinx cats. She stuck with notable traits. "New mage to the area. Prosthetic hand..."

He snapped his fingers. "Oh! I think I know the one. Has he yet proven his ability to provide for you with such a handicap?"

There it was—the expected old-fashioned question mixed with a non-human notion she'd anticipated. "Yes, he can provide. But I don't need providing for, remember?"

Guessing he wanted a cider, she popped open a can and handed it to him. Since Sasquatch didn't much like having to glamor themselves to fit in within human cities, they traded timber, ore, or services with Jacob or the Assembly for things they wanted. That meant Sitkum drank for free on the few times every year he visited The Sanctuary of Spirits.

The Sasquatch became serious and lowered his voice. "You might think otherwise when you are with his child."

Naturally, this was when Finn arrived and took the seat next to Sitkum, dressed in his "full kit" as he called it. Tonight's outfit had a decidedly Celtic theme: dark hunter green pants and vest, gold buttons with the Celtic harp emblazoned on each, and gold buckles on his patent loafers. Everything matched perfectly. As if anything less than perfection was even a choice for the leprechaun fashionista.

Finn, startled by the end of Sitkum's last statement, asked, "Esme's what now?"

"In no way, shape, or form am I... *that*!" she yelped. "So shut your mouth right now, leprechaun, because I know where your tongue might lead, and it's not safe for you in my bar. Should I go to the back and grab you a booster seat?"

That cat-got-the-cream smile he was famous for crept back onto his face. "'Twas worth it to rile ya up."

Yikes. She needed to walk far away from that conversation as soon as humanly possible.

The constant fear of being targeted and dealing with the planning around finding the culprit had left Esme with no room to think about Miles' confession of love. The years she'd spent working for the Assembly as a handler had given her plenty of practice at suppressing emotions that could hinder her focus, but the nightmares the Alp had trapped her in still clung to her, even in the daytime, refusing to let go. And now, after Sitkum's comment, a new kind of torment awaited her—visions of their child together. Images of what could be, of the simple joy of it, would mock her as she lay awake that night, desperately trying to sleep.

Finn turned to Sitkum and introduced himself.

Perfect—this was her escape. "You two should chat. I need to check on other customers."

In the time between leaving Sitkum and Finn and greeting her next conversation partner, she made a whiskey sour, a gin and tonic, and a Negroni. Each was a fairly standard drink, so the time flew by without much hassle.

"Hey, Charity Case!" Maureen's classic greeting remained unchanged, even after everything they'd been through. Esme had expected at least a little respect from her. Apparently, her expectations were too high.

Maureen took a seat at the far end of the bar, a spot most people avoided because it was right in front of the box where they stored garnishes. She usually preferred sitting where she could hold court among the commoners, so maybe Maureen was there on business, not just to bust Esme's non-existent balls.

"One extra dry martini with no vermouth, shaken?" Esme asked. And just like that, Maureen cast a ward of silence over them both.

"Fake it with water. I have a meeting with the New York office before the opening bell. Let's cut to the chase."

Esme started making the "cocktail" as Maureen continued.

"Here's the situation. Someone's been masquerading as me, taking old talking points I've made and twisting them to stir up trouble. It should be no surprise to you that cambions are the principal topic of choice. Something about 'poisoning the community' and all that nonsense."

Esme handed over the drink, surprised her hands weren't shaking. Was Maureen actually trying to protect her by using the "Charity Case" nickname to throw off suspicion that she was… gods above and below… on Esme's side?

"Now, here's the part that scares me. Whoever this is, they're also trying to get Jacob ousted. They're throwing around the idea that he's too old. They're spouting that he's an unfit leader because of his questionable morality, past and present, if you catch my drift. It would be a bad idea to leave a power vacuum with the malevolent threat worse than we've ever seen it. And without Jacob as your primary buffer against the hate they're spewing, your life would also get way worse fast."

Recognizing the strain that maintaining a ward of silence around them must be taking on Maureen, Esme quickly asked, "So what do we do?"

"Hell if I know. I just thought you should hear it first—or second, since you're the one under fire. I've already talked to Jacob. If this escalates, we're in deep shit, girlie."

All that, and Maureen didn't even know about the planned attack. Gods below, this was getting worse by the day.

Abby

Abby watched as Colin eyed Cerys suspiciously from his spot on the couch next to her. Gwyn seemed to enjoy the newfound wariness that her brother had around him after meeting the gwyllgi. She couldn't help but be amused as he shamelessly flaunted their connection by casually lounging on the floor with both dogs nearly atop him. Miles did a good job of ignoring Colin and Gwyn, leaning on his kitchen counter, listening to Jacob speak.

Jacob stood up and readied himself to go. "I'll sum up the evening. The leprechaun is with Esmeralda now, and we've also made sure that Katia is safe. We have a plan to expose the imposter by setting up a trap. That's it. I'm going home."

Cerys and Lily stood from their spots on the floor, following Jacob to the door. He patted them both on the head and, in parting, declared, "Next time, you all can meet me at my place. Bring the hounds."

The moment he was gone, Miles wasted no time stuffing a few things into his gym bag and attaching Lily's leash. "I'm picking Esme up from work and staying at her place again. Gwyn, you know the rules. Colin, you want a ride? We should talk."

Colin's expression showed his displeasure at leaving Abby alone with Gwyn. But it was probably the "We should talk" remark that stopped him from saying anything else. With one last, threatening glance back at Gwyn, her brother left. Miles technically outranked Colin in the Corded Brotherhood, so his acquiescence made sense. Abby dearly loved her brother, but his overprotective behavior had gotten out of hand. She was the older one.

"Wow, so Colin's joined the 'we hate Gwyn' club, huh?" she asked. "At least Miles has chilled out since the Alp thing," she added with forced nonchalance.

Gwyn's nose crinkled in distaste. "Yes, Colin attempted to show how much he disapproves during training today."

Abby couldn't help but smile. "Esme told me she almost broke his nose. He can be an idiot sometimes, so I can't blame her. We fought like cats and dogs as kids, but things are better now. What exactly is he so pissy about?"

Gwyn shrugged, pausing before answering. "He doesn't want me 'sniffing around his sister,' like the stray dog I am."

Her temper immediately flared. She could practically feel the steam rising from her skin. It wasn't just Colin's words—it was what they meant; the assumption that she couldn't look after herself. "He seriously said those words to you?"

She was fed up with the constant assumptions from damn near everyone that she couldn't handle herself. It wasn't her personality that made people treat her that way. She knew she could be aggressive sometimes, so it had to be her appearance. She knew she looked like the stereotypical ingénue—small and innocent—but she couldn't help that. Was she supposed to start wearing biker jackets and cursing like a sailor just to get them off her back?

Abby also had a personality feature of resisting whenever she was challenged, regardless of whether it was appropriate at the time. So, she said exactly what was on her mind with savage glee. "Colin can shut his stupid mouth. If you're a dog, then I don't mind you sniffing around me, Gwyn. In fact, I like it. 'Cause I can be a real bitch sometimes."

She watched as his whole body froze. There was no taking it back now. Gwyn had the right kind of cockiness to redirect the conversation immediately if he was put off by her comment, but he chose not to. Instead, he offered, "It is still early. Would you care to watch another movie? You said there were three."

"Are you only asking me because you haven't figured out how to use Miles' television yet?" she joked, a bit shocked that he hadn't suggested she go home already after that last comment.

An unhurried, slightly mischievous grin spread across his face, easing the tension in her chest. He replied, "That, and I wouldn't mind doing some further sniffing."

Her eyes involuntarily widened in surprise. Abby was absolutely down with some tit-for-tat flirting.

It was a modern-day miracle. Had her temper and inability to shut her mouth finally led to a positive outcome? As they moved to the couch, Abby's stomach fluttered nervously. Even though their conversation had been fairly direct, she still didn't know what to expect.

At first, they sat at opposite ends of the couch, a polite distance between them. But the gap felt too inviting. Slowly, almost imperceptibly, they inched closer—an arm resting on the back of the couch, a knee brushing against hers, until the space between them disappeared. Less than halfway through the movie, she decided she'd had enough of dancing around the issue.

Abby glanced over and caught him watching her. Gwyn's gaze locked onto hers with such intensity that her breath hitched. All the right signals were there, but he still wasn't doing anything about it, damn it. Her heart beat faster, the anticipation building with what she knew she was about to do. Being bold had worked once before...

She reached out, lightly resting her hand on his thigh. "Gwyn," she whispered, "if you want to kiss me, right now is the perfect time to do it."

Cerys perked up at the first words either of them had spoken in a while, but seeing nothing of interest, she closed her burning red eyes and returned to her nap.

Gwyn lifted a hand, gently tucking an errant curl behind her ear. Instead of pulling away immediately, he trailed the tips of his fingers along her jawline with a reverence that made her racing heart skip. As he closed the gap between them, she tilted her head up slightly to meet him.

Her breath caught, and when their lips met, it was as if the room stilled around them. Her entire body sparked with approval. Gwyn's kiss was neither desperate nor hesitant—it was steady, reassuring, like something she hadn't known she needed. It felt like finding sanctuary, like slipping into the familiar coziness of your own bed after a long time away from home.

It made her want to melt into his skin and never leave. Far from being dull, it generated a delicious heat within her that she just barely kept in check. Their kiss was a thrilling blend of passion and familiarity that eluded her comprehension.

The movie played on, but she couldn't have cared less. Given everything that had changed in the past few weeks, this was too new and fragile to jump headfirst into. She never went further than briefly caressing his skin under his shirt, and he followed her lead. Their height difference made it easy for her, a little trickier for him, but they managed. An hour later, she drove home alone, with swollen lips, a stubble-scratched chin, and a grin that refused to fade.

CHAPTER TWENTY-TWO

THE TABLES TURN

Esme

"Ya know, y'all talked a big game a few weeks ago about how I wasn't going to be involved in anything dangerous and yet... here we are." Will emphasized each word with a tap of his fist on the table.

Esme, Will, Abby, and Gwyn were killing time in the Assembly's main conference room, waiting for the others to arrive. Everything about the space was unremarkable—standard gray walls, generic furniture, a pull-down projector screen at the far end of the table.

"Brujo," Esme countered, "if you were a better teacher, we wouldn't be running into this problem now, would we? Oh, and be nice to Abby's brother. He's hot and available, so that might improve your behavior."

Gwyn barely glanced at Esme before Abby's sudden gag made him freeze. His hands fluttered awkwardly for a second, then dropped. "Abigail?!"

When she caught his concerned look, Abby sat up straight, smiled, and rubbed his arm reassuringly. "I'm fine. Esme is disgusting, but I'm used to it."

Esme's gaze narrowed, and her lips pressed into a thin line. Over the past fifteen minutes, those two had found a couple dozen excuses to touch one another—hands grazing, shoulders bumping. Something was definitely going on. Esme bit back a frown, but not for long.

"Hey!" she snapped, drawing their attention. She needed to address this before Jacob, Miles, Colin, and Finn showed up. "Y'all better not have gotten naked on Miles' couch. That's my naked spot."

Will dissolved into giggles. Gwyn's eyes bulged. Abby rolled her eyes and said, "You're nasty, Morgana. And no."

Gwyn, seizing the chance to shift the conversation, asked, "Morgana?"

Abby answered, "Her middle name."

"Ah, the name is very familiar for some reason," he said, regaining his composure slightly. "Esmeralda, I assure you, nothing of the sort occurred."

Will didn't know of Gwyn's true identity, so they all kept mum on the subject of his slip-up—even though it physically hurt to keep quiet after he dangled that scrumptious bit of information in front of them. Could he have been referring to Morgan le Fay, King Arthur's older sister?

"Yeah, okay," Esme replied dubiously. "Just cool it with the touchy stuff before Colin and Miles get here. We don't need either of them grumpy today."

When Miles asked, she'd pretend like she didn't see Abby's wink out of the corner of her eye.

Within minutes, the rest of their small team arrived. From their body language, Esme could tell they'd been plotting. Normally, she'd be bothered by being left out, but today, she was just eager to get this over with so she could get back to being able to fall asleep without overwhelming anxiety.

Jacob came in first, dressed in his full regalia, his black robe sweeping the floor. Miles followed, striding in, looking sharp in dress slacks, a crisp shirt, and a perfectly knotted tie. Colin was right behind him, similarly dressed.

Will nudged Esme excitedly, whispering, "You brought me the best present. He's beautiful. I'll be on my best behavior, I swear."

"Told ya," she whispered back.

But her attention shifted to Miles. Even from a distance, she could tell he was wound up tight—like a spring ready to snap. They had talked about everything Maureen said when he picked her up from the Sanctuary, so she'd hoped they were on the same page. Either something new had come up, or they'd learned something no one would be happy about. She wasn't looking forward to finding out which.

"Where's Finn?" Esme asked as they approached the table. The leprechaun had been noticeably absent during recent events.

Jacob made a dissatisfied sound close to a grunt, and Miles just shrugged. Neither seemed too concerned, so Esme assumed he'd mist walk into the meeting at the worst possible moment.

Jacob quickly got down to business. "I've called you here primarily to observe, but you may also need to act as containment if something goes awry. Gwyn, I must admit, I do not know how best to use you today, but I've just had an idea. Is your hound with you, by chance?"

"No," he answered, clearly confused. Esme noticed he'd inched his chair a bit further from Abby's. Good boy.

"I want you to leave immediately and fetch her. She'll be the object lesson for our meeting. Don't worry—no harm will come to her in my presence. I'll even buy her a large steak for the trouble. You can make it to Miles' house and back in less than an hour, correct?"

Esme chuckled. "Maybe not with the way he drives." She remembered the one time she'd seen him behind the wheel—he'd driven so slowly it had been painful to watch. Then again, if he was over a thousand years old, which seemed likely now, maybe he had a reason for driving like a grandpa. She was sometimes struck by how ordinary he seemed, even with his noticeable accent, considering the mystery surrounding him and Miles.

As Gwyn stood to leave, Jacob added, "Do not forget that you are a Corded Brother visiting from Wales."

Gwyn nodded, and Abby tossed him her car keys. He left without another word.

Jacob addressed the rest of the group. "The topic today is the increasing frequency of malevolent activity. Not all seated members of the Assembly are directly involved in handling this problem. They're all capable of defending themselves against a personal threat, so if something happens, focus on containment, not their protection."

"Will Sylas be here?" Esme interjected, trying to sound casual, but her voice caught.

She hadn't seen Sylas in what felt like forever. She thought—hoped, really—that a threat to the Assembly, or even just a threat to Jacob, might bring them back together. They had too much history to give up on each other completely.

Jacob paused for an awkward moment, his eyes flicking to the floor, before answering cryptically, "I hope not."

Shifting back to the main topic, he said, "This will be a real meeting, so keep quiet about everything you hear in that room. Colin is my excuse for convening. He and Miles will be seated in the conference room when the Assembly members file in. The rest of you will watch through conveniently placed cracks or keep an eye out for any external disturbances."

That answered a question she'd had for a while. The higher-ups must be well aware of the crucial role Miles played for the Assembly as a Corded Brother if he was going to sit in on this meeting so casually.

"Mr. Cruz," Jacob continued, "you're here to help us see through the imposter's glamor. If you notice anything suspicious, inform your partner for the day, Ms. O'Malley, immediately. Esmeralda will have a few conjurations flitting around, searching for signs of trouble. Fionn!" he shouted, calling out the only missing member of their party.

To nearly everyone's surprise, Finn suddenly appeared, sitting in what they thought was an empty chair.

"Yes, yer grandness?" the trickster asked, twirling in his seat.

Jacob said, "He will skulk in much the same manner as you've just witnessed."

Finn made a kissing face at Abby. So, he had been in the room the entire time. That snake. Esme made a mental note to remind him to keep quiet about the new couple.

"Miles, Colin, are you fully armed?"

"Yes," they chorused. Both patted their wrists, hips, and chest as if they needed to make absolutely certain they hadn't forgotten that one special dagger that might come in handy during a fight.

Jacob stood, declaring, "We have less than thirty minutes before the seated members arrive. Let's get moving."

Miles and Colin stayed in the conference room with Jacob while Will and Abby found places to watch the meeting through cracks. As usual, Finn just poofed out of sight. Esme found a storage closet to sit in. It crossed her mind that it could be the very same closet where Katia sought refuge during the ghoul attack.

There were more comfortable offices to hide in, but she didn't want anyone stumbling upon her by accident. Besides, using four conjurations at once was easier when sitting down. She could control multiple conjurations while standing or even fighting, but it split her focus. She didn't want to miss anything important. Choosing the closet's security, she settled in and enjoyed the oddly comforting scent of copy paper and floor wax.

For today's mission, she decided to use her pixies. Normally, these resembled a cartoon fairy, complete with pixie dust. She'd make them some shade of pastel, and each stood around six inches tall. But now that she could reliably tap straight into the infernal realm for power, her conjured pixies were the goth version of the adorable creature. Tiny black thorns dotted the skin on the backs of their elbows, knees, and spine. A crown of spikes had replaced their beautiful flowing locks, and their teeth had transformed into jagged fangs.

To be extra cautious, she shrank them all down to the size of moths. Her plan was to have them fly an evenly spaced circuit around the building with the goth version of Irritella in the lead. They would serve as her eyes and ears—sort of. While she couldn't precisely see or hear through her conjurations, she could sense what they were experiencing like an echo, a disconnected and subtle representation of their experiences. It would be enough to alert her if anything was amiss—hopefully.

Miles

Just before the meeting, Miles made the mistake of asking Jacob about the rumors surrounding Esme. Jacob's typical unwavering honesty now had Miles seething with anger, undermining his attempt to appear as the calm and collected soldier he was supposed to be.

He knew he should be more upset about the attempt on her life than petty insults, but his dreams of late had been a non-stop stream of Elena—if that even was her name—fighting duels and enduring relentless taunting while the king gritted his teeth and did nothing. It almost felt like the dreams were egging him on, pushing Miles to do something—anything—to stop the past from repeating itself. Yet, with no direction to aim his wrath, all he could do was pretend to be the good soldier and hope that Maureen's imposter revealed themselves during the meeting.

Not all seated members of the Assembly would be present that day. Miles knew that at least two humans, a nymph, and a svartálfar would not be in attendance. Since these members seldom attended events, their absence wasn't a significant loss. He'd hoped that Sylas would finally stop raging for Esme's sake, but it wasn't to be.

Josiah was the first to arrive. He was a First Nations man who Miles had only met in passing. No matter the weather, he could always be spotted wearing slip-on sandals. With his reputation for nature-based magic preceding him, he gave Miles a nod of acknowledgment and found a seat. Abby and Colin's mom, Christi, filed in next. Colin stood to embrace his mother before she sat next to Josiah. It was evident that Abby and Colin had gotten their lack of height from their mother, as she barely reached five feet tall. But the siblings' blond hair must have come from their father, because Christi had vibrant ginger hair. Miles was uncertain of her magical specialization, but he intended to ask about it whenever he got the opportunity.

Next was Ved, a garuda man. His work with illusions—covering light, sound, and smell—was impressive. His feathered form was breathtaking—gold, white, and blue plumage covered every inch of his body. He also had an avian beak, so when he spoke, it came out in a voice no human could replicate. "Jacob," he bowed solemnly. "I am afraid that I may only remain for a short while."

Jacob replied, "I understand, Ved. We'll try to make the report quick so you can get the gist of things before you leave."

Maureen followed in after Ved, wearing one of her signature pastel tailored suits, and her hair was set so tightly it looked uncomfortable. Miles was still working on resetting his opinion of her. The stories he'd heard from Esme about how Maureen used to treat her grated on his nerves, especially now that his dreams were stuck on the theme.

But he was taking Esme's lead on this one. If she was willing to let bygones be bygones, he'd... try. That was the thing about Esme. Everyone was a potential friend, even if they regularly spit venom in your face. He loved that about her, but he could already tell it would be a source of endless frustration for him.

Maureen sat down, and a familiar selkie entered, carrying the first aziza he'd ever seen. Standing at less than a foot tall, Winnie still somehow possessed the kind of surpassing human beauty that was fascinating to behold on such a small person. Her wings were a leafy shade of green with brown stripes along the edges that led to two streaming tails from the tips. The rest of her looked completely human, with rich brown skin and hair.

Her host was a selkie that Miles had, unfortunately, met several times before. Winnie found a perfect resting spot on her waist-length, wavy gray hair. Sorcha was the forward type who either didn't read human body language well or ignored it entirely, so you had to be blunt with her. Luckily, she was never upset by his lack of interest, but she also never gave up. Without hesitation, she took the seat closest to him, signaling another encounter he'd rather avoid.

Next up was Jon Doe. Miles had verified that Jonathan Doe was indeed his actual given birth name—poor sod. Jon was a human in his forties, maybe ten years older than Miles, and mild-mannered. He was an alteration mage like Len. However, unlike Will's roommate, who was an artist, Jon Doe was interested in material chemistry. His dozens of patents hinted at a brilliant mind behind the unassuming exterior that hid just how wealthy he was. Miles mentally filed away a potential invitation for a future drink, already imagining how Jon's work could advance prosthetic technology.

Not long after Jon's arrival, Jacob started the meeting. He reported the number of malevolent sightings, terminations, and the state of their victims over the past six months. Everyone knew who Colin was, so he didn't need to be introduced when he started the slideshow displaying multiple graphs on the subject. The point of this show was to drive home the point that they needed support.

"There's no doubt about it," Jacob said. "The problem is getting worse, fast." He paused for dramatic effect, then continued,

"Ah, yes, good timing. Everyone, please do not react poorly to what I am about to show you. The creature you are about to meet is tame. You have my assurances on that." He raised his voice and said, "Please, come in, Gwyn."

Gwyn made no sounds that Miles could hear, so Jacob must have set up perimeter wards that alerted only him. Still, Miles knew Jacob had good reason for his paranoia.

A second later, Gwyn walked in with a glamorless Cerys on a leash. Her glowing red eyes cautiously surveyed the room, wary of the mixture of fear and anger she undoubtedly smelled. Her ears were alert but not pinned back aggressively.

When they had weighed Cerys the week before, she clocked in at over two hundred pounds and was still regaining weight. Before they found her, Cerys had struggled to secure sufficient food after her release from the magical prison that held all malevolents. The game in the Cascade Mountains where they found her was scarcer and larger than what she would have hunted in Wales a thousand years ago.

The group's reactions to Cerys varied. Winnie hid under Sorcha's hair, who, Miles just noticed, had inched even closer to him until their chairs touched. Ved's feathers stood on end, but he remained seated. Josiah folded his arms and grunted, seemingly amused at the sight of a hellhound in the conference room. Miles liked him more already. In contrast, Jon Doe froze like a stunned creature, not moving a muscle.

Christi and Maureen had been informed about the gwyllgi, so their reactions were limited to small smiles. As far as Miles knew, neither woman was aware of Gwyn's supposed true identity and connection to the Wild Hunt, so perhaps they'd been told a version of the story close to the one they were about to hear.

Jacob waved Gwyn to the front of the room. "This is Gwyn. He is a Corded Brother visiting us from Wales. As you can see, he has a companion helping us track malevolent creatures. We are working on a method to detect malevolent magic, not just sense it. Our new friends may hold the key to curtailing the growing malevolent problem."

Jacob sighed and spoke gravely. "My friends, we are at a point with the malevolent disruptions where some of you—or your chosen representatives—may be called upon to help in the fight. With what I'm about to say, I'm being cautious, not predicting any future events. There has been speculation that the high concentration of mages, especially powerful ones, at the Solstice Gala could act as a homing beacon for unknown malevolents in the area. I am coordinating discreet security efforts with my team of agents for the event. While I'm not asking you to take action, I am asking you to be aware and keep your eyes and ears open."

This was good. The growing consensus was that malevolents were drawn to powerful magic users. Jacob had used that information to plant the idea that something could happen at the gala without revealing they suspected a plot. Knowledgeable people were prepared people. All Miles could do was hope it paid off in the end.

Abby

It certainly wasn't luck that placed one of Jacob's "convenient cracks" for spying on the conference room in such a strategic position. Jacob mentioned that the room was soundproof, but they should still avoid making too much noise. He showed them an office with a tall, thin bookshelf, which had hidden casters underneath for easy movement. When they pushed it aside, it revealed a hairline crack, barely wide enough to see through, that lined up with the wainscoting on the other side. Some optical trick provided a wide, clear view of the entire room.

The meeting was blessedly short. After Colin's slideshow, there were a few minutes of show and tell with Cerys. Ved was the first to leave, and everyone else seemed in a rush to follow once they saw him go. At least Abby knew that her mother's mad dash wasn't from fear but because she was almost late for her joint therapy session with their dad.

Abby poked Will hard in the side. "Do you see anything?!"

Will whined slightly, "No, chica, damn. Your bony finger is sharp. I already told you—I think this plan is a bust. I can't believe Josiah pet your boyfriend's terrifying dog like it was nothing."

Abby couldn't argue with that. Sure, Cerys looked terrifying, but beneath her hellhound exterior, she was just like any other dog.

Sorcha and Winnie took about fifteen minutes to stop bothering Miles after that. Abby knew exactly how that selkie could act around attractive men. Josiah petted Cerys for five more minutes while Jacob and Jon chatted excitedly before leaving together. With the door shut, Maureen turned her intense expression on Miles and Colin, grilling them about something.

Abby was hoping the quick meeting and failed plan to trap the imposter meant she and Gwyn could end the day watching the last movie in the trilogy at her place.

But then she heard the unmistakable sound of hooves frantically scratching against the hallway tiles.

Not again.

Chapter Twenty-Three

ABSOLUTELY NOT

Gwyn

Gwyn couldn't help but enjoy the interrogation Maureen was putting Miles and Colin through. He relaxed in a chair, gently massaging Cerys' neck, barely containing his amusement as he watched their futile attempts to steer her away from her chosen topic.

"Dr. Goodwin, I know all about the malevolent problem, but this meeting felt wholly unnecessary—and Jacob doesn't do unnecessary. So, what's really going on?"

Miles shifted restlessly on his feet and replied, "I think with all the rumors flying around, he wanted to provide context to the situation."

She scoffed. "Context, my ass," and made a rude sound that caught both Corded Brothers by surprise. "It was smart bringing the hellhound for show-and-tell. But I think this was a power move to solidify his place at the top."

Gwyn silently agreed; it was a shrewd power play. This woman was sharp—he liked her already. He now understood that she was the "servant" who'd ushered him and Finn into Jacob's home at their first meeting. As a precaution against Gwyn, Jacob had strategically placed a potent evocation mage in his home.

Maureen lowered her voice. "I'm working on some cambion counter-propaganda."

At this, Miles' restless feet stilled, and he took a half-step back. Finally, Gwyn saw a flicker of genuine emotion break through Miles' carefully constructed mask. Gwyn noted it—there was history or tension between Miles, Esmeralda, and this Maureen. He'd have to ask Abigail about it later.

Moving under his hand, Cerys shifted into an alert crouch, her ears perking up warily by his feet. The gwyllgi tilted her head, her glowing eyes fixed on the entryway.

His heart went from a steady, relaxed rhythm to a frantic war drum in an instant. When he'd gone to retrieve Cerys, he had remembered Abby's gift. This was the perfect time to use his new weapon. Reaching into his coat, his fingers closed around the cold leather handle of the Dullahan's whip in one hand and the weight of his short sword in the other. He shot to his feet.

"It is time," he warned.

Miles

Miles considered ignoring Gwyn's warning but changed his mind on seeing Cerys' alert stance, and nodded begrudgingly. He'd been too distracted by Maureen to notice anything amiss. He snapped back into leadership mode.

"Right, malevolent incoming. Welcome to the party, Maureen. I know you're capable." He drew both push daggers strapped to his forearms, gripping one in each palm. Colin mirrored his movements. "Spread out. We don't know what it is."

"You all were expecting this!" Maureen accused, her voice sharp with frustration. The briefest flicker of doubt crossed his mind about her, but he quickly dismissed it. She wasn't acting. Maureen was not in on this malevolent attack.

Miles didn't have time for a lengthy discussion. He cut straight to the point. "Correct. But we thought it would happen during the meeting."

Without waiting for her response, he ordered, "Stay at the room's perimeter and keep both sides of the door clear for an exit."

He heard Maureen mutter something about "been doing this for a long time," her low grumble laced with weariness, before quickly complying.

Gradually, his ears picked up persistent scratching and snuffling coming from the hallway. Whatever it was, it was hunting. Fearing the worst but needing his team ready, Miles warned, "There may be more than one."

Gwyn muttered, "Abigail."

"Exactly," Miles responded quickly. "But it's headed our way. Colin, stay near the exit and be ready to bolt. We have too much firepower in here and not enough out there. Find your sister and Will first."

The snuffling and hoof-like scrabbling grew louder on the smooth tile. Whatever it was, it was massive. The breathing was as loud as a horse's.

Gwyn looked ready to argue with Miles' orders, but there wasn't time. They had vulnerable people outside, and debating who was best to protect them was useless. Still, Miles felt like he owed Gwyn something for the forewarning. "Colin's an excellent sprinter," he said with a nod. Then, "I'm opening the doors on three."

With a surge of magic, Miles flung the doors open, welcoming the monster in.

The dire boar charged through the open doors with its three sets of arm-length tusks at the ready. It was easily the size of a rhinoceros and armored like one too. Interrupting its coarse fur were black, bony plates of armor. Its rippling muscles flexed underneath them as it pushed for a fight.

While the others moved to surround it, Colin slipped away unnoticed, thanks to Cerys springing into action. She was a blur as she expertly maneuvered around the boar's hooves, nipping at the boar's side, though her dagger-sharp fangs slipped off its armor.

The three of them moved to surround the dire boar as it mindlessly charged toward the conference table at the center of the room.

With another flash of the hellhound's teeth, the vicious crack of a whip echoed in the enclosed room as Gwyn struck at the beast from the right. Miles hadn't known that Gwyn had brought the weapon, but he was glad that he had because the dire boar immediately turned his way.

Maureen launched her first attack. Given the boar's current preoccupation with Gwyn, her timing couldn't have been better. Miles stood more than ten feet away from her, but he could feel the air temperature around her drop suddenly. Maureen's magic sucked the moisture out of the air and condensed it into an ice lance that she aimed at the boar's hindquarters.

When she loosed it, the blast drove home into the creature's backside, cold enough to burn its surrounding skin. But Maureen wasn't finished. She cooled the air in the room so rapidly that even within the climate-controlled interior, an unnatural fog formed.

Bloody hell. Now Miles understood why she was a seated member of the Assembly.

Disoriented by the fog, the dire boar lashed out, shredding the nearby furniture instead of charging at people. Within moments, the conference table had fallen to pieces, and only a few chairs remained upright. Miles managed a single stab, but its thick hide nearly cost him his weapon. There was no way he could match the speed or agility of the gwyllgi nipping at its heels.

He needed to do something fast. Gwyn whipped at the beast repeatedly. The few strikes that landed on flesh instead of armor ripped into its body, but it paid little attention. The sheer size of the creature meant that Miles' typical up-close fighting approach would be ineffective and dangerous, especially since he had neglected to bring a firearm.

Miles watched, awestruck, as an invisible lance of air pierced a spot near the creature's heavy, distended stomach—Maureen's work again. Her fog had been an invaluable distraction, but he needed to find a way to end this.

"Gwyn, toss me your sword!" he shouted. Seeing Maureen's icy lance gave him an idea.

As he prepared to do something reckless and, quite honestly, foolish, Miles felt a wave of adrenaline rush through his veins. Gwyn threw the sword, hilt-first, with skilled precision. Not being an expert swordsman himself, Miles plucked it out of the air with telekinetic magic.

He channeled all the power he dared into his shield and forced the rest into his muscles, ligaments, and bones so that they could withstand the force his madness was about to put them under.

Abby

"Will," Abby tried to keep her voice calm. "I am going to leave and check out that sound. I need you to stay here. Got it?"

"Uh, you're scaring me, chica."

"Good. Stay here," she said, pointing firmly at the ground.

But the moment she opened the door, she realized she was too late. The hallway lights were out, and a man—or something resembling one—was striding toward her. But behind the stranger was another. With each step, her brother's unmistakable silhouette grew closer to the stranger, moving swiftly and silently to catch up.

To the creature, Abby's arrival in the hallway was probably like a burst of light in the darkness, instantly catching its attention. Fueled by an instinct as ancient as humankind itself, it surged forward as soon as it caught sight of its preferred prey—her. But so did Colin.

Closer now, the creature's breathtaking beauty—raven hair, blue eyes, angular jawline—made it hard to look away. But Abby was a scholar. She knew the nøkk's features were molded just for her, to lure her in, to create a false sense of security. She used the most basic yet effective method to break free from its snare—she glanced down. The stranger's lower half was... just wrong. His legs had a grayish-green hue and were adorned with shimmering scales, resembling those of a fish. Plus, he was completely naked, with every part of him on display—literally hanging out. Gross.

Colin must have accidentally alerted the nøkk to his approach, because the beautifully hideous creature turned away from her toward his pursuer. She had to give Colin a chance. Without closing the door behind her, Abby shouted at the top of her lungs, "Hey!"

The nøkk turned to her with that same hungry look back in his eyes. If Colin couldn't get to the creature in time, she'd have to try her last-resort magic on it before it tore her apart. She hoped that the malevolent Fae was humanoid enough for her secret talent to be effective.

Without a sound, another blond-haired figure burst into existence less than three feet from her face. Abby stumbled backward in shock. She barely had time to register the leprechaun's identity before burning-hot magic erupted from him. Gods above, now she understood why people made horror movies about his kind—their sudden appearance alone was enough to stop a person's heart.

Her heart raced once more as someone or something yanked her roughly to the side, slamming her into the wall. Yet she still managed to keep her eyes on the fight. Finn's hands reignited with blazing flames, and he hurled a lance of ifrit magic straight at the nøkk. It was undeniably foolish to use fire magic indoors, but Finn turned pyromantics into an art form rather than a danger. His unexpected arrival had bought Colin precious seconds. Now, they might actually have a chance of getting out of this without needing Miles' magic touch.

Colin was finally close enough to it, but the nøkk whipped away from the fiery magic with such speed that both his daggers missed their intended marks. Instead of striking where the nøkk's lungs should be, one dagger barely grazed its flank before clattering to the floor. Colin and Finn had hurt the Fae, but it wasn't dead yet. With scorching fire on one side and cold iron on the other, the nøkk frantically sought an opening—and took it. Abby watched as its scaled legs prepared to flee. But another pair of legs, the same ones that had pulled her to safety, were faster.

Will shot past the others and threw himself on the monster. As he tackled it to the ground, Abby used magic to pull Colin's dropped dagger to herself, standing just a moment behind her brother. Meanwhile, Finn waited, watching for the right moment to strike.

The nøkk struggled to rise, but Will, larger and more skilled at wrestling than it was, held it down. Struggling, Will grunted, "Pretty boy, come kill this thing!"

Calmly, Colin approached the struggling pair. "Give me a clear shot at its neck," he said.

Will firmly restrained the creature by gripping its arms and wrapping his legs around its thighs. He shuffled down the creature's body, carving out an opening for Colin. Her brother kneeled over the nøkk and swiftly plunged the dagger into the base of its neck.

Gods below, the Corded Brotherhood had turned her baby brother into a cold-blooded killer. The transformation from the boy she'd known to the man she now witnessed with blood dripping from his weapon was stark and unsettling. It made her wonder how much *she'd* changed since the Dullahan attack.

She hadn't even needed to use her secret magic to force Will to respond. His actions revealed a strength within him she hadn't expected to see. If she was tired of being underestimated by everyone, she couldn't keep underestimating her friend.

Her friend... Still holding Colin's dagger, she turned and went in search of Esme.

Esme

Esme was bored. So bored it was starting to hurt. Her pixies flitted around the offices, doing nothing of note. Her leg was numb from sitting too long—surveillance duty sucked.

The only thing even remotely exciting was seeing Gwyn and Cerys enter the building.

As expected, she sensed them with one of her conjurations, but she hadn't expected her infernal pixie to detect traces of malevolent magic on Cerys.

She remembered what Finn had said a few months ago when he described how he knew the banshee was real and not a conjuration. He'd known, "in the way that like recognizes like" because of the ifrit magic running through his veins. Maybe Esme's infernal magic recognized its offshoot in the traces of the malevolent magic.

She started eating one of the protein bars Will had given her after the Alp attack, saying that she needed to "pack some meat back on her bones." He'd bought her a gigantic box of all of his favorites. This one tasted like a candy bar, with nougat, caramel, and nuts covered in chocolate. For now, she was happy to delude herself into thinking that it was healthier than an actual candy bar. Anything to pass the time.

When the seated Assembly members began to file out, Esme wasn't certain if she should stay put or head out to see what everyone else was up to. After one of her pixies sensed the selkie leaving, she decided she'd had enough. She dismissed two of the four pixies and kept the remaining pair circling.

Just as she was stretching out her hamstrings to leave, she felt it: Something was subtly off in one hallway. Her job was surveillance, right? Time to survey.

Esme opened the door and stepped into the hallway. The lights were off, and with no windows in this section of the building, it was nearly pitch-dark. Had everyone forgotten about her? It was times like these when she wished telepathy wasn't just made-up magic for television so she could reach out and ask someone what was going on.

Still, an unsettling intuition prickled in her subconscious. To be on the safe side, she summoned a blade and crept down the hall. If Gwyn had seen her, he'd have been proud of her footwork. She barely made a sound as her pair of pixies flanked her front and back, enhancing her awareness.

With each step forward, the uneasy feeling worsened. She hissed into the dark, "Finn! If you're out here, show yourself!"

Nothing. No sound, no movement, no response. Just as she was about to round the corner, the pixie behind her picked up on something. Esme stopped and planted her feet firmly, twisting her body into the ideal position to confront whatever awaited her from behind. Her lessons were paying off.

Still, there was nothing. Letting out the breath she had dumbly held in anticipation, Esme swiveled around 180 degrees to make absolutely certain that she was alone. Just to get her point across, she whispered, "Finn, if you're messing with me, right now is not the time. Believe it or not, this sword is sharp."

A faint scratching sound, like footsteps on tile, echoed from the other side of the conference room. Maybe it was someone coming to tell her they could all go home now. But Esme's gut told her she was hoping for too much.

Miles

Cerys was no longer visible in the thick fog, and Miles had to trust his instincts to avoid running into her as he sprinted ahead. Clutching Gwyn's sword, he was ready to get close to a monster that could end his life in a single blow. It was lunacy, but necessary.

The dire boar thrashed wildly, its tusks slicing through the air as the other mages saw what Miles was doing and tried to keep it distracted. Ice shards clattered off its bony plates, and the crack of the whip echoed through the room. Miles took a deep breath, feeling the strangely familiar weight of the sword in his hand, and charged in.

The shield around him shimmered, absorbing the impact as the boar's tusks skimmed it. Miles ducked low, rolling beneath the creature's line of sight. He felt the heat of its breath as its lungs heaved in fury. The stench of its fur and the metallic tang of its blood filled his nostrils. Heart pounding, he slid to his knees, aiming for its underbelly, desperately hoping to find a weak, unarmored spot.

Every muscle, every nerve, had to be perfectly positioned. The success of his mad plan, not to mention his survival, demanded absolute precision.

With a scream, he drove the sword upward, channeling all his strength into the strike. The blade encountered resistance before smoothly slicing through the boar's tough hide and into the softer tissue beneath. The massive creature let out a roar so loud that it shook its entire body as it tried to rid itself of the object.

Miles clung to the sword's hilt as he was tossed around like a chew toy. The fear of aggravating its grievous wound was the only thing that prevented the monster from outright crushing him. Every movement the boar made ripped the hole he'd created wider, deeper, and more jagged. The magic he was expending to maintain his protective shield and grip on the sword was immense. He was growing more fatigued by the second.

Breathless, he tried to shout, but all he managed was the vague phrase, "Push!"

Either one or both of his allies understood what he meant, and the relentless sound of the whip and biting cold ceased abruptly. Suddenly, he felt a powerful jerk. Their telekinetic push on the sword thrust the weapon forward, aiming for the creature's vital organs. The blood oozing from around the sword turned bright red, and the dire boar's thrashing immediately weakened. With a final, violent shudder, the beast collapsed in a heap on the ground, forcing Miles down with it.

He barely had enough strength left to yank the sword free. He swayed backward, but his hands refused to let go of the weapon, holding it as if his survival still depended on it. Right before impact, a surprising savior grabbed him, preventing his fall and steadying him. Gwyn held him up by the shoulders as Miles stumbled again while trying to regain all of his senses. He was shaking and covered in blood from the waist up, but still managed to say, "Esme. Abby."

Hearing this, Maureen darted through the obliterated doors and into the hallway. Gwyn shook Miles violently, his voice urgent as he commanded Miles to stand under his own power. "Yes. Now, let's *go*."

Miles compelled his legs to carry him into the dark hallway, loosening his sodden tie as he walked. Cerys kept pace alongside him, none the worse for wear from the fight. Whether she was there of her own volition or her master's was yet to be seen.

Esme

In another hallway, pitch-black and leading to the conference room, Esme desperately hoped all of this was just another one of Finn's particularly excellent tricks. She was already plotting all the ways she could scare the life out of him using one of her conjurations.

The sound of approaching footsteps caused her to release a slow breath, trying to ease the mounting tension. It was probably one of her friends coming to meet her so they could all leave together; nothing more. She could just breathe and relax.

But as a stranger approached, Esme's hopes of heading home vanished. She stood at the intersection of the hallways as a vaguely familiar mage approached her slowly.

She dismissed her sword with a flicker of magic and greeted him tentatively, trying to play off the fact that she'd just been holding a conjured weapon made of freaking brimstone. "Uh, hi. How was the meeting?"

Because her attention was entirely on the man in front of her, she didn't notice the pixie behind her had detected another, more familiar and far more comforting, presence.

Her greeting was met with an unsettling smile from the stranger. His mouth was far too wide and his face unnaturally plastic, like something trying to mimic human expression.

From behind, she heard Abby scream, "Esme! Run! That's not Jon!"

Esme whirled around just in time to see her friend crumple to the floor. Witnessing Abby's collapse ignited her fury. She turned on the imposter, her eyes blazing with rage. In a flash, she conjured her blade from the shadows.

But her opponent had already made his move. Not-Jon shifted into a bear-like creature and was already loping away.

In a fit of unanswered rage, Esme screamed, "Absolutely not!"

As she spoke, a tiny fraction of the fear and desperation she felt for her friend escaped into the air. With her arm and shoulder infused with infernal power, she hurled her sword at the creature, unsure how long it would retain corporeality out of her grip. She'd never attempted this move before.

However, her throw was off. The creature weaved aside, dodging most of the blade. Still, one edge grazed its hind leg, giving her a fleeting glimpse of something gray beneath the glamor. It moved far too fast for her to catch up, so she dismissed her sword and ran to Abby.

The best-case scenario was that Abby had merely exhausted herself from using too much magic too quickly.

After no small amount of pestering from Esme after the Dullahan attack, Abby had taught her basic first aid and how to make an initial emergency assessment with the ABCDE approach. So Esme made certain that Abby's airway was open, she was breathing, her circulation was good. She skipped the "D" and "E" checks in the acronym, though, since Abby immediately woke up ready for a fight after Esme performed a painful sternum rub to gauge her responsiveness.

It didn't take long for everyone to find Esme and Abby sitting on the floor in the dark hallway. First, it was Colin, Will, and Finn, freaking out that Abby was still curled up in a ball on the floor.

Next, Maureen, of all people, flew into sight, only slowing when she saw them calmly sitting or standing together. She looked like she'd just walked out of a rainstorm that had coincided with a tornado. Her hair was in wild disarray, and bits of wood, plastic, and something that looked like drywall were scattered across her pantsuit. Finally, Gwyn appeared, trailed by Miles, who seemed to limp slightly with Cerys at his side.

With all eyes on her, Abby sat up and groaned, covering her face with her hands. "Ugh, I'm fine. Stop staring at me!"

Maureen threw her hands up and stormed off, muttering about calling Jacob.

Seeing that everyone was fine, Miles went straight to Esme. He seemed to realize he was covered in blood only a second before pulling her into an embrace, so he settled for holding both of Esme's hands. His intense stare made her feel like every inch of her skin was being scanned for harm. Knowing him, it probably was.

In his silence, she found comfort, as if they didn't need words to understand each other anymore. She realized then, with a sinking feeling that came from dread and jubilation, that there was no turning back for him. She just hoped she wouldn't let him down in the end.

CHAPTER TWENTY-FOUR

THE BETRAYER AMONG US

Esme

Apparently, while they were busy fighting malevolents, Jacob had left to share investment strategies with the real Jon Doe. Like the others, Jacob had believed their trap had failed, only to realize it had been turned against them. Since no one was seriously injured or dead, Jacob ordered those involved to reconvene at his house.

Jacob assured them they could leave the bodies of the dire boar and the nøkk in the Assembly offices as "someone would be by shortly to take care of them." The cryptic statement made Esme want to stay behind just to see what they did with the corpses. She thought Jacob was joking about the containment unit and the Dullahan, but now she wasn't so sure. Did the skeezy mortician come and pick the bodies up, or did the Corded Brotherhood actually have a team dedicated to hiding mass casualties?

Gwyn had dramatically lamented that no one would let him butcher the dire boar. Finn even backed him up, saying, "I have to agree with the pouty one on this. Imagine the amount of bacon that one has!"

Everyone else shuddered in disgust.

The blood covering Miles from the waist up had begun to dry, forcing him to remove his shirt in the parking garage before getting into the car. Will was so engrossed in chatting with Colin—about either football or wrestling, Esme couldn't tell—that he didn't even glance at a shirtless Miles as he wiped himself down with a clean cloth and grabbed a spare shirt from his trunk. It was a day for minor miracles.

Gwyn assumed his storytelling persona while recounting how they killed the boar. Esme knew that Maureen was a badass, but he made it sound like she was a rampaging goddess. Esme had to take a momentary pause when he mentioned Miles' killing gambit, trying to suppress her urge to scream, "What on earth were you thinking?" at him. Gwyn seemed slightly disappointed that he hadn't personally achieved the kill. And then the story of the nøkk.... Now she understood why Will and Colin were best bros all of a sudden.

Then, thanks to Miles' exhaustion, he even asked her to drive them to Jacob's house. She'd always wanted to try driving his brand-new electric car because it seemed so zippy compared to her doddering hatchback.

She adjusted the seat and mirrors while Miles fell asleep, the rhythmic turn signal merging with the quiet music. For a few precious minutes, the simple act of driving, something so normal and familiar, became her tiny refuge. She could forget about the malevolents. She could forget about the threats on her life.

For a little while, she could even let go of her gnawing sense of inadequacy.

She'd been useless during the fight. All she did was scream and throw her sword. She couldn't stop whatever magic the malevolent had used on Abby, and her friend had paid the price—the extent of which they still didn't know.

The glimpse of gray beneath the bear's glamor gnawed at her guilt. It made her wonder if she was to blame for everything that had happened since the Dullahan attack.

Esme parked, reclined her seat, and took a moment to center herself before waking Miles. This was going to be a rough meeting for everyone involved.

Miles

Across the library, Abby shouted at her brother, "Colin! Shut up! Half the people in this room know, and I trust the other half."

He'd been trying to stop her from telling them all something, and she was having none of it. They sat in a large circle that Jacob had set up in his library before everyone arrived. Maureen was now officially part of the plan regarding the trap they'd set for their unknown adversary.

Miles noticed Gwyn place a soothing hand on Abby's knee. Esme noticed too—she tried to distract him by poking him in the side. Bloody hell. Esme knew something was going on between them and was trying to hide it from him. She was probably right. Now wasn't the time to focus on that. Miles exhaled slowly, calming himself, and waited to hear what Abby had to say.

Abby leaned forward in her seat. "Here's the situation. I can't remember a single thing about walking up to Esme. It's like the memory's just...gone, Colin. Just like how Mom does it."

A thunderbolt of understanding hit Miles. That's why Christi sat in the Assembly, yet no one knew what her specialty was. No one knew, because her talents were mostly illegal to practice. Either that, or she could simply pluck any inconvenient memory of her actions from their minds. The messy story behind Abby's parents' divorce was suddenly making a lot more sense.

Colin shot back, "Yeah, except this time you passed out right after, so it's not the same at all."

In the way only siblings could provoke, Abby's face turned bright red with anger. Esme had joked about calling her a harpy when she became agitated. Now Miles could see why.

Surprisingly, neither Finn nor Will said anything during the entire exchange.

With a deathly calm, Abby told her brother, "Colin, I could make you forget everything that happened today and put you to sleep right now. And you know it."

Miles saw Gwyn's eyes widen in sudden realization, mirroring his own. Abigail wasn't just an enchanter; she was an Enchantress, with the power to manipulate memories and control others—magic that was highly illegal, right next to necromancy and blood rites.

Esme muttered under her breath, "Gods below..."

Miles couldn't agree more.

Jacob broke into the argument. "I think I understand your point, Ms. O'Malley. But you can rest assured, your mother is not behind this attack. I can guarantee that."

Abby shot back, "Then why did it spare me when it was hunting Esme?"

Jacob reasoned, "It's easier to alter a memory than to fight multiple opponents."

Esme began pacing—something she always did when a revelation hit her hard. Gesturing emphatically, she declared, "This is getting us nowhere! We haven't learned anything new from this counter-ambush."

She stopped pacing and met Miles's gaze, inhaling a long, steady breath before slowly addressing the others. "I have two things to say that none of you are going to like... for various reasons."

Miles kept his expression neutral, but he saw Maureen fold her hands with a look of dark, expectant satisfaction. Esme began pacing again, and Jacob tried to encourage her. "Well, go on, darling."

"One. I can sense malevolent magic with my conjurations if I infuse them with a bit of infernal power. I figured it out when Gwyn brought in Cerys after I supercharged my pixie sentries. When one of my pixies looked at Cerys, it felt like what smelling a familiar smell feels like. Like, you know immediately what cookies baking smells like versus pot roast... Alright, that was a ridiculous example, but I hope it makes what I mean clear. There's just no comparison. My infused conjuration instinctively recognized malevolent magic in Cerys, and I felt it through our bond."

She stared at Maureen, daring her to challenge the statement. "I think we can use it to track malevolents."

Maureen appeared dubious but didn't object outright. Miles considered that a small victory.

"And second?" Jacob prompted.

Esme returned to her seat next to Miles and clasped his hand, silently asking for strength. He appreciated that she trusted him enough to lean on him. The warmth of her hand reassured him that he'd done the right thing in opening up to her.

"I think our villain is Sylas...which means everything is my fault."

He asked, "Why?"

Esme bit her lip before responding. "When I flung my sword toward the bear-like creature that fake Jon Doe had transformed into, the blade cut through the glamor, exposing a gray body underneath. It was the same shade of gray as Sylas. He's powerful enough for all of this. Jacob—could it be him?"

Miles watched as Esme shrank into herself, her voice growing smaller with every word. Miles tightened his grip, silently reminding her he was there. If Sylas was behind this, everything was well and truly screwed. He was incredibly powerful, intelligent, and worst of all, he knew all of their weaknesses.

Jacob's silence was unsettling. Gwyn and Colin spoke over each other, saying, "Who is Sylas?" and, "Sylas wouldn't work with malevolents."

Will buried his face in his hands and muttered in Spanish. The fear rolling off him was palpable. Even Finn, normally so lively, sat calmly—dare Miles say, even sedately—in his chair.

Jacob's slow, deliberate response added years to his appearance. "Esmeralda," he began, flipping the pen he was holding over and over, alternately tapping the end and the nib on the desk, "it worries me that you might see this situation more clearly than I do. I hate to admit it, but...it's possible."

He continued, "Colin, Gwyn, you're both involved now, so here's the short version of events. A few months back, a pishacha possessed a local dryad. That dryad was Sylas' girlfriend, for lack of a better word. The pishacha used her body to imprison Will and Maureen. Esmeralda, Miles, and Finn rescued them."

"And I killed her," Esme added weakly.

Miles watched as Gwyn studied the mage who could see magic and the elemental powerhouse sitting across from him. Will still had his face buried in his hands, but Maureen was glaring at Jacob, clearly resenting being presented in any way that could make her seem weak.

Jacob explained for Gwyn's benefit, "Sylas is a seated member of the Assembly. He's a leshy who's quite adept at multiple forms of magic."

Gwyn questioned, "A leshy? A powerful life event like losing a lover could cause him to undergo the change."

Jacob ordered, "Explain."

Esme's admission of guilt seemed to have no impact on Jacob. Miles sensed that Jacob was deliberately ignoring it, silently signaling that he believed her actions were justified. But Jacob's tough-love approach, though well-intentioned, wasn't working for Esme—she seemed oblivious to his intent, withdrawing further into herself. He'd have to bring it up if there was ever a natural opportunity.

The sight of Gwyn sitting up straighter in response to the command brought a smile to Miles' face. At least someone was forcing him to heel.

"Beings like our friend here, whose very essence is made of magic," Gwyn pointed at Finn, "may change based on how they use it. It's similar to how Fae magic and malevolent magic are distorted reflections of infernal and general magic. Their bodies and minds can twist and change if they become consumed by hatred and aggression."

Finn came alive at being singled out and bitterly added, "Hey, now, that doesn't really happen to my kind." He stuck his nose in the air.

Gwyn said, "I'll grant you that, Finnegan. Yet, creatures straddling the line between malevolent and not are highly susceptible to magic's sway. Abby mentioned you had a pooka chef at The Sanctuary of Spirits—he'd be at risk, just like Sylas."

With a slap to his knee, Jacob declared, "I finally heard something useful come from you. I'd heard of this happening, but hadn't considered it here. If it was Sylas, it would explain his fixation on Esmeralda and our other cambion. You've earned your paycheck, Mr. Gwyn."

The flippancy of the conversation seemed to push Esme deeper into herself, causing her to pull her hand away from Miles. Either she was withdrawing, or her temper was about to flare again. It was hard to tell with her—maybe it was both.

"So, what?" she asked. "Am I supposed to kill Sylas now, too?"

No. If it came down to it, Miles had already decided he'd pull the trigger for her.

That evening

"Thank you for driving, lovely. I don't think I could have done that otherwise." Miles knew he was grinning like a fool, but it was worth it to see Esme's face after he said it.

She made a pleased sound and rolled onto her back. Her skin was so soft and warm that he already wanted her close again. The more time they spent in the room together, the more it felt like they were reclaiming the safe, familiar space it had once been. The lingering tension from the Alp attack had almost entirely disappeared.

Esme joked, "If a nap is all you needed to do that, I'll drive us everywhere."

Probably sensing his lingering fatigue, Esme had offered to drive again after the meeting at Jacob's house. Miles had made a herculean effort to stay awake so they could talk about how Sylas fit into the grand scheme of things and her feelings about the possibility, but he'd ultimately failed, having used too much magic during the fight earlier. That day, he'd been grateful for a rare break from his usual dreams.

"I had to make up for missing your birthday."

She nipped his shoulder. "It was my thirty-second birthday. I'll take thirty-one more make-up sessions. Thank you very much." She nipped him again. "To be clear, that was a challenge."

"I've got at least a few days to get to thirty-two, correct?"

She pursed her lips and shook her head slightly. "I'll think about it."

"Well, while you're in a good mood, riddle me this, Esmeralda. What's going on with Abby and Gwyn?"

She lightly swirled a finger over a scar on his ribs, trying to tickle him, but his nerves were deadened there. "That's not gonna work, lovely."

"Ugh, alright." She shifted back to place her head in the cradle of his shoulder. "This might surprise you, but I actually know as much as you do. I guessed the same thing, though, and warned them off using your couch as a naked spot since I've already claimed it."

The much-needed moment of levity brought laughter bubbling to his throat. "Okay, okay, I agree," he said, not resisting the urge to play with a lock of her hair. "It's your spot. What are we going to do about it?"

Her answer was quick, punctuated by a hard poke to his side. "Nothing."

The answer didn't sit well with him, but he chose to leave it be... for now. They had more pressing matters to attend to. "Fine, I'll leave it... but only for my muffin top."

She playfully nudged him. "Muffin top? Is that my new nickname? I swear, I make one joke... Wait, no, that's payback for the poke during the meeting, isn't it?" She snorted.

He felt himself grinning again. The muscles of his cheeks weren't used to this much exercise. "Maybe."

"More seriously, though, I think we should start working with Abby to see if we can determine some way to either resist or limit the effects of the neuromancy the malevolent has already shown. I also think it's time to put more pressure on Will to make a breakthrough."

Yep, he was talking shop in bed.

Esme sat up, the sheets falling in her haste, providing him with a stunning view. "So Sylas is now a malevolent?"

"We actually don't know if it is Sylas yet, love." He needed to remind her of that. "I hope it isn't. Jacob said he'd feel things out with him. Let's wait and see what he finds out, yeah?"

With a sigh that disturbed her hair, she conceded. "Yeah, okay. I guess I can be patient about this, especially since it keeps you living with me. But, there's another matter that I'm finding it very difficult to be patient about... You ready to reduce your debt by one more?"

In response, he pulled her toward him, guiding her slowly, eagerly, down.

CHAPTER TWENTY-FIVE

SHOPPING

Esme

Esme and Abby finally had a day just for themselves. It felt like it had been months since they'd spent quality time together. They planned a day of dress shopping and pedicures—manicures being a lost cause for two mages who worked with their hands.

Abby's blue Beetle had barely parked when Lily started prancing and wagging her tail excitedly at the front door. Esme wondered which of the three car occupants the dog was most excited about—probably Cerys. Lily's routine with her gwyllgi friend had been disrupted since Miles had moved in with her.

Now that she thought about it, today was a day out for all the girls, including the dogs, who had their own adventure planned. Gwyn had cryptically mentioned he'd be off on his own shopping adventure for a few hours. After that he'd take both dogs on a long hike—a special treat for Cerys, who couldn't go to dog parks because maintaining her glamor was too taxing.

Esme watched Gwyn, feeling that she couldn't figure out what was off with him. He was definitely up to something.

But today, she noticed a change in his demeanor and armor of confidence—his previously icy glare had softened. He also wasn't showing his usual brand of arrogance. The change felt more like a shift; a recalibration.

Miles' constant arguing with Gwyn had to stop; she needed to convince him to talk it out for everyone's sake. It felt especially pressing now that Gwyn and Abby seemed to be hitting it off.

Esme opened the door for Lily and stepped onto the porch. The December weather was typical—damp and cloudy, but not too cold. As soon as Abby opened her car door, Lily pranced over, hoping for pets, but ended up sniffing the bag she carried instead. With a laugh, Abby said, "As Lily can tell, I brought pirozhkis!"

Then Cerys and Gwyn jumped out and the dog festival was on. The two-hundred-pound hellhound with glowing red eyes chased the oversized wolfhound in frantic circles in Esme's miniature front yard. Luckily, ordinary people usually dismissed minor magical events as figments of their imaginations. They shuffled them inside, where they'd stay until Gwyn picked them up later for their hike.

While Abby was in the kitchen putting away the pirozhkis, Esme began the inevitable grilling from the living room.

"Gwyn, do you even have a driver's license?"

He reached into the pocket of his coat and produced a card. To her eyes, it looked legitimate.

"How?" she asked, but he tapped the card once, and the glamor he'd placed upon it faded, revealing a grocery store loyalty card instead.

Esme raised her voice so that it would carry to the other room. "Abby, you're messing around with a criminal!"

Gwyn's eyebrows knit together in a frown, but it wasn't defensive—not entirely. He stared at the fake card a little too long, as though caught in some unspoken memory. When he pocketed it, his movements were slow, almost reluctant. Had she hit a sore spot she hadn't known existed? It was meant to be a joke, but then again, she didn't know that much about Gwyn's past.

Abby's voice, intermittently singing and humming the theme song of a popular cop television show, signaled her return. Abby shrugged and said, "Eh, he drives too slow to be pulled over, anyway."

Esme grinned. "And I know you're fine with a bit of a bad boy. If you're going to kiss goodbye, please do so outside so I can maintain plausible deniability with Miles on the subject."

Sure enough, they walked out of her living room, hand in hand.

Just as they were preparing to leave for the salon, Finn arrived, juggling garment bags, which he failed to keep from dragging on the ground, and a rectangular box.

"Heyo, lovely ladies. I come bearing gifts!"

The two women exchanged dubious looks but remained silent, just waiting for whatever insanity he was about to drop onto Esme's doorstep.

"Uff, I suppose I should explain myself. Can we go inside so I can show ya? I promise there's no mischief in these bags."

Abby said, "Say it two more times, and we might believe you."

Esme raised her hand, and as it connected with Abby's palm, they shared a satisfying high-five at Abby's slam-dunk of a comeback. Despite Finn's initial skepticism, he begrudgingly went along with it, and Esme welcomed him inside.

"Let's get started!" he said, clapping his hands and giggling like an excited child. "I've missed a few birthdays, and honestly, when ya get to my age, ya stop thinkin' about 'em." He stroked his beard thoughtfully, then said, "I'm not even sure when mine is. Maybe we'll celebrate this spring—with plenty of alcohol!"

Esme gave him a side hug and said, "If you can make a hangover disappear, sign me up for all of it. If not, maybe just a drink or three. Now," she pointed at the bags, "what's this?"

"Right!" His hands made a racket again. "So, on top of the birthdays I've missed, I heard you were in need of some fancy attire for the Gala, so I took the liberty of making these for you both. Didn't have time for shoes though, sorry."

He pointed to the left bag and said, "Esmeralda," and then the right, "Abigail."

Abby's arm shot out and gently grabbed Esme's wrist. "Wait..." she muttered, eyes searching the living room for something that lived only inside her memories. "Promised attire..."

"What? Abby, what's wrong?" Esme whispered, "You're kinda freaking me out."

Abby shook her head, as if trying to free herself from whatever negative thoughts plagued her. "No, nothing. Never mind. Just something that has..." she hurried through the end of her sentence, "absolutely nothing to do with Finn's generous gifts."

Trying not to offend him but barely able to conceal her skepticism, Esme asked, "You made us dresses?"

A bit smugly, he replied, "Aye. Just where do ya think I get my clothin' from? Go ahead, open 'em."

Esme cast a sidelong glance at Abby before warning Finn, "Okay, if something jumps out at us when we unzip these bags,

I will swear, all the way to my grave, I saw nothing after Abby removes a few precious memories from your head."

"Threat taken, lassie." He was practically bouncing with excitement. "Just open the bags!"

With cautiously eager fingers, Esme and Abby did as he bid. With just one peek, Esme's jaw dropped. "Holy..." was all she could say until her gown was fully out of its bag.

It was made of silk in the darkest blue of a moonless night. The fabric was extraordinary, but it was the bodice that stole her breath. Black mesh, so fine it was nearly translucent, was embroidered with onyx and genuine gold beads, strategically arranged to cover what needed covering. The beads formed swirling patterns, nearly identical to the wisps of brimstone that accompanied her infernal conjurations. These swirling mists cascaded off the bodice, creating an off-the-shoulder look that was somehow flexible despite the weight of the materials.

She'd never seen such a finely crafted, personally styled piece of clothing. But when she turned the dress around, her breath caught again. On the back, the head of a shadowcat—just like the first infernal conjuration she'd made under Finn's tutelage—was formed from the same beads. Oatmeal roared her fury to the night sky. The beadwork continued down the back, tapering off into a pattern of shooting stars that looked to be made of more gold and diamonds.

Esme nearly choked in shock.

She turned to Abby's dress, which was equal in quality and personality. They were of a similar cut, but had a completely different feel. Abby's was also silk, in a shade of pink champagne, with a matching fine mesh bodice. On it, a pair of wings formed from gold beads and tiny pearls took flight, the tips extending so far they fanned out at the shoulders. Her dress had a belt made entirely of gold beads. When Abby flipped it around, Esme saw a crown of the same gold and pearl beads, with a halo of gold extending from its peaks.

Finn had taken Esme's nickname for her, "harpy," and created something extraordinary out of it. The crown was confusing, but maybe it had something to do with Finn worshiping the ground she walked on.

Esme and Abby exchanged delighted looks. Esme said, "Finn, these are amazing. The amount of work that you put in is spectacular." She stopped just short of saying thank you, even though she felt it was more than warranted. After all, even if he was a friend, he was Fae, and she'd taken the thing he said about scorpions to heart.

Abby added, "Seriously. Finn, can you make my wedding dress one day? Calling these stunning feels like an understatement."

The dresses—just the fabric, gems, and gold beads alone—must have been worth thousands of dollars. Add in the craftsmanship, and Esme felt faint. The only thing keeping her grounded was a nagging suspicion about how Finn had gotten their measurements to craft these masterpieces. On second thought... Esme decided she didn't want to know the answer to that.

That same joyful giggle burst out of him. He was overflowing with happiness. It brought a wide smile to her own face. "You'll need to try 'em on to see if alterations are needed," Finn said excitedly.

But Esme pointed at the box still sitting on her couch. "What's in the box?"

"Ah, yes." He hurried over to grab the last mystery item. "This is from yer ole geezer. It's his birthday present for ya. I said I'd deliver it along with my own. He had somethin' else to do today."

Esme couldn't shake the unease she felt, knowing that Finn must have a truly ludicrous piece of mischief in store for her. He was being remarkably well-behaved for a leprechaun. Despite everything, she hoped he was reserving at least some of his energy for a more important task, like helping them figure out how to see magic or thinking up ways of fighting the malevolents.

While Esme untied the red ribbon around the box, Finn and Abby chatted about her upcoming birthday that spring, so he could mark it on a calendar. The last thing she expected to see was wood shavings. She pushed a cautious finger into the pile and yanked her hand away sharply. Blood was streaming from her finger and she felt slightly faint. Instinctively, she sucked at the cut and worried at her overblown physical reaction to such a small cut.

With matching expressions of concern, the leprechaun's bright eyes and the enchantress's knowing ones settled upon her. With her finger still in her mouth, she muttered, "Be right back," and went to the kitchen to wash up.

Esme walked back into the living room with a bandage on one finger and a basting brush in her hand. It wasn't meant for this, but it would do the job to brush aside the wood shavings so she could see what she was dealing with.

A few swipes later, she found the handle.

Lifting it into the air, she saw that Jacob had made her childhood dreams come true. It was a slimline dagger with a rosewood handle inlaid with a swirling gold pattern. The blade resembled Damascus steel, but the pattern shifted unnaturally in the light. Definitely magic.

Gods above and below, she owned a magical dagger.

Abby walked over and bravely sifted through the wood shavings to find a matching thigh, forearm, and waist holster for it.

Abby remarked, "That is far better work than I've ever seen, even from Ivar!"

Ivar, a svartálfar blacksmith with jagged, stone-like skin, was a great guy but also a frequent professional pain in Esme's ass at The Sanctuary of Spirits.

Esme agreed. "I can feel its magic, but can't tell what it does. Any ideas, Finn?"

"I can guess." He seemed reticent to answer.

"Please..." She stopped just short of begging.

"My guess is that it's vampiric."

"Excuse me?" Her eyes flickered toward the dagger, a touch of wariness seeping into her voice.

"It takes a bit o' magic from whatever ya stab, lassie. Not blood. Humans..." He rolled his eyes. "The ones I've heard of can release the stored magic durin' a fight. How, I dunno. You'll have to ask your old man. But that thing is worth a pretty penny, by any standard."

Esme jabbed the dagger into the open air and restrained herself enough to squeal in delight only once—Abby and Finn were well used to her by now. "Now I just need to find something to stab with it."

"On that pleasantly bloodthirsty note," Finn grinned, his eyes lingering on her dagger, "I'm off, lassies. I was told in no uncertain terms that it's supposed to be your ladies' day. Toodles!"

He just, poof, disappeared.

The friends settled in Esme's living room, their dresses draped over the back of the couch. The thought of stuffing their breathtaking creations into garment bags, unseen until the

Gala, was unbearable to both of them. They'd rescheduled their pedicures to an earlier time, since they no longer had shopping to do, and decided to spend the rest of the afternoon relaxing at Esme's house eating cheese and chocolate. Gwyn had dropped by to pick up the dogs while they were gone, so it was just the two of them, like old times. They poured themselves some sparkling wine, toasting to a day free of monster-fighting and drama.

It was nice to chat through the usual catching-up topics. But after a while, Abby pointed an accusing finger at Esme, "So, you've been all smiles today, lady. What gives?" Abby glanced upward, then amended, "I mean, other than spending a marvelous day with me and having magic hands at your beck and call."

Esme gave a full-force wicked smirk. It felt like it had been a million years since Esme had gone to Abby for advice after her first night with Miles. Abby's comment had poked fun at Esme's reverie over Miles' use of magic in... enhancing his prosthetic hand for her benefit.

Esme sighed contentedly, then said, "No, he still does that, but I think it's because I'm happy. You seem happy too. Stressed out, sure, but happy. Finally, I feel like I'm doing something with my life, ya know? I finally realized that I've spent far too long just passively floating through it, with no real intention. Now, with all this malevolent stuff and learning about my powers, I feel like I might be uniquely suited to do something about a problem."

Abby raised her glass in salute. "Hell yeah, lady. You are a badass."

Naturally, Esme took the moment to drop another bombshell, because she was a drama queen at heart. Grinning like a fool, she said, "Also, Miles told me he loves me."

Abby's eyes widened. "Finally! How do you feel about it?"

"Finally? We've been together for like two months!"

"Together, sure, but you've been spending time together for like eight, ten months now? Plus, you've basically lived with each other since day one of your relationship. So...have you said it back?"

Esme silently shook her head. She thought she might love him, but the emotion was so big, so... overwhelming that she shrank away from it. Even if he already felt like home...

Abby accused, "You're worried something is going to go wrong, aren't you?"

Esme grimaced in a way that probably looked a bit comical.

"Gods, Esme. Nothing will go wrong," Abby reassured her, taking a sip of her wine. "You two are solid. Plus, you've got me to back you up."

Esme smiled, feeling a weight lift off her shoulders. "Thank you, Abby. I'm lucky to have you in my life. Speaking of romance, what's going on with you and Gwyn?"

Abby chuckled, shaking her head. "We've only kissed, Esme. And we went on that one date before we even knew who he might be. I don't know what we are yet."

"Do you want it to be something more?" Esme asked gently.

Abby paused, considering her words. "I think so. He's different from anyone I've ever known. But it's complicated, especially with all the secrets."

"Secrets or not, you deserve happiness, Abby. And if Gwyn makes you happy, then you should go for it." She shrugged. "I approve. I think Gwyn's a badass."

"So many badasses in my life!" Abby exclaimed. Then, turning serious, she asked, "You don't think he's crazy with all he says about Miles?"

Esme bit her tongue so hard that she tasted copper and forced a nonchalant shrug. Miles' dreams weren't her secret to talk about, so she deflected.

"So, you got super mad yesterday and dropped a bomb-shell on us all, harpy. One: I need you to tell me everything. Two: I need you to try it on me so I know what it feels like."

As predicted, Abby's bewildered look suggested she thought Esme had lost her mind. The diversion from the topic of Miles and Gwyn's pseudo-past had worked, so it was worth it.

Abby collapsed sideways onto Esme's couch with all the drama of an A-list movie star, her body sinking into the decorative pillows. Face still smashed into a pillow, she groaned. "I really can't keep my mouth shut, can I? Remind me to tell you what I said to Gwyn about sniffing."

"Oh, I absolutely will remind you of that. But for now, dish the story, Enchantress-mine..."

Gwyn

Gwyn gazed with fanatical admiration at the beauty before him. The modern world had truly created wonders. Her body was a sleek work of art, all curves and lines that spoke of elegance and strength. Her slender arms promised both grace and deadly precision. She gleamed under the dim light, a soft, alluring sheen that invited his touch.

He traced a finger along her smooth surface, feeling the perfect blend of power and pliability he craved. The tension within her was palpable; a coiled force waiting to be unleashed. He couldn't wait to see what she'd do when he finally released her restraints. In Gwyn's hands, she felt both powerful and responsive, an extension of his will. As he held her, he could almost hear the whispered promises of silent, lethal efficiency.

This crossbow wasn't just a weapon. She was perfection. She had a magazine that could fit eighteen bolts, and Gwyn was deeply in love.

Since the Corded Brotherhood had set up an account for him, he'd made exactly two purchases from it. The first was a Latin dictionary with a handwritten note tucked inside that he'd posted to a run-down inn in the middle of nowhere Caernarfonshire. The crossbow was the second. His gambling winnings were nearly exhausted, but they had managed to sustain him thus far. Fortunately, that was a lifestyle he was happy to leave behind.

Now, hunting for the Brotherhood gave him purpose. It was the closest thing the modern world could offer to a career that resembled his past existence—or at least what little of it he could recall. His transformation from mortal to something more remained an unfathomable puzzle. He knew his affinity for magic had been far stronger in ancient times, but how? Delving too deeply into the mechanics of his transformation, or the arcane nature of magic, seemed to push his fragile human mind to its limits.

He could remember fragments of his childhood and his time as a man, but his ascended life remained shrouded in mystery, only vague remnants flickering at the edge of his mind. Desperate for answers, he'd recently experimented with his connection to Cerys, hoping it might unlock some understanding of his past. Yet each time, the effort proved fruitless, leaving him with more questions.

As he stared at his new weapon, he considered that focusing on the past wasn't the best use of his time anymore. The shadows lurking at the edges of his mind were always ready to pounce and steal away his peace of mind. It had been over a thousand years since he had felt any semblance of happiness, but now, things were changing.

He was, at his core, a hunter. Though it was a role he had first taken on somewhat reluctantly, forced upon him without choice, fighting the malevolents had filled a void he hadn't realized existed. He needed the purpose. He needed the fight.

He hadn't lied when he told Abigail and Esmeralda that he was taking the dogs on a hike—he was. He was simply adding to their exercise by practicing with his new weapon along the way. The dogs eagerly retrieved the bolts, tails wagging with joy after each shot.

Seeing their unbridled delight, he realized he might have been looking for his power in the wrong place. Instead of seeking answers externally, through Nudd, perhaps he needed to reconnect with those aspects of himself that made him Gwyn ap Nudd, psychopomp and leader of the Wild Hunt.

Both dogs went completely still after he retrieved his last shot. Their ears perked up at attention. Mirroring them, he froze, his senses heightened. He felt it as much as he saw it: a streak of ruddy brown fur in the snow just off the mountain path.

The bowstring was already in place upon the cocking hooks, primed and ready to shoot. He clicked off the safety, aimed, and let loose.

CHAPTER TWENTY-SIX

MIND GAMES

Abby

Years Before

Abby's dresser was in disarray. Clothes and accessories were scattered everywhere. The thought of cleaning it up later filled her with dread. Abby's hands trembled with fury as she rummaged through her closet, tossing aside shirts and random trinkets she had stashed away. Frustration burned inside her like a tornado made of fire and flying glass shards, ready to rip apart anything that came into her path.

Being a preteen girl meant a constant whirlwind of emotions, and each second she couldn't find her stupid mp3 player only fueled her fury. How many times had she told Colin to stay out of her stuff? Yet here she was, again, searching for the one thing that could calm her down. She threw a winter boot across the room, and it crashed against the door loud enough to snap her out of her rampage, if only for a moment.

She heard a faint scuffling outside her door and braced herself. Would it be her mom, barging in to scold her, or Colin, sticking his nosy face into her business? Sure enough, Colin walked in, trying to look innocent but failing miserably.

"What are you doing?" he asked. "Mom is going to be mad when she sees what you've done to your room."

Compared to other kids his age, her little brother's tiny frame made him seem even younger. At eleven, he was too young for his magic to manifest, but at nearly fourteen, Abby expected hers to kick in any day now.

Abby glared at him. "You little..."

Then she exploded, jumping up from her spot on the floor by her closet. "Where is my mp3 player, Colin?"

Her anger propelled her feet further. He stepped back, but she grabbed his arm, her fingers digging into his skin as she reached into his pockets with her other hand.

"I don't have it, I swear!" Colin protested, squirming in her grasp. But then something happened—something neither of them expected.

A surge of power pulsed through the fingers clutching his arm. It was like nothing she'd ever felt before. It felt like heat and electricity all wrapped up in one zinging package leaving her fingertips. Colin's eyes widened in shock, then glazed over. His body slackened.

"Tell me where it is," Abby said, her voice dropping to a hushed, controlled tone now laced with a foreign feeling—compelling authority.

Almost robotically, Colin replied, "It's in my room, under the bed." His eyes remained fixed on her face.

Abby's heart pounded unevenly. What had just happened? She let go of him, and he blinked a few times as the strange, vacant look in his eyes faded.

"Don't... Don't touch me!" Colin screeched, his voice tinged with fear.

But the power had felt nice, and Colin actually listening to her for once felt even better. Before she could think twice, her hand shot out again to grab his arm. She tried to replicate the bit of magic she'd just unleashed.

Quoting a half-remembered line from a movie as the power flowed from her, she commanded, "Drop and give me twenty, weasel."

Colin's ungainly pre-teen body dropped to the floor and began doing pushups. Abby felt triumphant until the moment her mother burst into the room, her eyes darting between them.

"What's going on?" she demanded. "Colin, get up now!"

Colin kept doing pushups, counting each one aloud. Only when he hit twenty did he stop and finally acknowledge their mother's presence.

"Mom—" Abby started, but her mother cut her off. Her expression changed to one of horror as she saw the lingering effects of Abby's magic on Colin. His eyes were still glazed over. Unlike the previous incident, her magic didn't fade away immediately. It held him in its grip even after the command was fulfilled.

"Abby, pull it back right now. If you can't do it, I'll force it, and that won't feel nice for any of us, " her mother ordered, sharp and urgent.

No longer triumphant, Abby tried to tug backward on the feeling she'd let loose on her brother, but it felt like she was pulling on a rope that had no end. "I can't, Mom. Help!"

Now she was afraid. Fearful tears streamed down Abby's face. At first, Christi embraced her daughter in a tender hug. It was a hug filled with understanding and a mother's compassion.

But two heartbeats later, that same mother used the equivalent of a magical cleaver to brutally sever the connection Abby had with Colin. Both kids stumbled backward, tripping over scattered clothes and stuffed animals Abby had kept as mementos.

Abby's head was pounding and Colin looked worse. When they managed to stand again, their mother's face wore a terrifying expression.

Christi warned Colin, "Remember, when your magic comes in, you'll likely do something similar to your sister accidentally, so forgive her now and move on. As punishment, she'll be cleaning your room for the next week. Go back to your room and return her mp3 player after we're done talking."

Colin looked a bit too smug as he left the room, but Abby felt too guilty to be mad about it.

Their mother closed the door behind him with a flick of magic, hammering home the seriousness of the situation. "I was afraid this might happen. You knew you had a good chance of being an enchanter like me, right?" she asked quietly.

Abby nodded mutely, still wiping at her face.

"Abigail... you can't use this other power openly, or even really tell anyone about it."

It was strange for Abby to have her mother seem at a loss for words. She normally knew just what to say and when to say it.

Eventually, Christi said, "What just happened with your brother means that you have the power to control minds. Some call it charming, domination, or even neuromancy."

The air in Abby's room suddenly felt too thin. She was struggling to breathe. A chill swept over her skin, the small hairs on her arms standing on end, and her stomach churned like she'd eaten something rotten. Abby was panicking. "But... but I didn't mean to. I didn't know."

Her mother's expression softened, though her voice retained a hard edge. "I know you didn't, sweetheart. But you need to understand that this power is dangerous. I'll teach you to control it, but you have to listen closely to what I'm about to say, and never forget it."

Abby shook her head rapidly, wanting to hear the words so they could dam the deluge of emotions welling up within her.

Christi sighed and sat down heavily on the edge of her bed. "Mind control is illegal, just like murder, because of the damage it can do. Think about it like this. If a person doesn't have control of their mind or body, how much better than dead are they?"

Murder? Abby's power was that bad?

"You must never tell anyone you can do this. Not a single word, Abigail. I'll help you learn control, but I need your promise that you'll keep this as secret as you keep magic itself from the mundanes."

Her mother added, "Don't worry, I'll make Colin and your father understand everything."

Did her mother mean that she'd help them understand or *make* them understand? Abby's mind swirled again, this time with fear and confusion. "But... you're just like me, aren't you, Mom?"

Her mother gave her a flat look, one Abby had only ever seen adults exchange. It asked a question she translated as, "How did you know?"

"I think our powers may be similar, but only time will tell if they're exactly the same. I have a feeling that we're different, though. It's a lot to keep closed up, baby girl. I've kept it a secret my whole life. Promise me you'll be careful. If you need to talk about it, I'm always here."

"I promise," Abby whispered, more out of fear than of understanding the heavy burden she'd inherited from her mother.

Esme

Present Day

"And that," Abby said, with a grin that didn't quite reach her eyes, "Was how I accidentally hijacked Colin's brain and made him permanently afraid of me. Not that he isn't still a pain in my side most of the time."

"So, what...? Christi taught you to control it in secret for years? Or did you learn that at your fancy private high school?" Esme asked.

"No, she was just being considered for a seated position back then, so it came out to all the top dogs. Jacob, Josiah, and a few others actually helped train me, too."

Esme braced herself before asking her next question. "Sylas?"

"Yep... he was my primary teacher," Abby muttered, a nervous tremor in her voice, clearly wanting to avoid the painful topic of Sylas, and Esme understood perfectly. "Anyway, once I started working as a nurse full time, all bets were off. I got tired of patients getting violent with me, so I started using small bursts of power to calm them. But only when I knew I wouldn't get caught."

Abby proudly proclaimed, "And that's how I became known as the 'Crazy Whisperer' at work."

"I've gotta know who is stronger, you or Christi?"

Abby paused, seeming to weigh how to answer. She settled on a single word. "Me."

That meant Abby was guaranteed a seat in the Assembly the second she wanted it. Esme wanted the specifics on their power difference, but Abby seemed uncomfortable, so Esme tabled that question for later.

"So, will you do it, Crazy Whisperer?" Esme asked instead, bobbing slightly up and down in her seat, hoping for a yes. "*Come on*, I want to know what it feels like. Make me do something ridiculous, something silly I would *never* do otherwise."

"Something ridiculous you would never do?" Abby made a sour face. "That's going to be impossible to come up with."

Esme took another sip of her sparkling wine and made a raspberry sound with her lips in Abby's direction. Abruptly, she grew serious. Tracing patterns in the condensation on her glass, Esme suggested, "Then make me forget something. I can think of a few things I'd rather forget forever."

"Esme..." Abby said cautiously. "I'm telling you 'no' on that before it gets stuck in your mind as a real option. If you actually see a mage psychologist and they approve, I'd do it. Otherwise, no."

Esme sounded sulky. "I guess I shouldn't have expected otherwise from my little rule follower."

Abby stood up and declared, "Woe-is-me doesn't quite fit a demon-blooded badass." She lightly touched Esme's shoulder.

Two minutes later, Esme snapped back to consciousness, finding herself in the middle of her living room in a ridiculous, contorted pose. Short and stout, she stood frozen like a statue mid-pour, mimicking the shape of a teapot. She hadn't even realized what she was doing while under Abby's control.

She had asked Abby to use magic on her, and she should have expected the feeling, but the reality of it was far more unsettling than she had imagined. And she thought her ability to touch the infernal power was terrifying... Esme felt a tremor roll down her spine.

Somehow, Esme had sensed the unlocked front door while she performed her little teapot show, but the knowledge didn't register into her consciousness until Abby's magic faded. As the door creaked open further, there stood Gwyn, his expression a mix of confusion and alarm. The realization that he had witnessed the whole thing nearly brought her to her knees, laughing. She could already imagine his horrified retelling of the ridiculous performance.

But that wasn't what froze her there, staring. It was what Gwyn was holding. Abby's sharp intake of breath meant she had noticed it, too.

Gwyn was carrying the freshly skinned pelt and blooded carcass of what looked to be a magnificent fox in one hand and a gigantic crossbow in the other as he stood on her front porch. In the middle of Seattle. During daylight.

Esme felt like she and Gwyn were probably even in the embarrassment department. He just didn't know it yet.

Esme was counting down the moments until Abby started howling at him for apparently hunting, skinning, and then bringing home the carcass of an endangered species.

Three... two... one...

Chapter Twenty-Seven

Dispense with the Pleasantries

Abby

When Abby felt the overwhelming urge to toss her most valuable possession out the window, she knew it was time to act. The champagne-pink dress, dripping with priceless metal and gems, had taunted her from the closet for long enough. She couldn't handle the constant anxiety of that "promised attire" comment without doing something about it.

She thought through her options. She couldn't do it in the bar. Her use of magic would not go unnoticed there, and the consequences would be severe. To magically interrogate a leprechaun, she needed complete privacy. But then she remembered that age-old saying: Keep it simple, stupid.

She'd bend the truth as far as she could.

Opening the door of her apartment, she braced herself. Esme was convinced that Finn was hundreds of years old and she'd seen evidence of his mist walking and firepower herself. Even if he could resist Abby's magic, she hoped he'd understand why she was doing it and forgive her later. Either she'd succeed, or she'd have an irate leprechaun on her hands.

"Hey, Finn! Thanks for coming on such short notice," she greeted him, her tone upbeat to try to mask her anxiety.

This time, unlike when Gwyn had visited before, she didn't have to clear piles of clothes out of the way to let him in. The extra duties with the Corded Brotherhood had finally pushed her to hire a weekly cleaner, and it had paid off.

"Aye, well, I was already headed to the bar and yer on the way. Happy to help."

"Come on in," she said, opening the door wider.

Dressed for a night out, he walked straight toward the dining table, nose leading the way.

She'd prepared everything while waiting for him to arrive. Two plates, two glasses of milk, and a pile of steaming crumpets awaited them. "I stopped by the crumpet shop earlier and brought a few home for us to snack on. I figured that some proper Irish butter might make the fact that they're English more palatable."

"Ah, it's grand, Abigail." He rubbed his hands together in delighted expectation. He really was a walking stomach.

Now came the test. She handed him a plate while subtly brushing his hand, allowing a tendril of her magic to flow into him through the contact.

"Finn," she said. He gazed at her with anticipation, his expression somewhat vacant. "Fold it up like a taco."

If he was resistant to her magic, she hoped he couldn't feel that she'd already tried something. Surely, he'd just think she was stark raving mad for making such a strange, albeit innocent, suggestion about the way to eat a piece of bread. But, if he followed her suggestion, it meant she had him.

Finn obediently folded the crumpet and took a bite. As he chewed, eyes empty, she moved her chair next to his and sat down. It was far more energy efficient to channel continuous small doses of magic into him by maintaining physical contact than it was to do it from a distance. Likewise, making someone talk, when all that was required was information, was far, far simpler than diving into their subconscious.

"Keep eating while we talk," she said softly.

He nodded, chewing slowly.

It was time to dispense with the pleasantries. His mind wasn't putting up much resistance, but that might not be the case for long, so she dove straight into her questions. "Did you have anything to do with the skogsrå?"

"Aye." As a bit of saliva dribbled down the side of his beard, she wiped it away with his napkin.

Gods, she'd expected a "no."

His answer forced her to frantically rethink her plan. This had been a stupid idea that only worked out well for her if he was innocent.

If he wasn't... Abby was in over her head. He could turn her into a pile of ashes in seconds if her control over him wasn't ironclad. She could turn him into a vegetable, but being judge, jury, and executioner didn't sit well with her either. She decided that, one way or another, he would walk out of her apartment with a few missing memories and she'd allow Jacob to take care of the rest.

"What dealings did you have with her?"

Finn's hands twitched, his fingers digging into his palms as if he was trying to keep something buried. His lips parted, but no words came out, just a shaky breath.

Abby's heart skipped a single beat, waiting for his answer. Reality was starting to crash down around her. She had made a mistake—a massive, possibly fatal mistake. But there was no going back now.

"I... I might've seen her." His brow furrowed, a look of confusion spreading across his face.

"Finn, focus. Did you or didn't you?"

"I saw 'er."

That wasn't a complete answer. Was this a sign he was resisting? Abby's patience was wearing thin, but the fear of what he might say still overrode her frustration.

"Why did you see her, Finn?" She leaned forward, her magic pulsing through her fingers, subtle but firm. She channeled a gentle stream of magic into him, careful not to overwhelm him.

"I wasn't seekin' her out." Finn's tone turned serious, his usual playfulness gone.

Abby leaned forward, her voice firmer. "Then why were you there?"

"I was followin' you lot."

Her heart raced. "Why?"

"For Jacob." His answer was like an open-palm slap to the face. She already hated herself for what she was doing to him, and his response just sealed the deal.

Finn's throat bobbed as he swallowed the last bite of his second crumpet. She already knew the truth. Jacob had sent him to spy on Gwyn and serve as backup if Gwyn tried something.

As she remained clutching onto his arm, her head drooped in despair, overwhelmed by a wave of terrible emotions. She felt like a monster. But she couldn't afford to let her emotions get the best of her right now. She had to wipe his memory of this conversation and rip a few beads off her dress so it looked like she'd invited him over for a quick repair and a snack.

She pumped a bit more magic into him and stood. "Let me go grab the dress."

"Abigail O'Malley," Finn announced, his voice pure and clear as she'd ever heard it.

Abby froze mid-step, her heart stopping. She turned to see Finn's eyes no longer vacant. He wasn't under her control. Anger was burning in his fully lucid, squinted eyes.

Gods below, she was done for.

"I know that dress made it to yer closet perfectly intact. I will take genuine offense if you purposely damage it ta further yer ruse!"

Abby grimaced, and she stumbled over her words as her mouth went dry. "Okay... I..."

An angry scowl twisted his face. Flames flickered in his raised hand, causing Abby to feel a true shiver of fear for the first time since they met.

She took a step back, instinctively retreating as a flop sweat broke out over her body.

Then, like a dam breaking under the pressure of a flood, he erupted into a boisterous laugh. The flames disappeared alongside the scowl. His laughter shook him, and he slapped the table, trying to bring himself under control. The plate holding the crumpets rattled and the butter dish nearly broke.

It took a long minute for her racing heart to allow her to speak.

"You were *acting*?" she asked, incredulous, understanding why Esme wanted to throttle him so frequently.

"Aye! Well, I'll admit ya had me at first. Kinda tingly." His whole body shuddered.

"Esme is right. You are a snake!"

With both hands over his heart, he theatrically declared, "But ya love me for it."

She exhaled forcefully to steady her nerves. "I'm sorry, Finn."

"I've already forgiven ya, *princess*. I sorta wanted to see if you'd have the jewels to do it. Glad ya did..." his voice trailed off like he considered adding more, but thought twice of it.

He seemed happy to chat, so she asked, "How did you shrug off my control without me knowing about it?"

"You're quite good! You've got a lot more magic in those fingers than ya think, don't ya?"

"What does that mean? I haven't forgotten that you didn't answer my question."

With a grin that stretched from ear to ear, Finn's eyes danced with amusement. "Just an observation. Ya come from strong roots... I'm a few too many things squashed together to not be slippery, lassie. I'm a leprechaun for one—we're naturally a bit more immune to mental enchantments. While I may look spry, I'm also no spring chicken. And I have that bit of ifrit in me. We should train ya up even more. We can make a party of it with Esme!"

Abby had acted like an ass, and he was happy for it? It was impossible for her to fathom the inner workings of his mind. He stuffed another butter-laden crumpet into his mouth.

"We don't deserve you," she said, forcing her tone to exhibit a playful lilt. "Seriously, Finn, how do you eat so much?"

He snorted. "That's for a different day of questioning. I've a bad feelin' we're gonna need your skills soon, dove. Lessons start now! Let's see if you can stop me from takin' another bite! No holdin' back."

Jacob

Seattle's concrete and asphalt soaked up and held onto the weak December sunlight, but it wasn't like that in the mountains. At these higher elevations, late autumn's cold resembled winter, with snow already blanketing the evergreens and starting to settle in the valleys. Jacob seldom left the city—his house, even—and he had forgotten how much colder it was away from the coast. He had only been there a few hours, but the chill had already settled deep into his bones, refusing to dissipate, even after two cups of coffee and an hour indoors.

Sylas sat across from him, cloaked in a blandly forgettable glamor. The magic used to reinforce it was unnecessarily excessive, which made Jacob wonder if Sylas was struggling to control his power due to grief over Juniper, or if the possibility Gwyn had mentioned might be true.

Inside the diner, they chose a table, as Sylas's true form was far too large for a booth. Standing almost seven feet tall, his gray skin and mossy hair made him practically invisible in the forest. Antlers like a stag's crowned his head, though his face, with its hazel eyes and laugh lines, was undeniably human. Jacob shifted uncomfortably, his back and legs throbbing in the stiff chair.

When the waitress brought the bill, Jacob immediately handed over his card. It was time to get to the heart of the conversation and then retreat to the ergonomic heated seats of his car. He had wanted to give his friend more time to mourn. It had been less than two months since Juniper's death. Yet he'd learned to place his trust in Esmeralda's instincts. If she was certain enough of her hunch to brand one of her oldest friends a villain, the weight of that accusation demanded he act accordingly.

"Right," Jacob said, reluctantly. He didn't want to have this conversation any more than he wanted to step back into the frigid air. Even so, duty called. He cast a ward of silence around them, then said in a neutral tone, "There have been two attacks on Assembly headquarters by malevolent creatures. And malevolents behaving oddly have been targeting mages in our community. There are those who think you might be involved."

A shadow passed over Sylas's face, but he kept his composure. "I'm mourning, Jacob. The only rage I have is for what I've lost."

Jacob nodded slowly, studying Sylas for a lie. "Grief has the power to make us consider things we wouldn't otherwise," he said, his voice softer. "I have a responsibility to confirm if you are responsible for these attacks, no matter how absurd that might seem."

He could feel Sylas's hands tense into fists under the table through the magic surrounding them. The leshy was either offended or guilty. Jacob's preference was the former.

"My aim has always been to protect our community," Sylas said, his voice tight. "I regret that my grief has isolated me. I do not seek vengeance on our community, Jacob. But the past... has a way of catching up with all of us."

Jacob sipped his coffee, his face neutral. The last statement felt like a warning.

"I understand. I hope you find the peace you seek, old friend. When you're ready to return, you know where to find me."

Sylas's smile was so small it could easily be mistaken for a mere twitch of his lips. "Thank you, Jacob. I hope the same for you."

Jacob wasn't one for strained pleasantries, so he quickly wrapped up their meeting. He left the diner, torn between wanting to clear his friend of suspicion and feeling like something was deeply off. Sylas's glamor was too strong, far too much magic poured into maintaining it. And then there was that parting comment about the past. It was a warning cloaked in familiarity, sharp enough to stick with Jacob as he walked away.

He barely made it a few steps into the parking lot before Sylas exited the building behind him. Instead of walking in the opposite direction, as Jacob had expected, the leshy, still in his glamor, approached and placed a gentle hand on Jacob's shoulder. "Sometimes the past doesn't just catch up—it walks right up and taps you on the shoulder to remind you of its power over your future."

Chapter Twenty-Eight

Q4 Meeting

Esme

Walking around armed was something Esme would have to get used to. She strapped her new dagger to her forearm under the navy blue blazer she'd chosen for the meeting. At some point, she'd have to give the weapon a name. The straps were mildly irritating, but the constant buzzing of the dagger's magic against her skin was worse, like tiny creatures with sharp, spiked feet were crawling up her arm.

She'd watched Miles arm himself that morning with two guns and at least four knives. It was almost amusing, comparing her first impression of him to what she knew now. Months ago, she'd thought he was just like any other mage—outrageously attractive to her, sure, but otherwise just a normal man. Now she knew about the scars covering his body, the enemies, both human and magical, that had put them there, and what made him the kind of man who kept running back into danger.

Despite the skogsrå's mention of "special attire," the quarterly meeting remained a gathering of mages, which people sort of dressed up for, making it a potential target for whoever was using the malevolents for their own ends. The only thing they knew for certain was that there would be another attack—the question of when weighed on everyone's mind.

The last open Assembly meeting of the year felt festive, with Solstice Gala buzz and families in tow. To improve attendance, the meeting was shortened and children's activities were provided in another room. The most anticipated party of the year was only two days away.

As always, the meeting was held in a mundane hotel conference room. Wards kept mundane eyes and ears out, often by convincing intruders they'd forgotten something or, in a more amusing twist, make them urgently need to use the restroom.

For this meeting, the room was set banquet-style with round tables instead of the usual rows of chairs. Esme and Miles had happily skipped the autumn and summer meetings, but things were far from normal now. When they arrived, they spotted Abby and Gwyn seated at a table near the front. Wanting to spread out, they chose a table on the opposite side of the room, also near the front.

The problem lingering in the back of everyone's mind was Jacob. He hadn't reported back to Miles, Colin, or Esme about his promised reconnaissance work in approaching Sylas. In fact, he hadn't spoken to any of them in the past day and a half. Though Miles hid it well, Esme sensed his worry. A tangible tension emanated from him, causing her anxieties to spiral.

As soon as she laid eyes on Jacob, Esme knew all her worries would fade away. He was, after all, a formidable mage and the Bastion of the Corded Brotherhood. Everything would be fine...

A few minutes after they settled in, Colin and Will walked in together, pretending to search for a place to sit. Esme was completely shocked. Will never came to Assembly meetings. Had Colin convinced him to come as backup? But when she saw Colin almost dragging Will to a table near the back, she reconsidered. Had Will and Colin become fast friends, or something more?

Finn was lurking somewhere nearby, and Esme felt on edge about that too. Last time he'd skulked around, he'd heard about Abby and Gwyn's budding relationship before they were ready to talk about publicly. What could he be up to? Even if it was an official skulking assignment, she didn't like the list of things that might go wrong. He was supposed to be watching for anything suspicious, but she had a feeling she was due for one of his pranks, so she watched her back. Esme wasn't sure if the seriousness of the situation would be enough to forestall his trickster behavior for the entire day.

Gradually, the room filled up, and more people joined their table. Miles was unusually taciturn, his silence a result of scanning the room obsessively, leaving Esme to handle most of the small talk on her own.

Just when she thought everyone had arrived, a completely unexpected figure stood before her—a towering, seven-foot-tall, hairy sasquatch.

"Sitkum! What...? Why...?" She was at a loss for words. Never in her life had she seen a sasquatch at an Assembly meeting. They were a rare exception to the rules: they weren't required to announce themselves or interact with the magical community, as long as they stayed within the US and Canada. Their pacifism and preference for isolation were the main reasons. The secondary, and far less talked about, reason was that the gesture was a bit of reparation owed for their slaughter when European colonists began settling the continent.

Sitkum pulled out the chair next to hers and sat down. "Esmeralda, it's good to see you."

"You too! Surprising, but good. What brings you to the quarterly meeting?" Esme remembered her manners and added, "Sitkum, this is Miles, my... uh, boyfriend."

Miles raised an eyebrow at her hesitation, but said nothing. His attention was still divided, focused on the activity in the room. The two exchanged pleasantries until the seated members of the Assembly filed into the room.

At their head was Jacob. Esme felt like cheering in relief. As Jacob took his place at the podium, Sitkum leaned in, cheerful. "I'm here to meet the woman my mother chose for my arranged marriage."

Esme felt elated. Overwhelmed by relief at seeing Jacob safe and excited for Sitkum finally having a chance at what he'd always wanted, she whispered back, "Tell me everything!"

Laughter colored his voice as he responded. "She's short, too! It's perfect. We'll meet for the first time at the Gala to see if we'll suit. I'm hopeful."

Finally, Jacob spoke, and the room gradually fell silent as the mages turned their attention to him. He smiled warmly, and the last scrap of Esme's anxiety vanished.

"Welcome, everyone," Jacob began, his voice steady and reassuring. "It's always wonderful to see so many familiar faces here at our last meeting of the year. Your dedication to our community is truly heartwarming. I want to commend each and every one of you for your contributions."

There was a round of polite applause, and Jacob continued. "As we look forward to the Solstice Gala, I—" He paused, a slight frown crossing his features. "I believe it's important to remember that the..."

An undeniable unease spread throughout the room as Jacob's pause lingered longer than expected. To the audience, this probably seemed like a social gaffe. Jacob was unfailingly poised. To Esme and Miles, it signaled trouble. He squeezed her hand and surreptitiously scanned the room for any clue as to what might have caused this strange reaction.

When Jacob spoke again, the whole room flinched in surprise. "As we gather to celebrate, we must also be vigilant about the... the caterpillar's cocoon is a symbol of our progress."

A ripple of confusion passed through the crowd. From across the room, Esme saw Abby exchange a baffled look with Gwyn.

"...It's crucial to the safety of our entire Assembly."

The murmurs grew louder, and some of the mages began whispering to each other. Sitkum leaned over to Esme, his heavy brow furrowed. "What is he talking about?"

Esme shook her head, just as baffled. "I have no idea."

Jacob appeared to struggle, his gaze distant and unfocused. "We must not forget the importance of the... tides."

Miles watched him with increasing concern. Esme asked quietly, "Is he okay? This isn't making any sense."

He nodded, his expression tense. "Something's wrong."

Jacob's next words were unintelligible. Something had to be done, fast.

Just as Esme was about to nudge Miles to ask what they should do, he rose and started walking to the stage.

Miles

Miles moved swiftly toward the stage, the medical side of his mind taking over. Jacob's symptoms, garbled speech and confusion, immediately raised red flags. A transient ischemic attack or stroke was at the top of his hasty differential diagnosis. Miles quickly assessed as he neared: Jacob's face showed no obvious drooping, and his arm movements seemed coordinated, but the speech issue was undeniable.

Still, he considered other possibilities. A seizure? Less likely given Jacob's presentation, but not out of the question. A tumor causing increased intracranial pressure? An infection like meningitis or encephalitis? Could it be metabolic—hypoglycemia or an electrolyte imbalance? He cursed the lack of immediate tools to rule anything out.

Reaching the podium, Miles said the magic word "Business" to the Bastion, using it as a diversionary tactic. For the Brothers in Seattle, "business" when uttered without explanation or context, was code for "drop everything and come with me right now."

With a brief nod to Maureen on the stage nearby, he gently placed a hand on Jacob's shoulder. "Let's step aside," Miles said quietly, offering a steady presence. Jacob didn't resist—a small mercy. Confused patients often became combative, especially in high-stress environments.

As they walked, Miles noticed a tremor in Jacob's right hand. Miles' pulse quickened—not out of fear, but urgency. A tremor could be a sign of an ischemic event. He scanned Jacob's gait, noting it seemed steady, though his eyes were glassy and unfocused. He did not like where this evaluation was headed.

Miles' heart raced, faster than when he faced malevolent creatures. This situation was more personal than that. Unlike during a fight, this might be a battle he couldn't do anything about.

Once they were in a private room, Miles guided Jacob to a chair and kneeled to meet his gaze. "Jacob, follow my finger," he instructed, moving his index finger side to side. Jacob's eyes tracked the motion, albeit slowly, but without the nystagmus or jerky movements that might indicate other neurological issues.

"Good," Miles said, his tone calm. "Now, smile for me."

Jacob attempted a smile, but it was lopsided. Miles' stomach clenched. A stroke was becoming more likely.

"Lift both your arms for me," he said, his gaze fixed on Jacob's movements. Both arms rose evenly, though Jacob's right hand trembled faintly. Miles frowned. A mismatch of symptoms. Was it an atypical presentation? Something more insidious?

He quickly pressed on. "Jacob, can you tell me where you are?"

Jacob blinked slowly, his expression wavering between confusion and frustration. "The... meeting?" he managed, voice strained and uncertain.

That answer told Miles two things: Jacob wasn't completely aphasic, but his cognition was impaired.

Miles glanced at his watch, calculating the time. Every second counted. That's when Esme walked in, followed by Abby and Gwyn. Thankful for the backup, he let out a sigh of relief. A year ago, he would have been completely on his own in this. He jumped up to meet them before they got too close.

Speaking quietly so Jacob wouldn't hear, Miles said, "Abby, follow stroke protocols. Esme, tell him a story—something about me examining him for a possible magical attack. Keep him calm. Gwyn... stay out of the way."

Abby and Esme jumped into action. Miles stepped aside and made some urgent calls. "Hey, Dr. Shenoy, can I borrow the

MRI off the books for a special one-off? Let's call it a... calibration."

MRI secured, he returned to find Jacob looking even more dazed. The Bastion looked around blindly, clearly confused. Despite Esme's efforts to soothe him, Jacob's gaze eventually fixed on Gwyn, suspicion flashing across his face. The sudden shift in Jacob's demeanor triggered alarm bells in Miles' mind. Perhaps it was the oddly focused way Gwyn, a relative stranger, was studying him that set him off.

"Who are you?" Jacob demanded, his voice lowering in pitch. At this, even the room seemed to hold its breath. Before anyone could react, Jacob's hand flicked in a subtle but practiced motion, sending a focused gust of wind that knocked Gwyn back a step.

Gwyn stumbled, but remained on his feet. He didn't seem surprised by the unprovoked aggression, nor did he retaliate. Esme quickly stepped between them, her voice soothing as she tried to calm him. "Jacob, it's okay. Gwyn's a friend. He's here to help."

Esme turned to Abby, pulling her aside. "Abby, you need to calm him down—before he hurts someone."

Miles knew she was right, even if he didn't like it. Jacob needed to get to the hospital, and quickly, but they had to avoid any more outbursts. Before he could respond, Jacob muttered incoherently, his hands twitching as though preparing to cast more magic.

Abby hesitated, visibly conflicted.

There wasn't time for that. Miles snapped his voice out like a whip. "O'Malley, serve the Brotherhood!" He hated this particular necessity of leadership, especially when he respected the person he was snapping at.

It worked. She started forward, just in time for Jacob to send another gust of wind into the open air. Or so Miles thought at first. When he looked up, he saw that Gwyn had deflected the second spell Jacob had flung at him... somehow.

Miles crafted a magical aegis around Abby. She noticed, nodded, and visibly steeled herself.

Miles softened his tone. "Jacob, listen to my voice. Abby is working under my orders as a nurse. You're safe."

Each word was a lifeline, pulling Jacob back from the brink of snapping again. Slowly, Abby crouched down and grabbed Jacob's hands. She spoke conversationally, "Hey, Jacob, did I ever tell you about the time that Colin tripped over a dead raccoon?"

She was trying to distract him, and it was working because his facial expression changed from one of aggressive fear to one of amused disgust.

In a brief moment of clarity, Jacob said, "Please tell me he didn't squish the poor thing."

"Yep, guts all over his brand new jeans. Dad hosed him off in the yard!"

Abby's expression turned to one of deep concentration. Then Jacob was quiet and still.

Abby's demeanor changed in an instant. Her breath quickened and her words wavered slightly when she said, "Let's get him in the car now! This is unbelievably tough. I can try to put him to sleep or we can drug him, yes?"

"We can drop by my place on the way for a dose of sodium thiopenthal to keep him sedated. Will that help?"

Esme groaned, recalling when Miles had used the same pharmaceutical on Finn during an interrogation. Her dissatisfaction with his usage of the drug on the leprechaun was so strong that she came close to using one of her conjured trolls to break his ribs.

With that thought, Miles realized they hadn't seen Finn in a while.

Abby, noticing Esme's reaction, asked, "Yes?" with a hint of confusion.

Gwyn

While everyone else around him had time only for reactions, Gwyn had time to contemplate. The events of the past few days took on a different meaning as he saw them through the eyes of the man he used to be: a prince. To his mind, what he witnessed unfolding resulted from a highly skilled strategist lining up events for maximum damaging impact.

He'd heard the whispers while Jacob was on stage. Most credited his behavior to his advanced age, dismissing the lapse as a medical issue. But the true plot became clear when he heard a few individuals citing it as a justification to demand his resignation. Like predators at a banquet, the idea caught on quickly and others joined in to feast on the corpse of his power.

This wasn't an assassination attempt. No, this was a carefully orchestrated attempt to destroy Jacob's reputation. This was an attempt to dismantle everything Jacob had built.

But why? Gwyn wasn't qualified to answer that question. Neither was he sure who was behind it, but the plan was clear. He could tell that Abigail was struggling under the strain of maintaining her magic. Esme was reluctant to leave Jacob's side, but with a bit of coaxing, he was able to ask her, "What is an MRI?"

With great difficulty, she tore her gaze away from Jacob and responded, "It's a machine that takes pictures of the brain so doctors can find issues."

"Can this machine see magic?"

Her lips pulled in as if tasting something sour, then she said, "Uhh, no, it sees the density of tissues... I think."

He had no idea what that meant, but it didn't sound magical. "But this is magic. The Bastion isn't ill."

She argued, "But none of us sensed malevolent magic."

"That is because the magic is deep within him. The magic of his life, of his... soul must be blocking our ability to sense it. Especially because his own magic is so strong."

"So if I ran out there and grabbed Will you don't think he'd be able to see *anything*?" She looked around wildly as if Will might appear and save them all.

"He might... But Abigail needs help right now and having two people looking around inside might allow one of them to see the problem—like this MRI but for magic."

"Gods! You're making no sense." She was angry with him, probably thinking he was wasting her time.

Then it was as if a switch had been flipped, and her full attention was on him. The words she uttered felt like a knife at his throat. "Explain. Now."

Gwyn didn't know how to explain something he barely understood himself, but he just knew somehow. If he were a more temperamental man, he'd rage at the injustice of his stolen memory, thrust upon him by Nudd.

Yet if Miles was Nudd... surely this wouldn't be happening. The more he observed Miles, the harder it became for him to cling to the notion that Miles was Nudd in disguise.

"Esmeralda, I can't explain it, but I have a strong feeling that it must be magic. I am going to get Abigail's mother to help keep Jacob restrained."

Esme's response was sharp and immediate. "Then run!"

Chapter Twenty-Nine

AN EXPENSIVE FIX

Gwyn

He ran.

Gwyn resisted the urge to burst in and carry Christi off over his shoulder, opting instead for a calm entrance. In just a few strides, he reached Christi's side, ignoring the curious glances and hushed speculations.

He bent close to Christi, his voice low but insistent. "Abigail needs you," he whispered.

Abby's mother rose from her seat, her movements sharp as she signaled for the meeting to continue without her.

The mages at the high table exchanged glances, likely assuming it concerned Jacob. Once they were alone in the hallway, Christi turned to him, her voice tense, commanding with urgency. "What happened?"

Gwyn felt his jaw tighten. "Abigail is physically fine. But we need to hurry because she is all that is controlling Jacob right now."

The color drained from Christi's face, her composed exterior cracking as his words sank in. Though she tried to mask her fear, her trembling hands gave her away. "Gods a-fuckin'-bove."

That single phrase, paired with her tense expression, made it clear to Gwyn where Abigail had inherited her pugnacity.

They hadn't gone far down the hallway behind the large meeting room before the fine hairs on Gwyn's neck stood on end. Halting suddenly, he felt the magic before he heard the faint popping that announced a new arrival ahead of them. If this delay caused any harm to Abigail, he would have no hesitation in hacking the leprechaun's limbs off, one by one, with a smile on his face.

The man who appeared not ten feet in front of him was familiar and, in this moment of crisis, most unwelcome. Flames flickered around Gwyn's left hand as he reached into his jacket for his short sword. Christi stood alert, tense, looking ready for battle herself.

"Nice. You look good dressed up." The stranger's voice and face were the same as before, though Gwyn knew it was just another illusion. He had the same black hair and high cheekbones that supported thick-rimmed glasses. On this occasion, he was dressed as a hotel worker.

Gwyn's frustration grew as he realized he still couldn't sense any magic from the other man, except for the magic that filled the room from his mist walking. He had initially assumed it was Finn's magic and had dismissed it completely.

"Stand aside," Gwyn commanded.

The stranger raised both hands in a gesture of peace. "You missed our meeting," he said, then turned to Christi. "Hello. You should probably run to go help your daughter. Second door on the left. Gwyn and I need to have a quick chat."

Without a second glance back, Christi hurried away. Gwyn felt a brief pang of something unfamiliar—envy, perhaps—that she'd shown her daughter more love in that moment than his own mother had ever given him.

Gwyn switched to Brythonic, partially as a test and partially hoping that it would convey his meaning with more efficiency than English. "Stand aside or fight. I have more important matters to attend to than yourself."

The stranger answered smoothly in the same ancient tongue. "I think I can help with your current predicament. But first, tell me why you missed our meeting."

Remaining in his battle-ready stance, Gwyn allowed the pyromantic magic he'd been holding to go out. This mage was clearly powerful. Pushing a fight without provocation would get him nowhere and most likely prove foolish.

"Our mutual acquaintance was indisposed. She took precedence over meeting with a needlessly clandestine stranger. You're not helping by standing in my way. Be aidful or be done with this conversation."

The stranger shifted on his feet in a way that suggested fatigue from standing for long periods rather than nervousness, and said, "You can call me Leon."

Before Gwyn could respond, Esme stormed out of the door Christi had just disappeared through. She quickly took in the scene, her eyes narrowing as she sized up the newcomer. With Gwyn still holding his sword, and the stranger in sight, she was instantly on guard.

Conjuring her own weapon before "Leon" had a chance to turn around, she took in his measure. Sensing her behind him, he raised his hands again, his lips curling into a disarming example of one of his too frequent smiles.

"Hello, beautiful. I'm here to help," he said in English.

Esme took a step closer. "Bullshit. You show up right before several malevolent attacks, vanish, and then reappear only when one of our own is in trouble?"

Leon turned back to Gwyn, switching to Brythonic. "I'm here to help the elder, Fair Son of the Mist. Allow it."

Leon said the meaning of his name rather than the words of it. This was confirmation that he was not only fluent in the now dead language, but knew exactly who Gwyn was... or at least had been. Who was this man to wield his proper name so casually? What was this stranger really after?

Gwyn said, "Passing strangers do not give aid out of the kindness of their hearts." Then in English, "What do you want, Leon?"

Esme, growing more frustrated, barked, "Gwyn! What did he say?"

In an attempt to exclude Esme or in a gambit to establish trust with Gwyn, "Leon" spoke again in Brythonic. "What I want? I am eager to get a good glimpse of him and make a good impression while I'm at it."

He replied in the same language. "If you already know that malevolent magic afflicts the elder, why do you want to examine him more closely?"

Leon chuckled lightly. "Your father, not the elder."

"Gwyn! Fill me in!" Esme snarled

Leon turned to address Esme again in English. "Ah, lovely, I'm not trying to be rude. Let me make you a promise. On my magic, if you allow it, I vow to aid your leader without causing harm to anyone today."

Gwyn hesitated, his grip tightening on the hilt of his sword. Trusting a man he barely knew, especially one as slippery as this one, felt like inviting a viper into his home. Leon's easy demeanor, his casual use of Gwyn's ancient title, all reeked of manipulation. But Jacob couldn't be contained forever, and with every passing second, the chance to fix whatever was happening to him could be dwindling. If Leon had ulterior motives, allowing him inside could lead to disaster.

But what if turning him away cost Jacob's life?

"Fine," Gwyn said through gritted teeth, "but she has the final say."

Esme shot Gwyn a wary glance, still clutching her conjured sword that was a duplicate of his own.

"Not until I know what he wants," she said. "Gwyn, I want to trust you, but you're not telling me everything. You can't have such a long chat with our new friend and not be hiding something."

Gwyn understood the value of keeping secrets, especially when he didn't have all the information. Every opportunity was crucial to him, and this man had the potential to help him find some answers he sought. Perhaps he had made a mistake the day he believed he should cease searching for his lost power externally, especially when a fortuitous opportunity repeatedly presented itself to him.

The promises Leon had made were solid enough to get through this situation. Gwyn could tell that this Leon was playing a long game—what he wanted probably wasn't available to him quite yet.

"Leon wants a chance to examine Miles' halo," Gwyn said. It was close enough to the truth for her to believe him. Mentioning Leon's knowledge of Miles' connection to Nudd would be counterproductive. Such an association would undermine their confidence in him, implicitly connecting him to Leon, a connection he wished to avoid—even if it meant lying.

"Leon?" she asked, still suspicious.

Leon was unruffled. He stepped forward, a small smile playing on his lips as if the entire situation amused him. He gave a courtly bow before her. "I promised, didn't I? My word is my bond."

His words were smooth—too smooth. Gwyn didn't miss the way Leon's eyes lingered on Esme. Leon spoke directly to her, his voice conveying warmth and earnestness. "I get it. You have no reason to trust me. But I'm here to help. Jacob has been a friend to our kind for a long time. Let me do what I can for him."

From the last two sentences, Gwyn gathered that Leon had been studying them for long enough to know more than he let on. He knew Jacob's name and his history, that Esmeralda was begotten before she had used her infernal powers around him, and he knew of Gwyn's suspicions about Nudd. Whatever game this man was playing, he knew too much about them. It made Gwyn feel an ocean's distance removed from comfortable.

Esme's eyes met Gwyn's, silently asking, "Can we trust him?"

No, they couldn't. But for now, they'd use him. Gwyn wanted to demand answers, to make Leon explain himself, but time was running out for Jacob, and they couldn't afford to waste any more of it.

Esme

Once Esme understood Jacob's peril, her fear and vulnerability morphed into anger, her usual defense against uncertainty. This stranger, speaking a dead language and asking to examine Miles' halo in exchange for helping Jacob, was raising all kinds of red flags. Gwyn had deferred the final decision to her, but it wasn't her trading a glimpse of an aura for a favor. Esme would be lying if she said she didn't want to growl like a feral dog.

A gentle touch on her arm pulled her from her thoughts. A calm, familiar voice followed. "I'll ask him, dove. Gwyn's right, this is magic at work."

She hadn't heard or seen the leprechaun approach, suggesting he'd been employing his stealthy Fae abilities to eavesdrop. Still, his presence was most welcome.

Finn tugged her sleeve, signaling for her to bend down to hear what he had to say. She felt and heard the weak ward of silence blossom around their heads.

He whispered, "Dove, my Brythonic is admittedly horrible, but I heard him say 'your father' to Gwyn. I just don't want ya walkin' into this blind. I don't know if we have much of a choice though, bein' honest."

Gods below. Esme shelved the bombshell for later: Jacob needed help. Gwyn stood nearly motionless, while Leon shifted impatiently, waiting for her response.

"Screw it. Drop the ward, Finn." The sounds of the world returned to their ears.

"Let's just go in. If this nutjob is desperate enough for a look, he could just glamor himself and stand next to Miles in a coffee line without us knowing. A binding promise just makes it safer for everyone involved. Make this worth my time, Leon."

"Yes, ma'am," Leon replied.

They reached the door, and, for a moment, Esme's hand lingered on the handle. One wrong move, and this could all go to hell. She took a deep breath, steeling herself for whatever lay ahead. Finn gave a subtle nod, and she pushed the door open.

Blessedly, nothing much had changed since she'd left a few minutes before. Abby was still kneeling with Christi, each holding one of Jacob's hands and Miles was doing gods knew what on his phone.

"Rhun, we've brought help."

Miles' attention snapped up at the sound of his middle name, hope coming to life in his voice. "Another doctor?"

"No, he's a mage who promised to help Jacob."

Miles squinted at Leon, studying him. His hand moved instinctively toward his gun, though he didn't raise it just yet. The hope she'd seen there drained from his face.

"His magic isn't right." Miles' voice was deep, in low tones she'd not heard from him before.

He was as on edge as she'd ever seen him, his body tensing like a coiled spring. But not having his gun pulled was a reassuring sign that he hadn't completely lost it. This was undeniably out of character for him. Miles was the rock-steady one, not trigger-happy in the least.

Leon's hands shot back into the air.

"Miles," Esme began, her voice calm but pleading, "I get it. He's suspicious, but we have to do something now. He made a magically binding promise to help Jacob and do no harm. Gwyn says this is malevolent magic affecting Jacob, not a medical issue. Finn agrees."

Leon chimed in, his voice calm and oddly cheerful despite the circumstances. "I promise, I'm here to help. Jacob is a friend to our kind."

Miles pulled the gun from its holster but kept it low. His grip was so tight on it that his knuckles were white. "What kind?"

"Begotten," Leon answered simply, holding Miles' gaze.

"Fine. Then who the hell are you, and how are you going to help him?" Miles' bedside manner had grown wings and flown out the window. Either Jacob's vulnerability or something about Leon was triggering his behavior.

Leon sighed, eyes flicking to the floor before answering. "I'll... untie the knots of the malevolent magic inside him. It's complicated. I'm Leon."

Esme cut in, "Are you an enchanting specialist?"

"Not exactly. I do have to touch him to work the magic, though."

Miles, incredulous, asked, "Esme, you don't even know this guy?"

In front of her objectively impressive boyfriend, her ignorance was definitely not a good look. But he said he loved her. She could give him the truth. "No. He ran into Gwyn and me at the library and has apparently been stalking us since. I completely forgot about him with the whole Alp thing..."

She caught herself before she could continue rambling, aware that the clock was ticking. "He said he wanted to help me with my demon problems, and now he wants to help with Jacob."

Abby finally spoke after her long period of silence while she worked. "We have to do something soon. He's fighting us now. They're right, Miles. This is magic, not medical." Esme noticed Christi sweating, clearly straining to control Jacob's magic alone so that Abby could speak.

Gwyn, usually the second calmest in the room, surprised them all by saying, "Miles, I suggest you hold your weapon to the back of his head during his examination. I don't trust him either."

Bloodthirsty, Gwynnyboy, damn, Esme thought. But there was comfort in the fact that his suggestion implied no collusion between Leon and him.

With a conflicted expression, Miles' eyes darted between Esme, Leon, and Jacob. Esme took a step closer to him, her voice low and urgent. "Please, just let him try. We have the promise."

Miles' intake of breath showed his resistance, but he gave a slight nod. Still not lowering the gun, he reluctantly agreed.

With Abby and Christi working on Jacob in tandem, Jacob wasn't doing much more than sitting, staring blankly at the wall. Christi's sweating hadn't abated with Abby joining back in the fight. Abby's fatigue was evident as she hunched slightly, a sign of her exhaustion.

Leon kept his hands in the air as he moved toward Jacob, his face with a more serious expression than they'd seen from him yet. Miles followed, the barrel of his gun aimed inches from the back of Leon's head.

Leon addressed the enchantresses, neck stiff. "I will touch him and count to three. On three, please release your control over him. I'm a bit nervous right now, so I'd appreciate verbal agreement from you both."

They gave their agreement. "One. Two." He hovered his hand just above Jacob's temple, hesitating for only a moment before making contact. "Three."

Both women sagged in relief as they released their hold on Jacob's mind. No one moved as the room fell into a tense silence. Leon's eyes were closed, and he didn't move a muscle. Time seemed to stretch as he stood over Jacob.

Eventually, Leon released his grip and rotated slowly, lifting his hands once again in submission as he faced the barrel of Miles' gun squarely. There was something unreadable in Leon's eyes, but the intensity in his expression matched Miles'.

Despite having a bullet mere inches from his brain, the cocky mage's face split into a confident grin. He said, "See you again soon," then disappeared before Miles' finger made its way to the trigger, mist walking to locations unknown.

Jacob's body slowly relaxed, almost as if he were coming out of a trance. His gaze moved around the room—first to Miles, still holding his gun only a few feet in front of him, then to Christi, Abby, and Gwyn. As Miles slowly lowered his gun, Gwyn ran to Abby's side.

Esme suspected Abby and Christi were close to experiencing magical burnout, as neither had found their feet yet. Finally, Jacob's eyes landed on Esme.

Jacob drew in a slow, deep breath, and released it while closing his eyes, looking for all the world as if he'd just suffered a broken heart. He opened his mouth. Closed it. Then hung his head.

Esme's heart shattered into a million tiny pieces as her mentor started weeping.

Miles

"Jacob?" Esme's voice was soft, almost childlike. She sounded so vulnerable, not like her normal, brash self. It made something twist uncomfortably in Miles' chest.

The Bastion rested his hands on his thighs. With his torso trembling with the weight of barely suppressed sobs, he whispered, "What have I done?"

Finn cleared his throat, clearly uncomfortable, and said, "I, uh, I'm going to grab yer boy for ya, Mrs. O'Malley. I'll just pop out then and... be right back."

With deliberate movements, Miles slid his gun back into its holster and then replied gruffly, "You did nothing wrong. This wasn't for you."

Miles didn't allow the wave of anger that rolled through him to show on his face. He had already acted more on emotion than wisdom. Leon's disappearance was likely his fault. Now they couldn't question him further about Jacob's condition or about how he'd cured it. Only time would tell what price they would pay for Miles' hotheadedness.

Every gut feeling told him that something was wrong with the other mage. He had stalked Esme, then showed up exactly when they needed someone with his abilities? The situation reeked of calculated interference. And yet... Jacob seemed to be cured. A cursory glance was enough to see that the focus had returned to his eyes.

The door creaked open again, Finn returning through it, leading Colin and Will. While Gwyn pulled Abby to her feet, Esme did the same for Christi.

Jacob sniffled and searched in the pockets of his robes for his handkerchief. Upon discovering it, he cleared his face, inhaled deeply, and visibly forced himself to composure. "I'm... I'm quite alright now, Esmeralda," he said, his voice steadier, though still tinged with lingering emotion.

Jacob met his eyes, and for a moment, Miles saw nothing but exhaustion and regret. There was something to unpack in that look. Jacob didn't need an audience for it.

"Everyone, out. I'm not asking," Miles ordered.

Esme crossed her arms and shot him the look that only spelled future trouble.

As feet started to move, Jacob spoke again. "Thank you, Christi. And thank you, Abigail. I appreciate what you did for me. I can imagine that it was a tough decision for you. You did the right thing. But Esmeralda should stay. She needs to hear what I have to say."

Miles wanted to stay, to support her and Jacob as the doctor and friend, but he also wanted to follow the departing crowd. He wanted to back Gwyn into an unoccupied room and start asking pointed questions with ample violence. He clung to Esme to stop himself; only the three of them remained.

CHAPTER THIRTY

WHY DOES THE TRUTH HAVE TO HURT?

Esme

Esme had never seen Miles lose composure like that. Abby had described his fury with the Alp, but witnessing it firsthand was entirely different. Normally, he was so logical and precise. But he'd stood there, ready to take a human life, in full view of everyone.

Seeing him lose control was a harsh reminder of how she must look to others when she let her own inner demon loose. Uncomfortable as it made her, Esme couldn't blame him.

Miles set out chairs and checked Jacob's vitals as they talked.

"I feel like myself again," Jacob said, though his tone was tentative. "But my memory of the last few days is patchy. My first concern is who that young man was. I caught a glimpse of him briefly as I came to myself."

Miles grunted, showing admirable self-restraint when agitated.

"His name is Leon," Esme answered. "And yeah, he's suspicious as hell."

She recounted how she and Gwyn had met Leon at the library. "He knew I was a cambion because he is as well. And, look… I think you both know that I've been team pro-Gwyn. But both times we've run into Leon, he and Gwyn spoke in some language I didn't recognize. They both said far too many words for Gwyn to have translated everything for me."

"Latin? Welsh?" Jacob asked.

"Brythonic. Finn said it and I recognize the name from my reading. I know you're both skeptical, but what if Leon is like Gwyn?"

Miles raised an eyebrow. "A lunatic?"

Esme's look made him raise his palms in the air and offer a quiet but, she noted, not shamefaced, "Sorry."

"I don't know if either of you got a good look at Leon, but that is nowhere near his real face. His glamor was impenetrable both times I saw him. Maybe he used one of those glamor potions you had me try once, Jacob."

"Perhaps," Jacob said, "but he could mist walk and remove malevolent magic from my mind. Those are not parlor tricks."

Miles gave a small nod of agreement, but he didn't look happy about it.

Esme felt the need to defend Gwyn. "I think we all have to agree that Gwyn is a magical badass. If this guy is like him, maybe he's even more experienced."

Anticipating her further arguments, Jacob asked, "I agree with you, Esmeralda. But do you know if Gwyn can mist walk? I'm just trying to gauge his skill level."

Esme hesitated. "I have no idea, but that's not the point I'm making." She was trying to piece together her thoughts, but it was difficult because of all the moving pieces. "What I don't get is, how could Leon speak Gwyn's gobbledygook language if he wasn't like him? If Gwyn is the Gwyn ap Nudd, reduced to humanity once again, his original language is lost to time. Yes, I've done my reading. Not even top linguistic experts know it."

Jacob turned contemplative. "Esmeralda, darling, are you saying you think Leon escaped from a malevolent prison like Gwyn claims to have?"

"Yes. But, if so, why doesn't he have an accent like Gwyn does? Why is he keeping tabs on us? And why did he go out of his way to help us?"

Miles finally broke his silence. "What did he say to you in the hallway?"

She recounted the brief conversation on her fingers. "He flirted with me again. I called him out on his creepiness. He and Gwyn talked unintelligibly for a bit. Then Leon made a binding promise to me to aid without harming anyone today."

Miles' expression darkened. She belatedly realized she hadn't brought up the flirting part before because it simply wasn't relevant... to her, at least.

"I know how you two feel about him, but Gwyn didn't trust Leon, either. He left the decision up to me about whether to let Leon help with Jacob at all," Esme told them.

"Did Leon want anything in exchange for helping me?" Jacob asked.

Esme glanced at Miles before admitting, "That's the only thing Gwyn translated this time. He said that Leon wanted to see Miles' halo up close."

Miles' eyes widened slightly, the only sign that he'd been affected by the revelation.

"We were desperate," Esme explained. "Leon could've inspected Miles anytime without us knowing. Plus, I had the promise of safety for everyone from him. I agreed to it because you were going to hurt someone, Jacob."

Jacob nodded without speaking, but Miles didn't look like he agreed. He was still uneasy about the entire affair.

Esme asked what was undoubtably burning in Miles' mind as well: "Jacob, did Leon do this to you?"

"No."

That was a relief, but she pressed on. "Then who did?"

Jacob paused, then said, "I need to tell you about your parents first."

Jacob

Thirteen Years Before

The cage rattled violently, the metal bars nearly bending under the creature's fury. Jacob had insisted that they use the Brotherhood's most remote warehouse. But even here, the nandibear felt too close for comfort. The cold, damp air seeping into the room carried a faint hint of mold and dust, adding to the unease that settled in Jacob's chest.

"Lauren, this is one of your riskier ideas. We should've started with something smaller, like the baby hydra."

Jacob had passed his ninetieth year of life. At this point, he knew that there was only so much you could do to hold back your top performers when they thought they should assume risk to reach a greater reward. As he stood face to face with the creature, he regretted not putting up more resistance to their idea.

With its strong, bear-like physique and the fur pattern and elevated front shoulders of a spotted hyena, the nandibear might appear to be a blend of the two powerful animals if one didn't know better. Its muzzle had the protruding fangs and lips of a baboon. Looking into its eyes, Jacob could discern a level of intelligence that rivaled that of a primate. The deadly combination of its strength and intelligence made it too dangerous for their use at this stage.

Lauren was facing the cage with her back turned to him and Robert. Behind her back, Robert made a silent gesture with his hands to Jacob that spoke volumes. It was clear from his expression that he had attempted to dissuade her, but both he and Jacob understood it was a futile effort. She was a quiet, reserved woman until she'd set her mind to something.

Lauren, unaware of their silent exchange, said, "It was what we could get. The cage is holding."

"Yes, but for how long?" He'd been too forceful with his tone, but fear had a way of making Jacob gruff and unpleasant.

Lauren's golden hair whipped to the side as she turned to face him. Her eyes, usually so calm, flashed with hurt and anger. She formed fists with her hands. He'd obviously struck a nerve. There was a breaking point that would unleash a side of her no one expected until they witnessed it firsthand.

"Sylas already gave us the third degree on it this morning. Do you know what he accused us of, Jacob?" Her volume was increasing with every word, her voice trembling with barely controlled emotion.

"According to him, we were negligent parents of Esme. He couldn't stop talking about our irresponsibility of potentially leaving her alone. He went on and on about the possible dangers she might face as one of the few demon-blooded in the region."

Lauren briefly shut her eyes, as if concealing a secret within them. When she opened them, the glimmer of sadness there threatened to overwhelm her resolve. "She's not a child anymore. He seems to forget how humans age. He seems to forget that we do all of this for her, for the kids."

"Honey," Robert said as he stepped to her side and wrapped his arm around her shoulders, pulling her into a side hug. His embrace seemed to ground her, the tension in her shoulders easing slightly. "How about we talk about the progress we've made so far instead of starting another argument? Jacob isn't telling us to stop our work. He's just being cautious."

Lauren sighed, leaning into her husband. Robert gave her a reassuring squeeze before releasing her and turning his attention back to Jacob. "I've been using illusions to help placate it, but that only lasts for a while and when it thinks we aren't here."

Lauren added, "During experimentation last night, we noticed it paused in a way that looked involuntary."

The creature was nocturnal, so the majority of their work took place in the late evenings. Intrigued by their first hint of progress, Jacob asked, "What method did you use?"

"We tried doing what Christi suggested the last time she dropped by. But neither of us has the right specialization for it to be that effective. She was able to establish a link with it. But she mentioned that its relatively low intelligence prevented her from sustaining the connection in a meaningful way. There has to be another solution."

Jacob's mind wandered to the fresh-faced college student whose conjuration magic might offer the right kind of connection to malevolents, but forced away the thought. He immediately chastised himself for even entertaining such an idea about someone so young. How could he, of all people, be so callous? But he knew the answer. He constantly found himself slipping in and out of a wartime mindset, a habit that had become ingrained after years of leading in different battles.

When he was Esmeralda's age, the Nazis were just beginning to rise in Europe. A few years later, he was walking on blood-slick battlefields, the screams of the dying echoing in his ears. Survival had meant hardening his heart, numbing himself to the surrounding horrors. Compassion had been a luxury he couldn't afford back then. Even now, it was sometimes difficult to find that part of himself again.

As the nandibear threw itself against the cage bars once again, a growl rumbling from its chest, Jacob felt like further caution was necessary. "I will be honest and say that I am concerned about your ability to contain this creature."

Calmly—too calmly—Lauren reassured him, "The cage will hold."

"Fine. If you insist on that, I will accept your expertise." A good leader shouldn't suppress their people when they'd earned the right to be confident.

The husband and wife standing in front of him held an entire silent conversation in a matter of moments, using only their eyes and one small nod.

Robert said, "Speaking of controlling this beast... and Esmeralda. We wanted to talk to you about what would happen with her if something did happen to us. Sylas is on board with our plan, and we were hoping to convince you too."

With a sinking feeling, Jacob bid them farewell. Walking away, he glanced back at the darkened warehouse. His fingers fumbled for the phone in his pocket, hovering over the idea of making a call, of issuing one last warning, but he stopped himself. Trusting them was the right thing to do—or so he told himself.

When he didn't receive a call updating him on any progress made overnight, he sent Maureen out to the warehouse. It was only a few hours later when she returned, pale and shaken. Her voice trembled as she relayed the grim news: Robert and Lauren were dead. The scene she described was one of devastation—a shattered cage, deep claw marks gouged into the floor and walls, and the lifeless bodies of two mages in his charge lying amid the wreckage.

Jacob's breath caught in his throat as the weight of the loss hit him. His chest tightened, the pain of grief stabbing at his heart. Robert and Lauren had been more than just colleagues; they'd been friends. Now they were gone, and all he could think about was the conversation they'd had only hours before their deaths. The thought of Esmeralda coming of age without her parents, of her learning the truth about their deaths, made everything worse.

There was no time to mourn; not properly. They would have to cover it up. The story would be tragic: a freak accident on a remote road; the kind of thing that happens every day but leaves behind so much sorrow. It was the only way to keep the secret of their work safe. It was the only way to protect the living from even more danger.

It was a lie, but a necessary one he could live with. If his friendship with Robert and Lauren had taught Jacob anything, it was that some truths were too dangerous to reveal at the wrong time.

Esme

Maureen's brash delivery of the truth weeks before had rendered at least one benefit: Esme managed to keep her composure through Jacob's recounting of events.

"Darling," he began, "I urged restraint, but your mother was adamant that they could work the magic together. And... there's more to consider about the situation that could have implications for our current predicament."

Esme accepted that there was likely a good amount of truth to what Jacob was saying about their bullheadedness. She had made a conscious effort to be less stubborn than her mother and not as biddable and easily swayed as her father could be, especially when it came to his wife. Exhausted, she said, "Thank you for telling me about my parents. Were they Corded Brothers?"

"No, but they volunteered to help—much like you. You deserved to hear the truth from me," Jacob replied, "not just Maureen, who only saw the aftermath of it all."

Trauma had a funny way of changing people; Esme knew that all too well. Now that she knew the truth, she couldn't help but wonder if the horrifying experience of finding her parents after the attack had somehow shaped Maureen's animosity toward Esme. Even if Maureen often projected the image of a self-assured soldier, her chosen career was essentially that of a desk jockey. That spoke volumes about her natural inclinations and finding something like that was bound to affect her psyche.

How entangled Maureen seemed to be with Assembly and Corded Brotherhood activities begged the question that Esme couldn't believe she was so late in asking. "Was Maureen Seattle's Corded Brotherhood field agent before Miles arrived?"

Jacob seemed to hesitate, considering how or even whether to answer. Quickly making up his mind, he said, "Yes. She's 'retired' from active field work now. Age comes for us all."

The major blow of learning that she'd been lied to by and about her parents had already healed. In the grand scheme of things, this was a minor revelation compared to everything else she'd been privy to over the past year. She was ready to move past it for now. Jacob's earlier concerns that she'd run headlong into unpracticed magic were still fresh in her mind but she couldn't deny the allure of exploring the type of magic they'd been researching.

"Alright, Jacob," Esme sighed. "This has been a long and winding journey to get to the point of who did this to you."

"I want to reassure you of one thing first, Esmeralda." He reached for her hands and she gave them happily. "I hunted the beast down myself the same day."

Nope, she wasn't going to cry about that... Grief choked her throat as she watched Jacob's fists clench, the white knuckles a testament to the furious rage still simmering after all these years. She returned her hands to her lap and waited.

"As I said, the background story is relevant. Many disapproved of your parents' actions, but it wasn't Maureen who voiced the strongest opposition. She was younger, less powerful, and less confident back then. It was Sylas who caused the most noise."

"Sylas?" Esme echoed.

"Yes. Sylas is a guardian by nature. He's fiercely protective of everything he considers his own. He couldn't stand the thought of you or any other mages being in danger, even if it meant going against his friends. I also wonder if his knowledge of your parents' aims could be how he is controlling the malevolents."

Jacob paused, then added, "Understanding the relationships of non-humans can be challenging for us. I think he felt more deeply for Juniper than any of us realized. I think Gwyn was right—her death broke him."

"Are you confirming that Sylas did this to you?" Before Jacob had a chance to answer, Esme fell into her usual pattern of pacing.

"Yes."

Luckily, she had already considered this a possibility, so the news didn't completely incapacitate her. She'd already spent days being sad about the possibility. Now, with confirmation of her fears, it made her furious. "I want to throw that chair into the wall," she muttered.

Jacob smiled, the first she'd seen in days. "Go ahead. I'll put it back together, darling."

The reminder of how she'd broken his chair after finding out that she was demon-blooded slammed through the dam that was holding back her emotions like a wrecking ball. The tears came rushing out and so did overdue words. "I've spent so much time being angry with you, and every time you forgive me. I'm sorry, Jacob."

He met her gaze. "You've forgiven me every time I've hidden something from you. We forgive each other. That's what family does. I'm sorry for my part in all this, Esmeralda."

Family. What she thought she had with Sylas. What a cruel lie it had been. *We forgive each other*. A near-hysterical laugh bubbled up at the cruel irony of it all. Now she wondered if Sylas had ever truly forgiven her or if he was simply waiting to strike.

Chapter Thirty-One

A Beginning

Gwyn

"Miles was a little rude at the end, don't you think?" Abby commented as Gwyn pulled into her apartment building's cramped garage. After nearly an hour of working magic on Jacob, she was almost drained. So Gwyn volunteered to drive her home while Cerys came along for the ride, reclining across the backseat. Abby playfully teased him about his improved driving. It being "less grandpa like" sounded like something he should interpret as praise.

Gwyn still couldn't understand why she and Esme expected him, a man from an era long before steel existed, to be good at driving. But, then again, maybe they still didn't believe that he was who he said he was.

"I think I understand his reasoning," Gwyn said, answering her thought about Miles' behavior.

Abby gasped, causing him to whip his head around to see what was wrong. She had her right hand clutched over her chest and her face showed an expression of such shock that he began to open the door to meet the threat.

"Did... did you just agree with Miles?" she teased, this time catching him off guard.

Her playful banter was going to cause his heart to give out one of these days.

"I think he wanted to protect Jacob's reputation, so he chose to examine his health in private."

"Oh, there's definitely some dirt there too, especially since Jacob wanted Esme to stay," Abby replied. "I'm not worried, though. Knowing her, she'll tell us soon enough."

If by dirt, Abigail meant that Jacob desired to confess his sins to Esme, Gwyn couldn't argue.

"Want to come in and watch the third movie? Or just hang out? It's still early," she asked.

What he thought was, "You are becoming the flame that brightens my darkness." But what he said was, "Okay."

He *was* becoming a romantic.

Less than two hours later, Abigail was already slumped over, once again falling asleep on his shoulder as they watched the movie. He did not begrudge her this. Single-handedly, she'd exerted control over an Archmage for an extended period. He regretted not acknowledging out loud just how remarkable that was. Cerys had also dozed off on the floor nearby.

On the screen, an epic battle between man and malevolent Fae raged. It featured an unconventional approach to cavalry warfare, but it provided an entertaining spectacle to witness. The clashing swords at the height of the battle must have awoken Abby because she sat up groggily, blinking at him.

"Gwyn, why don't you have like… pock marks all over your face, screwed-up teeth, and scars?"

He blinked slowly, confused. "What?"

She reached for the remote and paused the movie. She pressed, face completely serious, "Why aren't you ugly?"

He squinted at her, trying to make sense of the question. "Abigail… I… What?"

Her wide eyes and alert expression didn't match the bizarre words coming out of her mouth. It was as if she was caught between a dream and reality.

"If you're from the dark ages, you should have smallpox scars, crooked and missing teeth, and be a helluva lot shorter."

She leaned in, inspecting him closely. "Show me your teeth," she demanded.

So now he was a horse up for sale. With a sigh, he grinned widely.

"They're perfect, Gwyn. I had braces twice to get mine even half as good as yours, and they're still crooked."

"Abigail, please ask your question plainly." He couldn't blame her for being skeptical about his identity. It was an incredible tale.

"If you really are who you say you are, why do you look so… perfect?"

He considered her question, unsure of its deeper meaning, but tried to answer.

"My height has always been my own. Probably because I never experienced the hunger that sometimes afflicted the peasants. My hair, my skin, my eyes are all the same. I remember having more scars. I had one right here from an arrow's fletching." He drew a line on the side of his neck.

"My father saved all but one of my teeth. As for smallpox... I do not know what that is, but I have suffered skin defects."

Frustration at his hazy memories made him grip the couch cushions. "I am changed, Abigail. The only explanation I can offer is that my ascension cleared away life's imperfections. And for some reason, my downfall didn't undo those changes."

Abby gently took his wrist. "Downfall? Hey, it's okay. I think I was just dreaming, and then I started wondering why..."

Her words trailed off as his hand covered hers.

"I am not perfect," he said softly.

"You're really, really close, though."

He didn't want to release her hand, which she hadn't pulled away. "Half of my memories are gone, Abigail. I don't even remember how old I am. How old my body is."

"This," she squeezed his hand to convey her meaning. She'd noticed his grip on the cushions. "Was about something more than simply forgetting your age. Talk to me."

He'd allowed his weakness to show, and now she was asking him to drag her into his darkness.

Gwyn sighed. "Perfection is a myth. I'm not the being I once was, nor the man I remember. I'm something in between—something imperfect."

"There's more, isn't there?" Her earnest expression made him want to tell the whole truth, to stop the lies.

"I'm afraid, Abigail. Afraid of what I might remember, and afraid of what I won't. Afraid that I'll never be whole again. This... humanity... it's new and old to me at the same time. I am now a pauper and yet I still possess an arrogance that is fit only for a prince. I am woefully ignorant of the simplest things, but I possess a deeper understanding of certain subjects than even the most educated scholars of this day. I have no skills that would translate to respectable employment in this time. I am an 'unemployed loser,' as your brother put it, yet I was once educated to rule a kingdom."

His words poured out like a long-held breath. He hadn't been that honest with anyone since her... At some point during his verbal purge, he'd turned toward her on the couch. He couldn't stop himself from reaching out with his free hand and touching a curl that framed her face.

"I am... undefined. I'm not asking for pity, and I'm not asking for you to fix me. But I do need you to understand that I'm still figuring out what it means to be Gwyn without ap Nudd. I want you with me while I do it."

A warm light filled her eyes before she turned her head and, featherlight, kissed his hand. Barely above a murmur, she said, "I'm sorry for everything you've been through. I'm here, Gwyn."

The kiss was unexpected, but it was exactly what he needed at that moment.

Following an intense moment of eye contact, she was the one to break it first. Abby practically vaulted herself up from the couch, speaking rapidly. "I'm hungry. Do you want some popcorn? Or I could get a pizza or sushi delivered."

Perplexed by her sudden change in mood, Gwyn stood and followed her to the kitchen, watching as she busied herself rummaging through the fridge, asking if he wanted a drink or if he'd prefer eggs and pancakes for dinner. He let her expend her nervous energy before approaching slowly, as one might calm a skittish animal.

It wasn't until he was almost touching her that he finally spoke. "Abigail."

"Yep? So, what's the plan?" She continued her frantic searching.

He placed his hands gently on her shoulders. "Yes, we should eat, but first, I think we should talk about why you ran away from me just now. Did I do something to offend?"

Had he been too honest?

Her cheeks turned a rosy shade of pink. "No."

Her tone turned more convincing. "No. You did nothing to offend. I... I'm sorry if I was too forward."

She backed up until her hips hit the counter. Abigail thought she was too forward? His favorite memory of his new life was the time they'd spent kissing. If anything, she wasn't forward enough for his liking.

He inched closer to her as he spoke. "Esmeralda gave me the impression that women had more freedom than men to be forward with their desires in this society. Was I wrong? Was that 'pulling an Esme,' as you described? Am I mistaken in my understanding of how relationships progress in this time?"

Abby made a weighing motion with her head. "Eh, I think it's evenly split between the genders on who makes the first move."

"So what makes you think you've been too forward with a single kiss to my hand?"

"I..." she started, then stopped, her words hanging in the air.

"Please, Abigail."

"When we went on that date at Pike Place before I knew about your past, everything felt easy. But now I know that you're still finding your footing here. Sure, we made out the last time we watched a movie together. But now that I know more about you, I can't help but wonder if I'm pushing something you don't need right now. I never stopped to ask if what you really need is a friend."

Gwyn moved even closer until their breaths mingled. He needed to show her. "May I do something?"

"Uh, yeah, sure."

Abby

Strong hands trailed down her arms, lingering at her ribs. Before Abby could fully register it, she was sitting on the countertop, eye-level with Gwyn. Her breath quickened as his hands stayed on her sides, the warmth of his idling touch unmistakable.

"I need a friend," Gwyn murmured, his voice low. "But I'd be lying if I said I didn't want more with you. I've made my move. It's your turn to decide what happens next."

She felt the weight of his abdomen against her knees and instinctively parted them to welcome him closer. What did she want to do next? She wanted to jump on him like he was the tree and she was a monkey.

But instead, she grabbed the nape of his neck and pulled him in. Seeing his eyes half-closed in anticipation before she even kissed him was the confirmation she needed—this was exactly what he'd meant by next.

It felt like an eternity before he pulled her closer, her chest pressing against his. That was better. Somehow, he always smelled like leather, hay, and a bit like Cerys. They were wild smells that didn't match the poised man she'd come to know. She couldn't understand how his past still clung to his skin, especially since she knew he wasn't spending his free time riding in the countryside.

Her hand lingered at the back of his neck, not wanting to let go. The calluses on his hands snagged on the fabric of her dress shirt as he caressed her through it. Another problem she could solve. His hesitancy and cautiousness were so apparent that she felt compelled to guide him along. She said, "I love kissing you, but if you want to touch me, I'd really like that."

Guiding both of his hands from where they rested at her waist, she slid them behind her back to tuck his fingertips under the waistband of her pants.

The "Oh" that slipped out of his mouth was undeniably endearing. But he still didn't move a muscle. His hesitancy made her wonder if she needed to "pull an Esme" to help him understand how far she was willing to go. The delicious sensation of his rough hands on her skin was enough to make her decision for her.

So, she pulled an Abby, pushing ahead and bluntly stating what should have been said delicately.

"I want to make it clear where this could go if you want it to, Gwyn. I don't know what you expect, but I'm not a virgin. Your hands are now beneath the waistband of my pants. I'm inviting you to go further, if that's what you want."

His entire body stilled. That same "Oh" reached her ears for a second time. With his hands still on her hips, he ducked his head to the side and muttered something entirely unintelligible to her ears. It almost sounded like a curse and a prayer all wrapped up in one.

"What was that?" she asked.

When he spoke, his voice was rougher, his accent thicker. "I am not unfamiliar with pain, Abigail. But barely touching you since we sat down has felt like torture. Your words are a... release. There's nothing I wouldn't give you if you asked."

"So," she said, her voice teasing, "I'm either jumping off this counter, or you're carrying me to the bedroom."

It wasn't what she was expecting, but she couldn't claim that she didn't enjoy the ride. Her "monkey hanging from a tree" metaphor lasted about three seconds before he mist-walked them straight into her bedroom. The sudden shift left her disoriented, her breath catching. Once she felt like she could speak again, she said, "I didn't know you could do that."

Supporting her weight with his hands on her backside, he raised a brow. "Neither did I. I had incentive."

"Were you trying to impress me or just impatient? Yes to both is a-okay with me," she replied, with a grin in her voice.

"Yes," he replied, his tone light but filled with intent.

"Good," she said, kissing him again, her arms around his neck, legs wrapped around his waist. She held on, enjoying the full contact their bodies had as he held her aloft.

When he adjusted his grip, her body instinctively moved against him, seeking friction. His pained groan was followed by soft nibbles from her neck to her ear. She sneaked a peek at the state of her room and was mostly satisfied. But there were two books and the shirt she'd changed out of while getting dressed before the meeting that morning scattered across one side of her bed. Feeling impatient herself, she used a bit of telekinetic magic to flick them onto the floor.

Leaning close to his ear, she whispered a command, "Just tell me if you don't like something."

Releasing her grip from around his neck, she slowly slid down the length of his body until her knees silently hit the carpet. She immediately set to work at freeing him from the confines of his pants.

When that same incomprehensible blend of curse and prayer escaped his lips, she knew she'd made the right decision.

The next morning, she woke up to the scent of something burning. Worried that she had left the stovetop on the night before, she jumped out of bed. But the empty pit in her stomach reminded her she hadn't cooked anything.

The frigid air in her apartment made goosebumps break out across her skin. When she opened her bedroom door, she realized why—it was freezing because all the living room windows were open. Gwyn stood in the kitchen, wearing only his boxers, the vent hood on full blast as Cerys begged at his heels for scraps.

With a sheepish grin, he tried to hide his embarrassment. "Good morning."

"What happened?" Clearly, he'd been trying to cook something.

Turning around, he grabbed a plate off the counter and presented her with what appeared to be a passable, unburnt omelet.

"I burned the first one. On Esmeralda's stove, I could see the flame heating the pan, but yours is different. I must also apologize for damaging the fire alarm to avoid waking you."

She looked up and saw that there was the telltale streak of black coming from where the smoke detection chamber was on the device. He must have caused a pinpoint short circuit in the wiring, damaging nothing around it because the housing for the device and ceiling all looked intact.

"How?" she asked, barely able to believe it.

"Similar to a tiny spark of lightning."

The skill required for fulminomancy, especially work as precise as he'd displayed, surpassed the relative simplicity of summoning fire. Gods above, maybe Jacob was right. Gwyn hadn't yet shown them the true magnitude of his magical abilities. And from the way he said it, maybe he hadn't remembered he could do it either.

CHAPTER THIRTY-TWO

A VILLAIN'S PROMISE

Sylas

"My magic binds me to leave after your task's completion. So complete it."

The nameless mage stamped his foot with the impatience of a spoiled child, his theatrics belying the razor-sharp cunning behind the glamor. This mage was petty, yet he showed remarkable sophistication in his abuse of power. Each command was precisely planned to inflict further psychological pain on Sylas, making him doubt his actions and his very being.

Sylas' greatest regret was that his formidable casting skills were no match for the maniac's relentless, overwhelming strength. He doubted even Jacob, with all his knowledge and power, could stand against this lunatic alone.

Every choice Sylas had made had come at the cost of his body, his soul, and his heart. Twisted by malevolent magic, his bones ached, and the joyful part of his soul was gone. Though he carried the crushing weight of guilt for what he'd done, he clung fiercely to the belief that his actions weren't meaningless; that the suffering he endured served a greater purpose.

But belief wasn't enough to silence the young faces that haunted him. Images of their hopeful, bright eyes clashed with the terrifying possibilities of his failure. Those visions haunted his waking hours and dreams.

"You can forget about the succubus. I know it's not her," the mage added, his tone far too casual for the topic of murder. "If she's collateral damage, so be it. Remember what you're trading for. One, maybe two, for the many."

Sylas had repeated the words to himself nightly, yet hearing them from the mage left a bitter taste in his mouth. The mage's soft laugh was more frightening than what he said because it spoke of the madness lurking just beneath his glamor.

"Have you always found success in scorning those who undertake your work?" Sylas asked in a low, clipped tone, devoid of feeling. He regretted speaking as soon as the words left his lips, his many years of power having made him too bold. Years spent as a respected member of the Assembly, making decisions that shaped lives, had ill-prepared him for this forced submission. He couldn't afford to be angry, but the changes his body had undergone made his rage unbearably difficult to control at times.

Tilting his head, the mage pondered the question, as if he found it rather amusing. "Oh, I wouldn't call it scorn. It's *incentive*. Everyone is so soft these days. I don't understand it! Your hatred makes you want me gone. For that, you need to complete my task. It's simple. Use your hatred to increase your haste."

With a hard swallow, Sylas looked down at his slightly trembling hands. He wasn't sure if they trembled from the strain of suppressing his magic, or from the thought of what he was about to do. The image of Esme's face—the dichotomy, the girl he helped raise to womanhood, the woman who had stolen so much from him—flashed in his mind. She was the closest thing to family he had left, and he was repeatedly being asked to harm her.

He'd dried her tears after her parents' deaths, abandoned his forest to help her come back to life. And now he put even his own student, Abigail, in the path of his destructive power because she saw the right in standing against evil, in standing with her friend. Now Sylas might have to be the one to break both of them permanently.

For a time after Juniper's death, he might have called what he was being forced to do justice. But he understood now what it meant to be without choice. This unnamed mage's oppression that shackled him was informative in its cruelty. Esmeralda deserved forgiveness for killing Juniper. She had no choice, and Juniper was probably already gone at the end. The thought of using his magic against them felt like a second dagger of grief, after Juniper's death, twisting in his heart.

Now he wanted nothing more than to tell his Esmeralda exactly that. Yet such a move would undoubtedly provoke another violent, and likely deadly, reaction from the raging madman. For Sylas, the thought of indulging his emotions at the risk of another innocent was unthinkable. The cost had been too high—too many sacrifices, too many fallen—he couldn't let personal desires eclipse what was best for all. If protecting them meant becoming the monster in their eyes, he would bear that burden. His body was already following suit.

He took one last look at the mage, then squared his shoulders. This man had already proven how far he would go.

"It will be done," Sylas said, his voice steady now. "Then you can leave in a cloud of regret."

The mage chuckled softly, his smile as brilliant as the midday sun. "Regret? Not this time around."

Chapter Thirty-Three

SNEAKY, SNEAKY

Esme

Esme poured the bubbly into the orange juice, demanding an answer. "Stop being cagey and answer the question, pipsqueak."

"Here we go *again* with the feminine interrogation," Finn muttered so quietly she almost didn't hear him. Then louder, he said, "I'm rightly wounded, lassie."

The bar buzzed with lively chatter and the clink of silverware as patrons enjoyed their special Sunday brunch after yesterday's meeting. For Esme, there was no better time than the present to grill Finn about his frequent disappearing acts recently.

"Where were you during the meeting? No one could find you. Plus, you deliberately waited for Leon to arrive before revealing yourself, knowing full well that... our mutual friend was in the next room, barely hanging on by a thread!"

Finn hung his head in defeat.

With a toothy grin that made him look more like a predator than the vegetarian he was, Sitkum approached the bar saying,

"She sounds angry with you, leprechaun." Then, with a smirk, Sitkum asked, "Want me to sit on him, Esme?"

While Sitkum had better hearing than a human, Esme hadn't done the best job of keeping her voice low. She looked at the sasquatch and said, "You know what? Yes. Sit on him."

Sitkum was ready to plant himself on Finn's chair when the telltale sound of mist walking filled the air. Finn appeared, cross-legged and smug, in the open seat next to his original one.

"Nice trick," Sitkum said approvingly.

Finn gave his own, less menacing-looking smirk and answered, "To answer your question, lassie, during the Assembly meeting... I was, well, distracted by somethin' I walked in on. The exact nature of which isn't suitable for chaste ears." He pointed at Sitkum.

The sasquatch didn't look the least bit offended. Instead, he surprised Esme and Finn once again with another unexpected modernism. "Different strokes for different folks," he said, and shrugged.

Finn burst out laughing. "*Strokin'* is right for you, my boy!"

She tried. Oh, she tried so hard, but she wasn't capable of holding back her own laugh. Thankfully, she'd already sat down the bottle of bubbly, preventing it from spewing everywhere during her convulsions.

Sitkum's laughter was a different thing altogether, however. The sasquatch laughed with his whole body and for a considerable duration. Every time he snorted, his knees banged into the bar, causing everything to rattle. The brownie sitting nearby grew increasingly irritated, squirming in his booster seat as he struggled to finish his waffles.

"Okay, okay," Esme gasped, trying to regain her composure. "Finn, that was good. Stefan," she said, turning to the brownie, "how about a mimosa on the house for putting up with us?"

This brownie didn't care about grand gestures or pretty words. Stefan's love language was all about saving money, finding the best deals, and getting the most out of a transaction. The thrill of outsmarting a seller was the only thing that truly made him happy.

"Just look at my plate! Food's practically ruined. Syrup everywhere," he whined.

More like he'd eaten half the plate already and there was a single drop spilled. But she knew where this was going. Making him feel like he'd negotiated a better deal would brighten his day considerably. Busy as she was, the payoff of seeing the pure joy on his face would be worth every second of work.

"Oh," Esme said, her voice heavy with regret. "You're right, Stefan. I can see that now. Really, really sorry about that. You deserve more than a mimosa. May I make you a cranberry spritz as a small apology?"

He readily accepted the human-sized glass she handed over and went back to polishing off his plate without another complaint. The food disappeared into the creature's stomach with surprising speed, leaving Esme dumbfounded at how such a small body could accommodate so much. Esme smiled at seeing how happy he was. Even as one of her longest relationships crumbled, she still had this.

Cleaning while she talked, she pressed Finn, "At least give us a hint about who you stumbled in on."

With a mischievous glint, Finn grinned. "Tattoos."

Esme immediately knew he meant Will. Of all the mages Finn regularly saw, he had the most tattoos. Inside, she squealed with delight. There was only one person he could have been with—Colin. Colin's steadfast nature was the perfect balance to Will's excitable energy.

Esme wasn't certain that Sitkum actually heard any of this because it took him a while to stop laughing. When his laughter finally subsided, Esme turned to him and asked playfully, "Will you save a dance at the Gala for your hairless friend?"

"Of course!" Sitkum beamed.

"Alright, I've got to get back to work. Finn, we need to talk later about our outfit coordination for the Gala, so come to my place in a few hours."

It was a bald-faced lie, but it was one of the three things guaranteed to get him to show up to her caper planning session other than food and drink.

Later that afternoon

"Give me the details!" Esme quickly realized the implications of this and backtracked. "Okay, on second thought, actually not details." Esme feigned a gag. "Just the glossed-over and dressed-up good bits."

Abby sat across from her at a table for two. They arrived at the restaurant just in time for an early dinner consisting entirely of happy hour appetizers.

"Well, I can tell you it didn't involve magic hands. But it did include getting rail—"

"Stop right there!" Esme thrust her arms out, palms forward, warding away Abby's next words. "Too much, even for me!"

Esme fanned herself dramatically. "But I approve of your happiness. Is it too early to ask what you two are now?"

Abby shrugged. "I wish I knew."

Esme confessed with a resigned grimace, "I wish I didn't know exactly how that feels. At least it's better now. But how was therapy? You just escaped!"

Abby made a weighing motion with her hands. "Mom started out being defensive but then broke down and apologized to all of us like fifteen times each. Dad hugged Mom for the first time in months. Colin complained about being left out of the drama, even though he didn't want to hear any of it in the first place. So, it was mixed."

"Abby, you are killing it right now. You've wrangled your entire family into therapy, you're dropping your work hours to regain a bit of sanity, you've hired a cleaner, and your dry streak is over."

"So, so over," Abby said, a grin stretching from ear to ear. "And how was work for you?"

Still playing the drama queen, Esme clutched at her heart and made an overjoyed face. "Finn dropped the most tantalizing bit of information in my lap that you need to know." She punctuated the last four words by tapping the table with one straightened finger.

Abby rolled her eyes, but a smile still tugged at the corners of her lips. "Spit it out, Esme."

"Finn stopped just short of saying that he caught Will and someone else making out during the meeting yesterday. That's why he was late finding us."

"That snake! I knew Colin was acting less wound up than usual."

"So you think it was Colin, too?"

Abby shrugged. "Maybe they're just messing around, maybe not. Guess we'll see. Will's a huge upgrade from his last girlfriend, though. We all hated her."

"Let's hope Will doesn't go all emo when Colin heads back to California," Esme added.

"Cheers to that! He's worse than a lost puppy sometimes, and I'd have to hear about the heartbreak from both sides." Abby raised her water glass for a toast.

Esme hesitated. "I hate to spoil the mood, but I'm glad you invited me here. We need to plan..."

Abby scooted forward in her chair, sensing the shift. "You don't seem too happy about it. Is this about that crazy guy, Leon?"

Esme shook her head while she mindlessly ripped small pieces of her napkin apart. "No. I think we might be the only ones who will want to save who's been hunting cambion," she mouthed the word instead of saying it aloud, "The one who messed with Jacob's mind."

Abby's expression grew serious. "So, we know who? Is that what you found out when Miles kicked us out yesterday?"

"Sylas." Just saying the name hit Esme like a punch.

Abby blinked once, then took a deep breath. Abby's reaction to big news was unique. She didn't react to it immediately with big emotions like Esme. She didn't leap to denial or counterarguments. Neither did she try to explain it away. She simply accepted it; a reaction that was utterly baffling to Esme's emotionally sensitive nature. Abby sat with the information for a moment, then seemed to gather herself.

Abby hung her head as she talked. "Miles won't hold back. Neither will Gwyn, especially with what he said about leshies. And Jacob's going to take this personally. What are we going to do to stop them from..." She looked at Esme and made a slicing gesture across her throat.

Esme shaped her fingers into a heart. "I knew you'd get it. We can't give up on him yet. So, let's plan…"

An hour later, Abby was fighting off sleep when Finn knocked at Esme's door. Esme smirked. "That's what being up all night does. I'll get the door."

Abby yawned, trying to stretch out her back and wincing from some unknown pain. "It was worth it."

Esme opened the door to see Finn, two sheets to the wind. He positively reeked of booze. "Finn! My buddy, my pal. You look like you need some water and a snack."

She shuffled him in, guiding him to the kitchen. "Why are you drunk? No. Better question. How are you drunk? Can't you burn away the alcohol like you did when you were drugged?"

He hiccupped. "I can. But I'm just a wee bit dry in the magic department right now."

"What did you do?" It was a valid question, considering she saw him less than six hours before.

"First, I had a drinkin' contest with Sitkum. He pulled out a soddin' nugget of pure gold as the prize!" The leprechaun's eyes went googly, blissful.

"But I lost that, so I suggested a round of magical darts. I didn't know the hairy one was so good at illusions. Plus," he hiccupped again, "I think that the judge was biased against me."

Magical darts was exactly like mundane darts except players could earn extra points for performing telekinetic or illusory tricks during the throw.

"Who was the judge?"

"Mr. Cruz." He said the name like it was a curse. "I kept upping the ante, but it was never good enough for him."

"Maybe if you hadn't broken in on Will while he was doing things behind closed doors, he wouldn't have it in for you!"

The leprechaun teetered to one side, nearly toppling over. "I see that now…"

Esme turned to Abby. "Can you give him a bit of magic? He's useless to us this way. I tried it a few times and my magic doesn't seem to play well with others."

At any other time, Esme might have felt the familiar sting of isolation, reminded of the bitter taste of her discordant magic, but the urgency of saving Sylas eclipsed all else.

"The scamp deserves a hangover," Abby suggested, sighing. "But, fine. We do need him to alter our dresses."

"It might work with me, Esmer-alda. Let's…" Finn fell backward onto the couch. "Give it a gooo."

There was no reason for her not to try. Abby walked her through the process again, patiently explaining each step. By the time Esme finished, Finn appeared to be much steadier on his feet.

Though her body ached as if she'd just completed a grueling half marathon, an uplifting sense of accomplishment filled her. Before Finn showed up drunk, she hadn't recognized her longing to fit in. In the end, supporting a friend was all she needed to help her feel less alienated.

Looking at Finn afterward, Esme couldn't help but wonder if he'd done it on purpose.

It took them half an hour of arguing, but they hatched a plan to save Sylas.

Jacob

Out of respect for her leadership at the last Assembly meeting, Jacob traveled to Maureen's house instead of summoning her to his. Now they sat in the Mitchells' sitting room, sipping weak tea that Eddie had scrounged up for their impromptu talk.

"I can still cancel our plans. Or Eddie can go on his own. He knows how I feel about visiting his parents anyway," Maureen said, rolling her eyes.

Her face fell, the change in her expression so sharp Jacob could almost hear the shift. "I've known Sylas for almost forty years. It's hard to believe he'd go this far. It feels like a betrayal of everything we've been through."

"Maureen, it *is* a betrayal of everything we've been through."

His surprisingly candid remarks left the usually quick-witted Maureen speechless. A flicker of surprise crossed her face before she spoke. "Do you think they'll be okay without either of us?"

Jacob waved his hand, brushing off Maureen's concern about neither of them attending the Solstice Gala that year. "I can't divulge the specifics, but let's just say a potential solution is on the horizon. It involves many moving parts. If that doesn't pan out, I trust them to handle it."

Maureen took a sip of her tea and eyed him over the rim of her mug. "Playing a sneaky game, old man. What's your angle with your other move?"

"Maureen, you're no spring chicken yourself. There's no game, I'm sorry to admit. I've lost face. They won't trust me anymore. That's it. There's nothing more to it. I'm retiring."

He'd led the Seattle Assembly for over four decades. That was a sufficiently long period for any individual to take on a forward-facing position while having his own businesses on the side.

"Are you stepping down as Bastion too?"

"I don't have much of a choice in that. As long as I am mentally and physically well, my vows remain intact."

"You would if you lied."

"True." He took a small sip of his tea. At the very least, the weak brew would keep him hydrated and warm—the Mitchells kept their house temperature at near arctic conditions. "I have serious reservations about pushing for that change at this particular juncture. Anyway, I'd rather die on my feet."

Maureen raised her mug in a casual salute. "Cheers to that."

"Who do you think will take over the role?" she asked. Her demeanor did not reflect enthusiasm regarding his departure.

"Although I have some preferred choices, the possibility of a foreign candidate remains."

"Who?"

He shrugged. "There has been interest from China, India, and the United Kingdom."

Maureen's laughter was filled with wicked delight. "You're hoping for your countryman, aren't you?"

Absolutely not. As the head of the London Assembly, the man already occupied the most coveted position in western Europe. With an almost unlimited budget, generation after generation of family members trained and willing to serve, and a mundane population eager to believe that the magic they were seeing was just part of a movie being filmed nearby, David Abington had no reason to leave London. All of that and yet Jacob's informants said David had already booked his flight.

There was only one possible motive Jacob could think of for David's desire to relocate to Seattle: Miles. David had carefully manipulated every aspect of the Miles' life for nearly twenty-five years. In Jacob's opinion, it had been more than long enough. He was suspicious of David's ulterior motives in sticking so close to his god-touched mentee. The things he could want out of the bargain ran the gambit from fatherly attachment, which Jacob counted as highly unlikely, to using the boy for his personal gain as he had for years. The moment that man set foot on American soil, he'd begin exerting control over Miles' and Esmeralda's lives. Not for the better, especially considering he wasn't fond of cambion.

Maureen's speculation would have to go unanswered. Publicly denouncing David would only further weaken Jacob's position.

"You're still going to be pulling strings from the sidelines, though, right?" Maureen asked.

He allowed a faint smile to touch his lips. Jacob had already booked his flight to London. "Not at all. I'll be lying low for now, waiting for Sylas to make his move. The word is that I had a temporary brain inflammation and am recovering."

"Sneaky, sneaky, boss."

Jacob only smiled.

CHAPTER THIRTY-FOUR

THE CONFRONTATION

Gwyn

Returning to Miles' home, even if it was empty, from the sanctuary he'd found with Abigail felt like stepping into the enemy's stronghold without so much as a weapon at hand. Abigail's family was in town for the Assembly meeting, so she had to meet her father for lunch, followed by a family therapy session. The notion of family therapy was entirely alien to Gwyn. Instead of discussing their issues, families in his time simply resorted to plotting and betraying one another.

Cerys squeezed through the gap between his legs and the door, entering the house first. Through the bond he shared with the hellhound, he could sense her impatience was due to something catching her nose's attention. After shutting the door, he discovered the tray of muffins on the counter was the reason for her singular focus. Assuming they were another batch from Esme, he snatched one, savoring the petty satisfaction of knowing it would annoy Miles.

It wasn't until he was nearly finished with the muffin that he realized he and Cerys weren't alone. A figure shrouded by magic rose from the corner of the room. Damn Miles for placing wards against his use of magic, and damn himself for thinking the trade-off was worth it. He didn't even have his sword, having left it at Abigail's. Gwyn was at a massive disadvantage.

When the figure stepped into the weak light streaming through the window, he saw it wasn't an unfamiliar face. It would have been more comforting to see a stranger than the man who stood before him.

"Time to talk," Miles said in low tones.

Gwyn dropped the mostly eaten muffin back onto the tray and rolled his shoulders. His one-word response of "Yes" carried the weight of his sudden descent from Annwn, his people's version of heaven he'd shared with Abigail, back down to the harsh reality of the present.

"Care to join me back at the table?" Miles asked.

Gwyn suspected what this conversation was about, but knew it wouldn't help to worsen his position by being uncivil. "Yes."

Miles dropped the last dredges of magic that shrouded him from sight and pulled out a chair. Gwyn couldn't see any visible weapons on Miles, but that didn't mean he wasn't armed.

Watching for any telling twitch of a muscle in his opponent's forearm, Gwyn chose exhaustion over anger in his voice. "What is this about?"

"Business." Miles' answer was swift. "I simply have the privilege of being the representative. Given our history, I can understand why you might find that hard to believe."

"So you took no pleasure in catching me off guard?"

"I wouldn't go that far." A lopsided smile tugged on Miles' face. "You answer my questions, maybe make a binding promise, and we leave here the same way we entered."

Gwyn doubted that was possible.

"I still have the binding promise I made to your Bastion hanging over my head," Gwyn said, leaning back. "I have been unfailingly honest with your Brotherhood."

Miles drummed the fingers of his prosthetic on the table, the rhythm almost identical to the one Nudd used when agitated. "You haven't been honest with Esmeralda."

This had to be something to do with Leon. Gwyn remained silent until Miles pressed further.

"Don't like the mirror I'm putting in front of you?" Miles scoffed. "The worst thing about all of this is that she trusts you, and so does Abby. You've been manipulating both of them since the second you laid eyes on them."

"No." He had tried with Esme, at first. But that effort had lasted all of one day. When he'd met her at the beach to share his suspicions about Miles, she'd already begun to win him over. By the next day, she'd become his comrade-in-arms against a troupe of Dullahan. To manipulate Abigail was unthinkable, and likely impossible.

"The second I started believing a fraction of your ludicrous story," Miles said, "you proved that you're untrustworthy."

Miles had always been wary of Gwyn, but this was the first crack in his distrust that he had seen. If Miles hadn't approached this conversation like a predator hunting its prey, Gwyn might interpret his words as a glimmer of hope.

"What convinced you that I might not be mad?"

With an irritated flick of his prosthetic fingers, Miles shooed the question away. "Nothing."

Feeling even more weary than he had been entering this tiresome conversation, Gwyn met Miles' gaze. "Something has changed, and I must know what."

Miles shrugged. "Maybe if I had more of your honesty, you would get more of mine."

Suddenly, Gwyn felt a wave of dizziness wash over him. His vision swam and the sounds around him faded. The last thing he remembered seeing was Miles' grinning face before his head hit the table, the darkness claiming him.

Gwyn awoke in a position he had never experienced in this life or the last. The room was dark, and as he strained his arms and legs, he could feel the rough texture of the ropes binding him to the bed. All was quiet except for the sound of his breathing and the faint, steady breaths of another person sitting mere feet from him.

A dim mage's light flickered to life, revealing the man who wore his father's younger face staring down at him with a malevolent smile.

"You should be embarrassed, mate," Miles said with a smirk. "It was easier to tie you up than the leprechaun. Though I did give you a significantly stronger dose. I was far less worried about accidentally killing you than Finn."

Gwyn felt his brow scrunch stupidly, unbidden. What had Miles done to him?

"I'm glad to see that my wards against your magic are working. I'll be back in a bit when you're slightly more lucid."

Miles manipulated a bag of water hanging from a pole before leaving. Before Gwyn fell back asleep, he realized that the bag was connected to a needle that pierced his skin.

Gwyn woke up sometime later; he couldn't say exactly how long had passed. His mind was sharper, more focused, likely the result of a potion, elixir, or other concoction Miles had dosed him with. Only fragments of what happened afterward surfaced in his memory. Fleeting visions of being tied up and incapacitated were followed by the sting of something piercing his skin before he drifted back into unconsciousness.

Gwyn had to agree with Miles' last statement. It was incredibly foolish of him to get caught in this situation so easily. His mind felt like a satisfied hound, fat with scraps of food after a feast—indolent. Spending the night with Abigail had made him feel so gratified, so comfortable, that it had made him drop his defenses. His predicament was entirely his own fault. There would always be a dagger hiding in the darkness, waiting for a moment of vulnerability. He just needed to remember that the next time he left their sanctuary.

Still, he couldn't help but wonder why Miles had waited so long to make this move. With his curiosity piqued and the potential shame of failure holding him back, Gwyn reluctantly decided against attempting to break out of his bonds. He wouldn't be a fool twice over. Seeing how this scenario played out could be quite educational.

At some point, he heard footsteps shuffling across hardwood, and a familiar figure darkened the doorway. No matter how tightly he squeezed his eyes, the blinding light still burned through his eyelids to sear his retinas, as the overhead light turned on unexpectedly. While his mind may have been mostly back to normal, his body was still experiencing the side effects of whatever Miles had dosed him with. His head throbbed painfully with every sluggish pulse of his heart.

"Nicely played," Gwyn murmured.

Going by the tone of Miles' voice alone, because opening his eyes would be torture, Gwyn thought Miles sounded unusually smug. "If you had only two words to describe how you'd murder me right now—if you could—what would they be?"

Gwyn hadn't intended to answer the question, but it popped out unbidden. His tongue felt thick and slow in his mouth. "Slowly, painfully."

Had Miles given him another potion?

When Gwyn opened his eyes, he noted with curiosity that Miles wasn't carrying one of his signature knives or daggers to complete the threat of his presence twice over. Interesting. He knew one was always nearby, however.

"So you're awake enough for a chat. I currently have no plan to murder you. But I could be persuaded to change my mind if you don't give me what I want." His smile was cold, humorless.

Gwyn needed to say something to stop the overwhelming shame building up inside him. He, a very proud man, would carry the disgrace of this situation until his dying moments. "I will admit... I didn't think you had it in you to go this far. Especially with a guest."

"Are hosting rules even relevant anymore?" Miles shrugged, then turned sardonic. "According to you, I have two men inside of me, so who knows which one is in control right now?"

Gwyn growled out, "What was in the bag attached to my arm?"

"Saline." Reading the confused look Gwyn was giving him, Miles clarified. "To keep you from dehydrating. I'm not a monster. You were out for hours."

"Are you sure about that?"

Miles studied him for a moment. "I don't have to play nice. One on one, we might be a match. But it looks like you don't have many allies. Maybe you're trying to make one with Leon. I don't know, but I can tell you he won't be enough. If I decide on it, I can guarantee that you won't make it out of Seattle alive. That's a threat and a promise."

Miles leaned over, his elbows resting on his thighs. Against all of Gwyn's expectations, his eyes held no trace of hatred or malice. His eyes looked just like his father's when he had been pressed to decide on the execution of a man, when all he had was a limited knowledge of his crimes—unhappy resignation.

Miles said, "To business. The Bastion has been compromised. The Corded Brotherhood wants to know how you're connected to it."

Gwyn strained to lift his head and met Miles' gaze, bonds restricting his movements. "I'm not," he replied flatly. "Serendipity is a fickle goddess."

"And your connection to Leon? Also just a coincidence?"

"Yes, to my knowledge." Gwyn lowered his head back to the bed.

Coincidence... like running into Miles and Esmeralda while searching for Cerys. Like meeting Abigail at The Sanctuary of Spirits. Like finding Esmeralda at the coffee shop with her. How had he missed the signs? Serendipity had been toying with him since his reemergence.

Gwyn was no closer to finding out the truth behind his imprisonment than he had been the day he saw Miles' picture at the pub in London. Something had to change, and yet, he'd gained Abigail. He had a friend in Esmeralda. He even more than slightly tolerated the leprechaun. Will was starting to make a positive impression on him, and he respected Jacob.

"You spoke of promises," Gwyn said carefully, his tongue more under control. "Upon my magic, I swear that I have no memory of Leon before the day we met him at the library. Upon my magic, I swear I played no part in the Bastion's assault or the planning of it. By my magic, I swear I have only encountered Leon twice, each time with Esmeralda. Now, I have given three promises."

"And yet you said so much that Esme couldn't understand," Miles retorted.

"It has been long since I spoke so easily. Yes, Leon speaks our language."

Only after speaking did Gwyn realize he'd said "our" without thinking. Miles raised an eyebrow.

His drug-addled brain finally registered the scarcity of connection that he had to his hound. "Where is Cerys?"

"Asleep," Miles replied. "She's fine. She's not the problem. You are."

Gwyn tugged on the bond between them, feeling Cerys peacefully sleeping curled up next to Lily a room over, without a care in the world. So, Miles still had some lines he wouldn't cross.

This conversation had reached a tipping point. Gwyn could either continue to indulge Miles' sadistic game or change his predicament to reset the gaming board. He chose the latter.

Miles

The empty bed before him and the dagger at his throat were... unexpected. Miles could feel the sharp sting of the blade against his skin, but Gwyn controlled his strength just enough to avoid drawing blood.

So, the rogue could mist walk. Somehow, his wards had failed or Gwyn had found a way around them.

Gwyn's voice was stable, sane. That was no small thing.

"I would like nothing more than to see your throat cut, but Abigail and Esmeralda would disapprove. Threats are not something I tolerate. I could stop this, but I want to enjoy seeing you wrestle with your doubts."

With the smallest pressure from his wrist, Gwyn pushed the dagger until a fine trickle of blood welled. Miles' pulse shot up. He lowered the dagger just as Miles was about to make a disarming move. "Let there be no doubt—this is my repayment for the life you spared."

Gwyn stepped back and released his hold on Miles. For a moment, they stared at each other. As Miles put space between them, he cast an aegis of protection around himself. Gwyn stood unmoving, gripping the dagger, not inviting a fight but also not backing down from one.

Bloody hell. While Miles could have easily disarmed Gwyn, it would have come at the cost of an injury to one or both of them.

Miles faced a choice. He could either dig in his heels, risking real confrontation, or be open to change. Flexibility might buy him a temporary alliance when they needed it most, while he feared that any more stubbornness would only backfire. The options for that ending were blood pooling beneath one of them (again) or the ashes of his house blowing away in the breeze.

Ready for action, but hoping for a calmer outcome, Miles said, "What can I offer you in exchange for more honesty? We still haven't moved past the undeniable truth that I am not your father. If I hadn't taken an oath not to swear on my magic, I'd swear it now. Not that my word means anything to you."

Miles could almost hear gears clicking and turning in Gwyn's mind.

"Deliver the fake identity papers that your people promised. Abigail made it clear that your organization has been intentionally stalling. I dislike being indebted to you."

"Done," Miles replied easily. If Gwyn wanted to leave the area assuming the identity the Brotherhood set him up with, so be it. They'd have tabs on him for the rest of his life.

"What did Leon really want?"

"He truly said that he wanted to 'get a good glimpse' at you. I said it was about the halo—what else would he be interested in?"

It sounded like a half-truth.

"And Esme? What did he say about her?"

There was nothing kind about the grin that spread on Gwyn's face. "In our language, nothing. He made the binding promise that you heard about and volunteered to help with Esmeralda's 'demonic problems.' No wonder, because he was quite open about his attraction to her. I think he even gave her a lover's name."

Gwyn was intentionally provoking him. "I think you mean 'pet name.' You've made your point, Gwyn," Miles said through gritted teeth, barely restraining the urge to lash out.

They stood, locked in a silent standoff. If Gwyn could use his magic again, he needed to proceed cautiously.

"The Brotherhood accepts your promises," Miles said finally. "I count us as even."

Showing his intent to deescalate, he discarded the shield he'd been maintaining. Gwyn's face briefly showed a flicker of surprise. He composed himself quickly, coming to a decision.

"This is far from over," Gwyn warned, voice as cold as the blade he gripped.

With a flick of his wrist, he deftly twisted the dagger in his hand, the sharp blade now pointed toward his body, and presented it to Miles. "I am content to be patient with us. Though you've been more of a disappointment than anything."

Miles took the dagger and nodded. Being trapped in a stalemate was a new experience for him. Malevolents gave no quarter, and the humans were always trying to kill him first. The truce between them was as fragile as the blade's edge he was now holding.

Backing away, Gwyn said, "But my time here has not been completely wasted. I have gained a friend and a lover. I don't trust this Leon either."

Miles swallowed his retort to hearing the lover part. It scratched at his throat the entire way down.

Filling the silence where Miles' objection should have been, Gwyn asked, "Have you found proof of Leon's meddling with the Bastion?"

"We know who did it. It wasn't Leon."

Miles' tone hardened. "For Esme and Abby's sake, I'll let this go—for now. Letting this lie means I'm giving you enough rope to hang yourself with if you step out of line. The Brotherhood will deliver on the forged identity, but don't think for a second that you'll be free of us."

Gwyn's devil-may-care smile made Miles want to roll his eyes and walk out the door of his own house.

"You're moving out of my house before the Gala. You also need to decide on a last name—tonight."

The news only fueled Gwyn's obnoxious grin. He asked, "Then what do we do about the one who attacked the Bastion?"

"I'm so glad you asked," Miles replied with what might have been his first genuine smile aimed at the other man.

Miles walked to the dining room and pulled the chair he'd been sitting in before Gwyn ate the drugged muffin and sat back down in it. As he folded his hands on the table, he said, "We need to find a way to kill a leshy that won't require Esme and Abby's forgiveness."

CHAPTER THIRTY-FIVE

NEWMAN, NEW WOMAN

Gwyn

Gwyn leaned on the wooden railing of the retired ferry boat the Assembly had rented for the Solstice Gala. The air was thick with moisture as the winter wind swirled around him, sending a chill through the layers of his rented suit. It was a welcome contrast to the stifling heat of the crowded boat's interior. He absentmindedly fiddled with the plastic card displaying his new identity. The picture of him on it stood out for how grainy it was, unlike the others he'd seen. He surmised that was the result when photographs were taken without the subject's knowledge.

"Thank you," he finally said to his sole companion on the deck of the ship.

Gwyn's eyes followed Abigail as she twirled and swayed with Colin, her head bobbing in and out of his view. He couldn't help but feel a twinge of annoyance, knowing that Colin had been the first to learn Will's method of seeing magic. Gwyn had secretly hoped that his past mastery of magic would continue to resurface, just like it had with his mist walking and his use of fulminomancy. Still, he could respect Colin for his skill and his attentiveness toward his sister.

Leaning closer, he whispered, "Their dresses are a stunning display of craftsmanship, leprechaun. I especially like the... emblems you've stitched into both."

"Do ya now?" Finn's eyes sparkled, not with joy, but with mischief. "I had to point out the knots on the shoulders of Esme's to her. Don't think she's noticed the dragons yet, either. Abby's original house sigil was easier to weave in, as ya can see."

The wings that made up the shoulders of Abigail's dress matched Creiddylad's household's emblem, a war eagle, perfectly. Add to that the image of a crown on the back, and the symbolism was as clear as a cloudless day to Gwyn. Esmeralda's dress bore Nudd's household knot on both shoulders, with dragons cleverly hidden in the smoky patterns on her bodice.

The dragons were well-documented in literature, but Nudd's knot and Creiddylad's house sigil had both been lost to time. Either the leprechaun had an excellent source of information that Jacob would literally kill for, or Finn knew far, far more than he let on.

Gwyn shifted his weight from foot to foot. "How did you know?"

Finn giggled. "Oh, are we bein' honest with each other now?"

"I'm unaware of any time I have been dishonest with you."

The leprechaun snorted. "So, it's just things left unsaid, huh?"

"On this topic, for good reason. Be plain, Fionn."

"All right, but only because I can't wait to see the look on yer face. We've met before, Gwynnyboy. It's been quite a long time, but I've got a good memory for such a momentous occasion."

Not receiving the shocked expression he'd been hoping for, the scamp pressed on. "Took me a bit to put all the pieces together, but eventually I worked it out. They're different, though, aren't they? The guardswoman was much more uptight and yer woman was more... repressed."

They had to be. The court was stifling for all souls. But Gwyn said none of this aloud.

Finn blew out an impressed breath, pointing toward the interior of the boat where Abigail and Esmeralda were. "The tale of how ya managed to get them both here... Well, that story is surely one for the ages, Mister Newman."

Gwyn liked the sound of his new last name. It was... fitting. He replied to the leprechaun truthfully, "When I remember how I did it, I'll let you know..."

Finn eyed him skeptically. Then, dancing a quick jig, Finn added, "Oh, and don't worry about threatenin' to kill me if I open my gabber. I won't say a thing—yet. Now the fun can begin! We've got some work to do, you and I. Ya just don't know it yet."

With that last cryptic remark, Finn started walking away.

In his wake, Gwyn said, "That is an awful lot to drop on me and then leave, Finnegan."

Finn giggled and sauntered off without a backward glance to join Esmeralda at the bar, leaving Gwyn pondering the trickster's schemes.

Yet, for the first time since the dream that had revealed the crime that landed him in a malevolent prison for more than ten centuries, Gwyn felt a strange peace as he sat with his sins. He just wondered how long it would last.

Esme

Esme's drink of choice for the night was sparkling apple juice, but it still took her brain too long to figure out why the name tag of the man in front of her at the bar was familiar. It read "Alan K." She could tell that the well-tailored man standing in front of her was wholly mundane. That wasn't completely unusual. To accommodate the needs of their extravagant gala, the mages of Seattle often relied on mundane volunteers who were in-the-know to assist as temporary staff for the evening.

Esme had to stop herself from smudging her makeup when her hands flew up to her face, realizing that the man had to be Alan Kim. He was the father of the wayward teen she'd helped guide back to the right path almost a year before.

"Gods above, Mr. Kim!" she exclaimed. "I'm Esme Turner. Is Grace here tonight?"

His smile, bright with perfect teeth, betrayed that he was indeed a good dentist. "Yes, she will be. That's why I'm here! She had a study group for a big exam after the break, so she's running a bit late."

Alan was still new to the world of magic. He'd only learned of it a few months before his wife died from breast cancer a little more than a year before. His daughter Grace's grief had sent her spiraling into a self-destructive path that lasted for months. Grace was a talented animagus/zoomancer (mage society was split on the title) who caused a bit too much trouble with her animal companions. The teen's repeated violation of the top edict against using magic in public just before her eighteenth birthday drew the wrong sort of attention from the Assembly, so they sent Esme to fix it.

Alan nodded toward the dance floor. "Andrew just came into his magic. I thought tonight would be a good time to bring them both out into society while I could be here—without it being weird for them both. Teenagers."

A young teen with dark hair was tearing it up on the dance floor. The way he effortlessly moved to the rhythm of the music suggested that he had been practicing dance for a long time. With a perplexed expression, Esme turned to Alan, silently asking for an explanation.

He shrugged, chuckling. "Jacob said something about his type of magic being even more rare than Grace's. Has something to do with enhancing his body? That's why he can dance so well. I'm already having to talk him out of doing ten sports at once. I'll be taking him home soon, but Grace will probably stay late. She's excited that she gets to wear her prom dress twice."

Jacob's early interest in Andrew's abilities did not escape Esme's notice. In less than ten years, the Corded Brotherhood would come knocking on his door, eager to hire a fresh recruit with the right skills for killing monsters. She shook her head, trying to shake off the pessimism. Who knows? Maybe, just maybe, they'd figure out how to stop the malevolents from returning by then.

The malevolents.

The waiting, the watching for them... Their looming threat had already stolen Miles away from her for half the night. When he arrived to pick her up, she felt like the leading lady in a romantic film. Miles, usually so articulate, had stumbled over his words when he first laid eyes on her. Though he always made her feel beautiful, tripping up the ever steady Dr. Goodwin had been a thrilling experience. She'd have to stuff that leprechaun full of baked treats to thank him for the dress.

She wasn't the only one missing her partner for most of the night. Will, Colin, Abby, and Gwyn were all stationed apart, ensuring a constant lookout. Colin had told her that Sorcha, the selkie, had patrolled around the ferry for most of the night so far. Similarly, Ved, the garuda, would switch between perching on the ship and soaring above, his powerful illusion magic concealing his presence during his patrols. She'd even spotted Winnie, the aziza, flitting around, seemingly more occupied with her duties than having a good time.

But nothing had happened yet, and it was getting late. Perhaps they'd been incorrect in thinking that Sylas was planning on attacking that night. Maybe he'd done all that he planned. She hoped...

Finn walked over to her, looking as dapper as ever. He wore an honest to goodness black tailcoat with matching slacks, patent leather shoes, and gold accents galore. Somehow, he pulled it off without crossing into gaudiness in the way only he could.

Alan stared at Finn as he walked over, his mouth hanging slightly open, just as he had been while gawking at the other non-humans during their conversation. Esme told Alan, "Yes, Finn is a leprechaun. They're usually shorter, though."

"Heyo, beautiful," Finn greeted her.

"Heyo, yourself, handsome." She tipped her flute of apple juice in Alan's direction. "Thanks for the juice, Mr. Kim. I can't wait to see Grace!"

With that, she tugged Finn away so the poor mundane man could continue to adjust his world view in peace. Which, in this case, meant away from Finn's prattling on about anything and everything.

"Any news?" she asked once they were out of earshot.

Finn shook his head. "Nothin'. Will is on the lookout and yer man is doin' his rounds."

"I'm betting nothing will happen until nearly everyone is gone, just like last time."

"Aye."

"When Miles picked me up this afternoon, he only had like… three daggers strapped to his body. That number is suspiciously low. He's also been way too calm for the past two days. Do you think they're plotting like we are? Or do they have intel we don't?"

"Aye."

"Since when did you start giving short non-answers? Whatever. You haven't used any magic tonight, right?"

The plan they'd come up with was straightforward. Finn would sneak up on Sylas, mist walk him to where Abby was waiting, and she would put Sylas to sleep. Then Esme's trolls would carry Sylas to her car, already prepped with the backseats down. Abby was confident she could keep Sylas asleep for at least thirty minutes—long enough to get him to the holding cell Esme had just learned they had for magic users at the Assembly headquarters.

From there, they could focus on his rehabilitation. Sylas would be contained and not dead. Everyone could go home safe and happy.

Instead of answering Esme's question about his use of magic, Finn took in a long swallow of air as his gaze shifted slowly away from her. He muttered, "I volunteer as breakfast, lunch, or dinner. Maybe all three, if it doesn't kill me."

"You volunteer as... what?" Esme asked, confused.

Then she saw what he meant. Katia approached, her arm linked with a brunette woman unfamiliar to Esme.

"Perv," she scolded Finn. "Don't be weird. Better yet, say absolutely nothing."

Turning to greet them, Esme smiled. "Katia! And Heather, I presume?" She wasn't certain what else to do, so she offered out her hand for a shake.

"Esme that dress is stunning! Correct! Heather, this is Esme. She's the one like me... but not exactly." Katia's usual sensual aura was toned down, suggesting she had recently fed and fed well.

Esme smirked. "Thank you, Finn made my dress! Unlike Katia, I just get angry, not sexy."

Finn's face was as red as a tomato as Katia's attention shifted to him briefly.

Katia chuckled. "I'd trade places with you any day, Esme. Anyway, we came to let you know Jacob wants to shut the place down early. The DJ's going to announce it soon." Leaning in, Katia whispered, "I'm staying as bait." Then, louder, "But Heather is heading home, right, Heather?"

Heather rolled her eyes and muttered, "She always gets what she wants."

Finn sighed dramatically. "She can have whatever she wants." His voice was filled with longing and a touch of desperation.

Esme smacked him on the shoulder, hard. If only Jacob didn't have to lie low at home to bring Sylas out of hiding, his mere presence would have been enough to control the leprechaun.

After a dance with Sitkum that involved him carrying her more than actual dancing, Esme found herself face to face with someone she hadn't seen in nearly a year. Unlike their first meeting, they were both free of bird droppings. While they'd exchanged the occasional text, their busy lives prevented them from doing much else. For Esme, that had meant her life being turned upside down and flipped sideways, but for Grace Kim, it meant a return to health, a light back in her eyes, and a scholarship to a university.

"So basically, you're winning at life, Grace," Esme exclaimed, doing a victory dance in her chair, her squeal of delight going unnoticed in the noisy room.

Grace smiled proudly. "Thanks to you. Thanks for kicking my butt last spring. I realize now that I needed it."

Esme sat back, relishing the gratification of a job well done. She rarely knew the outcomes of her enforcement work for the Assembly because it was typically negative and conducted in secret at every stage. She allowed herself to celebrate this small victory and enjoyed the moment of peace that came with it before the night's inevitable chaos erupted. "You did all the hard work. I just gave you a little nudge."

Before Grace could reply, her expression shifted to concern, her eyes darting behind Esme. Turning, Esme saw Alan approaching, carrying Grace's younger brother, Andrew, limp in his arms.

Esme's smile vanished as she stood up. "What happened?"

Alan was practically trembling with worry. "I don't know! One minute he was fine, asking for water. Then he went back to dancing and just collapsed. Someone said not to worry, but I'm taking him to the hospital! These mages are crazy!"

Grace quickly gathered her things, her earlier pride now replaced with concern.

Esme moved closer, hands raised in a calming gesture. "Mr. Kim, if someone told you not to worry, it's probably magical exhaustion. He's just tapped out. He's used too much power, too quickly. If he hasn't vomited, he'll be fine within a couple of hours. He just needs rest."

Alan looked at Grace for confirmation.

"Yeah, Mom mentioned it to me several times," she said. "I've never passed out, though."

Esme did her best to reassure them. "Just take him home and let him rest. I can have my boyfriend meet you on the way out to be sure—he's a doctor."

Alan nodded, struggling under the teenager's weight.

"His name is Miles Goodwin. I'll tell him to meet you by the ferry ramp. Go, go!" She shooed them off, understanding that Alan needed to feel like he was taking immediate action. Grace's concern mirrored his. As they hurried away, Esme pulled out her phone and dialed Miles.

Chapter Thirty-Six

A Ship in Port is Safe... Right?

Will

Will squinted to block out the city lights in the distance, wishing he could pluck his eyes out with one of the garnish spoons at the bar. They stung like a wasp had attacked each eyeball, while his head throbbed with a pain that felt like that same wasp had built a nest inside his skull.

Sure, everyone else was there for champagne, awkward small talk, and the faint hope of looking like the size of their magic was bigger than the next guy's. But not Will. No, he was on a mission, playing unwilling soldier.

The DJ's set wasn't helping. The pounding beat only made his headache worse and reminded him of the fun that couldn't be his. Adjusting his tux collar for what felt like the hundredth time, he wondered why beauty had to be so painful. He made a mental note: Move to Puerto Vallarta. Take Colin with him. Join a cult. Anything to avoid this.

He tried to recall why he hadn't protested more about lookout duty. Oh right—Colin, Esme, and that harpy, Abby, had guilted him into it.

Well, to be fair, Colin hadn't exactly guilted him. The idea of a night out with him had sounded great, but things hadn't gone anywhere near planned. Since Colin had learned how to see magic, the strategy had changed, splitting them up for the entire night. For Guillermo Cruz, the Solstice Gala would hold no secret kisses in the coat closet or grinding on the dance floor. At least he'd been able to spend more of the night indoors than outdoors, unlike poor Colin, because it was cold as hell and it looked like it was going to snow.

Will couldn't even imagine how tough it must've been for Esme to learn that Sylas was behind the malevolent attacks. Then again, he wasn't exactly surprised. The leshy had always made him feel uneasy. His one redeeming quality was that he would probably hold off on attacking until the kids had all gone home for the evening.

As a steady stream of people flowed out, Miles approached. Will asked, "Did Jacob decide to shut the party down early?"

With a grimace and a casual shrug, Miles said, "Apparently there was a problem with the pumps in the ladies and gents, so we can't hold a party any longer by health codes, or some such."

Will joked, "I'm not completely certain Jacob's one hundred percent human. With all the sneaky stuff he comes up with, there's gotta be some Fae in there somewhere."

To his surprise, Miles nodded, half in agreement. "I came by to tell you to take a break for a few while everyone files out. We need you fresh."

"Aye, aye, Captain," Will said with a mock salute.

"Major," Miles corrected with a smirk.

"Oh, excuse me. Major. Does that make Jacob a Field Marshal of Bathroom Sabotage?"

Will forced a grin as Miles walked away. Fresh for what? For the first time, that damned beautiful, reassuring smile wasn't enough to make the lingering feeling that something wasn't quite right go away. A growing unease, adding to his throbbing headache, plagued him as he went in search of Colin.

Abby

Abby reapplied her lipstick, grateful for the rare moment of peace in the now-empty ladies' room. Jacob's clever ruse had exceeded their expectations in clearing out the place. Not a single person was willing to risk their party clothes to use their magic to repair the toilets.

Gwyn's status as a newcomer to the area, combined with his natural resting glower, had saved him from having to make too much small talk throughout the night. Though he seemed to enjoy the party in his own detached way, Abby noticed his interest was almost academic, as if he were observing the attendees through the lens of a sociologist rather than being genuinely fascinated by the spectacle of the gala. At least he hadn't looked like he wanted to murder someone, which should be counted as progress from her experience.

Abby tore off the skirt of her dress in one swift motion, folded it neatly, and slipped on the boots she'd stashed beneath the counter earlier. The forecast called for snow, and in hilly Seattle, snow was nothing to joke about. She and Esme had prepped for a fight, wearing leggings beneath their skirts. Finn had worked overtime to modify their dresses so they could tear the skirts away at a moment's notice. Long skirts, after all, were a death sentence when dealing with malevolents. Now dressed for action, Abby grabbed her jacket and headed for the ferry's outer deck, where everyone was supposed to be waiting.

Gwyn met her halfway across the dance floor. With an expression of grim warning, he pointed toward where she could see Esme and Miles practically sharing a coat on the other side of the windows. "They're having a romantic moment."

"And Colin, Will, and Finn?" she asked.

Holding up two fingers, Gwyn answered, "Probably having their own romantic interlude." He ticked off one finger. "Or sneaking around, following the succubus," he added, lowering the other finger. "I'm avoiding all of them."

She looped one arm through his and pulled him close. "We can have an interlude of our own, ya know."

Abby couldn't decipher the reason behind his searching eyes or his words when he said, "You are a perfection I do not deserve." But she accepted them anyway, because that was romantic as hell.

She reached out, her fingertips brushing against his cheek, and pulled him toward her for a tender kiss. With a sly smile, she declared, "Now you're stuck with me. Come on, let's disrupt the lovebirds. We need to go out there and decide if we're officially calling this a bust. I know Winnie quit hours ago, and I think Sorcha and Ved went home."

When Gwyn opened the door, a blast of icy air hit Abby, instantly causing her to break out in goosebumps. But it wasn't just the cold that made her react. It was the unsettling feeling of being noticed; a strange prickling sensation that broke out on her skin as they stepped outside. Whether it was instinct or her sense for magic, Abby glanced over her shoulder.

The shadowed ferry interior revealed nothing unusual. Still, the sense of being watched clung to her with every step. Will and Colin arrived at the same time, their footsteps creaking on the ferry's wooden floor.

Esme and Miles stood hand in hand by the deck railing, watching the city lights shimmer on Lake Union. They didn't seem to notice the cold—or anything else.

Abby rubbed her arms for warmth. "So, is this a bust? Gods, please tell me it's a bust."

Gwyn wasted no time in removing his overcoat, draping it around her shoulders, pulling her close. The gesture was sweet, unexpected, and she adored every second of it. The newness of it didn't matter. In a night full of uncertainties, this felt like something she could hold onto.

Colin spoke up, "The seated members seem to think so."

While Abby regretted the lost opportunity to help Sylas, she was happy to make that sacrifice to ensure nobody was harmed. Perhaps Sylas had already recognized his mistakes and was actively trying to make amends. Grieving people often acted impulsively without considering the consequences. If she and Esme could find it within their hearts to forgive him, their forgiveness could inspire others as well.

"I won't argue with their call," Miles said. "Let's head out."

Esme

The ferry rocked gently beneath their feet as they rounded the corner. Esme's sudden halt created a bottleneck of traffic behind her. Before her, Grace, now dressed down in casual city attire, stood beside an imposingly tall man. When he turned, she realized it was Sitkum in his human disguise. He looked like a twenty-something Native American man wearing the casual clothing of a tech sector worker in the city, just taller.

Grace greeted them with a wave. "Hey, Esme! I'm helping Sitkum find a ride that can handle his height."

Grace tilted her head back to meet his eyes, and a soft chuckle escaped her lips. "I came back because I realized I left a few things while we were in a rush to leave earlier. Dad's pretty lax about curfew since I'm eighteen now."

Looking down at the dagger sheathed on Esme's now unskirted thigh, Grace commented, "Nice knife."

Esme glanced down, having forgotten that she was wearing a rather intimidating magical dagger out in the open. "Thanks," she mumbled. Whoops.

Grace smiled. "Oh, by the way, Andrew woke up before I left. He's fine. Thanks, Dr. Goodwin, and thanks again, Esme."

Believing the danger had subsided, Esme concluded it was safe for them to return to the boat for long enough to grab her things. She plastered a fake smile on her face and said, "It's no problem at all. I hope you had fun tonight."

"I did!" Grace replied.

Sitkum added with a shy grin, "Same! It was worth coming into the city to meet Matika."

Esme asked, "Think I'll have a wedding to attend this spring?" The arranged couple had talked most of the night.

"I hope so." The sasquatch was practically incandescent with happiness.

Before anyone could reply, a desperate cry turned every head toward the opposite end of the boat. It was a woman's voice filled with pleading. The only person left that it could be was Katia.

Esme bolted toward the scream. She wasn't the only one. Colin and Will outpaced them all. The faster pair halted in front of them, blocking their views.

Pushing past Will, Esme tensed, her eyes now fixed on the unfolding chaos.

The interior of the ferry was a nightmarish scene: hundreds of spiders the size of dinner plates swarmed around Katia and Finn. While he fought off the majority with precise bursts of fire, Katia, armed with a broom, smacked away the few that got too close. A gaping jagged hole in the ceiling nearby marked the spiders' likely entry point.

The moment the spiders sensed fresh prey, half of the swarm shifted toward Esme and the others. Esme's heart faltered when she realized Grace and Sitkum were right behind Gwyn and Abby. With his head towering above the crowd, Sitkum immediately saw the problem and dropped his glamor, probably to preserve his magic. This startled Grace, who took a step back in surprise. She recovered quickly, but her shock proved she hadn't been aware that he wasn't human. Yet, she still couldn't see the chaos that lay ahead because the swarm was eerily silent.

"Took ya long enough!" Finn shouted, his voice gravelly with strain.

The spiders were approaching fast, only twenty feet away.

The spiders' bodies, swollen with varying patterns of yellow and black, were covered in needle-like hairs. A vivid blood-red stripe ran the length of their abdomen, all the way down to the spinnerets. Their long black legs had yellow stripes of the same color as their grasping mouth appendages, which had a fang-like appearance rather than the wooly graspers of regular spiders.

Arms stretched out on either side, hoping to lead anyone behind her away from the danger, Esme backed away from the approaching cluster. "Sitkum, Grace, run!"

But Grace had surreptitiously circled around Gwyn, Miles, and Abby to catch a glimpse of whatever the fuss was about.

"No!"

It turned out that Grace had a secret heroic side just waiting to be revealed. The young mage thrust out both arms, palms facing forward, with fingers extended. Her whole body thrummed with magic. Her arms were trembling—from fear, inexperience, or the strain of what she was trying, Esme wasn't certain. Surprising them all, she ordered, "Fight!"

As one, the spiders ceased moving. With no pause, everyone leaped into motion, ready to carry out the young mage's orders.

With a flick of his wrists, Miles activated two wicked push daggers that had been concealed under his cuffs. With the fluid grace of a dancer, he moved effortlessly, cutting the spiders down two by two. Gwyn did likewise, swinging his short sword in great arcs to cut through masses of arachnids at once. Esme had no idea where he'd hidden that, but that probably accounted for his rigid posture all evening.

Esme pulled her new dagger out of its sheath and started stabbing. It would take time to summon her blade and that was time they might not be able to afford. One blade and two booted feet would have to do while Grace's control held. Abby was close behind her, pulling out the knife she'd stolen from Colin, but never returned, weeks before.

Finn continued his assault with pinpoint-accurate streams of fire. Katia started using the pointed end of the broom to skewer them, one by one. Will picked up a chair and started crushing them, late-night wrestling style. Sitkum was using his enormous feet to smash them, a couple at a time.

It was disgusting. The spiders burst like overripe fruit, splattering a nauseating yellowish-blue ichor across the ferry's wooden floor. It was impossible to avoid stepping into the mess, so Esme didn't try. She'd have to thank Abby later for telling her to bring snow boots.

Esme stabbed and stomped through the mess, shouting, "Abby, what in the nine hells kind of spiders are these?"

It was understandable that Abby sounded exasperated. She wasn't the talkative type when riled up like Esme was. "Jorōgumo babies. Only the adults are venomous."

Even without venom, the sheer size of their fangs meant their bites would be intensely painful. Add to that the fact that they were attacking en masse like a pack of rabid dogs, and this situation did not bode well for them.

"Babies?" Esme gasped, silently pleading for more information. "Gods, I do not want to see the mother."

Esme should have shut her big fat stupid mouth because the woman who had to be their mama promptly halfway crawled, halfway fell out of the hole in the ceiling in an ungainly pile. There was simply no other explanation for why an unharmed, beautiful woman emerged from the same place as the spiders. Her black eyes were open but unfocused and glassy. She seemed only halfway awake. Her head barely moved as those same eyes looked around the room.

The woman wasn't a threat—yet. Everyone ignored the still form of the woman, now lying on her back in the middle of the spider mass. Esme continued stabbing without pausing to investigate the thumping sound behind her.

But as the tips of several spiders' legs nearby started twitching again, Esme glanced back, dreading to discover what the sound had been. Grace was sprawled on the ground, breathing gently but otherwise motionless. Sitkum hovered over her, stomping the nearest spiders as they approached.

"Grab her and run!" Esme shouted. Sitkum studied her for a moment, his eyes flickering with uncertainty as he weighed the wisdom of her orders. Finding whatever assurance he needed there, he swiftly scooped Grace up in one arm, cradling her like a human-sized football, and sprinted away.

They'd killed roughly half of them in the time Grace had bought them—that glorious girl. With hundreds still left, it was time for Esme to call her conjurations because the spiders were waking up. And so was Mama...

Miles

Something felt off. Amid the chaotic spider attack, Miles detected a shift in the room's magic—an unexpected stillness that couldn't be ignored. In the periphery of his vision, he saw something near the jagged hole in the ceiling, but he couldn't afford to look away from the swarm.

He caught a glimpse of a woman emerging—no, falling—into the carnage. For a split second, Miles wondered if she was another victim, then realized she was something else entirely. She was something much, much worse.

Relying too much on their agent delivering on his promise had been a grave mistake. That reliance had made Miles sloppy and far less organized than he should have been. Sure, he'd drafted surveillance schedules and had gotten people on board with his backup plan, but that was the problem. He'd treated it as if it were merely a contingency and not the most likely outcome—and that was inexcusable.

The room was full of people Miles had to trust, and that trust weighed heavily on him. And he couldn't afford to be careless again. The lives of his friends were too precious to gamble on a hope that everything would turn out fine. If they weren't at their best, if they didn't fight like hell to stay safe, none of them would make it out alive.

Neither his magic nor his short weapons were well suited for fighting dozens of opponents that he needed to keep at arm's length. Of course, he couldn't have predicted that hundreds of spiders would be what Sylas attacked them with, but even so, it was awful planning on his behalf.

Miles reached down and pulled a longer dagger from its ankle sheath, gripping it firmly in his left hand. In his right, he still held the push dagger he had used while the creatures were asleep—but they were waking now. At least with the shorter blade, there was some comfort: if the spiders bit, their fangs were just as likely to strike his prosthetic as his actual arm.

Determined to make the most of his abilities, he sent a surge of magic through his muscles, quickening his movements while keeping one eye on Esme. He wielded both blades simultaneously as he cut through the swarm. But power always demanded its price, and he could feel the approaching debt with every magical push.

Out of the corner of his eye, he saw Esme hesitate. His heart didn't just lurch when she paused—it stopped, suspended in a moment of pure terror. He couldn't lose her. Not here. Not now.

But then the way she nodded and the eclipsing of her eyes told him that she wasn't hesitating; she was calling up a conjuration. With a second push of magic, he cast a protective shield around her, holding off her attackers while she summoned her minions.

He couldn't wait to see the destruction she would unleash upon them.

And what of himself? He could already feel the strain on his body from pushing his magic to its limits. There was no room for error. Preparation wasn't just about having the right weapons or magical skills—it was about the psychological resilience to stand when everything seemed hopeless.

As he moved to face off with the rising Jorōgumo mother, he had to ask: were they prepared for what might happen if one of them failed?

CHAPTER THIRTY-SEVEN

But That's Not What Ships Are For

Gwyn

By all the magic... A living carpet of murderous beasts separated him from the greatest danger in the room. Gwyn watched in disbelief as ten-foot-long spider legs emerged from the woman's back. He had witnessed much evil, but this would rank among the most disturbing.

Gwyn breathed a small sigh of relief when Miles, the closest to her, stepped closer still to address her threat. He trusted Miles to keep her occupied until he, or one of their many allies, could assist. Gwyn's main strategy, perhaps his only effective one, was to remain with Abigail and eliminate as many of the smaller spiders as possible. Beyond that, there wasn't much more he could do than cut them down with slashes and stabs now that they were awake.

The sheer number of them, combined with their erratic movements, made crafting a battle strategy impossible. He'd never faced anything like this before. The largest spider he'd seen in his life was no bigger than a child's hand. These were the size of small dogs. Finn was burning through them with his fire, but Gwyn doubted that his own precision was equal to the leprechaun's, so he would rely primarily on the strength of his arm.

"Abigail, please keep your back to me."

Her breathing was heavier than usual. "No argument here."

Behind him, he could hear her doing much the same as he was: relentlessly lunging and stabbing. The spiders were still sluggish and disoriented from the mage's earlier control, but Gwyn knew they wouldn't stay that way for long. Except for her growing limbs extending from her back, their mother was almost motionless. Miles battled through the throng to get to her.

"I need to get to the furniture over there," Gwyn said, nodding toward an antique table where he'd hidden his crossbow.

They were only about twenty feet away, but the mass of spiders made it feel farther. His crossbow could be a game-changer, giving him a ranged option if any of his allies were ambushed.

"You brought the fox-killer, didn't you?" Abby emitted a soft snort of amusement, teasing him again.

He winced at the reminder. He'd already apologized for that. The notion of preserving beasts of little commercial value was entirely unfamiliar to him. He thought he was presenting his dearest friend with a gorgeous fur. Something a lady from his time would fairly swoon over. Instead, he'd acquired a valuable lesson, in a manner of speaking.

"Okay, let's go," she said, her feet already moving. "I need something to enchant."

Spiders swarmed around them, but Gwyn cast a sheet of fire to ensure the safety of her advance. The flames barely kissed the floor; just enough to keep Abigail safe without causing damage. She couldn't perform her magic effectively if she had to continue kicking and stabbing. She was most effective as a ranged combatant. He needed to get her up and out of the midst of battle.

Gwyn had a choice. He could attempt to walk through the mists of magic to take the Jorōgumo mother by surprise with the edge of his blade. However, he wasn't confident that plan would work, and it might even endanger him. Or, he could place Abigail in a safer, more effective spot.

"No, we're taking the faster way."

Abby

Abby wished she had more than just one knife as she fought the spiders off, but she had to make do. Kicking them away worked. But one after another, they filled the gaps left by their fallen comrades. She had a hunch that her hot hands spell would be effective against them, but she was scared their biting fangs would still break through her short-range heat barrier.

After Gwyn's initial burst of fire subsided, the approaching spiders gradually became less wary. She'd expected to have to fight the entire way to Gwyn's crossbow, but he'd delivered them there with a bit of magic instead. It was her second time experiencing a mist-walking journey, and she hoped it wouldn't be her last. She definitely had to learn how to do that.

As soon as they arrived at the cabinet, Gwyn spun to face the oncoming spiders and Abby opened the only door that appeared large enough to store his crossbow within and found it immediately. As soon as she stood with her prize, Gwyn unleashed a second burst of flames all around them. He was clearly tiring, but he was controlling the flow of his magic better than when they'd fought the Dullahan. Maybe some of his memory *was* coming back...

After handing the crossbow over, she found herself being lifted by her hips and placed on top of the cabinet. At first, she bristled, thinking he doubted her abilities. But then she saw she had a clear path above the horde of spiders to the bar from where she stood.

"I'm going to leapfrog over to the bar," she told him.

The spiders had demonstrated their ability to scale walls, but the bar offered a wider range of objects for her to enchant and reaching it wouldn't be time-consuming.

Gwyn gave a brief nod, his focus split between fighting and watching her out of the corner of his eye.

Abby leaped onto a nearby barrel that was acting as a cocktail table. Barely pausing in her movement, she reached down and imbued it with a bit of her enchanting magic.

Once she made it to the bar, a spider scuttled up the side. She kicked it off. From her elevated position, she saw Colin had teamed up with Will. They had twice the number of spiders around them than anyone else in the room. That indicated that the folklore was true—Jorōgumo preferred hunting men.

Their mother was showing the same proclivity. Her eyes locked on Miles, the closest male, who was cutting through the throngs of baby spiders to get to her. Abby had to believe that Miles had a plan because she didn't like how exhausted

Colin already looked. He would be the first to receive some help—other than what Will was already giving him by swinging a chair around like he was a madman.

Will

Surrounded, Will could only hope that his weakness for a well-dressed man would ultimately be worth it. None of his personality traits were well suited for this. But he'd surprised himself once by tackling the nøkk with zero forethought. He could do it again.

So he did his best with what he had. Will grabbed a chair and started swinging. He swung wildly, not with grace, but with enough force to get the job done. Colin stayed with him, back against his, slicing and dicing with the skill of a real-life ninja. If Will hadn't been literally fighting to stay alive, it would have been the hottest thing he'd ever seen.

To their right, the sound of a glass shattering grabbed Will's attention. Then another. Thank the gods he'd not worn his soft-soled shoes. Glancing up, he saw Abby on the bar, hurling glasses, one after another, at the approaching spiders.

"Abby! We need to be able to move! What are you doing?" he shouted.

She kicked out with one booted foot, sending a spider body flying off the bar.

"I know! Arms in!" she called back.

Will didn't understand, but Colin reacted right away, suggesting some sibling mind reading. Colin kicked away the nearest spider, its fragile body sailing through the air before hitting the ground with a soft thud. He surprised Will by wrapping him in a tight bear hug. *What the…?*

Then the glass shards scattered around them rose from the floor and began to spin rapidly. Abby had conjured a tornado of broken glass that tore through the surrounding spiders. She must have enchanted the glasses beforehand, using her telekinesis to wield them as weapons. Gods above and below, he never wanted to see Abby in a bar fight.

Her face was tense when Will stopped staring at the glass tornado to look up at her. With her focus elsewhere, she failed to notice the spider creeping dangerously close to her leg once more. Before anyone could warn her, a crossbow bolt struck the spider, pinning it to the bar top. Will looked over to see Gwyn, sword in one hand, crossbow in the other.

From his relative safety inside the eye of the swirling vortex of glass, Will could see Miles dart under the mama spider's lightning-fast assault. The disgusting, spidery legs extending from her back lashed out, their barbed tips aimed at him. Miles was nearly as quick as she was, his shield deflecting most blows with a satisfying thwump.

Abby sustained the glass tornado for a solid minute as the numbers of the surrounding dead piled up. But the destructive vortex of debris started to slow, and Will realized what that meant: Abby was tiring.

From his back, Will could feel the sound reverberate from Colin's lungs when he shouted, "Abby! Stop!"

As the tornado faded, Esme's summoned trolls arrived, their thunderous crashes announcing their entry into the battle.

Miles

The Jorōgumo yōkai moved unnaturally fast, her feet scraping against the ferry's wooden floors as the spider legs lifted her human body off the ground. She surged forward on eight legs, each strike narrowly missing Miles as he twisted and ducked.

He was still wearing his tuxedo jacket, and sweat was already pouring down his face. Breaths coming quickly, he countered again and again. Arm up barely in time, a clang echoed as chitinous barb met dagger.

That last hit had been too close, penetrating his shield. Shifting low, Miles swept at her underbelly. She twisted upward, bending impossibly to counter with a downward strike. With a desperate heave, he barely strengthened his shield in time to block. The smooth hardwood floor offered no resistance as his feet skidded, the force of the impact driving him back.

"Drop the shield!" Esme yelled.

He hesitated only briefly. Despite his worry, he had to trust that she had good reason. He felt immediate relief at the reduction in his magic output.

As Miles moved to meet the yōkai's next move, a huge gray arm swung forward and caught the blow in his place. It was one of Esme's trolls.

A second troll stepped forward, flanking Miles. The woman he loved was a saint.

Undeterred, the Jorōgumo matriarch struck out at both trolls with her two front spider legs. Esme's infernal magic had altered the trolls so drastically that he could no longer distinguish between them. Instead of the usual yellow and humanoid troll form, these were gray, had spikes covering their joints, and possessed a gorilla-like, muscled, and stooped physique. The newer addition was unable to dodge the blow in time. Miles watched as magic rippled and faded slightly where the blow landed.

The next frantic thirty seconds proved that Esme was using these trolls as a shield for him. Any approaching baby spider was swiftly crushed underfoot. Every blow intended for Miles was stopped. She was giving him a chance to make his move.

Miles moved with practiced speed, driving his dagger into the matriarch's leg. With a hiss, the Jorōgumo's mouth stretched, revealing monstrous mandibles that folded out of her mouth like the spider legs had out of her back.

His body flooded with adrenaline as eight legs sent her soaring toward the ceiling. A menacing click echoed as her legs briefly struck the overhead beams. In a blur, she launched herself at Miles again, this time from above, fangs reaching.

Fuck.

Esme

It almost felt like too much to forgive. Esme's anger and hurt that Sylas had actually gone through with his attack after all they'd been through fueled her magic.

After sending George and Tom to protect Miles, she had Bert lift her onto his shoulders, carefully avoiding the spikes. Even though her head scraped the low ceiling, she ordered him to start stomping. Held away from the majority of the baby spiders, she could focus on her connection with her conjurations.

From her higher vantage point, Esme could see that Finn and Katia were still chipping away at their opponents. She was worried about the leprechaun. The strain of using so much magic was causing his face to droop. Gwyn was standing on a cabinet, fox-killer in hand, while Abby fended off spiders from the bar. Will and Colin were using the pile of corpses around them from Abby's glass tornado as a makeshift protective bulwark.

Esme could feel all three of her conjurations taking bite after bite from the fang-like pincers at the spiders' mouths. At this rate, they would lose corporeal stability quickly. Despite only practicing it in training, she might need to try magically reinforcing them on the fly.

A sudden movement—a streak of black hair and legs darting toward the ceiling—caught her eye.

She had always been confident in Miles' abilities. He was the protector, the healer—never the one in need. But then she saw him, a lone man silhouetted against the looming shadow of the monster, bracing himself for impact. Angry with herself for not doing more, she increased the power she provided to Tom and George. Every ounce of her attention went into holding her trolls in place to take the blow for him.

The Jorōgumo mother's body slammed down before Esme could take two steps in Miles' direction. And through her trolls she could sense what had happened before seeing it.

Her trolls had successfully absorbed most of the impact. Under her guidance, they staggered up to their feet, tossing the malevolent who was still trying to attack Miles several feet through the air.

Miles had been bitten.

Panicked, barely knowing what she was doing, Esme leaped off Bert's shoulders. Eyes only for him, she saw Miles as he raised his remaining dagger, ready for her next attack, defiant despite the blood soaking through his now torn shirt.

Others must have been watching too, because Finn and Katia arrived first. Flames curled from Finn's hands as he hurled a wave of fire into the swarm of baby spiders. Katia, grim-faced and tight-lipped, persistently swept away any that got too close.

With a brief nod of thanks, Esme reinforced her faltering trolls with more infernal magic, the conjured forms solidifying just in time to block another deadly strike from the mother. Empowered, their mouths became so crowded with fangs they could barely close them and their eyes turned a sinister red with blackened sclera.

Her conjurations fought on, protecting her, Katia, and Finn as the three of them went to Miles. She could feel that George and Tom were almost gone. As Miles tried to stand to meet the malevolent again, she saw that his legs were no longer moving properly.

Then a god-forsaken roar ripped out of Bert. Esme's conjurations were completely silent unless she created the illusion for it.

But she hadn't.

Esme could feel it. Her troll's odd behavior reflected how close she was to losing herself to the insanity of her demonic blood being so soaked with infernal power.

She couldn't lose control again. Not like when... Juniper...

Think.

But she couldn't, not clearly. Only Tom and George were losing stability more rapidly than her.

She had to get Miles out of the room. He couldn't take another bite. She ordered Bert to fetch Miles, then sent them rushing through the sliding doors to the outer deck. There, Bert would protect Miles from any stray spiders that ventured into the cold.

Overwhelmed and on the verge of losing herself, Esme concentrated her rage into summoning her blade as she charged back into the fray. She would be Miles' first line of defense.

Her sword returned to her hands as quickly as ever. But like her trolls, it had been twisted by the infernal power leaking through her emotions and into her casting. Its once-smooth edge was now serrated like a monster's teeth, a twin to the blade from her first Alp-induced nightmare.

Right then, she was beyond caring exactly what its transformation meant; beyond caring that her infernal-infused trolls matched those of her dreams.

She swung the sword anyway.

A heavy realization that was warm like a thick wool blanket, yet as weighty as lead, was all that anchored her to reality. Why had she held back those words, letting them build up inside her until they felt like... *this*? Like she might be too late to say the one thing that living demanded.

The mantra, repeated silently with each swing, was a lifeline, a tangible connection to reality against the pull of the infernal. She loved Miles. There was no denying it.

Gwyn

As the leprechaun unleashed another wave of fire on the dwindling number of baby spiders, the matriarch charged toward Gwyn on spiked legs. Outpacing Finn's retreat, the mother lunged, venomous limbs slicing through smoke and heat, sending him reeling back toward a broken bar stool.

Barely thinking about the intelligence of his decision, Gwyn mist walked for a second time in one evening. His split-second decision was justified the instant his blade sliced all the way through her front leg. The same horrifying fangs that had injured Miles struck out at Gwyn as he pushed Finn and Katia out of the way.

"Get back!" Gwyn barked as he stepped into Miles' place. Finn wisely vanished, carrying Katia away through the mists of magic. Gwyn's brief glimpse of the succubus proved that she'd earned her battlefield scars that night. Her legs were badly bitten; the pain must have been excruciating.

Enraged by the loss of her limb, the Jorōgumo mother spat venom at Gwyn, the glob hissing as it hit his arm. Gwyn winced, but pressed forward. Esmeralda's continued training sessions had allowed him to keep his swordsmanship sharp. The next strike of an uninjured leg met his blade. The baby spiders were even fewer now.

With a bow in one hand and his sword in the other, Gwyn felt more like himself than he had in ages. He needed more of this. More of the Gwyn from before. As he fought, a smile never left his face.

The malevolent crouched low, her legs poised ready to leap again to the ceiling. Gwyn had learned from the devastating aftermath the last time she tried that move. Hoping to distract her from her aim, Gwyn threw a jet of pyromantic fire in her direction.

She jerked back. The stench of burned flesh filled his nostrils. Gwyn had nearly depleted his magic, but he could still muster one final effort. The fire had worked, but he needed to be more careful inside this wooden structure. Having seen firsthand the devastation caused by fire countless times, he was cautious with his power.

Having blocked the malevolent from completing her devastating leap, Gwyn prepared a safer but more magically draining electrical surge. Just as he was about to unleash the magic on her, the matriarch lurched backward a second time. A huge barrel, nearly half his height, slammed into her chest, sending her sprawling a dozen feet back.

Gwyn didn't pause to think. He raised his crossbow, aimed, and loosed. The first shot took her in the chest. Reload. He shot again.

As the matriarch tried to stand, Gwyn's second bolt pierced the space between her fangs. She fell silently to the floor.

His allies were safe. Away from the fray, Finn stood protectively over Katia, who had collapsed due to the pain of her injuries. Back to back and sporting only minor injuries, Will and Colin killed each spider as they approached. Abigail stood tall above them all. Her swift thinking had allowed Gwyn to take the fatal shot.

Esmeralda's trolls were nowhere to be seen. Only she prowled the room, seeking death after death with her blade. Although her form lacked polish, the intensity she brought to her movements evoked memories of his lost friend, Elena.

In his youth, Christianity was still a young religion, but Gwyn had already been educated about its doctrines and stories. Now, with certainty, he could say Esmeralda looked like a vengeful angel of death. Her strikes were merciless as she cut through the remaining spiders. His student was learning the dance macabre.

Abigail noticed, too. She shot Gwyn a concerned look. He mouthed, "Not yet." Their demoness wasn't safe to approach at the moment.

Abigail nodded emphatically, her eyes widening in agreement.

None of them were truly threatened by the remaining spiders. This frenzy she was in had to end.

"Esmeralda!" Gwyn's voice was commanding, meant to cut through the chaos of the battlefield. "To Miles!"

She looked at him, eyes black as coal, but didn't truly see him. Then she sprinted out the door.

CHAPTER THIRTY-EIGHT

FEVER DREAM

Miles

His mind was plagued by yet another dream, one that pulled him into Nudd's world—if Gwyn was to be believed. Just like every other time, he was thrown into the midst of a story without warning.

Nudd, or rather the version of him that haunted Miles' dreams, feigned sleep atop a feasting table, his breath unnaturally even, limbs limp as though his body wasn't experiencing the tension swirling within. Miles felt the pulse of the king's concealed alertness thrum in his chest as if it were his own heartbeat, every twitch of the king's fingers echoing through his own nerves.

With folded arms, he discreetly peeked, his eyes scanning the room for something. The action was so out of character for him that Miles mentally straightened, his curiosity piqued.

The room looked the same as it had so many times before. Stone walls, held together with clay, a thatched ceiling, and a long firepit at the center. Nudd sat upon a raised dais at one end of the fire.

On his right, Gwyn, looking the same as he had in the last dream, sat on his right, while a woman about Gwyn's age sat on his left. Yet, aside from himself, every soul seemed to be asleep. Most had fallen where they sat, their heads resting on the table. Some people were on the floor in uncomfortable positions, either falling straight backward or slumping to the side.

It wasn't until he caught sight of movement that Miles realized why Nudd was paying such rapt, secretive attention to the room of sleeping party-goers. In the flickering torchlight, a figure shifted near the room's entrance. It was unmistakably masculine. Magic surrounded the intruder, saturating the air and clinging to his every movement. The intruder's glamor was impenetrable, even to the king's sight. Still, Miles could feel the suspicion, maybe even a hint of familiarity, rise within Nudd.

With each passing second, the intruder's gaze remained locked on the high table, as if searching for any sign of danger that might come from there. Still, Nudd chose not to take action. After experiencing the king's violent victory in this same room in a previous dream, Miles was perplexed at his inaction now. As a reluctant passenger, he could only wait and observe inside his host.

After the intruder seemed satisfied that those on the dais were truly asleep, he first inspected the sleeping party-goers nearest the doors. He paused occasionally, hovering his hand over certain individuals as though searching for something. Then, bolder, he moved deeper into the room.

Miles felt the king's sword hand clench at the open air as the man neared the dais, yet still Nudd did not act. Then the intruder's attention abruptly shifted to the guards' table. The sharp contrast of golden-brown hair intricately braided like that of any lady at court against the much darker leather of her armor was a striking sight. It had to be Elena—if Gwyn's story was true.

The intruder's attention lingered on the guardswoman, his breath turning shallow, predatory, as though tasting her essence on the air. Through his bond with the king, Miles sensed the intruder had detected Nudd's magic on her.

Carefully, the intruder reached out, fingers brushing a braid of her hair, rolling it between his fingers like a hunter savoring a kill before the strike. Miles sensed the king's barely contained agitation, yet he remained motionless to avoid arousing suspicion. The moment the intruder's fingers made contact with the skin of her neck, the king erupted from his spot, sword in hand.

Miles awoke with a start, his hand instinctively reaching for a sword that wasn't there, the sharp clang of steel still ringing in his ears. For a moment, the world was blurred. The flicker of torchlight from Nudd's hall overlapped with the muted gray of the night. The cold biting into his skin grounded him in reality, but the weight of the sword that should've been in his hand still lingered, as though the dream was trying to leave something behind.

Above him, the sky was a canvas of gray, lit by the city lights as snowflakes drifted down onto his face. It was peaceful; quiet. Soon, footsteps drew near.

Esme's presence washed over him like a distant echo of warmth, because his body refused to respond. Her face hovered above him, her eyes as black as the night sky without clouds. As he tried to lift his hand toward her, Miles found he couldn't move. The realization should have alarmed him, but it didn't. He could only watch as her eyes slowly returned to their usual violet.

She checked his pulse and breathing, then shook him lightly. As far as Miles could tell, it was only the two of them out on the deck. Through muffled ears he heard her say, "Rhun... your eyes are open. Talk to me."

She lowered her voice slightly, leaning in to hug him briefly, whispering, "When I came over, you were glowing the color of your magic all over—not just your hands. Please, *please*, talk to me."

Her voice was breaking down from strain or emotion. He didn't know.

His head ached horribly and his body felt like lead, every muscle frozen, leaving him achingly aware of Esme's proximity yet unable to reach for her. Had Miles had the ability to scream, he probably would have; the pressure behind his eyes made it feel like his head was primed to explode.

Then all at once, when he thought he might pass out from the pain, the pressure moved from his brain to his eyes. As the pain lessened, he felt a wetness on his cheeks as tears started to flow from the outer corner of his eyes.

Except Miles wasn't crying.

Esme's expression changed to one of horror. Her head whipped toward the boat's interior. She screamed, "Holy gods, Abby, come!"

She tore open the top of his shirt, sending the top button flying. Miles felt her hands searching, searching frantically. But he already knew that she would find nothing. He was healed. *But how?*

With the liquid now streaming down his face, Miles discovered he could feel his body again. Summoning every ounce of his willpower, he managed to just barely lift a hand to wipe his eyes. His fingers came away black. Esme looked back down at him, the alarmed look on her face likely mirroring his own.

The only logical explanation was that his body, or his magic, had pushed the venom out through his tear ducts. The weight of his trembling hand, slick with black venom and filth, became unbearable, so he let it fall to his side.

Tears—thankfully normal—welled in Esme's eyes. Her hands carefully cradled his head, supporting its weight because he couldn't quite do it for himself.

"Miles, can you hear me?" Her words came out as a broken whisper. "I'm so sorry. Gods, I've been so scared, but watching you nearly die today..." Her voice cracked all the way then.

"I love you too," she breathed, leaning down close enough that he could count her eyelashes. "And not just because you're brave or amazing in bed." A soft laugh escaped her lips, though her eyes never left his face. "It's the way you see through the world's darkness and yet, somehow, your moral compass never wavers. You're this monolith of stability when I'm drowning in disorder. And even when I am, you consistently support me. Miles, I need you. You're my home now. No, you're not just my home—you're my north star, my certainty in the chaos. And I thought... I thought I was about to watch my world end. Please, say something. Anything."

Hell, what a thing to hear when he could barely move and was covered in filth. They were a mess—her hair was matted with spider ichor, his clothes with his own blood, and both of them probably reeked. All he wanted was to hold her and never let go.

Esme was one thing when pushed—brutally, unapologetically, herself. There was something so beautifully Esme about confessing her love while they were at their worst, no pretenses possible, nothing to hide behind. Two people, stripped bare in the aftermath of chaos. If only his damn body would cooperate so he could show her exactly how much those words meant to him.

He reached up with his cleaner prosthetic and slid his knuckles along the side of her face. Esme's eyes fluttered closed at his touch, and she leaned into his hand, pressing her cheek against the cold metal as if it were the most natural thing in the world. One tear rolled down her cheek, retracing the path of his touch.

His power of speech finally returned. "Lovely... I'm glad... it was me." He pointed to the stain the venom had made on his shirt. He longed to kiss her, to express far more, but his body was still slow to obey.

She whispered back, looking pointedly at the stains, "The glowing... you think..."

Realization dawned on her face as the reality of what happened to him sunk in. They stared at each other, both unable to voice the impossible thing they'd experienced. Something told him he should be dead, yet he still lived. He should have been drained, hollowed, and spent from the self-healing following the fight. Yet even if his body was still slow to respond to his commands, he could feel a well of energy inside him he hadn't known was there.

His magic had always obeyed his will, but it had just acted beyond his control, without warning, without permission, knitting his wounds and purging toxins from his body. His magic had moved on its own. Not for the first time, it scared him.

Lost in the space between the dreamscape Esme's confession of love had created and the nightmare of losing control over his magic, Miles barely registered the approaching footsteps. Looking over, he breathed a sigh of relief, seeing that everyone seemed largely alright. Miles propped himself up on one elbow, signaling to Abby as she ran to his side that he didn't require assistance.

Before the group made it all the way, a vibrant streak of red and gray appeared in the air between them. Then the sound—a heavy thud and wet squelching—of the object hitting the ferry's deck twisted Miles' stomach into a knot.

The red was a trail of blood. The gray was the vacant eyes of Sylas' decapitated head staring up at him accusingly. Beside him, Esme's breath hitched—a tiny sound in the vast silence that followed the thud. Miles reached for her without thinking, pulling her back as if distance could somehow make this horror less real. Miles had seen death, too much of it, but he hadn't been prepared to shield her from this one.

Esme screamed.

Miles grabbed her and pulled her back again as she lunged forward, trying to either confirm her suspicions about the identity of the head, touch it, or gods knew what. He spun her away from the sight, rolling on the deck of the boat with her in his arms.

That bloody bastard had made his delivery dramatic, that was for certain. And he'd deliberately waited until after the spiders had been cleared out before doing it. Miles had hoped that their help would leave the body wherever Sylas had been hiding, allowing them to stage the area for "discovery." Those hopes were now irreparably dashed.

His eyes met Gwyn's, who was holding Abby in much the same way. The same realization passed between them: there was no escaping the consequences of their choices now.

Ten feet away, Will, Colin, Finn, and Katia stood in horrified silence, yet still wary. As far as anyone knew, the fight might not be over. They waited for the other shoe to drop, taking turns not looking at the twisted face of the man they'd once known staring blankly up at them.

They waited and waited.

"Finn," Miles urged without finishing his thought.

The leprechaun pursed his lips and removed his coat. It was too small to cover the outstretched antlers, but served as a temporary death shroud for the leshy.

As Esme trembled, Miles still waited for the rogue to show up, gloating about his success in killing Sylas. But the moment never happened.

Esme

"Come, come on, lovely."

Miles had just been injected with venom that probably should have left him in a coma or worse, and he was already on his feet, supporting her.

She felt Miles' arms lifting her, pulling her away from Sylas, but it was as though she was only half there. The shock wasn't like the anger she always kept hidden. This wasn't like her parents' deaths, where she hadn't seen the bodies. This was a brutal, unforgiving atrocity dumped at her feet.

She was shaking all over. Walking without consciously willing her legs to move, she asked, "Was that Sylas?"

Miles inhaled deeply before answering. "I think so."

"What happened?" She didn't turn to look at him, too focused on putting one foot in front of the other.

He remained quiet while her legs moved her body. Until they didn't.

"Come on, lovely," he urged again, his hand resting low on her back, gently massaging.

Her feet moved once more, halting only when they rounded the corner of the boat. The sight of Sitkum, without his glamor, jolted her back to reality. He was sitting at the end of the dock, cradling Grace's limp body across his lap. One hand supported her head while the other fumbled with a cell phone.

The sasquatch looked up as they approached. "Esme! You're okay!"

Even though he stayed in the same place, holding Grace, his shoulders eased, his face relaxing. Esme's anxiety roared back to life as she looked down at Grace. The teenager—the young woman now, really—looked pale, but appeared to be breathing steadily.

Miles squeezed Esme's hand and stepped over to them. Sitkum lifted Grace's head for him to inspect. "I think she just passed out from using too much magic."

"I agree," Miles said, then turned to Esme. "Is that her phone? Esme, should we call her father to come pick her up? Or should we have Jacob brief her first?"

Watching Miles take charge felt like a bucket of cold water being splashed on her face. She knew Sitkum and Grace; they were her responsibility, not his. She pushed down all the horrible emotions that were trying to choke her and concentrated on the present instead of things that couldn't be changed. Esme found her voice. "Her dad."

Then a thought struck her. The spiders hadn't fazed Sitkum in the slightest. Instead of freezing in shock like most people would have, he sprang into action and started fighting.

"Are you okay, Sitkum?" she asked, hoping he caught the subtext of her question.

"I'm fine, Esme. They couldn't get through my fur."

She must have stared at him a bit too long because he added, "The People have always known about the malevolents, Esme. We've always fought them."

"Oh..." Well, she doubly understood why sasquatch drank for free in Jacob's bar now.

Drained and sickened by the night's events, Esme wanted nothing more than to go home. But duty called. She surveyed everyone who had fought alongside her and realized that, of them all, Katia was the most covered in blood.

"Gods, Katia, do we need to call an ambulance?" Esme's shrill voice made every head turn to the succubus, who was leaning on Finn. After the fighting and healing, she didn't think Miles was in any shape to heal her.

Katia lifted the hem of her skirt and surveyed her legs. She winced, and except for Miles, everyone else winced with her. "I... I'll be okay."

What the...? There were massive gouges in both of her calves and one thigh. She definitely needed stitches; probably staples.

Katia scoffed dismissively, in a unique blend of Russian accent and Chinese mannerisms, gazing at the gore on her body. "The wounds will seal overnight. I just need a shower and a booty call... Or three tomorrow."

Finn sighed, and Esme shook her head, blinking rapidly. It took her fatigued mind a long moment to remember that Katia had said that she could heal rapidly if she fed. Everyone else would be fine with a bit of cleaning and minor first aid.

Medical problems out of the way, she called Alan Kim, asking him to come pick up Grace because his daughter had also passed out from magical exhaustion. Returning to the ferry, she found a single untouched piece of paper and carefully wrote a note, tucking it under Grace's wrist, hidden beneath her hair tie. The note read:

> *The monsters must remain a secret for everyone's sake. Talk to me first. Thank you.*

CHAPTER THIRTY-NINE
ARRANGING MURDER

Miles

Days Before the Solstice Gala

"You want to kill the leshy without the women knowing?" Gwyn asked, pushing aside a tray of drugged muffins. He displayed neither surprise nor disgust at the idea.

Miles nodded silently. Even with the lingering tension, he was attempting to set aside the threats. The less he said, the better chance there was that both of them could leave the house alive. Plus, the thought of Gwyn getting in trouble with Abby or Esme for referring to them as "the women" was amusing.

Miles had stopped questioning whether doing what was necessary was the same as doing what was right far too early in life. But Esme's feelings about the outcome of this particular decision had cast a shadow, darkening the morally ambiguous space he usually operated in.

"Leshies are territorial. Why do we not simply go to his forest and execute him there?" Gwyn suggested.

"He's abandoned his territory. We don't know where he is now."

Gwyn's eyebrows furrowed, a hint of surprise flashing across his face as he processed the irregularity of Sylas' behavior.

"You mentioned that beings of magic can change based on how they use it. Can Sylas be saved?" Miles asked.

Gwyn refrained from gloating about having the answers when Miles didn't. The choice earned a small measure of grudging respect from him.

Gwyn leaned on the table, hand to chin, before replying. "Let me make sure I understand correctly. Abigail says she's known the leshy since childhood and he helped train her. Esmeralda has a strong, almost familial bond with him?"

Miles released his grip on the knife he was still holding, placing it on the table between them and then shoving it off to the side, mirroring what Gwyn had done with the muffin tray. Gwyn's eyes tracked every move.

"For over ten years," Miles confirmed.

At this, Gwyn's eyes read something uncomfortably close to compassion—for him or Esme, he didn't know. "Then the man she knew is gone. He is feral. I would not doubt that his body has transformed as well."

Miles' suspicions were confirmed. Esme and Abby's affection for the creature Sylas had changed into was keeping them from seeing the reality of the situation. The night after Leon dispelled the magic from Jacob, Esme had spent hours devising ways to save Sylas. Miles had doubts about the possibility of rehabilitation at that point, but he was willing to try it for her. He had listened, nodded, and hinted a few times it might not be possible, but she'd been adamant. Her heart had been broken too many times, and he wasn't eager to break it again.

Gwyn leaned back in his chair. "How would we do it? Jacob?"

He seemed so relaxed suddenly. Maybe planning a murder helped Gwyn unwind.

Miles had a plan to address multiple problems. "Not Jacob. He's lying low to see if we can draw Sylas out if my plan doesn't work. We ask Leon to do it. Jacob has already agreed to the scheme, with money to back hiring him."

Gwyn's surprise was unmistakable. His chair creaked as he leaned forward, his eyes widening in disbelief. "Leon?"

"Why not? Everyone has a price, and he's shown that he's capable of advanced magic. He's openly declared his loyalty to those with demon blood, and now Sylas is threatening his kin."

Miles shrugged. Everything fit into place perfectly in his mind. He'd never imagined himself hiring a hitman, but this wasn't about what he wanted—it was about what needed to be done.

Gwyn shook his head, scratched the back of his neck, and blinked rapidly.

"You have reservations?" Miles asked.

"No... I am unsure if surprise is the right reaction to your constant dual nature."

Miles silently pleaded that he would avoid the "father" subject.

Miles reasoned aloud. "Esme said he's been watching us. We need to know why. We need to know more about his motives. If we can get him to handle Sylas for us, he'll be more likely to interact with us out in the open instead of taking us by surprise again. We can solve two problems at once without getting our hands dirty and without having 'the women' angry at us."

This was the best thing he could do for them, even if they never understood. Sometimes, the correct thing wasn't always the virtuous thing. Sometimes, it required going to dark places, making the choice, and living with the consequence. If it meant protecting Esme, and everyone else, then the trade-off for the mark on his soul would be worthwhile.

Miles leaned forward. "We can make it seem like one of the malevolents he's been using caused his death. Leon clearly wants to talk to you, so you're going to have to be the one to lure him. Are you in?"

Miles knew that Gwyn likely had his own reasons for wanting to get close to Leon. With the added benefit of exposing some of Gwyn's underlying intentions, this plan would actually tackle three of his problems at once.

Gwyn studied Miles' face for a long moment. His eyes were assessing, in a way that could either be challenging him to flinch or wondering at his own motives. His voice came out steady, assured when he finally answered, "Your idea is not bad. I'll do it."

Planning how they'd lure Leon into a conversation was simple. Now, the only thing that would be complicated was the outcome of his choices.

As Miles prepared to leave for Esme's, Gwyn inspected a muffin. "You baked these?"

Not receiving an answer, Gwyn suggested, "Let's keep one or two of these for when the leprechaun becomes unbearable."

Was that a joke from Gwyn? He appeared serious, making it difficult to tell, so Miles replied, "Freezing should work."

Gwyn

Gwyn went to the library where they'd first met Leon with a sign that read "come talk to me" on it in Brythonic.

He scribbled the phrase in his mother tongue on a piece of paper, folding it into a small triangle tent, and set it on the table in front of him. Then he settled in with a few books he'd been reading the last time.

Two hours passed before Leon finally sat down, clumsily plopping himself into the chair in front of him. Now that Gwyn knew his carelessness was a performance, he wondered if his ever-chipper, eager attitude was as well.

"Yo, what's up, little bro?" Leon greeted him, sunshine in his voice.

But Gwyn was the gloom of a cloudy winter morning. "I am not your brother."

Leon rolled his eyes, a gesture Gwyn had seen Will do countless times. "You asked me to come here," Leon said, pointing at the sign. "I was gonna keep my distance for a while, let tempers cool, but... How can I help?"

The man carried himself with the swagger of a traveling merchant, always ready with a smile and waiting palms. It irritated Gwyn to no end. "You assume we want your help?"

Leon flashed a brilliant smile, revealing a set of perfectly aligned, pearly white teeth. Not bothering to speak quietly, he said, "I do. You want the leshy killed?"

Gwyn discreetly glanced around to see if anyone was paying attention to their conversation. He struggled to keep his voice low. "So, you knew about him? And you've just been watching, doing nothing?"

The stillness in Leon's posture spoke volumes. He sensed the tension, primed for a confrontation. With feigned nonchalance, Leon replied, "He's not my problem."

"But he's been hunting your kind," Gwyn pressed.

Leon shrugged dramatically—another performance. "So far, they've come out the other side alright."

"We can pay."

Leon tapped a rapid staccato on the table with his right hand. "I do appreciate money."

Gwyn lowered his voice, offering a small dose of honesty in hopes of gaining something in return. "There are valid reasons we can't handle it ourselves. Discretion is key. You said we could be allies. Let's work together. We can provide backup if needed."

Leon switched to Brythonic. "Backup? Would you send your father? Or my new begotten friend?" he asked, seeming a bit too hopeful.

Gwyn was surprised it took Leon this long to make the switch. "Involving him is not an option. Approach her, and the deal's off."

Leon reverted to English, his tone light once more. "I don't need backup. When do you need the job done?" There was no trace of doubt in his comment or question; it was delivered with absolute certainty.

With an expression meant for the card table, Gwyn asked for more than he thought he would get, "By the solstice."

Leon drummed the same rhythm on the table. "That's not a lot of time, my friend."

"And yet you already know so much. I assume that you already know where the leshy is hiding and exactly how you'd kill him if required."

Leon grinned. "True. I haven't been on a good hunt in so long. I'm expensive."

"How much?"

He wrote a number on the paper. "Get the clearance for this amount and your problem will be packaged up and delivered, all nice and pretty."

The amount wasn't outrageous, but it wasn't small either. Thankfully, Jacob had authorized Miles to use Corded Brotherhood funds for this job. It was doable.

"We can pay your fee."

"Great! Promise me one more thing, and I'll deliver evidence of the deed by the end of the solstice."

Gwyn considered. "I can give a promise without binding—perhaps. What would you ask of me?"

Leon switched back to Brythonic, a move that made Gwyn even more suspicious. Was he testing Gwyn with these verbal games? "After your deal with the Bastion is up, you'll listen to what I have to say. I meant it when I said we could be allies."

How did Leon know about his binding promise to Jacob? This stranger had too much mystery surrounding him.

Ultimately, it didn't matter—not yet. In order to resolve their current problems, Gwyn had to close this deal. The leshy tried to kill his friend and resorted to using mind magic on Abigail. Those were more than reason enough to murder the feral creature. That he planned a further attack on innocents only cemented the rectitude of them taking action.

"Deal." Listening cost Gwyn nothing. He didn't have to act on anything Leon said.

Leon beamed and handed over the account details for the payment.

Miles

Naturally, Miles watched the entire meeting. Gwyn just hadn't known he was there.

Throughout their conversation, Leon frequently switched languages. He either suspected someone was eavesdropping or he was toying with Gwyn. Though Miles loathed it, he couldn't hold Gwyn responsible for this because he was never the one who initiated the switches.

Learning that he could understand what they were saying in both languages was unsettling. Had his brain acquired Brythonic through over twenty years of dreaming in it? That was the most logical conclusion. Alternatively, was this part of the package with his healing magic and "god-blessed" status? He'd keep his knowledge of the language to himself for a while—he might need a card hidden up one sleeve.

Now Miles knew that Leon also thought he was Nudd Llaw Eraint. Did he think this because of the halo? As far as he knew, Gwyn hadn't revealed his ability to heal to Leon. Whatever accident of birth or chance had given him, Nudd's magic was certainly making his life interesting. Time would determine how he would handle this situation with Leon, be it with words or a dagger in the dark.

Other than that Leon was completely untrustworthy, Miles learned one thing from the meeting: Leon's magic was off. But not in the way he initially thought Esme's was when they first met, so this wasn't a begotten thing. Yet it also wasn't like malevolent magic. It was something else entirely. It felt... strange. Dirty was a word that came to mind.

For now, the Miles of the present would use the tool that circumstance had placed before him to protect those he loved, even if he dirtied himself in the process.

CHAPTER FORTY

END THE NIGHT

Miles

"I'm not here to be prescriptive," David Abington's voice exuded reassurance, "but I have noticed a pattern in how these things tend to play out."

Miles highly doubted that. If David wasn't trying to impose his will, he would've remained in London leading the Assembly there. Yet, here they were, leaving Miles with no other option than to listen.

The two huddled beneath the deck awning, shielding themselves from the increasing snowfall. Behind them, through the windows of the retired ferry that had hosted the Solstice Gala, nisse workers silently stacked the still leaking corpses of hundreds of Jorōgumo yōkai for disposal in the Sound. The tiny people had abandoned their traditional pointed red hats and red wool sweaters in favor of the personal protective suits the Corded Brotherhood provided for them.

The world around them had gone to hell, and still, David's appearance remained mostly untouched. Miles' old mentor was an unmistakably, as Miles thought of it at least, aristocratic English man with a tall and slender frame, silver hair, and an aristocratic aura that had become more pronounced with each passing year. Everything about him was flawless, except for the fact that he appeared to have aged significantly since Miles departed London.

In comparison, Miles was unkempt and disheveled. His tuxedo and hair were a mess, stained with yellowish-blue blood and dotted with black and yellow spider carapace. To add to that, his prosthetic right hand was on the verge of losing power. He'd used so much magic during the fight that he didn't want to risk using telekinesis to sustain it, even if he felt surprisingly good due to some accident of magic.

"You've always been clever, Miles," David continued. "I'm just offering you the benefit of my experience so you can avoid any more missteps like this one."

There it was. The jab. The reminder that Miles had failed. Again.

It had been barely a week since Sylas's attack on Jacob, and already the calls for new leadership were growing louder. Jacob's reported condition, a brain injury, and not the malevolent magic attack it had been, left a power vacuum. One that David had flown across the world to fill.

His arrival from London during the biggest social event of the year was nothing short of a spectacle. David hadn't been at the party long enough for Miles to introduce Esme to him, but he wasted no time returning when he heard word of the malevolent threat. People were already whispering that he might even give up his powerful, well-funded position in one of the world's top Assemblies just to help Seattle. At least, that's how most of the magical community saw it: David being a savior.

But Miles knew that there was more to David showing up than met the eye. David thrived at the top, reveling in the privileges and loopholes that power brought. The fact that he was pushing for Jacob's relatively minor leadership position didn't add up. David wanted something. And Miles would have no choice but to find out what, because David would figure out a way for Miles to get it for him. The temptation to shut David down immediately was strong, yet his ingrained instincts and years of submission forced Miles to hold back. David's voice still carried the weight of countless commands he'd once followed without question.

"I'm all ears." It was the most Miles could say without asking for David to put the leash back over his head, there and then.

He thought he'd left the worst parts of his life behind when he crossed the ocean to take a new job, but the misery he'd escaped had followed him. The man who had once ruled every aspect of his life, every flicker of his magic, now stood before him, trying to re-exert control.

"My boy, you're disgusting. Go home for the night. I'll be responsible for leading the cleanup going forward."

Miles had a feeling that the last part contained a touch of double meaning, but he would take the offered out. "I'll need the head frozen for burial in hemp fiber cloth, if possible," Miles said.

"The leshy?" David appeared surprised by Miles' request.

As if David didn't know all about Sylas before even stepping foot on the plane to Seattle.

"Yes. He has mourners."

"Jacob, or your demon-blooded girlfriend?" Proof positive that David knew everything, even if he pretended that he didn't.

"Yes," Miles replied, his tone leaving no room for discussion.

A flicker of unhappiness, there and gone again in an instant, appeared on David's face. It left Miles wondering if David was unhappy about the man he was trying to replace, Jacob, or the woman who'd replaced him.

Esme

Esme was freshly showered and changed into evening loungewear. Exhausted as she was, sleep wasn't an option. She wouldn't be able to rest until Miles came home. It wasn't only about the comfort of having him around: They needed to talk about what had happened to Sylas.

But, of course, Miles had stayed behind with Colin and Gwyn to arrange the cleanup. Jacob was supposed to come out of hiding to help piece together the details of what had transpired. But Esme wanted nothing to do with any of it. Boundaries were supposed to be healthy, right? And this was one she was setting for herself.

Seeing someone she loved torn apart was something she never wanted to experience again. The memory of Sylas's fate ate away at her. She could still see the blood, smell the iron tang in the air. How could she even begin to talk about it?

If the last year had taught her anything, it was that she could survive this. The only trick she needed to pull off was doing it without sinking into the darkness that always threatened to pull her back down. So, while she waited for Miles to return home, she busied herself by doing instead of feeling.

She spent the time tearing through closets, looking for a gift box large enough to hold a plastic sword. She'd saved plenty of gift bags and boxes over the years, and she knew one had to be hidden somewhere. It took nearly twenty frantic minutes before she finally found one the right size, along with a bag of tissue paper.

Grace deserved it. The plastic sword was a relic of the first time they'd met. Then, Grace had sent flocks of birds and waves of wildlife to make Esme's assigned task of speaking with her nearly impossible. To avoid hurting the animals, Esme had grabbed a toy sword left behind by a tourist to fend them off. When she'd finally convinced Grace to sit down for a heart to heart, the teenager had wanted the sword, but Esme refused. Now, after Grace's heroics with the spiders, she'd earned it—and then some.

Footsteps on the front porch made Esme jump. She darted to the door, her heart pounding, expecting to see Miles when she threw it open. Talking with him, being with him, was exactly what she needed to ground herself.

But the face that greeted her was not the comfort she sought. It was Leon.

She instinctively stepped back to get further behind her wards. She was alone, and he probably knew that. The numbness from the night's loss had somewhat muted her feelings, but her throat still tightened as a cold sweat prickled her skin. Leon had already proven that he was a powerful mage. His appearance at her house in the middle of the night pointed at something unsafe to her well-being going on.

"Hi," he greeted with a small wave. He wore a plain black jacket, dark jeans, and sneakers. His hair was wet, as if he'd just showered, and with the snow now steadily falling behind him, he had to be freezing.

"It's—" she touched her phone to bring the screen to life, "two in the morning." Her secondary emotion of anger was creeping into the spaces where her fear hadn't overcome her. Her pulse thudded in her ears, but she kept her voice steady. "What do you want, Leon?"

"Well, lovely," Leon said with a casual smile, "I came by to see if your boyfriend was happy with my job performance."

The way he persisted in calling her "lovely" like Miles always did grated on her nerves. It was made worse by the fact that he used the term of endearment with a knowing smile, fully aware of its significance to her.

Her frustration burst into life on her face. "I have a feeling you already know he isn't here."

"Actually, no. What is it with you all assuming I know way more than I do?"

Esme folded her arms, a smirk playing on her lips. "Ohh, I don't know, maybe it has something to do with all the stalker-ish information you keep dropping on us."

A smirk replaced his smile as he feigned curiosity. "Yeah, I was also kinda wondering how your boyfriend survived a fatal bite."

Fatal? Gods below, something hinky was definitely going on with Miles' magic. Whatever it was, she was thankful for it because it meant he would return home that night.

While she appreciated what Leon had done for Jacob, his constant caginess and showing up randomly were getting annoying. But she couldn't deny her curiosity: the information he had just dangled in front of her was too intriguing to resist. She couldn't help it. She took the bait. "What job?"

She stepped back even farther into the threshold, adding space between them. Leon smiled as his eyes roamed over the door frame.

"Your wards are impressive."

"Thanks. Not my work," she said, half-closing the door. "Now, answer the question, or we're done here. It's cold, I'm tired, and you're too... fishy."

Leon smirked, pride evident on his face. "The job? Being the hero of the hour, of course. The leshy." His tone implied that it should be obvious.

"You..." She struggled to maintain her ability to speak.

The slowly burning candle of anger that ultimately led to a stick of dynamite within her instantly fizzled out, to be replaced by shock. The words barely made it past the lump in her throat. Sylas was gone. Just like that... "You killed the leshy?"

Leon showed perfectly straight white teeth and used both hands to point at himself in a display of triumph that sickened her. "As requested."

Leon

"Leon" had planned this night with every detail calculated to exploit grief and a sense of false security. Sylas' death wasn't the endgame. It was merely his second step.

His first had been to ingratiate himself by "curing" Jacob of the malevolent magic he'd forced into the Archmage's mind while in the leshy's guise. Now, with the leshy actually gone, Leon had earned himself time—time to integrate deeper into their fragile alliances, study Esme and the others, and ensure Nudd remained blind to his true intentions.

Leon had given them exactly what they'd requested: nothing more, nothing less. His deal with Sylas had never precluded harm or death, and it certainly hadn't required him to act with honor. Dealing with the bereft had its advantages. Rash decisions born of grief were as predictable now as they had been fifteen hundred years ago, and Leon knew precisely how to exploit them.

Some might think a creature of Sylas' caliber deserved a more heroic end. But there was no glorious battle or epic confrontation. There was only a swift, ignominious execution. Leon had allowed the leshy to set up the attack on the ferry, then stalked through the mists of magic, borrowed strength reinforcing his body, to sever the twisted creature's head from its shoulders.

It had been anticlimactic—too swift, too clean. While he'd benefited financially from it, Leon had relinquished his opportunity at seizing the leshy's power with the swiftness of his death. But the anticlimax was by design. Any hesitation risked Sylas revealing truths Leon wasn't ready for the others to hear.

As Leon waited for the leshy to complete his work, he'd studied all of them in action as they fought. Leon noted the decline in Gwyn's power, mirroring his own in some ways, though Gwyn's reemergence into the modern world was still quite fresh compared to Leon's own. That was fortunate, as Leon preferred avoiding a confrontation with Gwyn should he regain his pre-ascension strength and side with his jailer.

Watching Nudd's fighting style, he was initially discouraged, wondering if he had chosen the wrong course. Was this "Miles" truly Nudd? Leon's uncertainty dissolved the moment he saw the golden glow purge the venom from his body. That moment alone was worth every delay, every measured step. He had waited, he had watched, and now, he was certain: he had far more in this group of mages than he had dared to hope for.

He probably could have ended it while Nudd lay on the deck of the ferry, unconscious. But he'd seen enough of Jacob's thoughts during their brief contact to know Esme probably possessed a skill—a dangerous, invaluable skill that her parents had tried for years to achieve but failed because of their magical specializations.

Leon wanted it.

He needed something from three of this group. But he needed to avoid two others. The first was the kind of dangerous that fooled you into thinking she was nothing more than a pretty face. Her harmless, beautiful facade hid a danger capable of destroying everything he'd worked for. As for the second one, that leprechaun was concealing something.

Years of experience had taught Leon to be cautious. The safest way forward was to avoid Nudd as much as he could while he went about his preparations. Only when Leon's plan was almost complete would Nudd realize the danger he presented.

People of this era had a saying: *history repeats itself*. Waking up in modern Hong Kong following his captivity, Leon resolved to prove that specific saying false by whatever means necessary.

By the time he reached Esme's porch, Leon had already begun the next phase of his plan. He carried no visible weapons, no physical reminders of Sylas' death, only the carefully constructed demeanor of a man who thought he had done right. He barely breathed, anticipating her response.

Seeing tears welling in her eyes, Leon realized he should give himself more credit. What he had done had been more than a simple assassination. He skillfully manipulated events, eliminating a dangerous ally of Nudd and triggering the unraveling of his remaining partnerships. His preparations had fooled his targets into requesting their own destruction.

Esme's reaction was immediate—a sharp intake of breath, a stagger backward. And yet she didn't slam the door. She didn't demand answers or force him to leave. She stayed rooted, vulnerable, doubled over, tears streaming freely down her face. Leon smiled inwardly. *Perfect.*

"Oh no, no, lovely. Don't do that. You didn't know?" Every word that escaped his lips was saturated with a carefully honed sincerity. "Gods below, I'm sorry... I didn't realize he meant something to you."

Esme shook her head, her hair falling messily around her face, strands sticking to her tear-streaked cheeks. She was softer, still lovely, but in a different way than before. It almost made him want to change his plans. Almost. This rawness, this openness, this vulnerability, was what made her so valuable to Nudd and so easy for Leon to manipulate.

Leon reached into his well of stolen power. As he stretched his hand toward the wards, he felt their dull pulsing. One sharp snap later and her protections crumbled like dust blowing away in the wind. The sound was soft but deliberate, a crack meant for her to notice.

Her breath hitched as he made contact with her, separated by only one layer of clothing. Her reaction as she clutched the doorframe was confirmation that he should not have been able to break through her protections, but revealing a bit of his strength was a calculated risk.

Gently, he caressed her back, a display that, on the surface, would express his care and concern. What he did next was an even bigger gamble, but he hoped it would pay off. He dropped his glamor.

The man standing before her wasn't the Leon she thought she knew. What she saw was a different version of the man she loved, but with sun-kissed skin, raven-black hair, and violet eyes just like hers.

Her voice wavered. "Who are you?"

His face wasn't the cheerful facade he'd worn during every meeting before. He'd made it solemn for the occasion. "Someone who cares that he lied to you."

He needed her to feel that emotion, that moment of shock and despair, so that he could more easily take and give in return.

Esme straightened up, her face still contorted with emotion, still reeling from the impact of his true face. Her movement caused his hand to drop from her back, lightly grazing the exposed flesh of her hand. The moment of contact was all he needed. He had achieved both things he'd set out to do during this brief interlude. What he had taken was only a small piece of what he needed, but it was enough for now.

Taking advantage of her temporary distraction caused by the magic he'd used on her, Leon snatched the dagger he had witnessed her imbuing with power while fighting the Jorōgumo. He extracted its siphoned power and put it back exactly as he'd discovered it—never knew when that bit of magic would come in handy.

Leon restored his glamor and released the magic that allowed her to make memories once again. "I shouldn't have come. I'm sorry."

His regretful tone hinted at vulnerability, portraying him as an unintentional accomplice. Before she could respond, Leon gave a small wave and disappeared into the night, leaving Esme alone with her grief and confusion.

She wouldn't remember his true face by the time she shut the door, but the seeds he had planted—seeds of doubt, of betrayal from within, of growing trust in *him*—would remain.

Tomorrow, he would visit the former demigod. He had gifts to deliver and a new game to set in motion.

The End

THE DAMNED AND DIVINE

SNEAK PREVIEW

Good Morning Gwyn

Gwyn

Gwyn's new apartment was little more than a narrow rectangle with only three doors. It came with unimaginative, sparse furnishings, but the fridge was stocked and the space was *his*.

It was his reward for helping the Corded Brotherhood, the undercover combative arm of the magical community, in their fight against the returning malevolents. Gwyn hadn't exactly put a dagger to Miles' throat when the promise for his new space was made, but the memory of the dagger's grip in his palm was still fresh when the deal was sealed.

Unable to shake the habit of rising with the sun, even after nearly a year of enjoying the luxuries of central heating and blackout blinds, Gwyn had woken far too early after the abysmal night before. Now that he was awake, he had to deal with the conundrum of how to make a still sleeping Abigail coffee when the foot of his bed was barely more than a meter from his kitchen counter.

A light knock on the door spared him from making a decision. Cerys had been nothing short of focused when the nguruvilu arrived at Miles' front door. Yet, this visitor disturbed her far more than the large malevolent had. Unease pricked at Gwyn—Cerys' instincts were rarely wrong. She bared her teeth and even growled—a behavior uncommon for hellhounds. From what he could recall, they communicated within the pack by either howling or barking. Growling was a threatening sound, and gwyllgi usually skipped over threatening to attack immediately.

Sitting at the edge of the bed, Gwyn looked back to see if the disturbance had awoken Abigail. She hadn't moved, so he felt confident that he could address the interruption at the door without her stirring.

To calm the hellhound out of her fight-ready state, Gwyn had to pull hard on their connection as he petted her. He conveyed the image of a hellhound guarding the sleeper and, on top of this, he layered the emotions of gratitude and pack. Cerys' mind swiftly grasped this idea, and she positioned herself as a guard, putting herself between the bed and the door. Taking this as a good sign, Gwyn tiptoed over and opened the door quietly.

Miles had called the man in the doorway a "bastard" more times than Gwyn could count this past week. He'd always meant it as an insult, and now Gwyn understood the modern meaning. Being a bastard wasn't about birth anymore. It was about being disagreeable—and Leon fit the term perfectly.

Their deal with the assassin had specifically required his discretion, and yet they had received a deliberate display of grotesquery. Dropping the leshy's head at their feet, right on the heels of their battle against hundreds of spiders, was nothing short of calculated. He just hadn't figured out Leon's reasons for it yet.

Gwyn briefly considered shutting the door in his face, partially because he wasn't wearing a shirt and partially because he deplored the man, but he stopped himself. If Leon was here, maybe Gwyn could finally get some answers. Without a word, Gwyn shut the door behind himself, leaving him and Leon alone in a deserted hallway for the second time.

In low, sharp Brythonic, Gwyn asked, "Here to crow about your victory? Your delivery was revolting. But I'll give you this—the cut was clean."

A single compliment, especially when given at the end, could soften the sting of insults, making it easier for a proud man to accept.

"More importantly, my delivery was on time." Leon deigned to match his tone, unlike at the library in the past. Every time they had met, he had sported the same glamor as a fit east Asian man in his thirties, complete with thick glasses and an ever-present wide grin.

"On time?" Gwyn rocked back on his heels. "The clock showed past midnight. By all rights, you should forfeit half your payment."

"Brother," the paid assassin put on a show of appearing offended, "the solstice lasts until the sunrise."

Gwyn didn't want to hear his excuses. Leon's ability to conceal his magic from him only heightened his frustration. "That is not how these people think, and you know it... Why do you constantly test me?"

Leon barely concealed a withering gaze, but shifted tactics before the expression could fully take root. Speaking in English again, he said, "I'm here to ask why *she* didn't know."

Behind him, Gwyn heard the soft creak of the door opening. Abigail was wearing one of his hoodies and a pair of his sleeping trousers that she'd rolled up the legs on.

She looked at Gwyn with a puzzled expression, silently seeking answers. Her eyes were still fatigued from the strain of the night before, but she was a woman who recovered from any setback quickly.

"She didn't know what?" Abby asked. She added, "I had to use some bacon I found in the fridge and a little bit of magic to convince Cerys that hanging out in the bathroom was a good idea. She was... tense."

Gwyn tore his eyes away from her long enough to notice Leon's lingering gaze on her. Aware of Gwyn's scrutiny, Leon gave Abigail one of his too frequent, too deliberate smiles that cracked at the edges.

"Hello." Leon gave her every ounce of his attention. At least he wasn't trying to charm Abigail like he had Esmeralda. "I don't think we've been formally introduced. I'm Leon, and you must be... Abigail, correct?"

Abigail offered her hand to shake his, but Gwyn quickly pushed it down with an accompanying shake of his head. After what he'd seen the other mage do to Jacob with a simple touch, Gwyn didn't want her anywhere near Leon. She gave Gwyn a look that unmistakably showed her disapproval of his action.

Leon, to Gwyn's surprise, chuckled and flashed another dazzling smile. Now he was trying to charm her. "Oh yes, your boyfriend does have the right of it, Abby. Best not to offer up your hand to those with magic that you don't trust—yet."

Thrown off for a moment, Abigail shrugged. She repeated, "She didn't know what? Are you talking about me?"

Leon mumbled, "I'm getting the sense that the answer is 'also, yes'."

Gwyn hissed, low but direct in Brythonic, "Answer that question and I will remove your jaw from your skull with a blade or my bare hands, whichever time allows."

As Gwyn spoke, Leon's fingers twitched at his sides, a gesture so quick it might have been imagined if Gwyn hadn't spent most of his life on the lookout for the threat of a hidden blade. Perhaps Gwyn wasn't the only one battling against ancient habits in this modern world.

Leon did not escalate the argument with petty defiance. He raised both palms in the air in a gesture of surrender—something he was quite good at pretending—and widened his eyes in false shock.

"Apparently, I am not at liberty to say. It seems that I have already erred in coming here. Gwyn, you have my number. We should talk, because you're about to walk into a very messy situation. Well, two very messy situations: one with your friends; the other..." He grimaced as if he'd smelled something horrible.

Gwyn's patience snapped. "You should leave."

Leon smirked, glancing at Abigail. "It was lovely meeting you, Abby. I'm sure we'll see each other again soon. Oh, one more thing: check your trunk. It's handled, mostly. But you'll need to deal with the rest. I just didn't know what to do with it on short notice with the sun coming up."

"My car?" Abigail seemed more confused than anything else.

Leon grimaced again. "The mess. I covered it with a trash bag. I just don't have the contacts you two do to finish the job—sorry. I'm happy to pay the cleaning bill. Gwyn knows how to contact me. I know you'll forgive me when you see it." He gave a shrug that seemed practiced.

Didn't have contacts? Gwyn wondered why someone so powerful would deliberately maintain such distance from the magical community.

"Okay..." But before Abby could utter a word of protest or question, Leon gave them a little wave and mist walked to the other end of the hallway, blatantly shirking mage law. They saw him again as he stepped through the door leading out, waving again in their direction.

"I can't decide if he's an ass or if I like him," Abby muttered.

"It's still to be determined," Gwyn said, "but I'm leaning heavily toward 'asshole,' as you Americans say."

Abby sniggered but quickly sobered. "What was he talking about, Gwyn?"

Gwyn rubbed her shoulders through the fabric of his borrowed hoodie, practically begging, "Cariad, please allow me to explain inside."

"Cariad, huh? What does that mean?" She arched a brow.

"Something close to 'darling.'"

She smiled. "Okay... but if this conversation is going to piss me off, I need caffeine and for you to finish the massage you just started. Please tell me you have a coffee pot."

Striking a delicate balance, Gwyn confessed his recent sins to the woman he was growing to care for deeply. He needed to make her understand his actions had stemmed from his deep affection for her and his friendship with Esmeralda. Unfortunately, that took longer than he'd anticipated, and Abby was growing impatient.

"Okay, Gwyn, you've reminded me how magical beings inclined toward morally gray areas risk losing themselves to the dark side—in detail. *I get it*. What does this have to do with Leon?"

"Abigail, I love your brilliant mind."

She gave him a mock withering look. "Thanks, Gwyn. You can shower me with compliments later—all day, even—but right now, I really want to know what Leon was doing here."

"I'm avoiding the truth because I don't want to hurt you. The truth is... Sylas was lost to us weeks ago."

"Okay..." she questioned, her face clouding over with caution.

"Malevolent magic twisted him too far. By the solstice, the man you grew up with had... died, for lack of a better term. He was replaced by something else. Abigail, the changes in Sylas were irreversible. He could never go back to being the man you grew up with; the man who helped train you."

Gwyn dropped to his knees, grasping both of her hands, pleading with her to understand. "Jacob, Miles, and myself took all of this into account in making our decision. Sylas had already attacked Jacob, the result of which could have been his death, had Leon not come along. Sylas was planning to take more lives. He wouldn't have stopped until Esmeralda was dead."

"Gwyn, I already don't like where this is going."

"Cariad, we truly had no choice. The choice was between the walking remains of your dear teacher or the living, breathing presence of your loved ones. Leon helped us remove the threat."

Her voice was flat, but not accusatory. "Did you have Leon assassinate Sylas?"

"Yes."

Abigail did not react in the way he expected her to. With her eyes closed, she tilted her head back, inhaling deeply. Gwyn was certain she was about to cry. Instead, sharp enough that her voice probably carried through his apartment's paper-thin walls, she yelled, "Fuck!"

After a moment of stunned silence, he kissed her knuckles, hoping it wouldn't be the last time his lips could touch her skin. "I am so sorry."

Abigail pursed her lips, shaking her head angrily, her blonde curls bouncing with the movement. "Esme is going to lose her mind, Gwyn."

"I fear that is what Leon was suggesting when he questioned why she hadn't known earlier. That may be the mess we will have to walk into."

Desperate for an answer, almost as desperate as his body was for his next breath, he asked, "Do you understand why we did it?"

Abby gave him a flat look he'd rather not receive again. Her serious tone left no doubt about her feelings. "Yes, but never lie or hide something this important from me again, or we're done."

In times like this, the simple, unadulterated truth was best. "Then let us not begin the 'us' with a lie. Abigail, I will do my best."

"No promises?" Her expression hovered on the edge of scorn, her eyebrows furrowed and lips curled slightly. His harpy clearly disliked their decision, but her logical mind stopped her from rejecting their reasoning, or him, outright.

"I have learned from some past mistakes that I will only make promises to you I know I can keep. Abigail, if it protects you, or

Esme, or even Finn, I will do whatever it takes, even if it means leaving out important details."

Abby puffed out her cheeks, blowing out an aggrieved breath. "*Fine*," she sighed with the word. "You make moral ambiguity sound so damn logical. I've begun grieving, but I think I want to—no, I need to—be with Esme. We both need the closure. Plus, convincing her not to leave Miles after this will require some serious effort on my part."

Although the talk went far better than expected, Gwyn didn't assume Esmeralda would react in the same manner. She was far more emotional by nature, and her connection to Sylas had been deeper. Despite their current discord, Abigail's family was all alive and maintained, from his perspective, good relationships. In contrast, Esme had lost all of her family by blood and had since taken to finding one for herself. Sylas and Jacob were both clearly in those ranks. If Esme had already found out what they had done, it would be a challenge.

He nearly asked if she really had to try to save their relationship, but he held his tongue. Abigail wrapped her arms around him, something Gwyn didn't know his confidence needed until he received it. She snuggled into his chest and murmured conspiratorially, "Let's go see what that viper left in my trunk."

Gwyn fully concurred with her assessment of Leon's forked tongue nature.

The building only had one small elevator, so after they both changed into their daytime attire, they took the stairs down to the parking garage. When they reached Abigail's small blue car—what she had referred to as a "Beetle"—Gwyn cautioned her. "Please allow me to open the trunk. I do not trust Leon."

Abby stood with her hands on her hips, ready for a verbal spar. "I can create a weak personal aegis if needed."

"Abigail... *please* allow me to do this." She'd reduced a prince to a beggar, but he had smiled more since relinquishing his title than during the entirety of his family's reign. A fair trade, he supposed.

On the verge of pouting, she conceded, "Fine. He said 'messy.' I guess I don't have another change of clothes here anyway. Gods, I hope it doesn't stink! I have to drive home before the family therapy session later."

He released the door latch to find something rather large concealed in a plastic garbage bag. Regrettably, it emitted a foul odor.

Abby groaned. "I spoke too soon."

He turned to her. "I am going to open it now. Agreed?"

"Well, it doesn't seem to be moving at least. Yes, just get it over with."

Whatever was inside was still warmer than the ambient air. He carefully untied the string at the top of the bag. Peeking inside, he saw reddish-brown hair. By all the magic, Gwyn hoped that the rogue mage hadn't harmed a child. He would rip Leon apart with his bare hands.

He opened it all the way; the blood pooling at the opening of the bag caught his attention first. The sight of all-too-human pale skin followed.

"What is it?" Abby pressed.

Gwyn steeled himself for seeing the worst. Seeing the creature's wrinkled, craggy face and the red hat still clinging to its head brought him immense relief that mixed with growing trepidation. He removed his hands from the plastic and sighed. "Our fork-tongued friend has left us with the still-warm corpse of a redcap."

Her hands flew to her mouth, her eyes wide with shock. "In Seattle? Gods below, where there's one, there's six!"

Gwyn nodded. He wasn't certain if they returned from their malevolent prisons in pairs or in groups, but in his time, the gnomes were a nasty bit of work when encountered in numbers. Indiscriminate, they would just as soon strip the meat from a living, kicking horse, as devour a human infant. The idea of hunting such creatures in a city the size of Seattle was daunting, but it had to be done.

It was time for another malevolent hunt. Following that, he'd search for the human viper responsible for the mess, considering the mess a gift. Perhaps Leon had spared them the effort of killing this creature, but Gwyn's gut feeling warned him against trusting Leon.

Still, Gwyn had made a promise to speak with the assassin after the solstice and Gwyn kept his promises. His damaged memory was a persistent fog, obscuring the clarity of his past. Their shared history suggested that Leon might be able to help him remember more.

Though Leon swore he desired alliance, his actions and strange behavior lent his words a ring of falsehood. When they next met, Gwyn would bring an abundance of caution and his sword.

Less than five minutes later, the hunters became the hunted—the redcaps found them first.

ABOUT THE AUTHOR

Urban Fantasy author Stella Hope blends myth, romance, and non-stop action in each of her novels. Her favorite stories feature strong female protagonists, their loyal companions, and a generous sprinkle of humor.

Before embracing her passion for writing, Stella embarked on an academic journey that began with bachelor's degrees in Latin and geography. Afterwards, she pursued a graduate degree in environmental science and worked as a scientist for a few years. Stella's love for books eventually led her out of the forest and into the world of libraries, where she had the pleasure of running two public school libraries.

She lives in the PNW with her family, where she occasionally has to leave her writing cave to thwart the neighborhood bear's attempts at pilfering food from her bird feeder. When she's not writing, she's doing her best to stay away from bears, bobcats, deer, and sometimes coyotes during her trail runs and hikes. Her efforts are frequently less successful than one might suppose.

If you'd like to receive sneak previews, updates from Stella, and free content available only to subscribers, please join her mailing list at stellahopeauthor.com